D0484006

ZONE OF FIRE

ALSO BY CONRAD DETREZ

A Weed for Burning

Conrad Detrez

ZONE
OF
FIRE

Translated from the French by
LYDIA DAVIS

HARCOURT BRACE JOVANOVICH, PUBLISHERS

San Diego   New York   London

Copyright © 1984 by Editions Gallimard
English translation copyright © 1986 by
Harcourt Brace Jovanovich, Inc.

All rights reserved. No part of this publication
may be reproduced or transmitted in any form or
by any means, electronic or mechanical, including
photocopy, recording, or any information storage
and retrieval system, without permission in
writing from the publisher.

Requests for permission to make copies of any
part of the work should be mailed to:
Permissions, Harcourt Brace Jovanovich, Publishers,
Orlando, Florida 32887.

LIBRARY OF CONGRESS CATALOGING-IN-PUBLICATION DATA
Detrez, Conrad.
Zone of fire.
Translation of: La ceinture de feu.
I. Title.
PQ2664.E84488C4413   1986   843'.914   86-4789
ISBN 0-15-199989-9

Designed by Beth Tondreau
Printed in the United States of America
First edition
A B C D E

Para ti, Chepe

And Cain talked with Abel his brother:
and it came to pass, when they were in the field,
that Cain rose up against Abel his brother,
and slew him.
                    —*Genesis* 4:8

Under the ground many fires are lit.
                    —Empedocles, *On Nature*, 52

Then his flint dagger, his sex, will fall.
                    —Chilam Balam,
                        Prophecies of the Tun Years

O N E

1

Central America is a tongue of land, a twisted, stretched, gnawed tongue, a swollen, pocked tongue, pale in some places and bright red in others. It looks like a snake, a short, misshapen snake—not rearing up to strike and not crawling on its belly, either, but lying coiled, stiff and crooked, between two monstrously large triangular stones.

The tongue hangs out and an ocean presses against it; the tongue curves in and another ocean presses against it on the other side. On the left, the water is cold and the land is black; on the right, the water is warm and the land is white. In the Pacific Ocean, you shiver and your feet sink down into the mud beaches. In the Atlantic, you are much warmer, and with other fat swimmers you roll around on the ivory sand, the kind of sand you see in travel posters. There are lumps on this tongue of land, hard lumps— and yet inside them are cauldrons of stone and fire. There are also cracks in the tongue and, inside the cracks, more stone and more fire, and water, too. Central America is a tongue of fire.

Chonco is extinct, but Santiago is still spitting, and so are Cerro Negro, San Cristóbal, and Momotombo—that "naked, bald colossus," as Hugo called it. At five o'clock in the evening, Momotombo's cone is violet; at dawn it is gray. In full sunlight one time it looked white—but the sky was white, too, and also the surface of the lake, and the three lagoons shining at the foot of the cone. When the weather is very hot, Momotombo's amazing peak looks as though it's covered with snow, as though the cone is wearing a gigantic hat. I'll tell you what it is, novice climber—it's a liquid, and it's a gas. Volcanologists know this, and poets imagine it. As for you, you say: It's a skull, a white skull, a bald skull; Hugo was right.

It seems there are thirty-three of these volcanoes. They form a chain, a procession of hot mountains stoking their fires, a chaplet of fire, an incandescent corset—for the Pacific is violent. And here and there by the roadsides, old people speak in tongues to the gods of ash and rock. The pious bend down, kneel in the mire, and recite a scrap of the Popol Vuh. Now and then the volcanoes in a neighboring country answer them. The earth groans. Far below, the Pacific plate grinds against the North American plate. Everything shifts. Rodents come up out of the ground; rats run wild. Dogs bark. The whole world shudders, while moths float in the moonlight, rocked by the turbulent air, as though nothing were wrong. The whole world, the whole of this world, this tongue of earth, goes into a convulsion. Everything cracks, splits open, gapes. In the sleeping town of Managua, everything crumbles. Below the moths, as they flutter among the stars, people go about collecting the twenty thousand, thirty thousand dead.

You arrive later. In France you started a group called "World Explorers": now you are coming to explore. You have taken an airplane. The volcanoes, the earth are calm again. The mountains are seated hunchbacks, comatose. As you arrive, you leap over

4

gulfs, islands, the ocean. You fly over plains, rivers, chains of mossy, pointed rocks, forests, and of course—this is a bonus—the thirty-three volcanoes. The airplane slips between clouds and bottomless valleys. You see little towns and fields. At last a runway appears and the plane descends. The airport is a cream-colored, flattened rectangle.

Now you have to face the humidity, the dust, the policemen, the entrance gates. You face them, you get by them, and just in time you rescue your bags from the far end of some large hall. You push on, you make some headway, and then you run up against the barrier of the customs officials. At last you're out, and now you find yourself in a no-man's-land, beside a road. A bus stops. There is something written on it: it was built in the torrid, festive year of 1946. You make your way in among the standing passengers, who are sweating, deliciously stinking. You hang on to anything you can, anyone you can. Various knees bump into you, a stomach swells against your kidneys, a hand palpates you, an elbow grinds into your hip, and you sway back and forth.

You have come from so far away! You sweat from every pore, and your heart and brain sweat, too. Your spirit exults. As the bus slows down, all the old ironwork, boldly patterned, repainted candy-pink, soldered and resoldered over and over again, creaks and clatters and loosens even more; the whole thing comes to a stop, and you get off. This elaborate piece of architecture, with its four wheels, its sheet metal, and its load of dripping men and women, starts up again: you are left standing by the side of the road, in a hollow that will fill with puddles during the rainy season. From down in the hollow, your bags between your feet, you look silently at the countryside. You explore it with your eyes, and you are moved: you have come ninety-three hundred miles to see this! At last you are gazing at these pieces of wall, these leaning towers, these attempts at Doric columns. You gaze at flags, trees with shining leaves, an empty square, a cake that is about to fall in (*la catedral, señor*), another handsome confection that is coming apart (*el palacio, señor*), a vast cube of hard bread (*el teatro, señor*), concrete benches, pedestals without statues, pale-blue-coated stone seats, corners of flower beds, holes in the ground, a slope covered with grass, a piece of a road, a few spans of asphalt, and there—at the bottom of the slope, beyond the piece of road, behind the fragments of asphalt, and between the little mounds of earth and bricks—a path begins. The path leads to a grove of false oaks. The false oaks grow on ground that is almost uniformly level, scattered with garbage and small stones. Then there is a clay field, a square of grass, a plain, more rubbish. You discover a column of ants, the first one. Fifteen thousand kilometers. Your bags drop from your hands. Do ants know how to swim? They are heading for the lake.

There are columns of ants everywhere. One advances over the still-visible paving stones of a road, another goes around pieces of small pedestals decorating a small square—or, rather, a sim-ulacrum of a square—another furrows through deserted court-yards, another emerges from a gaping cavity at the base of a wall. The ants plunge forward over the cement ice-floe. They reach a doorsill, climb it, pass under a door, and file down the corridor of the house, where you have at last deposited your bags. You are intrigued by the fate of these little creatures. Are they lost? After the waters of the lake, they now confront the bare stone; there isn't a trace of food or even of excrement on it. You think that perhaps they are killing themselves, that this is a mass sui-cide—after all, even a termite may despair. Except that in the insect world one throws oneself from the nest of eggs straight into the grave.

And yet the procession continued, and you followed along be-hind. It seemed to you that the ants were attracted by the light outside the house, which was so hot, so imperious. After half an hour of walking, the column re-emerged through the back door onto a bright cement patio embellished with pots of earth that had no flowers or other kinds of plants in them, but were filled only with loam and pebbles—a desert after another desert. The column stopped abruptly, for no reason. There was no more to eat here than there had been in the hallways of the house—not a trace of a dead fly, not a scrap of dogfood, not even any crumbled piles of dung. Yet the ants stayed where they were: a ball formed, a quivering, shining ball. A little pile of coal particles seemed to have been created out of nothing and was coming to life in the desolate space of the courtyard. The ball swelled: one by one the tiny creatures were melting into it. The nest was like a bouquet on the stone, and the bouquet was feeding on nothingness; it was flowering like a monstrous plant under a sun that was dangerously white. The wad of ants did not move; it anchored itself onto its bank of hardened mortar imperturbably, as though the entire group had decided to die, either of hunger or of dehydration.

Hours went by. The seething black ball took root; the nest continued to live, feeding on hot air, transparent nothingness, and then shadow—the shadow of the wall a few yards away, opposite the door. The sun plunged behind a low, flat-roofed hut, and night invaded the patio. You, the traveler, turned away. You left the exotic crowd of ants, saying to yourself, I'll come back tomorrow. But by dawn the fat flower had disappeared.

T H E R E is also the city. They call it a city, but it's actually no more than a field, with a section of wall here and there, or some bricks piled up, or half a garage, a hovel, another section of wall. The center of the "city" is this field. Here the visitor strolls through the underbrush on shreds of asphalt. He clambers over mounds of earth, jumps across gutters, walks around various holes—sewer openings, dry wells, old cellars. He sometimes gets lost in what used to be a network of streets, looking for a landmark, a reference point, roaming the empty spaces, no longer knowing where he is or even what he is doing there. This unreal city fills him with distress; it is really a hallucination.

7

Managua: a city for a surveyor of the imaginary, a stage set for a metaphysical tale, a fiction. What could be more abstract than this surface, crisscrossed in every direction by monotonous two-lane roads, roads traced over one another, obsessively copied and recopied? What could be more abstract than these straight lines arbitrarily segmenting one another, outlining neighborhoods, sectioning bunches of houses and gardens? What could be more abstract than the way these addresses are written: "To Mr. Lopez y Lopez, starting from where the Aurora Pharmacy used to be, then going three blocks of houses to the east and two toward the lake"? Or these directions: "Take a left at the intersection where the Cristóbal Bar was, cross about a quarter of an acre of the old drilling grounds, then turn toward the lower part of town, walk the distance of two and a half surveyor's rods, and you will come to the square where the oak tree used to stand"? What could be more abstract than a place without monuments, without numbers, without street names, without a public meeting place?

Two cities were quarreling because one wanted to remain the capital of the republic and the other wanted to become the capital. What they did was build a third city, and they built it on a fault line, precisely on the seismic epicenter. The city was inaugurated, and called the first city of the country. But the city had been built to be destroyed, and for that reason we can tell certain stories about it today:

—Once there was a house. The earth trembled. The house collapsed. All that was left was some stones, a basement, a few bones.

—Once there was a barracks. The earth trembled. The barracks caved in. It was rebuilt. The earth trembled again. The barracks is now that vacant lot you see over there, to the right of the stall where combs are sold.

—Once there was a street stall made of planks and cardboard, isolated, like that other, in the middle of a field. The earth trembled. The stall held up but the comb seller died of fright. He was buried right there, along with his combs. If you look carefully you can still find a few—pink ones, yellow ones—buried under the rank weeds and the filth.

—Once there was a chapel. The earth trembled. The priest was saved. Now God comes back to prowl among the ruins at night.

—Once there was a prison yard.

—Once there was a column—of beautiful blue stone—and this column embellished a garden.

—Once there was a brothel, and twice the brothel rose from its ruins.

—Once there was a (clandestine) residence of counterfeiters and a (clandestine) residence of conspirators. The conspirators survived; they are living in exile now. The counterfeiters survived; they are in power now.

—Once there was a sidewalk, a simple sidewalk connecting a road and some warehouses. The tremor was brief but violent. The ground opened. The sidewalk still exists, unbroken, beneath the city.

Everyone is fully aware of it—the "zone of fire" runs through here. The beginnings of emergency settlements have been laid out, but there wasn't enough money to go on. There are rows of slums and government offices—housed in the slums—as well as brothels and music halls. Young trees have been planted in lines; they will die during the next rainy season. The city sits in the twelfth degree of latitude, and this means the land is infernally hot. Daisies burn on their stems, coral trees proliferate, and if a narcissus should risk sprouting it will die as soon as it is born. Only colors do well amid this poverty: the tropics explode in shades of red, ocher, blue, in fat purplish-blue petals. And like the flowers, the people lavish bright colors on their creations. One man has coated his door with orange, another his windowsill. The authorities have had the backless concrete benches in the square freshly painted. There are eight of them, low and massive. The colors chosen for them were the colors of the country's flag, so

9

that you see, in succession, white, blue, green, and a little red. Now the men out of work can lie down and go to sleep on their nation's colors. When they and the bums aren't napping, they watch the square. They stare at the brown-painted kiosk with its egg-yellow scalloped roof; and on this roof, the statue of the half-naked woman in her khaki-colored veils; and at the foot of the structure, green dragon heads with protruding eyes, turquoise teeth, large blood-red nostrils; and on either side of the heads, moldings of green and red, white and blue—the colors of the republic again—which lie between ornamental balls, also egg-yellow. And all of this—the seats, the kiosk, its architectural features, its gaudy color scheme—stands out against the dusty roads, the grayish background of the ruins that still surround the square, and the ill-defined pieces of land covered with patches of leaden pavement.

T H E R E are long lines of solidified ash, zigzags of rubble, snakes of stone, and, if you see it all from above, broad stripes dividing the black earth. The lava flows look like ropes coiled up or trailing over the sand, gray sand where just a few plants grow. You walk around. For hours at a stretch, for days, you are haunted by the enigma of this corner of the earth, which has barely been examined at all. Questions crowd into your head: what kind of cactus could this be? It grows on a rock and doesn't seem to have any roots. What is this gray mass, this swelling—a stone or a mushroom? You don't know anything.

You don't even know the scientific name of the chilamate. And yet there is no plant more prolific, more imposing, more beautiful than this tree, with its broad, dense leaves that shine like lacquered wood. Festive, regal, it injects some color into the gray shadows of the valleys, the roadsides, and the fields at the base of the mountains. It takes the shape of an ample, high-domed cap, an enormous emerald skullcap, a gigantic bell, a parasol

sheltering an entire hamlet, ten houses. In this landscape of volcanoes and lakes, no other tree is greener or more opulent than
the chilamate; no other tree promises such protection—against
the sputterings of lava, perhaps—or such strength, such coolness.
You wander along the dusty, monotonous roads, you go down the
slopes of a hot, ashy hill, you make your way through wretched
plowed fields, you ramble over wastelands, and then all of a sudden you see before you the massive, maternal breast of leaves.
You take heart again. You continue on your way, enchanted and
also relieved, because, after all, the majestic chilamate is there
keeping watch—a luxury, the cedar tree of Central America.

Here it is known only by its Indian name. Amazingly enough,
even the scientists have no idea what its other names might be—
in Latin, or Castilian, or English, or French. In the course of
your trip, you keep asking. You question, in turn,

    a botanist
    a geologist
    a quasi-ambassador (and former herbalist)
    a vagrant
    an old priest
    a young beggar
    a second beggar
    an agronomist
    a fallen woman (who speaks your language)
    some Protestants (one of whom is a volcanologist) `
    a philologist
    a myrmecologist

and—really!—it turns out that no one is able to tell you what this
beautiful tree is called in his native language or the language of
his area of expertise.

You are particularly amazed by the myrmecologist. As one will
have guessed, he is studying the habits of different species of ants
and the work they do. The wingless genus is his specialty, and

now he is examining the path of a double line of females. He asks you to slow down, make no noise, advance cautiously, with velvet steps, as though you were in enemy territory. He bends farther down. You bend down, too. One line of ants is walking away from you, each ant carrying its bit of twig, its particle of bark, its fragment of dry leaf. The second line of feverish little black dots is coming this way, perfectly parallel to the first, having unloaded its burdens.

"Interesting, isn't it?" you say, just to say something.

The myrmecologist doesn't answer. He looks annoyed. He frowns, shakes his head, and then, answering "No," leaps on the double line of ants. In a fury he tramples the ground, crushes the ants, and finally says crossly, "Absurd! It's all absurd!"

The scientist goes off and leaves you there with the wreckage of the ant hill, surrounded by the plant life, by nature. The man leaves in the same spirit with which one abandons God, or one's wife, or a teacher one has worshipped for years. The myrmecologist has left the shade of the chilamate, gone back to the road, and headed for the first town. The traitor hasn't turned around once. At first you were depressed by this scene—the man losing his faith, the carnage. Then you recovered. If some people manage to live without religion, you can certainly continue to live in ignorance of myrmecology.

C L E A R L Y, you think, nothing is so wonderful as stone— stone in itself, by itself. In this state of mind, you decide to go off again. You are curious about things; your curiosity is always new and yet always the same. You would like to go and see other hills of lava and black rocks, another volcano. There, high up, far away from the cities, you don't know what is happening in the places where men live. But for some time now, serious things have been happening in this country. And one day these things are explained to you as you stand at the very base of Concepción.

The immense volcano dominates an island in Lake Cocibolca. You are waiting for a boat to take you back to the mainland. You are sitting down, recording your impressions—as a volcanophile—in a notebook. Just then two men come by. They stop and say hello; they seem quite pleasant. They have come here from another island, one that lies closer to the middle of the lake, and they are also trying to get back to the mainland.

"We're in a hurry," they say. "Duty calls. We have to go and join those who are fighting for the people."

"Are you soldiers?" you ask.

"We're theologians."

The theologians aren't wearing tonsures or soutanes. The older one, who is middle-aged, has on blue jeans and a large white smocklike peasant blouse hanging loosely over them. The other, much younger theologian is dressed in dark-blue city slacks and a black shirt. He seems rather morose, defeated. He talks very little and defers to his colleague. Later you will learn that this man is a foreigner, like you. He comes from the general area, however, and speaks Spanish, and his country has as many lakes and volcanoes in it as the older man's country, so he should feel stronger and more confident than he does. But, as he explains, he was born in Guatemala and in Guatemala there are really two nations—the nation of Indians and the nation of Imbeciles. And since he isn't an Indian, he sighs, he has resolved to atone for it. This is why he has chosen to go into exile and fight. For the moment, the young man will not say anything more about it. His companion will monopolize the conversation during the entire crossing. Being a theologian, he will naturally talk to you about theology. He will refer to the creation of new sacraments, and he will go on to speak of:

horizontal sanctification
baptism by fire
politics

the eucharistic avant-garde
popular theophany . . .

He will also quote his favorite theologians—Carlos Marx, Federico Engels, and Pedro Teilhard de Chardin. He will utter certain propitiatory names: Lenin, whom he calls "the modern Saint Paul, my dear"; Camilo Torres, the guerrilla-priest; and the pure martyr Guevara. This Scriptural scholar will explain to you that the forms of religion must change. The Mass, today, is history; the Introit is actually a call to revolt; the Gospel is actually the seventeen-point manifesto of the party to which he has clandestinely belonged for years.

"Yes, it's astonishing, isn't it?" he said. "In Europe you rely on old-fashioned ideas, you don't invent anything. The Eternal City is a dead city, the Vatican is a museum, the Pope is a relic. Now, there are many humble Romes on *our* continent. These Romes are persecuted—that's why they're so numerous and so small. We have catacombs in the suburbs of our capitals, in the factories of our cities, in the plantations of our countrysides. And we have our widows, our symbols, our martyrs. . . ."

The boat bobs along, drawing away from the volcano. The waters of the Cocibolca turn from blue-green to gray. You listen to the theologian. Like many other people, you used to be a Catholic. The man confuses and irritates you. Should you blame him, should you attack him? You decide to challenge him instead.

"Father, you're proclaiming, 'Hallelujah! To arms!' But will you yourself bear those arms? Will you be in the vanguard? Will you fight?"

"The question pains me," the doctor admitted. "Unfortunately, I'm too old to fight. Look at my white hair, my large stomach, these glasses—I can't see a thing without them. But if I can't enter the fray, my colleague will do it for me and for all of us; won't you, Comrade Second?"

Comrade Second, budding theologian, expiator for his country, answered sadly and resolutely: "At your command, Comrade Superior."

"May the revolution bless you!"

There are four of you in the boat, including the ferryman, who is an aging, bad-tempered fellow with stiff hair and a glum expression on his face. He doesn't seem very interested in listening to the conversation. Anyway, he is sitting in the stern, away from the others, and all his attention is concentrated on maneuvering the oars. It is taking a long time to cross the lake, which is larger than some seas. By now the volcano is just a tall gray triangle sitting on the perfectly flat horizon of the vast stretch of water. The vegetation that grows tall at the base of the volcano has vanished, and the plants by the edge of the lake can't be seen, either; the mainland is no more than a few wavy lines, some low, rolling hills separated by broad valleys. The air is wet and the small waves make almost no noise. The serenity of the landscape inclines the men to be quite open with one another.

"Do you have a religion?" the theologian asks you.

"In a way. I believe . . . I worship stones."

"Marvelous! God is also present in the heart of stones. For stones do possess a heart, and God is that heart. There, darkly, within every rock, in the very center of every pebble, God throbs like a heart—as Pedro Teilhard de Chardin has described so well."

"Are you saying that God is a mineral?" you ask.

"God is matter. Matter is holy. There exists only one kind of glory—the glory of matter. Federico Engels is right: present-day theology ought to be called materiology; pure spirit is an illusion. The spirit that lives, lives only materially—and this is just as true for the spirit of stones as it is for the spirit of the Revolution."

You can meditate on this, you who are a captivated pilgrim to the sanctuaries of lava and fire. When you walk around craters bordered with volcanic slag, you are really walking around God, you are seeking Him, and when you are drawn to a natural well, with its eddies and its turbulent depths, you are again really drawn to Him. You can meditate on this, for we have never stopped probing the mystery of things and the mystery of our own actions: we know very little about what we are and even less about what we really want, what we want in the deepest part of ourselves. And so we spend our time running around senselessly. We think we love the heavens, and it is really the earth that we try to understand; we think we love mankind, and yet we kill one another; we think we love peace, and yet we make war.

The boat slips between wooden posts fixed in the water to warn of inland sea reefs, actually lumps of lava, the edges forming a vast, thick, jagged brownish crown. Nothing grows on these sharp, pocked, weatherbeaten rocks—no grass, no reeds, not even a little moss. The boat comes alongside a rock that has been cooked to a cinder, ground down by the elements, that is naked, irrecusable, something like the absolute in stone. The passengers leave the boat as the ferryman, grumbling, holds out his hand to help them. They walk hesitantly along the hard, irregular bank, which is full of pockets of water clouded with flitting mosquitoes. They reach the ground, which is dry and crumbly, and turn onto a path that leads to a hut where a fat woman with ashen skin, yawning repeatedly, serves them drinks. This barkeeper is the ferryman's wife, and her little bar is an obligatory stop for his passengers before they continue on their way. It is only now, with a drink in his hand, that the man brightens up. At last he emerges from his silence, turns to the doctor of sacred science, and asks: "Is God also present in a glass of rum?"

"Yes, but only in the first glass," says the doctor, half serious and half playful.

"Well, in that case your religion is worthless."

Thereupon, the ferryman swallows a second glass. The theologian refuses another.

"Come, come, Father," declares the woman at the bar, "only the tenth glass belongs to the devil."

"You keep your mouth shut," her husband interrupts. "The

tenth glass belongs to God, too. Every glass of rum belongs to God."

And he asks for a third. The man will end up quite smashed, like so many country people, pathetic creatures who are found dead drunk in bars or vacant lots, by the sides of roads or on plantations. The theologian stubbornly sticks to his first glass, as you do, and as his colleague does, too. You pay your share. All three of you leave, over the protests of the ferryman, who is already tipsy and repeats over and over that God is a fish who lives in alcohol.

2

The three of you enter a town, the first town you come to as you go north from the great lake. The novice theologian and the older man separate. Comrade Superior has a rendezvous with a leader of his party in a secret place. He will join the younger man again in the evening, in front of the squat yellow church of uncertain style that sits in the middle of town. While you are waiting for him, you and the younger priest have a chance to talk. You sit in a square in the shade of a half-dead chilamate that leans over several benches, and Comrade Second tells you his troubles.

Even though he was born into the imbecile segment of the population of Guatemala, he misses his country. He is sorry he can no longer go roaming around in the villages, the fields, the Indian communities.

"I would so much like to have the same color skin they do,"

he says, "and speak their language, and wear their costumes. In my secular life, my name is Julio César Ramirez, and in my religious life I'm called Ignacio. I would so much like to have the name of Qo-Cozom or Tecum Uman. And to be descended from the lines of the great Cavik, or of the Nihas. And to know how to use the medicinal plants *xocoyolli* or *xarimbacuas*. And to be able to make *cacao pek* and *tapal* pies. And to read the future in kernels of corn. And chant the verses of Chilam Balam . . ."

"And worship the Spirit of Lightning and the Spirit of the Earth?" you ask, intrigued.

"Why not?"

"And idolize the sun—or Chak, the god of rain?"

At that the priest's face darkens. True, the question is somewhat provocative. Ignacio, embarrassed, hesitates to answer. He thinks for a few moments, and then suddenly his face brightens. He declares, almost sententiously: "Rainwater is pure matter, the sun's fire is pure matter. The Indians have made gods of them. Comrade Superior, I believe, would say they are right. He would simply put the word 'gods' in the singular. The Mayans' theology has always been a materiology."

Ignacio talks on and on to you about his wish to have a different culture and skin color.

"If you only knew," he laments, "how the hearts of the white men in my country are full of complacency and contempt! If you knew what they think of the Indians and what they say about them! If you had heard everything I have heard and seen everything I have seen, you would understand that among the race of masters there is only stupidity and hatred." And the theologian reaffirms his vow of expiation.

Now the Superior comes into sight again. He is with two men, one of whom is talking and gesturing vigorously. The three head for a car parked to the right of the church and get in. As the car comes to a stop a few yards from our bench, the young priest is at least reaching the end of his complaints. The older of the two strangers is at the wheel, a gaunt, long-limbed, swarthy man with thick eyebrows and a badly shaven chin. He is still young, and his name is Itamar. The theologian identifies him as "a history professor." His friend sitting next to him, Abel, is barely twenty.

Itamar and Abel have been with the priest at the secret meeting. They are on their way back to the capital, which is where you and the two theologians are going, too. You will therefore travel together, joking around, talking about the heat, the countryside, about nothing important—because as long as you are in the car, the professor and his friend are guarded. The latter, who has said nothing, goes to sleep. Night is falling. The sky turns gold, then red, then black. The countryside becomes completely dark.

The car arrives at Managua. It makes its way through a succession of neighborhoods with dirt roads, huts, and often windowless fiberboard shacks where usually a dozen people live in two rooms surrounded by roosters and dogs; these neighborhoods, dotted over fallow land, empty lots, and dumps, are known as "colonies." After the "colonies," the car passes through a field of ruins, then a stretch of wood shanties. It stops abruptly in front of a shanty that is taller than the others and graced with a second story, an exterior iron staircase, and a sign above the door bearing the words Pensión La Perla.

"Well, we're here," the driver announces.

The inn where you are staying, now that you are back from your wanderings, is nearby. Itamar and his friend leave. The priests set off on foot for a parish where, they explain, a colleague usually puts them up for the night.

T H I S pension, along with other small inns made of planks and stuck between bamboo hedges and behind clumps of banana trees and masses of bougainvillea with gray leaves and dusty flowers, lies in a part of town—*your* part of this odd city—that has adopted the name of the only monument it contains; it is known as El Estadio, "the stadium." Nothing remains of the stadium but some blocks of broken concrete piled up between sections of walls, enormous boulders impaled on twisted, rusty steel bars, and some sections of tiers of seats that have collapsed along with their roofs, their ramps, and their halls. All that is still standing is a sort of circular pyramid whose upper part has fallen in, and so what remains, in the middle of the neighborhood, is this image of chaos, which, when seen at night, is reminiscent of the vast, stony disorder around the craters of volcanoes. In the daylight, the rubble loses its eerie quality. With the sun shining on them, the ruins are prosaic, and desolate. Whenever you pass through the neighborhood on your way to a bar, a store, a new rooming house, you have to go around the colossus. Then you choose one of the larger roads that lead toward the four cardinal points, all covered in cracked, broken asphalt.

One of them, which is also full of potholes, is lined on both sides by palm trees that have been ravaged by age, drought, and lightning till they are no more than bare trunks. This alley of smooth, rooted poles ends in a modest square shaded by real trees, with a few benches and a small basin that is always dry. The few cheap restaurants here and the one bar, El Olímpico, stay open very late. They inject a little animation into the square, where prostitutes come to prowl at night.

This is where you like to spend the evenings, now that you have come down from your mountains. You leave your inn; it's dark out. You take a left, a right, go around the square. You head for the restaurant that serves what is called "home cooking"—dishes of rice, beans, onion, and fried bananas, plates of thin slices of beef, pieces of chicken, or chopped meat cooked in oil. You eat your dinner slowly, because you are afraid that the evening will seem very long, as it usually does. You drink orange juice—or guava or mandarin—and, always sitting at the same table, you look out the window.

Three poles topped with fat white glass balls stand among the trees on the square. Two of the globes radiate a milky light. The third, whose bulbs have burned out, reflects a little of the light from the other two. A few women and some solitary men cross through the puddles of light. The men eventually sit down on the benches. They wait for the prostitutes to come up, they invite them to sit down, they chat a little, and they allow themselves to be led away. Some of the couples that form this way argue for a long time, then stand up and separate, the man and the woman going off in opposite directions.

This evening only two women are hanging around the square. One is pacing back and forth between the lampposts. She swings her hips and smokes a cigarette. When cars drive around the ruins of the stadium and pass nearby, the prostitute beckons to the drivers. The other woman is leaning against a tree, also smoking and apparently biting her nails. If you had to choose, you would talk to the latter. She's more reserved. Who knows? She might be content just to have you talk to her. But what would you say? That you're married, that you sometimes miss your wife, even though for the past few years you and she have hardly made love with each other at all? Wouldn't it be ridiculous to long for your wife when you're with a whore? Do other men also talk about their officially sanctioned and quite proper loves, their past joys, their present difficulties? Do they indulge in such confessions?

You're the only customer left in the restaurant, which is about to close. Your mind is still dwelling on these questions when you see a man walk up to the woman leaning against the tree. What disturbs you is that you know this man, you recognize him—it is the priest Ignacio. He is wearing his usual dark clothes, distinguished from ordinary people's only by the cleanliness of the shirt and pants, a certain sobriety they have, and the quality of the cut of the pants. But this distinction has an effect. The prostitute, who was leaning nonchalantly, wearily, against the tree trunk, now lifts her head, straightens up with some pride, detaches herself from the tree, and walks a little way with her potential client, the first of the evening. Ignacio seems to be at ease and speaks to her without hesitating, without betraying any nervousness or wariness. He talks to her as though he knew her already, as though he saw her regularly and was simply coming to meet her this evening. After a brief conversation, he leads her to a bench near the lamp with the burned-out bulbs and they sit down.

The scene makes you think strange thoughts. It bothers you to have caught the priest in a place like this, and it irritates you, too; you are more upset than he is. Apparently the proprietress of the restaurant has noticed this; in any case, she is on her way over. You get up from your table—you have nothing to say to her. In order to cut short any questions she might ask, any remarks she might make, you pay your bill and leave.

Outside the air is mild, not so hot as in the restaurant, which suddenly seems to you dirty, unwholesome—you're sorry you ever set foot in it. The mildness of the air makes you want to stroll around, though you don't want to run into the priest. You would like to slip away and at the same time remain here. You want to watch them without being seen. A section of fence standing between the restaurant and a house in ruins serves you as a hiding place. Here, in what used to be a courtyard, piles of bricks lie on the ground. Some of them have rolled against the fence, breaking through a few boards and creating narrow openings, convenient for someone who wants to keep an eye on the neighborhood.

You sit down on some blocks of stone and cement, facing one such hole, and you watch the gestures of the couple who are staying on the bench for so long. The theologian and the prostitute actually seem to have a lot to say to each other. Is the prostitute confessing her sins to him? Or is it just the opposite—is the priest making a confession to the prostitute? You will never know. The expiator from Guatemala might be telling her about his birth, the prosperity of his race, and its wickedness. Because the woman listening to him is dark-skinned, he would be all the more frank in revealing just how despicable the whites are in his country.

Of the two prostitutes, Ignacio has chosen the one with darker skin. Again and again you will see him come back to this square. Every time the priest will reject the women with good figures and light skin, and systematically choose the ones contemptuously called *negritas* even though they are either mestizas or pure Indians.

The fact is that you will return to this "dirty, unwholesome" restaurant. You will often watch through the window as Ignacio hangs around the square. The ladies of the night will pace back and forth, more numerous on some evenings than others, some old, some new to the work, chubby, thin, elegant, flashy, and sometimes shamefaced and dowdy. From this crowd of professionals, the priest will always choose the one with the darkest skin, who will also generally be the poorest. With each of them Ignacio will launch into a long confabulation, as tonight with the girl who is smoking and biting her nails.

You haven't left your hiding place. The pile of bricks under your bottom is hard, and your buttocks are beginning to ache. You don't want to leave until the couple stand up. You are tormented by curiosity, which is rare for you when human beings are involved. But people change. You have to find out—though you have no idea why—where the theologian is going to allow himself to be taken.

When their clients are in a hurry, some of the girls take them into the ruins of the stadium. Others lead them into the tall grass and rubble of the vacant lot that adjoins the square. The girls reappear after a few minutes, adjusting their skirts, brushing the dust and twigs off their clothes, and fixing their hairdos. Their clients emerge behind them—not satisfied, to judge from their grimaces, their air of frustration, the way they spit furiously on the ground, and the curses they hurl at their partners before slinking sheepishly away in the shadows cast by the trees and the sections of standing walls.

The priest Ignacio would never, you think to yourself, consent to betray his vows under such risky conditions, in such sordid surroundings, where he could be surprised by bums, prowlers, thieves, peeping Toms. It is inconceivable that this clean, impeccably groomed, delicate man would give himself to a woman in the middle of a ruin or a dump. And yet you can't imagine him bringing the dark-skinned woman back to his parish and into the rectory, either—even if they sneaked in—and then shutting himself up with her in the room where he sleeps under a large plaster crucifix with its writhing, bloody, Spanish Christ. It is easier to see Ignacio renting a room with an air conditioner and a shower in one of the three or four hotels that have resisted the earthquake. You will soon have your answer.

The hours pass. The prostitute accosting the drivers has already gone into the ruins of the stadium three times, and the third client spent a while with her before letting her go. It is growing late; you would like to go back to your rooming house and sleep. At last the priest and the woman stand up. They walk away from the bench and then stop. The priest seems to be giving the woman a last piece of advice, or they may be agreeing on a rendezvous, deciding on a password. Then, abruptly, he goes off. Resuming her nonchalant attitude, the girl goes dutifully back to her tree.

The same scenario will be repeated every time. The priest will come and wander around the square, pick out a dark-skinned woman, sermonize her—or tell her his life story, or complain to her, or try to reason with her, or pour out obscenities at her. Who knows? Then he will leave his recruit there and go away alone. Tired of these comedies, acknowledging that your behavior is rather voyeuristic, you will stop beguiling your loneliness in such dubious meditations. You will switch to another restaurant, you will find another square to stroll around in, and, if possible, another city. Since your wife is far away, you will no longer think of anything except leaving again for the region of the volcanoes.

3

But the city won't let you leave. Suddenly you are fascinated by certain men—their lives, their passions. Ignacio, Itamar, and Abel outwit you and take you prisoner.

At first you are consumed by loneliness: in the evenings this loneliness is enough to drive you to seek any kind of company you can find. Then you move out of your inn and into La Perla. You discover another world—deceptive, many-layered—and you let yourself be drawn into it. The pension, with its badly cared-for banana trees, which are choked with dry brown leaves, lies within Ignacio's parish, in the heterogeneous area of the city, where half the buildings were spared by the earthquakes. The labyrinthine and, for some, hospitable vestiges of the stadium stand here also, though farther down, at the edge of the field of debris. Here you will see the theologian come back and hover around the dark-skinned women, and you will cross paths again with some of the men who live in La Perla—quite ordinary, interchangeable men, except for the two militants.

The pension is filled with teachers, civil servants, and students. At breakfast you are likely to run into: a geometrician, married, of regular habits, the early-to-bed type, from a department in the north; a bank clerk, thirty-seven years old, divorced, determined to remain a bachelor from now on; a mechanics instructor who teaches forty-eight hours per week, his hair always untidy, always overwhelmed with work; two high-school boys, brothers, unrepentant skirt-chasers, the offspring of a landowner.

You also meet up with Professor Itamar, who is currently teaching history in one private school and two colleges. You won't see Abel at breakfast: he's a night watchman at a construction site in the southern part of the city and comes back to La Perla after everyone has left. As for you, you hesitate to go off again on your volcanological wanderings. So for hours at a time you and Itamar's friend are the only ones in the house.

The young man begins to trust you. The two of you joke around and get along well together; he asks you about your ideas, your tastes, the trips you've taken. He tells you he has broken with his family. He has a brother named Alvaro, a father named Jeremías, a mother named Fermina, and a sister named Alba. The brother is violent, the father a fool, the mother and sister Catholics. Except for the brother, they all live in Corinto, the commercial port on the Pacific coast. Alvaro has gone into the mountains to fight with a group of guerrillas.

Abel lived with his family until he was seventeen, when there was a scandal and Jeremías threw him out of the house. He worked for a while as a porter on the docks of Corinto, toying with the idea of joining the dockworkers' union and sleeping in warehouses, but then another scandal, this time provoked by his father, forced him to leave town. The runaway came to seek his fortune in the capital, and a third scandal nearly ruined him. Luckily, Itamar saved his skin at the last minute. From scandal to scandal, the young man was making a life for himself that was aggressive, passionate, perpetually within an inch of total destruction.

This is what Abel suggests, without explaining anything. It's all very mysterious, and you are perplexed, bewildered; you don't know what to say. In the course of these so-called confidences, the word "scandal" keeps cropping up—arbitrarily, it seems. This irritates you. Finally you risk saying:

"What are these—what do you mean by scandals?"

"Love affairs."

With his ambiguous, peremptory answer, he has reduced you to silence. You won't fully understand until weeks later, after yet another scandal, which occurs in a village not far from Managua where Abel has taken you to see some cockfights.

Abel is fascinated by cockfights. They're very important; they count for a lot in his life, in his friends' lives, in the lives of the people in the area. In Nicaragua, cockfights are as common as are elsewhere fights between men and bulls, between buffaloes and dogs, between drunken women, and between men drunk and sober. In his home in Corinto they had three cocks. His brother trained them, taught them to rise to heights of passion, entered them in all the championships in the region. And the cocks often came back the winners. Alvaro won a lot of money betting, which the family used to buy meat, shrimp, cases of beer. His mother and sister, of course, gave their tithe to the church, and his father and brother spent whatever was left at the brothel. The cocks were beautiful, with their gold-tipped green and brown feathers, their piercing eyes, and their steel spurs. Their names were Alvaro II (naturally), Macho, and Jesús.

In fact, there is a tradition in the town that certain cocks are always named Jesús. The women, who are Christian, take offense at this, and the priests protest, but the men simply laugh. For a long time Fermina begged her son to change the cock's name, but Alvaro would only tell her to go back to her prayers.

It's Sunday. The pension, like the whole neighborhood, is plunged in lethargy and idleness. For men who live alone—bachelors or widowers, lost boys, troubled adolescents either too shy or too young to go out and conquer the city—life is reduced to nothing, or almost nothing, or at best to an inadmissible, halting desire, or to something that can never be. For these lonely people, Sunday takes an infinitely long time to pass, like a night of insomnia. And so they behave like moles: they go to ground and curl up in their holes. Families, on the other hand, are finally together again, finally complete, finally mended after six days of dispersal, and they leave their burrows. In great, pompous numbers, like an occupying army, they invade the dusty spaces of the streets and squares.

It's Sunday, and night is sill far off at the other end of the desert. One can act like a vagabond—sleep until evening and then make up for it feverishly and far into the night. One can leave the city, wander through the fields and villages, or go off into the woods and hunt or fool around with a woman—but what woman?—or have a picnic.

According to Abel, one can also jump on the bus that goes to a place famous for its cockfights—Nindirí. Abel was told about this place by his brother, Alvaro, before they quarreled. Alvaro would go there to enter his bravest bird, Jesús, and once, thanks to Jesús, he won all the bets.

So, you and Abel head for Nindirí. When you jump off the bus and look around, your mouth drops open: the bus has stopped right across from the Santiago volcano. It has never before seemed so massive, so crushing, so menacing, and so frightening to you. A thick column of smoke rises from the crater. The people getting out of the bus pay almost no attention to it: they walk away toward the nearby villages, they don't stop or say anything about it, they go on laughing, chatting, teasing one another, complaining about the heat and their other problems. No doubt these people are used to living with such signs of danger—the rumbling of the earth, the emissions of sulphur and gas. One has to come from far away, as you have, to be afraid of an eruption. And you are afraid of it, though you don't dare say so. You look uneasily at Abel, who says, mockingly, "It's spitting again, the old bastard! As long as it doesn't start spitting boulders . . ."

And it's true that the Santiago sometimes vomits clouds of stones. It rains slag, lumps of hardened lava, and hot black dust over the fields, the road, and the houses. And this heavy shower of hail destroys trees and crops, punctures roofs. It falls on the chila-mates that line the road, tearing off their beautiful protective, polished leaves, breaking the young branches, and turning the old branches into thousands of gaunt arms reaching toward the sky. One time the fragments of granite and balls of compressed ash raining down destroyed the enormous thatched dome set on wooden columns above the arena where the cockfights took place. Fortunately, this accident happened after the match was over and the birds and the spectators had gone home. One Sunday a few years before, however, Abel adds, another eruption had flattened the roof of the enclosure, crushing the cages full of roosters and killing all the gamblers.

"And you're not afraid," you ask, "that this will happen again . . . ?"

"No need to worry," the boy interrupts. "The smoke is white."

You can usually tell there is going to be an eruption, Abel explains, when a gray or even black wreath of smoke billows up. But he doesn't know if a spotless cloud like this one can turn black while the volcano is spitting, and he doesn't seem to care much. He leads you to the arena.

The fights at Nindirí are crueler than elsewhere, it turns out. Women and children are kept away; the only people you see jos-tling one another at the ringside are boys and men. Priests in the area forbid their parishioners to come to this village because of the way people gamble, drink, swear, and get covered with blood; it is a place that encourages men to cultivate base appetites—a lust for vengeance, undying hatreds, and self-destructive impulses. The priests fulminate, and families stay away from Nindirí.

Abel says he likes certain powerful pictures you see there. When you go into the enclosure, the tiers are already filled with men of all ages, all sizes, all conditions. They press forward, elbowing one another like the passengers in the bus where for an entire hour you breathed in the smell of tobacco and sweat, the acrid sweat that emanates from bodies packed in together for a long time. And now you inhale this same smell of dried, curdled milk around the low railing on which the first-row spectators are leaning. Abel makes his way through the crowd, and you try to follow him, bumping into the gamblers and drinkers in the front. The boy takes his place behind a man who is holding up a foaming bottle of beer trimmed with feathers and brandishing it like a trophy. You take your place next to Abel. The referee moving around in the middle of the ring calls for the first pair of birds. Two young men go into the ring, carrying their birds in their arms and coaxing them like mothers simpering over their babies. Then suddenly they raise their voices, abusing and insulting the birds to excite them. They release them in the middle of the ring.

One of the cocks is white, the other red. Both have clipped heads: at Nindirí only cocks whose crests have been removed are allowed to fight. The red cock throws himself at the white cock, who jumps to one side, trying to dodge his adversary's spurs, claws, and kicks. The red cock gashes his neck. A jet of garnet-red liquid spurts from between his feathers. The blood soaks his neck feathers and the down on his chest and splatters over his wings. Everyone thinks the bird is beaten and is going to fall, but he recovers and begins running. The other cock runs after him. The white one turns around suddenly. The red one stops short and now the white cock leaps and plunges his beak into the other's neck. The neck is the part of the body the fighting cocks always try to attack; they are trained to do this by their owners.

And the white cock, who is no doubt excited, even maddened, by the smell of his own blood, strikes more powerfully than the red. The red cock goes down in a pool of blood, and his furious owner scoops him up, calling him a good-for-nothing, brainless hen.

Clearly the second fight is going to take longer. At first the two cocks behave like boxers. They sway back and forth, bob their heads, watch each other closely, dive at each other, and then, just as they are about to come into contact, dodge to one side. They run in all directions, flap their wings, try clumsily to fly away, and fall back down in opposite corners. This contra dance annoys the spectators. The owners of the birds pretend to be astonished. They make apologetic gestures at the referee and fatalistically let their arms drop to their sides. The bettors lose patience. They swear at the birds, who nevertheless persist in their haughty and pitiful parrying. At last, after a quarter of an hour, when everyone has given up on it, the fight breaks out. The two cocks turn on each other in a frenzy, but because they are well matched in strength and liveliness, neither one manages to wound the other seriously. The fight continues, the two cocks recovering their feet again and again. They back away, attack, and then, as though by tacit agreement, they break off the fight.

The birds huddle over, fold their feet under them, and sink down. The owners hurry over, grab them, and lift them up. Each man squeezes his bird's head between his fingers, turns it toward him, and brings it close to his own face, blowing on it as though it were a spoonful of scalding-hot soup. He forces the bird's beak open and inserts a metal bar so the bird can't close it. He blows more fresh air into the bird's mouth and, taking the horny mandibles between his lips, floods the mouth with his own spit. After a moment's pause, the birds, refreshed, dive at each other again, peck each other, tear out each other's feathers. This kind of scuffle often ends in a kind of tie. The bettors, annoyed at having shouted their heads off for nothing, at having wasted their time and their saliva, retrieve their bets. With their birds under their arms, the owners make their escape, to the hooting of the men and the gibes and shouts of the boys.

At this point, anxious to soothe the public, to make up for their disappointment and dissipate their ill humor as quickly as possible, one of the organizers announces "the main attraction of this cultural and sporting event." The village of Nindirí prides itself on drawing the most famous owners of fighting cocks in the country, the ones whose birds go into the arena gorged with rum. The crowd returns and applauds. The owners come forward, holding their birds by the tail in one hand and a bottle of alcohol in the other. Each man uncorks his flask, raises it to his lips, and swallows a mouthful of the strong, fragrant liquor, which is brilliant, the color of tobacco: the birds are given only the most expensive, brown rum, cane-flower rum. The men spit the next mouthful of rum and then another and another into the birds' mouths, which are kept wide open with the same metal bar. Little by little, the bottles empty. The drunken cocks thrash about in their owners' arms. Before putting them down on the ground, the owners hug them and walk around the ring cradling them and dancing. In Nindirí this puppetlike dance is called the "dance of death," because when the drunken cocks fight the loser must die. And this Sunday the three pairs of cocks being presented all belong to famous owners: the first pair consists of the cock of Pedro Lumbí, champion of the district of Jujugalpa, and the cock of Sancho Sánchez, owner of a brandy factory. Next will be the birds belonging to the two González brothers, who are inseparable but equally devoted to their respective birds. Third and last will be the cock who shares his owner's nickname, El Diablo, and the cock belonging to the big-time winner of bets, the famous Muy-Muy.

The festival of rum, blood, and virility lasts for hours. The bets increase until people are betting all they have—not only their money, but their bus tickets, their watches, their bicycles, their motorcycles, even their mistresses: they pledge to give up their turn at the brothel to the winner if they lose. They get excited, drink, jostle one another; some of them, soaked in sweat, alcohol, and the birds' blood and infected by an ambivalent sort of enthusiasm, hug the men next to them. They exult or they collapse. With shouts and hugs they show how much they admire an owner, flattering him and slapping him warmly on the back; or they are envious of him and turn away, as dejected and full of hatred as a dog that has been beaten. The atmosphere is tense; people are on edge, and they quarrel over nothing, make friends over nothing. In this overheated climate, Abel gets excited, slips in between two men, rubs up against them. One of them pushes him away roughly and shouts, "Beat it, fag!"

The crowd hears this and reacts: other men repeat the insult, brandishing their fists, and threaten to punch the shameless bastard in the nose if he doesn't clear out this second. There is a mixture of indignant remarks, jokes, exclamations—"Another one! And of course he's from the city! Those sons of bitches, they always try to take advantage." An old man mutters that these days people won't let you have a good time undisturbed. . . .

Abel himself has turned white. Like a cornered animal, he has stumbled backward and is looking around uneasily. You must have done the same, and now they assume you're another failure, another guy without balls, as someone has exclaimed, good for nothing but rubbing himself against people. The two of you make for the door, reach the road, and run on and on. . . . Abel is the first to collapse, on a grassy mound by the roadside. You can't breathe, you can't make a sound. Your throat is tight and dry, and it hurts. You expect Abel to say something, make some excuse, give some kind of explanation, but he says nothing.

Night has fallen. The two of you get back on the bus going from Masaya to Managua. A lot of the passengers are lovers: they like to spend the evening in the capital, where there are dances and movie theaters showing adult films, which are very popular.

You have seen some of them yourself at the end of your afternoons of wandering, when, instead of continuing to roam around
in the underbrush where the center of town used to be—roam
around and maybe get lost—you have chosen to enter one of these
dark theaters. Here you learned about the sort of love stories in
which people paw each other in bathrooms behind frosted glass
or Plexiglas, or embrace in the hallways of buildings, in kitchens,
in bedrooms, or in sheds. In the darkness, you imagine them
doing all sorts of things: chasing each other around in cornfields,
indulging in peculiar and painful contortions as they fondle each
other in cars, or lying down on the floor between the shelves in
department stores.

The movie over, you go back to your pension. As for the lovers
in the audience, they come out moved by what they've seen—and
more knowledgeable about which gymnastics lessons are fashionable in which countries. They leave the theaters and go dancing,
many of them heading for the section of the capital known as the
Rotunda. Within the narrow boundaries of this night district, one
can go to the Lolo Club, where so-called international music is
played, or the Quizás, or the Paramaribo, where they play a med-
ley of lewd and crazy songs. One can go to the Infinito, which is
delightful—according to the divorced man in the pension—and
which specializes in rumbas and boleros. The lighting there is
subdued. Even so, the dancers are supposed to observe a certain
decorum: they can rub up against each other when they sway their
hips, but they aren't supposed to stand still. Only in the bus on
the way back, packed tightly together, plunged in darkness, do
the couples lock in an embrace, the men and women fuse together
and become rigid, like statues of lovers sculpted out of a single
block of marble.

You stand wedged in as the bus inches ahead. In front of you
is a woman's back; behind you a boy who consists entirely of
shoulderblades. The mass of people is packed more thickly together than a bundle of firewood. It is impossible to move. If

someone pivots even a few degrees, the people around him protest, hit him below the belt, order him to keep still. You put up with it, and your friend does, too. His thighs are riveted to a woman's behind—it juts out like a pumpkin, swathed in polyester, but luckily there isn't enough room for her to wiggle around. Quite resigned, the two of you travel along twenty miles of broken road in the dark.

Once you have arrived, Abel still avoids commenting about the incident. The neighborhood where the bus has let you off is silent, the square deserted. You both wish you could walk off by yourselves, return alone, go in through different doors. As though moved by a tacit agreement, the two of you walk more quickly. Abel hesitates at the door of La Perla, says good night to you abruptly; his co-worker, he explains, another night watchman at the construction site, is waiting for him.

4

At first you're tempted to go away, to leave the pension and turn your back on the dissolute man and his group. You think to yourself: Look what happens—you leave home, you move away, you dream of living in peace with people who are relaxed and sympathetic, and now this relaxed attitude turns into vice and this sympathy turns into complicity. You've never really stopped and thought about men who like other men, have you? It's foreign to your life, to your way of thinking. What goes on in this sort of love—what people do, say, and feel—is hardly more relevant to you than the sensual pleasures of Africans or Javanese. By chance, you've landed somewhere alien to you, you feel out of place, and you're filled with distrust rather than curiosity. Yet it is impossible for you to forget the scandal, the stormy atmosphere in Nindirí, the visions of carnage, and the ominous presence of the volcano. And you also wonder exactly what it was about the scene that aroused Abel. Was it the heat, the sight of blood, the smell of rum, beer, and sweat? Or was it the proximity of danger, the smell of sulphur floating in the air? Desire is mysterious, and no doubt it works differently in every man. But why pursue it any further? What's the use of trying to decipher such enigmas? Your way of life is different, and so are your desires and your needs. It is inconceivable that one day your sensual orientation will change. The way you use your anatomy is regulated, fixed; it operates in a very modest way, while your ardor and ambition are directed at other kinds of conquests.

You hesitate. The desire to escape nags at you, but where would you go? In this city you are somewhat familiar with the center— a no-man's-land—the shores of the lake, the small business district—nowhere to sleep there—and the stadium neighborhood. You think of the names of a few rooming houses, and then you think of a few rooming houses with no names.

There's a knock at the door. It's Itamar. His white cotton shirt, open over his narrow chest, floats above his brown pants, which are too short. The man seems even thinner than when you first saw him. But this time his expression is gentle, despite the thickness of his eyebrows, which meet to form a coal-black bar curving down into a point above the top of his nose. His visit drives away your irresolution, starts you thinking of other things. For the third time in a few days, he has come to "talk politics." This is the price you pay for being French. Every militant in the world feels he must, when in the company of a Frenchman, bring up the storming of the Bastille, Robespierre, *Ça ira*, Louise Michel, the Communards, and the barricades. To this list, Itamar adds:

the writings of Babeuf (who's he?)
Gavroche
Les Misérables
Proudhon's saying: "Property is theft"
Marx's, Lenin's, and Bolívar's visits to Paris . . .

And from Bolívar he goes on to talk about Martí, who was also a great revolutionary and a visitor to Paris.

You say, "I'm not from Paris."

Itamar pays no attention. Martí, he continues, had fifty different lives. He was a traveler, a poet, a lawyer, a journalist, an art critic, a translator, an orator, a thinker. . . . The author of *Nuestra América* (what a tome!) was a perpetual exile, a conspirator and soldier. Most of all, Itamar points out, he was a Great Revolutionary Leader. The man spent time in Cuban prisons, studied in Spain, visited France and England. He met Victor Hugo, wrote for newspapers and magazines in Mexico, taught in Guatemala. In North America, Martí headed a Cuban Revolutionary Committee. The indefatigable wanderer next emigrated to Venezuela, where he settled in the capital and returned to teaching. He wasn't there long, however, before he went back to New York, to work successively in business and as a Spanish teacher, lecturer, and translator from English and French.

Martí also published several volumes of poetry and one novel, and served as consul and head of chancellery representing Uruguay, Argentina, and Paraguay, "those distressing Latin American republics," as he called them. During this period, his wife, tired of political turbulence, left him and went back to the colony of Cuba. Now Martí was all the more free to prepare a war of independence against Spain. He founded the Cuban Revolutionary Party, went to Jamaica to enlist compatriots in exile there. He started an uprising that failed, started another, and finally landed on one of his island's beaches, where his fellow fighters bestowed on him the title of major general of the National Liberation Army. One month later, while he was sitting on his white horse, our man was killed. Three years after that, in 1898, the colonial power lost the war and Cuba submitted to sovereign rule.

"Yes, of course . . ."

"Of course what?"

A lot of questions occurred to you: this man Martí must not

have been very interested in anything to do with the earth—or
what was under the earth—or anything to do with love. In his
heart of hearts, he must have been quite unmoved by volcanoes,
oceans, tidal waves, earthquakes—and perhaps also by women.
He preferred the company of other men, and what gave him pleasure
was agitation, conspiracy, war. He was as little tempted by sex
as he was by elegant clothing or the accumulation of wealth. This
rebel was shaped from the same clay as Itamar. But as for you . . .

"What an exhausting life," you remark.

"One could do less and still do well. Politics . . ."

Politics again! Does it always come back to that? People think
about it—and you yourself have thought about it; then they read
manifestoes, essays, programs, take the risk of handing out leaflets, and put up posters. They shout "Down with Dupont!" during
a meeting. Some of them shout "Down with Dupont!"—or Fulain,
or Sicrain, or Beltrain—until they are sixty years old. After they
die, their grandsons take up where they left off. Now it is the
grandsons' turn to consider politics, think it over, read manifestoes, and attend meeting after meeting. They proclaim "Down with
Dupont!"—Dupont being the son of the first Dupont. And all this
ends in producing a new decree. History is changed in a modest,
honest way. And a certain friend, the sort who puts up posters,
who is still putting up posters, though for another son of Dupont—this friend sighs at dawn one day, saying that he would
have liked to do "big-time politics." That was the expression.

Dupont was a minister, Fulain a senator, Sicrain the mayor of
a large city, and Beltrain is still a deputy. In another place, in
another time, they would perhaps have become guerrilla leaders,
condottieri, heads of movements. . . . You yourself were excited
by "big-time politics" when you were eighteen. You, too, were
drawn to the idea of going on excursions, to the lectures given by
the World Explorers group, and also to a certain girl you met,
your future wife. For a few months, you tried out the activities

going on in the neighborhood. Then you cut yourself loose and went on excursions that took you farther and farther from home. You left your street and took flight.

Now you're flying in circles around Itamar's world, coming very close to it. One can't join in conspiracies, one can't revolt, in isolation. One can't rebuild the city on a rocky, desolate mountaintop. Volcanology, my dear comrade, is geologically a lofty science. Standing apart, above, beside the rest of life, it is like an angel—sexless, universal, ignorant of ideology.

This is shocking. People protest—it smacks of amnesia, abandonment, omission. Abel, who has just learned the ropes, adds the clinical, faddish word "alienation." It is the end of the day, and the lamps are lit in the pension. You are all sitting around the table eating supper. The history professor—his shoulders stooped, his eyebrows pugnacious—has once again started everyone talking about politics. The early-to-bed geometrician isn't listening. The bank clerk is paying attention despite the skepticism he has adopted toward all enterprises ever since his divorce. The mechanics instructor, who is always in a hurry, says "yes" to every denunciation—it's more practical, it saves time, and this way everyone knows he's progressive.

The two high-school boys disagree. "We're in favor of women," they announce. "There isn't any better platform."

Words spoken by the privileged class, Itamar retorts. The brothers insist; they laugh and turn the conversation to the topic of sex. The geometrician bridles and scolds them. He is a Christian, and he speaks like a Christian, praising the tranquillity of marriage. The divorced man makes sly allusions to whores. The man in a hurry cleans his plate, finishing up his beans, his rounds of fried banana, and his chopped meat mixed with rice. Abel keeps quiet about what he likes; his friend Itamar says nothing, either. At the age of thirty he seems to be ignorant of love, yet he has a heart—given to the revolution—and his hands are beautiful—good for writing pamphlets. His expression can be very gentle—that's useful when he is recruiting. As for you, you are a foreigner, and you say that as a foreigner . . .

"I would be an internationalist," Abel interrupts. "Auscultators of stones, mountain climbers of all countries . . ."

"Come off it!"

The inhabitants of La Perla indulge in a little banter. Then the mechanics prof takes off, the geometrician goes up to his room, the divorced man goes out, and the high-school boys head for the Rotunda. They like to dance and flirt with the girls. It's Saturday night. At the Lolo Club, apparently, there is also a lot of touchy-feely while people pretend nothing is going on. The younger of the two militants has a night off: no construction site for him tonight, no night watchman's duties, no . . . The boy breaks off in mid-sentence. These words—guarded, suppressed as they are—hint that he has a story to tell as long as a novel. And he will tell you his story. Soon, Abel will take you aside and tell you. . . . He thinks the incident in the cockfighting arena has prepared you for it. Is he wrong? Is he right? He feels close to you; this bothers you. He feels you are ready. Tonight, tomorrow, the day after tomorrow, very late at night, when you are alone, the troubling young man will tell you that:

He is confused. Yes, there is the revolution, and, yes, there is love. There are also Itamar's lessons. And it is true that in the past he has gone on strike. He has shouted "Yankees go home!" at the cops. Once he even threw a Molotov cocktail at the military police. Abel has one life, two lives—it's hard to explain; he really should begin at the beginning. And at the beginning there weren't any politics and there wasn't any pleasure, either.

The boy loved one thing, hated another, but in the beginning what he really loved was sports. Abel tells how, in the town where he grew up, he used to go to the Cristal, a soccer club. He was sixteen years old, and he went to every game. Rooting for his team, he cursed if they lost, shouted in triumph if they won. Then the game would end, and the fans would rush to the locker room, Abel along with them. He congratulated the players, slapped them on the back, on the thighs, trailed after a dribbler or a goalkeeper as far as the door to the showers. And one time he went into the shower stall and let the door shut behind him. A strange thing to do—he himself was surprised at it. Yet something in him, something at once vague and powerful, impelled him to do it. Toca, the center forward, came into the stall streaming with sweat, a towel wrapped around his hips. Abel panicked, excused himself, and tried to get away.

"You're not the first," said Toca. And the center forward took Abel's hand and put it. . . . Abel had trouble breathing, and kept trying to leave. It was there, it must have been there, that his senses, that everything, a fire . . .

Unfortunately, he returned to the soccer club. Again he rooted for his team and disappeared into the locker room. Then there was a catastrophe. The coach of the Cristal was prowling around. He burst into laughter, poked fun at the soccer player, and threw the fan out. The news spread. People said Toca had an unusual sort of mistress. Abel says the rumor reached his brother's ears. Alvaro was mad, and right in the middle of a meal, in front of their papa, mama, and little sister, he asked Abel about it.

"I'm not a tart!" said Abel.

After all, Toca—and this was the Toca who became so famous two years later during the world championships—Toca was married.

"You're the other woman!" his brother roared.

"You idiot!"

His mother was horrified—her daughter, Alba, innocent Alba, was listening.

"So which of you opened your legs to the other?" asked his brother.

"Alba, cover your ears. Shame on you, shame! Leave the room, Alba."

And Fermina tore Abel's sister from her seat, dragged her off to her own room, and stayed there with her. At this point the father—he was trying to be solemn, you should have seen it—spoke up: "Anyone who acts the man with another man is twice as much of a man. Tomorrow, son, you'll do it at the whorehouse."

And Abel did it. Five days in a row, his father took him there and forked out for him. Abel did it against his own will, and every time his mother cried, "It's not Christian! It's not Christian!"

To put an end to all this, the son lied: "Father, I liked it."

The old man answered: "Now find yourself a sweetheart and get married."

There was a big scene between the mother and the father. His brother insulted him, threatened, invoked honor, and talked about death. And poor naïve Alba wondered what was happening, and kept crying because her mother was crying. A big drama—and Toca got off scot-free. Public opinion said he was still a man, a tough guy, the one calling the shots. His fans knew him well—he was a big womanizer, a real ladies' man. Of course, at one point people had talked about his escapades with a pansy, but what was the difference? He played well, scored often, had given his wife a pretty little girl.

Abel and Toca met again, at night, far away from the club. The soccer player had bought himself a motorcycle, and he would pick Abel up at the water tower at about eight-thirty. They would take off down what was called the River Road even though there was only a little stream next to it, and *that* was dry except during the rainy season. Toca would stop the motorcycle and they would walk into the fields. Toca knew all sorts of ways . . . all sorts of acrobatics.

Abel would go home. His father would sometimes ask him, "Well? Did you find a woman?"

"No."

"Damn it to hell! There are women all over the place. Where were you?"

Abel said, vaguely, "I went for a walk outside the city, on the other side of the river; the air smelled good, the trees, the plants; I walked. . . ."

"You fool!" his father broke in. "Do you think broads go walking around in the middle of the country at night? Do you think they go out to look at the stars? Do what everyone else does, you silly bastard—go to the square and pick one out!" And he growled, "What do you want? An heiress? A general's daughter? An actress?" Things were turning nasty again between them. The father suspected the son of not really looking for a woman. Point-blank, he said, "I forbid you to go to the soccer games."

"I . . . I haven't been going to them."

"You're lying. Your brother saw you there."

"Only one time."

That was too much: Jeremías was furious. Toca, that hypocrite—he had to be expelled from the club. Jeremías would make sure it was done. Since he knew the coach, he went to see him and made a scene in front of Toca, yelling "Tart!" at him. The coach defended the champion, grew angry, and attacked the old man. As for Toca, who was full of arrogance—the arrogance of a star—he hurled four words in the old man's face, four short, emphatic words. "Like father, like son," he said, and turned on his heel. Jeremías thought he would drop dead of apoplexy right there in front of the other soccer players, who were arriving for practice. Oh, that son of his, that damned son of his.

"Yes, coach, I knew it, my son, that rotten son of mine, that failure of a son, I swear I'll strangle him."

The strangling did not take place. Yet his father did shake him and hit him. His mother, seeing blood spurt from Abel's nose, fainted, whereupon Alba fell to the floor, too. At that point his father stopped hitting him, and Abel fled from the house. The man who had brought him into the world cursed him.

All day long the boy wandered through the city. He wanted to go find the soccer player, but he hesitated. He roamed around in Toca's neighborhood, pacing back and forth, circling the block of houses. Finally he made up his mind to knock at Toca's door. The champion opened it. He looked at Abel and spat on the ground. "Do you want me to finish you off?" he said.

And now Abel says to you, "After that I became a socialist."

"Oh? After the scandal?" you ask.

What was the connection—was his father a conservative? His brother is with the guerrillas. And what did the soccer player think?

"Yes, I became a socialist . . ."

"In opposition to what?" you insist, irritated.

"To nothing. I stopped seeing my parents. I went to live with the dockworkers."

"Who were socialists, right?"

The boy's only answer—and it isn't a very logical one—is that he had then looked for a job. He went down to the port and found work on the docks unloading wood, coal, barrels of oil, sacks of salt and rice. For the first few weeks he slept with the other workers in a warehouse. But the other men didn't do much sleeping. A lot of them came from the back country, and in the evenings they would talk endlessly about their problems, reminisce about their villages, and complain about the shortage of women—what they wouldn't give to eat some pussy, and it drove them wild that they didn't have enough money to go to a whorehouse. Then they became edgy: they would punch holes in the sacks of salt, thrust their penises into the holes, and discharge. The salt would burn them and they would whimper. The men watching these exercises would burst out laughing: "Pussies filled with red pepper!" they shouted.

Abel had to do the same as everyone else. He stretched out on a bale, penetrated it, rode it. The white powder in the sack ground against his foreskin, burned his penis. He was afraid of hurting himself, but the tingling excited him—this was better than banging a whore.

At last he received his first paycheck, but he didn't rush to a brothel: he rented a room in the house of a widow, and he bought himself a new shirt, a shirt with pockets that buttoned. The buttons were important, he said, because he needed a safe place to keep his cigarettes, his identity card, his photos—one of himself, one of his mother, one of the team, and, yes, one of the Cristal. Abel also bought a notebook and a ballpoint pen—one sometimes needs to write down one's thoughts.

Abel didn't last long in the widow's house, because of another tenant, an aspiring postman who came from the same village as the woman's late husband. Abel tried to get along with him, but he turned out to be rather stupid. The young man had sat for the qualifying exams twice and failed both times. He wasn't a very good sport about his failures: he was sure there was a plot against him and claimed the examiners were favoring the city people over the country people.

"Besides, they never ask any questions about plants, or animal husbandry, or religion, and those are the subjects I'm best at."

"Well, what do you expect? You're not taking a test to qualify as a farmer or a catechist."

"But those things are important."

"Not for working in a post office."

"Really? But sometimes nuns or gardeners or farmers come to the windows."

"And so do housewives, cooks, hairdressers. Christ! Learn mathematics!"

"That's hard."

"Well, then, go back to your hole in the country, become a horticulturist, raise chickens."

"People are poor there. They don't buy flowers, they steal them."

"And what about raising animals?"

"That's boring, and it's dirty work—you're always shoveling manure."

"Be a priest, then."

"I'd like that. I'd sit in the confessional the whole time. I'd open the window."

"And instead of selling stamps or certificates you would hand out penances and benedictions. . . ."

"It's fun to bless people."

"It's stupid."

"Abel, how can you say that? It does good to people to bless them. When I receive a benediction, it's as though someone is putting a fine cap on my head—the kind a postman wears—or stroking my hair and covering me with perfume."

"What are you waiting for, then? Why don't you enter a seminary?"

"You have to study a long time, and that's hard. You have to learn Latin."

Abel got tired of this maniac. He took his bundle of possessions and moved from the widow's house into a boardinghouse.

How he digresses! It's enough to make anyone yawn—and you're certainly yawning. It's enough to make you lose the thread of the story—and you're certainly losing it. Tell about your conversion to socialism, my friend—or maybe there wasn't any conversion.

"Sure there was! I'm coming to that," Abel protests. "When I was a docker . . ."

"You moved all the time," you say ironically.

Be patient, foreigner! Young people in Europe must have fewer ups and downs in their lives. As for Abel, he landed in another seedy establishment in Corinto—a backward town in a backward land. A low-roofed, badly maintained structure, it looked like a boardinghouse, but at the moment no one was living there, an old man sitting in the office told him. Abel asked if he could rent a room anyway. The old man got up, grumbling, and limped off to get him a registration form to fill out.

"No visitors allowed here," he announced. "I don't want to see anyone go upstairs, and I mean no one—no whores and no pretty boys."

"And why would I have boys coming up to see me?" Abel asked, afraid his reputation had preceded him.

"You're young," said the old man, "and you don't know about the filthy side of life yet. When you've been in the hotel business for thirty years . . . In the beginning, naturally, I wasn't suspicious. My lodgers brought in visitors. They would tell me that this guy was an old buddy from the regiment; or this one was the son of that old buddy; and this girl was the daughter of an old schoolmate. . . . And then one evening I heard someone shouting. The so-called buddy from the regiment was pissing blood from every hole in his body. That threw a scare into me: I thought I was going to have to smuggle a dead body out of my boarding-house. I guarantee you, human beings are capable of anything."

The hotelkeeper was an old busybody, and what he said was disgusting. Furthermore, everything in the place was ugly—the entrance hall with its sagging, chintz-covered sofa; the office with its filthy curtains; the door of the office, decorated with an out-of-date, yellowed calendar showing a picture of a naked woman astride a racing bicycle.

Everything was ugly, but it was late in the evening, the streets around the boardinghouse were deserted, and Abel was exhausted. He filled out the form, and the old man repeated the rules. Abel promised himself he wouldn't stay at this place very long; he didn't yet know how few places there were to stay in the city. He did know he could get a room in an assignation hotel, as some boys did, only there you had to pay in kind. Abel felt rejected, he was miserable, and from time to time he would think of Toca. Every time he came back to the slummy boardinghouse, he cursed and tried to think how he could get away. What if I went back to sleeping in the warehouses? he asked himself. The docks were full of life; the hovel where he slept smelled of death.

After work, Abel would hang around with his friends. They would take him to parties, where he learned of a budding underground trade-union movement. The leader of the movement was a man named Chepe (José) Monimbó. The man was always damp with sweat and would frequently peel off his shirt, so that on the docks he was known as Chepe the Shirtless. Abel listened to what Chepe had to say. He also read tracts. At night he plastered the warehouse doors with slogans, and he wrote on walls "Down with the National Guard!" and "Death to the dictatorship!"

It was during this period, and with these friends, that Abel—yes, now we're finally getting there—felt himself turning toward socialism. He tells you there were numerous discussions, and even talk of going on strike. Some of the porters sat down on the job, some of the stevedores stopped work, and a lot of the workers complained. They grumbled that there wasn't enough of anything—meat, rice, housing, public transportation. One of them added one evening that, to top it all off, the poor men in this damned town didn't have any women. This man was a bachelor, like most of the dockers, who were young, strong, valuable workers. Now they applauded, jokingly, but convinced he was right. Chepe the Shirtless, who could never keep his mouth shut and who was by nature a ladies' man, applauded, too, but he pointed out that the only solution was a socialist one. As he had said in an earlier discussion, socialism was "the only pigsty where everyone had a right to amuse himself as he liked."

This idea of a great egalitarian pigsty had won Abel over. He had never before really espoused any political ideal. Like many people, he called himself a patriot or a nationalist, but the issues the trade-unionist raised made him pause and ask himself some hard questions.

So it was this man Chepe who had awakened him. If he had

gone on working and living near the port, he would probably have turned into an activist very soon. Unfortunately—or maybe it was all for the best—a fresh scandal that resulted in the usual fuss, the usual outcries, sham attacks, and false remorse, drove him to leave his seedy boardinghouse, the docks, and the city itself.

5

It is Sunday again. You take a walk and head for the lake. The morning is beautiful, the town empty. By noon the streets have begun to fill with families—holy, raucous Sunday families—who are also heading in the direction of the vast body of water. After the midday meal, they leave the table and go down in a group to the Xolotlan. Fathers and mothers, sometimes grandmothers, and long strings of children pile into the buses. Huffing and puffing, the multicolored buses pass through different neighborhoods, some hastily rebuilt, some under construction, and some simply empty. The buses come to a stop and everyone climbs down at the edge of an empty field that lies between the road and the lake.

The families set off resolutely, picking their way among the heaps of garbage and the bushes. Two little girls tear the hems of their dresses—pretty pink-and-white dresses that float above their calves—on the remains of twisted, rusty metal or pieces of wood.

They whine and refuse to go on, and they have to be dragged along or carried. Several little boys vanish behind piles of dirt, fake sand dunes, the few shrubs that grow here. Wives and mothers-in-law try hard to avoid ants' nests, holes in the ground, and animal droppings. They kick aside sharp stones and dog turds that have dried into rocks. Now and then the women catch their feet in tangles of creeping plants and trip, perhaps breaking the straps on their sandals or the plastic ornaments on their shoes. They scrape their toes and bruise their heels. They curse their husbands or sons, or whoever else induced them to come to this field, which is fit only for mangy dogs, dead animals, tramps.

By the time the families reach the lake, a swarm of little boys have already taken possession of the shore. The kids throw themselves into the filthy water, where they horse around and knock one another over, while the little girls withdraw in alarm. Mothers and grandmothers arrive and collapse on patches of grass, catching their breath. Fanning themselves, they shout a string of warnings, orders, and counterorders to their children. The men joke around, dip their feet in the water, and dry off with their handkerchiefs, socks, or shirttails, or simply put their boots back on their wet feet. As the sun starts going down, the families leave. With the same loud laughter, the same oaths, they cross back over the empty field.

This is when the beggars arrive—five or six of them—filthy, ageless men accompanied by a younger one who seems mentally retarded. At the water's edge, the beggars take off their rags and wash. The oldest among them teases the retarded boy; another knocks him down and pounces on him; they roll around on the ground like clumsy wrestlers. The beggars insult one another, laugh, and immerse themselves in the water. The presence of a stranger doesn't seem to bother them, and this mixture of innocence and promiscuity makes you uncomfortable. From now on, you will come to the shore of the Xolotlan only in the morning.

Everything is clean in the early hours of the day. The sky is pristine, almost white, the lake uniformly pearl-gray; the hills beyond are lined up in descending order of height. The waters of the lake have receded, uncovering the debris along the beach. A rather odd beach, with its heaps of mortared bricks, stones, and lumps of concrete extending for hundreds of yards.

After the earthquake, the streets were cleared and mountains of rubble were emptied into the Xolotlan. A strange line divides the land from the water: fragments of building façades, balconies, and stone ornaments lie among pieces of wall, enormous quarry rocks, and scraps of iron. A large section of what used to be the city is now here, on this beach; the ruins stand out as solidly as a new construction. The air hardly stirs; the waves are slight. Not a stone moves. The water laps gently against the chaotic rampart, and this sound falls sweetly on your ears; it upholds the silence like delicate music. You find the vast body of water, the line of stones, and the emptiness around you soothing. It's good to be alone again; you can think things over, weigh the pros and cons of various situations, examine every possibility. Was it really necessary for you to end up with those people? Was it written in the stars? And where is it going to lead you? Itamar with his speeches, his little plots, his "sense of history." Abel—so irritating, such a propagandist, so good at pushing you toward . . . And those women in the stadium square, and their odd theologian friend with his mysterious ways and his obsessions. You're not here to get involved in conspiracies, or to reform the world, or to change your sex, or to alter God's nature.

The rainy season has started earlier than usual this year, and the slopes of the volcanoes are nothing but mud: it's dangerous, in fact impossible, to climb them. You have to wait for what they call the "dog days," when there's a pause in the downpour, and the dog days are late in coming. Cloudbursts empty on the mountains and the fields. Benches of lava, pyramids and banks of volcanic slag collapse. Storms break every day. The earth turns green again. Grass grows in places where before there were only stones and dust. A carpet of wild plants hides the rubble, the holes, the pieces of masonry that choke the ground. The long dumping area looks like a meadow. Beyond the meadow and the road, at the top of a slope, the cathedral springs up from a tuft of green. It actually stands among the debris of dressed stone and the banks of gray sand mixed with gravel, broken bricks, and mortar. But from far away all one can see is the rank weeds and bushes growing on these heaps of earth and rubbish. One can also make out the caretaker of the ruins sitting in the square in front of the church. In a sudden downpour, you run to join him.

The roof is still intact in one place, behind the choir and to the right of the apse, in the sacristy. The two of you take shelter here. From this spot you can see the roofless nave with its two aisles, the vaults, and the arcades, which the caretaker tells you have turned into aviaries and refuges for iguanas and bats. During the earthquake the roof of the church fell in, along with the cornices and the friezes. One of the two towers lost both its clock and its steeple. The other, cracked from top to bottom, may collapse at any moment. The ground in the central nave is now a garden, an ugly garden crammed with pieces of rotting beams and broken tiles and invaded by untidy vegetation, including shrubs and even a palm tree. Rats, dogs, and snakes make their way over the loosened flagstones of this garden. In fact, the cathedral has been reduced to serving as a hostel for ghosts, a dormitory for beggars, a motel for couples who either have no money, are in a hurry, or are having an illicit love affair. A free motel, the caretaker adds. And he laments what man has done to the house of God.

"If only they would at least have some respect for the confessionals!"

"Why the confessionals, rather than the altars or the fonts?"

"An altar is made in one big piece; you can hide behind it, but you're not protected. Whereas you can shut yourself up in a confessional, sir. And the pigs take advantage of that, especially the soldiers who hang around here at night with their tarts."

Before the earthquake, the caretaker was the sacristan here. "Ah, sir," he says, "there used to be such beautiful Masses in the cathedral, with the archbishop and his golden chasubles, and the canons, and the young seminarians, and the abbots. Everyone came to watch—Protestants, even communists. Forty-eight wax candles burned on the main altar, sir! Forty-eight! And there was the same number of vases filled with flowers, and there were streamers everywhere, and flowers made out of onionskin paper— blue, yellow—and banners and garlands, and at Christmastime there was flossy white angel's hair. The Sisters of Mary sang, and the men from the League of the Sacred Heart, in white surplices, swung forty-eight censers back and forth. Forty-eight! One for each parish of the diocese. Beautiful. You were transported some- where else—you weren't on this earth any more, sir, you were already up in heaven. Tears would come to my eyes. You could feel the spirits ascend, the souls of the blessed hovering over the heads of the choirboys. You would have been happy never to leave the church again.

"And that day, the day of the calamity, I left the church after everyone else, after His Excellency and Canon Bravo, who always did so much praying—God rest his soul—and even after the peo- ple who were making long thanksgivings; I stayed because I had to snuff the candles—all forty-eight of them!—and fold the vest- ments, and empty the censers, and put away the hymnals and the banners. Then I closed up the sacristy and walked across the square.

"That evening they had celebrated the Benediction of the Holy Sacrament. This was unusual for the middle of the week. It was as though people felt the need to ward off some misfortune, as though we all knew something strange was going to happen. I said to my mother, 'I feel uneasy. I can hear rumbling coming from far away, from deep down, very deep down.' The poor thing—she started to tell me I was hearing things. She said I'd done something to my ears while I was washing them. And then my poor mother died before she could finish her sentence. The ceiling burst open, the walls fell outward, and the roof dropped down on top of her.

"The shock snatched me up into the air and threw me outside; I found myself lying in the street, but only my legs were broken. This was Christmas Eve. It was dark, and the houses were caving in like stacks of jam jars. Lumps of concrete were rolling in all directions, people were bawling, people were dying, some women and children were half crushed and calling for help, some men were trying to lift the beams or the slabs of reinforced cement that were pinning them down. The whole city, sir, was just one great howl. My legs kept bleeding, and I couldn't get up. Whole buildings were still collapsing. And the people who weren't dying were going crazy, running around and pulling parts of bodies out of the ruins. One would find his child's arm, another would pull out a leg, or a head. . . . The survivors, those who could walk, would scuttle around clutching these pieces of the bodies of people they had loved. And they would trip over other bodies, or climb up piles of rubbish, crushed furniture, and flattened cars. They were trying to find their way to the parts of town on higher ground, or to leave the city altogether. I tell you, sir—sitting there on the ground, in the midst of the rubble, I was watching the end of the world. And it was Christmas Eve. My mother's feet were sticking out of a little heap of tiles and stones. Well, God is good to us."

"Perhaps He is rather—how shall I put it?—rather harsh?"

"God is kind, sir."

Is it his faith? Or has he gone crazy? No doubt his mind was unsettled by the shock, and the loss of his mother, and the infernal visions he saw that night. And he never quite got over it. The caretaker of the ruins is to all appearances tired but calm, even affable. He speaks in a steady voice. Is that enough reason, though, to believe he couldn't be crazy? In the same steady voice, this man asserts that in spite of everything, God's house is still serving God's purposes.

"People only come here to commit sins now," he says. "But other creatures gather here to do honor to religion, especially the iguanas. Yes, it's true, sir: those creatures sit up there where the rood loft used to be and organize councils and discuss theology. It is said that the animal kingdom is shut off from the affairs of heaven, but the iguanas are an exception; they have a natural aptitude for speculation. Though the cathedral is in ruins, divine interests are still being defended here. Is it mere chance that these lizards have always been respected in Central America? Iguanas have been venerated from time immemorial, sir. It doesn't matter to them that this church is dilapidated. It's still a sanctuary, and it is natural for them to live in a sanctuary."

M O R E storms break, and you return to the sacristy to seek shelter. The caretaker continues to tell his stories.

"Are these pious reptiles the only living creatures," he asks, "who discuss dogma and liturgy under the sacred vaults? Well, I don't think so—the bats, too, it seems to me . . ."

"No! Absolutely not!" says a fellow who has also taken refuge in this corner of the cathedral.

Like the caretaker, this old man survived the earthquake—and buried his wife and six children with his own hands in a crack in the ground. He agrees that quite possibly the iguanas discuss religion. But bats, never! If they discuss anything, the little beasts, it's politics.

"Do you think so?"

"Especially now, with all this agitation. Everyone's protesting. And the priests are not at all ardent. They preach about rebellion right inside the churches."

"It's true," you begin cautiously, "these days the theologians . . ."

"They're like those kids who are joining the guerrilla fighters. What are they called? 'Marchers'?"

" 'Marxists,' my dear fellow."

"And you think that the bats are . . ."

"Why not? If the iguanas are capable of arguing about the proofs of God's existence, the bats can certainly talk about this new doctrine—what's it called again?"

"Marxism, my friend. But that's an atheistic doctrine."

"Exactly. Bats find all religious convictions repugnant. They're heathen creatures—that's well known."

"Except for the ones that nest here," the former sacristan corrects him. "The bats in the cathedral have been listening to the iguanas, and that's why they are asking themselves questions."

"Or it might be the other way around, my friend, and the faithful are allowing themselves to be influenced by the heathen. Of all Catholics, aren't the priests the first to doubt? These days we see more clergy becoming Marxists—and therefore atheists—than we see Marxists becoming Christians."

Actually, the conversation is not entirely unreasonable. One image might seem too bold, another allegory too extreme, but you can't help thinking of Ignacio and also of his superior, a theologian devoted to the idea of matter, and a friend of the revolution. You can't help recalling certain remarks they made, certain articles of faith they had concerning the world, the divine and palpable forces of the world. These theologians would be quite at home in the ruined arcades of the cathedral. Of course, the iguanas would have nothing to do with them, but these doctors of theology would get along perfectly with the bats.

T H E storm is still raging. The rain comes down between the walls of the structure just as abundantly as it does outside. Masses of water pour in through the broken doors, the gaps in the walls, and the windows, which have no panes or sills. The water gushes down from the towers. The niches in the walls, now that their statues are gone, spit water like rainspouts. The holes where the organ used to be anchored have turned into gargoyles. On the ground opposite the main altar, a stagnant pool has formed. One arm of this pool extends into a stream and flows toward the wasteland of the nave. Other puddles have appeared in the choir and in front of the confessionals. One step separates the sacristy from the inundated area, but the beautiful, single piece of gray stone is cracked. And through the crack a bright thread of water is trickling, then running on into the grooves between the flagstones.

"That water . . . it's odd," the caretaker remarks absently, as though talking to himself.

"Water is water," says the other man, matter-of-factly.

"For now, yes."

"What the dickens do you expect it to be?"

"What if it changed to blood—if a deluge of blood began to fall on us, on the houses, on the ruins? This new, original cataclysm would fit in well with the others and make the whole thing perfect. Managua would acquire a very special status, an eminent position. It would be a capital of capitals, a unique city, strengthened by all kinds of baptism—by fire, by water, by blood. A chosen nation, a holy city."

"Still more ideas worthy of priests. Morbid, too."

"The iguanas . . ."

"To hell with the iguanas! There are better things for a city than martyrdom!"

"Like what?"

"Setting up neighborhood committees, carrying on the struggle, the insurrection that is brewing."

"Blood, in other words. Admit it—your politics also calls for blood, but blood that comes from below," the pious man pointed out. "I prefer blood that comes down from heaven."

6 0

"An illusion!"

"I have hope."

"You're talking nonsense."

"God's reasons are His alone."

This is certainly just how the iguanas must talk. And these animals never change their minds. If they start out raving, they will go on raving forever. The argument between the caretaker of the ruins and the other man seems likely to be endless. Neither one will give in. Long after the storm is over, the debaters will still be hurling their arguments and their obsessions at each other. Night will fall, and they will still be involved in their polemics while the bats swoop down on the vegetation in the nave, skim over the ground, and assault the imprudent men in the sacristy.

You would like to leave, and that should be easy—what reason do you have to hang around? You're not a beggar or a survivor of the earthquake or a partisan of any one particular species of animal. The rain stops, your shelter is half flooded, and you leave the ruins. It is still light. The sky has recovered its various shades of blue. Taking a detour along a slightly elevated path, you go back down toward the lake.

6

Is it really true? Will there be an uprising soon? At La Perla people argue: they're either afraid of it or eager for it. Everyone has a different opinion: the bank clerk couldn't care less—except for women; the geometrician, a good Christian and a married man, does his duty: he surveys plots of land, jots down measurements, examines files and boundary marks, writes to his family, and says his prayers. He has neither the time nor the inclination for this sort of thing; he is indifferent to events. Besides, he says, when you think of eternity . . .

And yet people are fighting in the mountains, organizing strikes, disseminating propaganda in the "colonies." And the two high-school boys, sons of the landowner—the two serious students of nightlife—can see nothing good coming of any of it. Abel apprehensively calculates his chances: he's fighting for the victory of the insurgents; he's afraid that if he were on any other side he would lose. He says *"Basta!"* to the dictatorship, the National Guard, the hired assassins. *Basta!* We've had enough of crime, death, swimming pools filled with whisky, gold-plated toilets, cut-off hands, and generals' tarts—give us *latinas, hombre, mujerísimas!* You've seen how those women brandish handfuls of eggs when military parades go by. *Basta* crimes! Yankee go home, go to jail, go to hell!

But men are dying, guys he used to hang around with, brothers, friends. A young recruit he knew well is deadly pale, fatally wounded, breathing his last. Abel won't see him alive again, and this is why he is torn: you may win battles in the street, but you're beaten in your own home. Abel is afraid, yet he continues to hope; he goes along with it, he joins in. Itamar comforts him— a few more months, comrade, maybe just a few more weeks . . . because progress is being made. The guerrillas are occupying the north and the south, and in the cities the passive resistance is having an effect.

News comes that the dockworkers in Corinto demonstrated and the National Guard responded. Chepe the Shirtless was thrown in jail, whereupon his friends went on strike and took to the streets. The police kept Chepe locked up for twenty-four hours, then released him. The man took up where he had left off—he organized meetings and discussions and made statements about resistance, tactics, and the hour of reckoning. Chepe roused the tired men, rallied the mistrustful citizens and the skeptics. He harangued them:

"What are we here for? To work ourselves to the bone? To spend our whole lives doing nothing but working and eating? Working hard and eating next to nothing? Work, eat, work, eat, all our lives? No, that's not why we're here! That's not why we're here in this shitty system, with no reforms, no mercy—no! Long live the new era! Out with the old structures, in with the new!"

"What?"

"Down with the old structures! Get rid of the old whores!"

"Oh, so that's it. Get rid of the old whores, bring in the new!"

It's working. The dockers are joining up, and there are a lot of them; the union is growing and active. A dozen guerrillas were apparently sent in to put a match to the powder keg, and the port rumbled; that part of town turned into a battlefield, the first of many.

I N the mountains, the rebels are growing impatient. Invading the woods, watching the paths, occupying the underbrush—that's fun for a while, but is it any way to conquer the country? The only way to take power is to take over the cities, and the guerrillas are anxious to seize control of the towns, ports, county seats; they dream of crowding into wagons or old trucks, their weapons held high, their hearts even higher, their banners and their hair tossed by the wind; they dream of the dazzling, flaming fresco that would be called *Entering the Capital*.

Today, however, they are sitting in the shady woods. Tomorrow they will take command of more forests, more hills, more fields, more thickets, more underbrush, but they are complaining: Look, comrades, they say, all this greenery is empty. We may be in control here, but we're in control of nothing! Abel's brother, Alvaro, is grumbling along with them.

Alvaro left his house and his roosters two weeks after his father tried to strangle Abel. His father was against his leaving, and his mother moaned, but Alvaro brushed the old man aside and laughed at the old woman. Jeremías followed him out into the street and called him a crazy man, a braggart, and a bandit, but Alvaro didn't turn around. He went off to join his friends, who were also preparing to leave. In the end, seven young men set out from Corinto along the road into the mountains.

Now that they're here, they're itching for some action. The reason they got into this business was to fight, not to play Indians, for God's sake, yet they're living in the mountains, eating and roaming around just like a bunch of Indians. Alvaro is fed up with it, and whenever he gets fed up he starts thinking about life in town, and about past pleasures—the little bordellos near the port, the cockfights, the drunken binges—and he dreams about his fiancée, Gladys, who is waiting for him. He sighs and groans— how soon will he be able to screw someone again? Not very soon if he stays holed up in the woods like this.

He could leave; he would steal off at night, find the road, and follow it down to the city. He might run into a sentinel, a solitary soldier, but he would cut him down, run off, and slip down another street, into another part of town. Casually, as if nothing had happened, this killer would then disappear into a whorehouse. And there, in front of Dora, Orfa, or Maritza—the expert Maritza, a woman who welcomed the whole world with open arms, as father and son agreed—in front of one of these girls he would unbuckle his belt, his thick khaki belt, and put his revolver down on the bed. He would laugh at the girl and tease her. Still on his guard, however, he would glance out the window, as he always did; the room was strategically situated at the end of a hall, and its window looked out on a back yard, the yard led to an alley, and the alley ended at the docks. He would look out the window, and the revolver would gleam on the crumpled, filthy, fringed eiderdown. And the sight of the weapon and the naked girl, coming after the long wait, the weeks of abstinence, would make Alvaro dream of death and destruction. The whore under him would moan. . . .

But this laxness of mind is no good. Comrade, you must stifle your imagination, harden yourself, encase yourself in cement, in concrete, drive away your bad thoughts. If you must daydream, daydream about heroes and martyrs, about the leader, about the prisoners, the people being tortured, mutilated. Remember there are no more militants, no more brothers, in the prison at Palo

Alto. One militant was castrated by his torturers; another suffered the same mutilation and killed his guard; yet another, a young one, smashed his head against a wall; and another . . . These were saints, comrade, and it is the saints who make revolutions.

"But my brother," Abel observes, "to judge by his habits . . ."

Each time he talks about his brother, you have the impression that he vacillates between being attracted to him and afraid of him. Alvaro has never known fear; Alvaro is sole owner of the family's three cocks; Alvaro is always sure of himself, in all kinds of situations: he moves his mother to tears, he impresses his sister, he fills his fiancée with admiration, he wins at the fights at Nindirí and Corinto and he has even won twice in the suburbs of the capital.

Alvaro is Alvaro! What a beautiful name! What a strong name! His father was the one who chose it. Jeremías has a predilection for the letter "a." Isn't it the first letter in the alphabet? The father gave his firstborn son—who was to become his favorite—a name beginning with "a." When the other children came along, he said to their mother, "You decide." To please him, Fermina also chose names beginning with "a." After Alvaro came Arnaldo, who died at the age of two, then Alba, then Anna, who was still-born, and lastly Abel. The family also used to have a dog named Anibal, but Anibal disappeared. Alvaro and his brother looked everywhere for him and came home empty-handed. Jeremías grumbled: "A dog isn't the same as a cock. Stop sniveling."

At the time, Abel was ten years old. He didn't like his name. In school, children made fun of him and called him Cain.

"Cain is my brother," he answered.

The children shouted, "Liar!" They liked Alvaro.

"Cain or not, if he had been with us at Nindirí," Abel observes, "the day of the scandal . . ."

"You think he would have . . ."

"He would have done what some of those guys do to their roosters. They grab them, call them failures, hens . . . and poof! My brother would have wrung my neck."

A L V A R O and his comrades in the mountains are waiting, and they're tired of waiting. They're obsessed by a single, powerful desire—for the confrontation to come, for the battle to be joined, for blood to flow. Then they will be able to forget everything else. But before that can happen, they will have to leave the forest, cross the fields, occupy the villages, and attack the cities. And the cities have never seemed so far away.

It's true that workers are organizing emergency rallies, students are agitating and handing out leaflets. But does this mean an insurrection, an offensive, a confrontation? Perhaps in the capital, where people are more excitable, more unruly, but in the town where Abel and Alvaro grew up, everything outside of the port area is calm. The people chatter and go about their daily chores as always, amuse themselves, get tired, and they mind their own business.

Every morning, Jeremías goes to the town hall. For thirty years the guerrilla's father has been a civil servant. Now using his age as an excuse, he has reduced the number of hours he works, and he sits behind the window only once a week. On the other days he sits at his table, bantering with his colleagues and from time to time stamping a declaration of residency or a birth certificate. Jeremías is over fifty; he has a paunch and occasional fits of insomnia. Sometimes he says he is old—though never at the bordello. He always sleeps with the same girl there, the all-embracing Maritza. Alvaro's father complains about his wife's menopause, and he makes fun of her piety. There is something even more serious that bothers him about his wife—she is growing a beard. It would be more decent not to sleep with her any more, he thinks, but is there room in the house for more beds?

Jeremías and his wife continue to sleep side by side on the same mattress. He may daydream about Maritza but he can't very well get up in the middle of the night and head for the whorehouse. The father of Alvaro, Abel, and Alba therefore does his duty as a husband, and he does it quickly, without any preamble or unnecessary talk. He simply mutters, "Come on, open up," discharges, withdraws, and falls asleep. For the rest, he keeps busy looking after his son's roosters. What son is that? Well, there's only one son now—the one who's off in the bush playing the hero.

Jeremías calls him names, sneers at him, and yet in his heart of hearts he admires him. Alvaro once challenged him:

"You know what you are? A civil servant of the dictatorship. The pigs—you slave away for pigs."

"How dare you, you snot-nose?"

"You've never thought of quitting, have you?"

Quitting! That's a fine way to talk! Of course, if he had to choose between the town hall and the whorehouse . . . But then who would pay for the food? And who would pay for Alba's dresses, and bottled gas, and bus tickets? And then there was pocket money—the fact that Alvaro got his pocket money from a "civil servant of the dictatorship" didn't seem to bother him very much.

"No, that's finished. I don't want your money any more. You can unload it on Abel."

"What! A real man doesn't give his money to a . . ."

It makes the father furious to hear anyone speak the name of his younger son. Whenever Alvaro mentions Abel, he does it to provoke his father, humiliate him, start a fight.

"If you quit, I'll pretend he's dead, too," the older son promises. "I won't talk about him any more."

Jeremías keeps his job. For better or for worse, he continues to stamp pieces of paper, record names, dates, and places, and sort files. From Monday to Friday, he lazily extracts "from the dictatorship" enough to keep the household going. And every Saturday from five to six, he goes to bed with Maritza. He tells her that he doesn't talk to anyone any more; he simply gives orders— to his wife, his daughter, his assistant at the office. He tells how Alvaro has left home—on a whim, because of a crazy notion, a taste for adventure. As for his other son, that one's dead. "He died some time ago. A shit, a disgrace, that's what he is. Well, that was before I knew you, my little beast. . . ."

W H I L E all this was happening, the mother prayed a lot and went to church with her daughter. For some time now, Fermina had suspected her husband of stopping in at the whorehouse, which made her think frightful things were going on. For her, prostitutes were like dwarfs or defrocked clergymen. The pious woman didn't dare question her husband, who was irascible the way his father, Jeremías the Elder, had been, and the way his son Alvaro was, too; she hated scenes.

Yet Fermina was worried. She didn't want to sleep with her husband any more, because whores were known to give their customers dreadful diseases. So now her religious fervor doubled: she paid for Masses and lit candles before the altar of Saint Rita, begging the saint to spare her. Obsessed by her fears, she wanted to confide in someone, but who? What kindly soul should she seek out? Her older son? He would laugh. Abel? He was still an adolescent. Alba? She still expected a lot from love, from a future husband, and Fermina would never forgive herself for spoiling Alba's dreams.

She became more and more uneasy: she couldn't sleep any more, and when Jeremías touched her she felt sick. Finally, she talked to her parish priest about it at confession. He reacted more calmly than she had expected.

"After men turn forty," he explained, "and sometimes before, many want to fornicate with younger women. Usually they have to go to professionals. At least they don't ask for a divorce; they don't do what rich men do—rich men have enough money to seduce honest young ladies, then they fall in love with them and end up by becoming so smitten that they get rid of their first wives and set up house with the new ones. Now, which do you think is better—to learn that your husband is going to a whorehouse, or to find out that he has moved in with his mistress?"

"I . . . I'd rather he went to the whorehouse. Except for the diseases."

"There's only one thing you can do about that, my daughter— cease all relations."

"If only I could. For a long time now, I've wanted . . . But I have to do my duty as a wife. Really, what a man does, my father! Frankly . . . And with such brutality . . . The most beautiful thing is to be a mother, and to believe."

"God bless you."

"But Jeremías still wants it. Can I refuse?"

"No."

"It's not fair."

"My child, you have to fulfill your obligations."

"Even if I might get infected?"

"Alas, yes. Continue to worship the good saint and put your contribution in the collection box."

From then on Fermina put twice as much in the box. She believed her offerings had a magical power, and became maniacally superstitious. She was always on the alert: if her husband came home late, it meant he had stopped off at the whorehouse on the way, and she would immediately run to put some coins in the collection box. If she felt him rubbing up against her at night, or if he actually took her, then she would hurry off to the church early the next morning and go into the saint's chapel.

In Corinto, Saint Rita is considered to be a last resort, the ultimate protectress of the afflicted. Now Fermina became her most fanatical worshipper, her most exalted devotee; from then on she forgot to pray to God, Jesus, or the Virgin Mary, her fear of gonococcus driving her to commit a kind of heresy—for Fermina the blessed saint was becoming a goddess. Yet the gonococcus microbes paid no attention, and ended up traveling from Maritza's crotch to Jeremías's rod, which was still perfectly spry but covered now with spots. He fretted and fumed and hesitated before he finally told his wife that he was infected. Fermina cried out, raised her arms to heaven, entreated the saint, and, praying all the way, went off to the town clinic. There a doctor examined her; he dipped in again and again, sniffed, raised his head finally, and congratulated her: "Madam," he said, "you are unpolluted."

Unpolluted? Fermina was thrilled, exultant, her heart full of adoration: from now on, the good Rita would always occupy the Omniscient's place in her spirit.

The devout woman hesitated no longer: she persuaded her husband to treat her like a sister from then on. Her husband went on to say that when a brother and sister grow up they stop living under the same roof, and he tried to persuade Maritza to leave the brothel and move into a little house with him in another part of town. The woman refused: she liked her job and was accustomed to her freedom. Besides, she confessed that she needed to sleep with younger men regularly and enjoyed initiating schoolboys—that was her way of being a mother. She couldn't do any of that if she got married.

"But we'll only be living together," Jeremías promised.

"I know men. Living together is marriage without legal documents, but marriage all the same."

"I won't be jealous. I promise."

"A politician's promise!"

"You'll be free—once a week."

"No!"

"Twice a week."

"Go back to your wife, my pumpkin, and if you like, come see me on Saturdays, as usual."

"Maritza, you know I love you."

"You silly goose!"

"When I die, in my will . . ."

"You, too!" Maritza interrupted. "What's the matter with all of you? You turn forty-five and you start talking about your wills!"

"What? Have other men said to you . . ."

"The old guys who come in here—it's always the same story. They fall for a girl, they stay all night, they start trotting out this business of their wills. They're all the same. A will . . . Paper! Even if it was a king's paper, what woman would trade her life for that?"

So that's what his parents are like. Abel had heard all these stores from Maritza, for he and the prostitute had become friends. But that, he adds, as though surprised himself, is another story. Maritza told him all his mother's and father's little secrets. For weeks the boy didn't know how to react. Should he be crying over it? Should he be calling them names? Abel had left home; it was better to get away—out of range, out of reach. But could you really do that? Could you succeed in cutting the ties, burning the bridges? Some people certainly didn't think so. They argued that you could get away from your family, but you'd be left with this pile of shit—memories.

"You must have a lot of memories," he says to you suddenly. "In France, your parents . . ."

You cut him off. "They died years ago."

"And what do you have left of them?"

"Hard to say—pictures, words, but it's all hazy. I've never really wanted to look back. Anyway, let's not talk about it, it's not interesting, and it embarrasses me."

Families. Are you going to become a sociologist and study families? One family in particular? From a small middle class, a small city, a small country? Descend from the rocky heights to examine four or five human insects, with their little gesticulations, their little wars—and your own little internal and external wars, and your gesticulations. After all, didn't you observe those ants for a long time—you hadn't planned to do that either. You could switch from volcanology to entomology again!

"Yes, I'm sorry, but it embarrasses me. In my family things were not so interesting, not so colorful."

Abel listens to you, but he is distracted: what he really wants is to get things off his chest. That's what happens: people ask you questions, you don't quite know why, and they don't, either—and then they talk about themselves, answer the questions themselves. And so the boy continues his story and tells you that in the end his father went back to his mother, though he didn't sleep with her any more. But the old man began to envy Alvaro's youth and vitality: "He's a fine figure of a man, my son," he would say. "If only I were his age! I would carry Maritza off, I would keep her running, work her ass off, and she would sign, the bitch—with both hands! All the papers! The papers from the town hall, the notary's papers—all of them! And with seals on them, too!"

Sadly, the father watched his son go off to the brothel or the cockfights. "As for me," Abel observes, "he was already suspicious of me, even though this was before the scandal. I was seeing Toca and I was also seeing Maritza. I would tell Maritza certain things and she would give me advice. She never breathed a word of any of it to the old man or the other girls. And the things she told me! About some of the other clients, about certain well-known people, about my brother, too. Alvaro thought she was terrific at her job, and she thought he was the spit and image of his father—the same faults, the same boastfulness—the only difference being that the son was talented. A smart guy, that cock trainer! But impatient—she pitied the woman he would marry. He would be sure to find his own Fermina sooner or later, because there were masses and masses of Ferminas; almost all women were Ferminas."

Abel had got to know Maritza when his father took him to prove himself. She had gone along with it, she had helped him, she could sense that he was meant to be something else. She was a real friend. And she also liked soccer—sometimes he would take her to see Toca play at his club. She rooted for the team, she shouted the names of the players, clapped, jumped up and down. In her opinion, none of the visiting teams had as many handsome men as the Cristal, and none of the others defended themselves as well. Maritza had a crush on at least four guys—the blond fullback, Gilmar; the guard Francisco Borba, whose nickname was Left Foot Paco (he was a lefty); and the brothers Nelson and Wilson Pérez, brown-haired and blue-eyed, well built, and as fast on their feet as champion racers. Toca, the center forward, was a famous dribbler, of course; in complete control of his movements, he could guard the ball, calculate his shots—he danced over the field. But Maritza thought he overdid it; the guy was a conceited puppy, she said, and people would put up with that for a while, but then . . .

Abel didn't believe it. At the time, he thought it would last, it would go on for a long time, and Toca would ditch his wife just like Falcón, the international star who had suddenly gone off to Managua the year before with a male sports reporter. Maritza was a shrewd woman, but the scandal cut him off from her. It was too bad. Maybe if he had gone on seeing her, his inclinations would have changed. But who knows? If one's inclinations are tied up with one's destiny . . .

7

Ignacio often came back to stroll around the Estadio neighborhood. You were loyal to the cheap restaurant you had first gone to, and you would sit there and watch him. The priest continued to approach women of a certain definite type—Indian, with dark skin. He would take the one he had chosen for that day and sit down on a bench with her. And there he would have those unimaginable conversations, utter those words you were never to hear—or so you thought.

You were quite wrong.

One evening, the exile from Guatemala took some sheets of paper out of his pocket, unfolded them, and began reading out loud. The dark-skinned woman next to him listened. She seemed interested, sometimes surprised. What did these pages contain that was so important, so captivating, you wondered. Was the theologian giving news of his country, was he reading confidential political messages? Was he teaching these women about religion or literature? Perhaps he was composing poems for them and reading them out loud. You would have given anything to get hold of those mysterious pages.

But to your surprise you didn't have to give anything at all. That same week, the priest came in to see you. In his hand was a book that had some sheets of handwritten paper tucked between its pages. He explained that these papers—rare, ancient texts—had been sent from his country by a friend in the seminary, and he handed them to you. You read:

Here is the Great Speaker, the Coyote. The ancients have said it. The tree has said it. Stranger though born on these stones, but not of these stones, man, you take the color of the earth, of the stones. Chukanel says this. Matzonel says this. The men of the dawn are not the men of the evening. The night is the Ancestress. Here are the sons of the Ancestress. Listen to the tree. Listen to the stone, the Coyote. Table of Knowledge is the name of the stone. And Speech. Its color is dark. The men of the dawn will go away. They are going away. They say: This is the land of the trees. This is the land of Hurakan and the House of the Jaguar. The sons of the Ancestress say: Go around the mountain that burns, go away from the names of *pelota*, off Nimxor Carchak. The men of the night drive out the men of the dawn. . . . Son of the dawn, go away. . . . Those from the House of the Trees take the color of stones, of the earth. Far away. Behind the mountains that burn, behind Hacavitz, Volcano. The sons of the dawn become the sons of the night. The Great Speaker, the Coyote approves. And at last Those of the Night, who have come from the trees, from the House of Hurakan, the Men, make war. The sons of the Ancestress are warriors, are Men. The tree has said it. Word of the Night, Balam Agab, has spoken.

7 6

"After reading this, I know what I have to do. . . ."

"Yes, these days we take 'war' to mean 'revolution,' don't we? It's easy to interpret that part. The rest of it, on the other hand, isn't."

The priest is surprised. "The rest of it? But it's perfectly clear."

"It's . . . poetic. The Coyote, the tree that speaks, the Ancestress—I don't understand any of that."

"And what about the men of the dawn opposing the men of the night?"

"I don't get it."

"The men of the dawn are the whites, naturally, the palefaces, my brother, me," the theologian exclaims.

And he takes the papers out of your hands and rereads these words in a loud voice: " 'Those from the House of the Trees take the color . . . of the earth. . . . The sons of the dawn become the sons of the night. . . . Those of the Night make war.' "

"The Ancestress is Mother Earth," he explains. "And the sons of the Ancestress are the color of the earth and the color of the night. They have dark skin, I have pale skin. So I have to change my skin."

"But how? By making war?"

"That's not enough, of course. You can fight and make fifty revolutions, change your beliefs and your party and your ideology twenty times over—you still won't change your race."

"That's exactly what I think," you say. "But how?"

"By having a child. By bringing into being a creature who, even though he will come from me, will also be related to the sons of the night."

What he is saying is clear: Ignacio is thinking of becoming lovers with an Indian woman or a mestiza. The conclusion you come to is also clear: his obsession with being descended from the Ancestress and emerging from the primordial stones and mud, of resembling them, of being the same color, is just a pretty excuse. The priest is feeling amorous; he wants a woman, and he is attracted to dark-skinned women. The idea of having a child of mixed blood is a complicated, clever dodge, and his reference to ancient mythologies only serves to justify his spending time with the prostitutes around the square.

"Having a child," you continue, "is a lovely idea. But you're a priest."

"That's a false obstacle," he breaks in, forcefully, suddenly on edge. "Priesthood is not consubstantial with chastity. What's more, at this stage in human history the greatest priesthood is revolution—my superior is categorical about that. And doesn't revolution imply love?"

"All manifestations of love, even carnal?"

"That can help. Don't you think so?"

"Everyone has a right to his own opinion. But what does your colleague think about it?"

Ignacio admits that Comrade Superior hasn't made any pronouncements on the question of physical love. But there is an instructive precedent: a monk they know who works for the Front had a child by a party militant, and the Superior did not disapprove.

"If the woman is a revolutionary, I can understand that," you say. "Since revolution is a priesthood, you're still within the bounds of your priesthood when you make love with a militant."

"That's true. I didn't think of that," the theologian answers, sounding worried.

Clearly this reasoning bothers him. Probably none of the girls soliciting in the square is a militant. What is more, the party condemns prostitution. Now Ignacio will have to go look somewhere else. Besides, if the most important thing is to have a child, why choose a whore for its mother rather than some other woman? You are careful not to ask the question. You hate embarrassing or hurting people, because it creates conflicts and complicates life. Then again, priests always have an answer for everything, whether they support the revolution or the counterrevolution, whether they defend continence or incontinence, whether they side with devout women or sinners. Religion is an elastic system; mysticism can embrace anything. No poet or scholar is more imaginative than a theologian; you don't argue with a theologian—you can't. You either give in or walk away.

You and Ignacio were still in your room at La Perla, and it was getting late. Now the priest left the pension, but not because you had quarreled—he had simply stopped talking, maybe because he had run out of arguments.

T H E two of you have resumed your conversation about the enigmatic text and its subject—the Balam Agab, the speaking tree. Some explorers had discovered a group of steles and pyramids in the middle of the jungle, and Ignacio received news of these discoveries regularly from his seminarian friend in Guatemala, an enthusiast for ancient cultures who was following the work of the archeologists and the experts in ideograms closely and with great interest: he would read the researchers' reports and transcribe the fragments onto letter paper for Ignacio. The story of the sons of the night opposing the sons of the dawn, he said, came from a city that had been buried for more than a thousand years under the tropical vegetation of the forest of Petén. The people indigenous to that place had invented hieroglyphs that were easier to decipher than those of other cultures.

"All the same," you say, "a lot of people claim that Mayan writing is still indecipherable."

"That's true to some extent, but it'll change soon. As soon as a method using a computer is perfected."

"Interesting! I didn't know about that."

"A whole literature, an entire history will be uncovered soon. The danger for me is that I'll feel left out of it. I don't want that to happen."

And the exile from Guatemala started in on his obsessions again, talking about gradually dying as a white man and being reborn through a son of mixed blood. This time you didn't keep raising objections. So many Catholic priests everywhere, in all periods of history, had had children, and that had never stopped them from being priests.

Was Ignacio goaded into action by what you had said? That very evening you saw him hovering around the prostitutes again. He chose the very darkest one among them, the shy, badly dressed young Indian girl you had seen him with before. The two of them crossed the square, plunged into the night, and disappeared into the streets, the ruins, or the recesses of the vacant lot nearby.

8

The seven guerrilla fighters are biding their time listlessly in the Marabios cordillera. They have their hammocks, their weapons, their courage, and a plan—to create a center *(un foco, compañero, un foco!)* the way Fidel did in the Sierra Maestra. Will they camp at the base of San Cristóbal? Or at the base of Telica? Or at the base of Chonco? Alvaro will answer that later.

There are seven of them, and then there are six—one of them has been having bad diarrhea and is too weak to stay. The six of them are bored to death sitting under the trees, surrounded by the cordillera's three volcanoes. These future combatants discuss strategic movements—they will establish a second center, politicize and arm the farmers, create a battle front extending between the two *focos*, form a column, conquer the territory. They talk about tactics, clean their weapons, and carry out training maneuvers. They kill deer, quail, and tapirs, and they hunt down iguanas, though this is a sacrilege; they make war on turkeys, agoutis, and opossums. The rebels have their plans—to attack the soldiers, the dictator's praetorians, the traitors and informers, to go forth and embrace the agricultural workers, organize them, instruct them, equip them, and strengthen their column of fighters. But for the time being they are attacking boars and armadillos and firing at the underbrush.

Their shots echo through the forest, and they are uncovered. The National Guard locates their position and launches a raid. The six of them charge through the vegetation. The underbrush is dense, and creepers hang down everywhere through a tangled mass of stems, stalks, and branches. The young men hurl themselves against the wall of foliage, stumble, gallop across thickly wooded hillsides, and leap over torrents and fallen tree trunks, trying to reach a place where the vegetation is even denser, where it is impenetrable, where they can hide. The guerrillas catch their feet in vines; they scrape their hands and faces; they tear their pants on thorns and trip over tree stumps, fall and roll over and over.

Some of them lose their weapons, their berets. One of them, nicknamed the Orator because he talks so much, trips over a root and loses his glasses. On hands and knees, the boy feels around for them in the ferns, swearing, cursing his blasted eyes, which are so nearsighted. He can't find the glasses. Now his friends have disappeared and the soldiers are getting close. He runs forward, bumping into tree trunks, going the wrong way. A soldier takes aim at the Orator and fires. Like a rabbit, the Orator leaps in the air and falls down dead.

The others scatter in different directions and keep on running. The soldiers hesitate. They don't know whom to follow, which one is the leader.

The guerrilla who devised the *foco* strategy, a student, decides to head for the base of the Chonco, because he knows the slopes of the volcano, knows where to hide in the slag and lava and the crevasses. Three others, who still have their rifles, choose to retreat to the bottom of a ravine. The deep, narrow gorge is hidden under luxuriant vegetation, and they think it's a good refuge: the soldiers won't come there. And the soldiers do keep to one side of it, but the ravine is swarming with snakes and one of the men is bitten. He can't call for help, because the soldiers are nearby, and the poison kills him.

Alvaro has left the woods for the fields. He has crawled through meadows, floundered into and out of ditches, and dragged himself across an endless plantation. Reaching a hamlet, he enters a hut. His shirt is in tatters. The man who lives in the hut gives him his own shirt in exchange for Alvaro's rifle. It is the middle of the night. Alvaro sleeps outside till dawn, then starts walking again. Eventually he hitches a ride on a wagon, and when he gets to a busy road, he flags down a truck. He is dropped off in El Viejo; from there he takes a bus to Chinandega, and from Chinandega he takes another to Corinto.

W H E R E should he go to get his strength back? To the brothel, or to his fiancée's house? Maritza's bed is like a beach—first the surging sea, then rest, true rest, the rest of a gunman, of a fighter. The girl can't cook, however. Gladys, on the other hand, is attentive and affectionate—but virginal. She loves to make herself beautiful for him, she talks about him, she concocts little dinners like the beautiful future wife she is, and she gazes at him tenderly. Alvaro goes to Gladys's house.

"My darling! How long have you? . . ."

"I'm here. Aren't you glad?"

He had just arrived. Nothing new in town—cockfighting championships here and there, fights in Diriomo, Masatepe, Diriamba. One bird wounded, the best one, Jesús, but he won. And then a visit to León, to a vet, and he ran into an old pal from the docks who had the sense to move, who got married and is renting a store, going into business . . .

"And what about us, honey?"

". . . and even thinking of moving to the capital some day. . . ."

"Do you love me?"

"And the guy is lucky, it's not . . ."

"Do you love me?" Gladys insists.

"What is this? You know I do. Do I have to say it a thousand times?"

"Well, there are other things you do over and over again, honey."

"It's not the same. When it's a matter of love, you say it once and for all and then you get married, sign the papers. With cockfighting, you move around, you train the birds . . . you have to keep starting over again."

"Do you love me, Alvaro?"

"I love you."

"And will you still love me tomorrow?"

"I will still love you tomorrow."

"And the day after?"

"That's enough. Ask me again and I won't love you any more. Do you want me to leave?"

"Stay here, my darling . . . Do you like my blue dress?"

"What blue dress?"

"The one Alba and I shortened. Don't you remember?"

"No."

"I'll wear it tomorrow night. Are you coming back?"

"I don't know . . . since you won't strip for me. . . ."

"Oh, be quiet! Shame on you! Listen, I've made some flan. Six dishes of it. I put pieces of banana in yours. Would you like some?"

Simpering, lovers' quarrels, and a lot of self-restraint! Alvaro is firm about that—an honest girl gives herself only after she is married. He's not interested in any woman who would be willing to lose her innocence. Jeremías, his father, always taught him that if you want to hold on to your wife, you take her when she's still a fool. And take her when she's very young, my boy, he said, or else very pious. Fermina had actually been a Daughter of Mary. She had never been with another man. He led her to the altar as if she were taking her first communion. The child became a wife, and the wife is a dutiful woman.

As for screwing, after spending time with Gladys, Alvaro goes to the brothel, like all the other engaged men in town. Then he sinks into a blissful sleep and dreams of his roosters, Maritza's body, and Glady's maternal flans. But during the past few weeks, he has been dreaming more often of rejoining the guerrillas.

N O W there are only four of them. They've found one another again. As for the nearsighted guerrilla, the only thing the soldiers brought back to town was his head: the rest of him was left to the vultures or the coyotes. Two of the guerrillas who got away retrieved the body—already stinking—of the boy who was bitten by the snake.

The guerrillas vow they will recruit new members. They scour the towns and villages. They go into bars, pay for drinks, chat with people there, try to talk politics. People listen to them and say nothing. There is distrust everywhere—in the countryside, in the markets, in the squares. The province has been terrorized. The National Guard has been through here, and people are silent in the hamlets, the little farming communities between Chinandega and Chichigalpa. In the cheap restaurants of El Realijo, Posoltega, and Telica, they look away, move to another seat, talk to someone else. The recruiters arrive in León empty-handed.

In this old city full of students, poets, patriots, Alvaro and his comrades relax; they argue and joke with the students. People at the university pay tribute to the heroes killed in the mountains; they have named a lecture hall after the nearsighted martyr; they praise the rebels' courage, favor armed struggle, but disagree with the strategy.

"Creating a *foco* gets you nowhere."

"It's suicide."

"Hold on!" Alvaro protests. "What about Cuba?"

"That was a different time, another story."

"And also Cuba is more Spanish than it is here."

"That's ridiculous! Cuba is full of blacks."

"I mean there aren't any Indians left there, and the objective social and cultural conditions . . ."

"Oh yeah, tell us, doctor."

"There's only one way—a people's war."

"A long one."

"Christ Almighty, this isn't China! You have to work with the cities—the middle class, the lower-middle class."

"And why not the upper-middle class, and the bankers, and the clergy, for God's sake!"

"Here's to a broadened Front!"

"Here's to the peasants, the peasants' war—let's surround the towns!"

"The revolution won't be accomplished by the peasants or the petit bourgeois. They can't do it," insists the man who was giving examples of so-called objective social and cultural conditions. "Only the proletariat . . ."

"Bravo! A socialist revolution . . ."

". . . is up to the proletariat! I've read the Bible, too, you know, Lolo."

"Let's talk science," Lolo protests. "Marxism is our guide."

"But our people don't know where they're going."

"Except for the proletarians!"

"Wrong. The country people are the only . . ."

"The middle class, obviously, damn it!"

"The working class."

"We need an armed uprising. In the cities."

"The countryside, the countryside first. Only the farmers will go the distance."

Sons of bitches! There they are, the ten of them, quarreling, and among them there are three tendencies, six subtendencies, four divergent strategies, two basic theories, four pragmatic tactical programs. Sons of bitches, every last one of them, Alvaro exclaims, and yet they're determined to carry on the struggle—they're all comrades. The core of survivors is ready. They really want to get involved in more actions. But how can they create a center, open a front, carry out different maneuvers—clustering, spreading, surrounding—with only four men? Even logistically it's not possible. So come on, sons of bitches, let's try to agree about something.

Who is the enemy? The ten men answer:

"The Guard."

"The Guard."

"The Guard."

"The dictator."

"The dictator and the Yankees!"

"OK, that's enough."

"And—maybe—the middle class . . .”

"Enough!"

"The Guard and the Yankees, *basta*. The dictatorship will fall by itself."

"And what about the *comprador* bourgeoisie?" the one man they call the "doctor" asks suddenly, worried.

"What's this shit?"

This shit, comrades, is a diversion. "Diversionist!" someone shouts. "We'll get rid of them, those *compra*-assholes." And as for the "doctor," it wouldn't take much to make the others choose him as the number-one enemy. But the "doctor" takes back the bad word. The incident ends with a promise of unity. The pioneers and the group from León—including the "doctor"—will arm themselves, leave the city, and head for the northern border. They'll make their way through that bitch of a cordillera, the Marabios, then cross the plain beyond it, and the rivers, and the haciendas—which belong to other sons of bitches. They'll settle in the mountains near Estelí.

T H E Y walk. It's raining. They walk but make no headway—the vegetation in this country! They sleep during the day, or try to; at night they move forward, get stuck in the mud, take the wrong path, go back the way they came. Just as they start off again, the sun comes up. There's one consolation: when it comes up, it shines on festive red coral trees, on a delicate-stemmed cane field, and on the most superb chilamates in the world. But at the end of the day, just as they are about to take off, the rain comes down again. Farewell, red blossoms, green shoots, great umbrellas of glossy flowers. The kingdom of light, the kingdom of the beautiful trees fades. The empire of the mosquitoes takes over the land. The rain and the growing darkness douse the men's laughter and their dreams as they struggle forward.

The path winds around, rising steadily. Alvaro is wearing shoes that don't keep the water out. Day in, day out, it pours. The air is getting colder. The men are leaving the tropical zone.

"Hey, look at that fog! Where's the doctor?"

"I don't know. At the back of the column, maybe."

Curtains of mist hang between the trees. The curtains are dripping wet, and it's impossible to avoid them. They enfold you. Your eyes sting. Your skin is peppered with droplets. With every step you take, you tear a hole in one curtain of fog and you run into another. The men don't say much; they just look straight ahead. They're saving their breath, doling out their strength. They have eyes only for the creepers, the stones, and the tangle of dead wood under their feet. One of them stops, briefly in the grip of an emotion—is it doubt, fear, regret? He looks back: the column is straggling. You can't see the head of it any more.

"Where in the hell is the doctor?"

"Him and his objective conditions."

"The spoiled brat!"

The guerrillas are moving slowly from thick and abundant vegetation to growth that is sparser, more characteristic of the temperate zone. But when the fog dissipates, the mosquitoes swarm just as badly here as they did in the tropical zone. The little creatures fling themselves on the human beings—rare prey in these remote areas—attacking relentlessly as the men swat them off their hands, their faces, even their pant legs, for the mosquitoes' darts pierce the cloth. The forest mosquitoes like the taste of ankles and thighs best of all.

Some of the men are allergic to mosquito bites: their skin swells up, their muscles change shape, their faces turn bumpy like old iron jugs, or their hands fatten suddenly, their fingers thickening into sausages. One boy is stung between the eyes and can't see; a little hump has grown at the top of his nose. With his eyelids blue and fleshy as prunes, he looked like a monster. He groans and staggers. "I'm blind! Help!"

Some of the comrades stop. Christ! This time it's serious—the boy has been poisoned. He has to be treated or the poison will go to his brain. Luckily, the doctor has brought along some medicine. They shout to him until they're hoarse, then one of them leaves the column, retracing his steps. The last in line is Paco from León, who is in favor of people's war. Paco is almost at the end of his strength, and he complains. Someone says:

"This isn't exactly the Long March, you know."

The theorist of protracted war clenches his teeth in fury, but he goes on walking.

"Hey, wait! Have you seen the doctor?"

Paco hasn't seen the doctor. No one else has seen him, either. They will never know what became of him, the so-called medic. Did he give up and slink off, ashamed? Did he get lost? Did he fall into a ravine or a jaguar trap? Did he get bitten by a rattlesnake and die?

The so-called doctor will be declared dead and eventually hailed as a martyr. The disfigured boy will be given into the care of some peasants, and the column will resume its march. A healer will treat the boy with herbs, the lump will shrink, the aspiring hero will go back down the mountain, find a path, reach some villages he knows. Once he is back in León he will prudently say nothing about his misadventure.

A L V A R O'S feet hurt; his thick boots have holes in them and the leather is coarse and stiff. They've been walking for five days and four nights, and now they're all sitting down to rest in a clearing, their shoes off. They yawn and knead their toes, their ankles, their calves. Another two days and they will have reached the place they're heading for, and they can start the operation. In Corinto, León, and elsewhere, their mothers, sisters, and fiancées are waiting for them.

"You're going, my darling? You're going away again?" Gladys had complained. And Alvaro talked about championships, said they were inaugurating a ring for all categories of birds at Ocotal, the other end of the world, on the border, almost in Honduras. And after that, he would go look for a place in the sun for the two of them, a business, and that would take weeks. But life was hard, and you had to prepare for the future.

Gladys cried—these plans for trips to such distant places— Ocotal! What an idea to go lugging his cocks all the way to Ocotal—such a crazy idea—and then down to Quilali, Jinotega, Matagalpa, and after all that trouble—oh, my darling—back to the capital—all this made her dizzy.

And now Gladys imagines her beloved sharpening the spurs of his cocks, elbowing his way through the crowd, placing his bets, stroking Jesús's feathers. She sees him strong and proud, but she knows that he likes to get into fights, and this worries her.

The girl pours out her worries to Alba. Alba is upset, too, but for other reasons—the boys will have nothing to do with her, she's too fat, her mother complains, her father lectures her, and she'll probably never again see her brother Abel, who used to sympathize with her. Gladys listens to her friend with half an ear, because she is embroidering the hem of her new dress with a garland of hearts. The dress is blue, like the one she wore the night before Alvaro left. If she had her way, all her dresses would be blue: she likes that color better than any other. Blue is tender; it makes you think of the sky, certain kinds of notebooks, the Virgin's clothes. And she also feels that blue protects her.

"Only, Alvaro likes white shirts. And when he left," Alba goes on, "he was wearing khaki pants."

"Goodness! Army clothes? I hope . . ."

"His pants were good and big. He likes big pants, with big pockets. He can put his hands in them."

"Alba! You make me blush."

"Why? That's what he always says. With big pockets . . ."

"Do you think he'll like these hearts?"

"Blue on blue—he won't see them at all. You know my brother—details. . . ."

"Holy Mary! I should have made them white."

"Or red."

"Or yellow. That wouldn't be bad. Yellow hearts."

Silk hearts, cotton hearts, nylon hearts—what does it matter? Alba asks. What counts is a real flesh-and-blood heart, a heart that beats for you, a heart in a man's chest—and as she says this, tears come to her eyes.

"No matter what color your embroidery is, you'll get married. I'm going to end up an old maid," Alvaro's sister whimpers.

"No, don't say that. In a few weeks, if you go on with your diet . . ."

"That diet's not working. I eat once a day and nothing but salad or white chicken meat, but I haven't lost an ounce."

"Some men like plump women, you know."

"Well, where are they? Dear God, where are they?"

The forlorn girl insists that everyone has someone, and everyone kisses and is kissed by this someone. Fermina has had her share. Gladys will have lots more kisses, and for a long time to come, and Abel was kissed so much it caused a scandal. And what about her? What man has Alba kissed so far? Only her father, old Jeremías. Every night, she briefly puts her lips to his hand, asking for his blessing. And what does he say? He says: "All right, all right, idiot, bless you."

Alba does meet young men now and then, but nothing happens. Sometimes she's too shy, her mother claims, and sometimes she's clumsy. Soldiers come marching past the house and the girl gets into a state: Should she go out? Should she sit in the doorway, go out for a walk? Should she cross the street in front of them? Look at them? Or would it be better for her to follow them, pretending she's on her way to buy bread or beans?

Alba hesitates. Just as the sound of footsteps gets close, she suddenly sees that her hair is a mess. The skirt she's wearing isn't pretty—she should have put on the green one with flounces, and her pink blouse, and tied a ribbon in her hair. She should have taken off her slippers—one of them is dirty—it's been sitting in the dust under the wardrobe for days—and put on her freshly whitened Sunday pumps.

But the soldiers are approaching fast: all she can do now is put on her apron. She opens the door. Her heart is beating fast. She swallows, hurries out, and just as she is crossing the street she trips and cries out, and the men laugh. She scurries back home, still in a fever, and hides in the kitchen. And this time her mother, presiding over her bowl of black coffee, flies into a rage:

"What are you afraid of, you foolish girl? Lots of men can't stand thin women. Just look at your father—doesn't he love me?"

"Probably, yes."

"Well, when I got married I weighed a hundred and sixty-two pounds and I wasn't any taller than I am now."

"That was the fashion then. Women wanted to be chubby. I read that in *You and Me* at Gladys's house. But nowadays all the models in the magazines are thin, and the actresses, too, even in newspapers like *Catholic Woman.*"

"Those magazines are for people who live in the capital."

"But men want girls who look like the girls in the capital. Do you think Alvaro would have gone after Gladys if she was fat?"

"A handsome boy gets a pretty girl. . . ."

"But I want my fiancé to be handsome, too."

"Oh, you featherbrain. You're not going to be picky, are you? At your age? When you're over twenty, you take whatever comes along."

This kind of talk plunges Alba into such a depression that in the middle of the day she goes straight to bed. She doesn't sleep: she simply lies there awhile, and then she gets up. There is a mirror on her wardrobe door. She plucks up the courage to look at herself: she's plumper than she was before she went on her diet, and her behind is gradually beginning to take the shape of her mother's; she will have to rip open her dresses and make them bigger. She takes out of the wardrobe the very same green skirt she used to think made her look thinner. She snips the threads and undoes the seams of the waist. The skirt changes shape—it looks like an old sack now. Alba shakes her head. Her heart is heavy, and her sight dims—she can't see the eye of her needle any more. She throws the scissors, the thread, and the skirt on her bed and walks out of the room. She heads for Glady's house, to bewail her fate there.

A L V A R O'S sister finds her friend sitting amid piles of back issues of *You and Me*. Gladys is leafing through the photo romances. She says she's looking for a good name for a girl.

"Who's the name for?"

"Me," Gladys says.

"What! You want to change your name? It's so modern, I like it."

"Thanks, Alba. But your brother doesn't."

And Gladys tells how Alvaro scolded her the evening before he took off again for the north. Gladys had done everything she could think of to please him. She put on makeup and powdered her face; she made cookies and bought clotted cream and served him out on the veranda. And as she was stirring her cup of coffee, also loaded with clotted cream, she asked:

"Do you like my cookies, dear?"

"They're not bad."

"And what about me? Do you love me?"

"Not again! Why do you keep annoying me with that question? Yes, I love you, but I don't like your name."

What a shock! Alvaro told her that a name comes from somewhere, like any other product—food, movies, cars. Either it's Nicaraguan or it's not. Either it's Latin or it's not. Either it's domestic or it's foreign. Every patriot knew that. And on his trips Alvaro talked to people, he listened to people talking, educated people, students, and he learned things. That's how he knew that the name Gladys was a pure Yankee name. And Yankee meant intrusion, domination, all that shit. The name Gladys was the same as a foreign trademark, an imperialist one, and that bothered him—her name didn't come from her own land, his own land. The name Gladys was a political statement, and an unpatriotic one. To call oneself by that name was thus a political act.

"But, honey, you know I'm not involved in politics. I don't understand any of it."

"You're involved in politics without knowing it. And your politics are bad."

"Really, I don't understand . . ."

"Too bad! Get rid of your name and find another. And as for understanding—later, maybe—who knows?"

"And what kind of a name do you want me to find?"

"A Latin name. Something like Antonia, Lucia, Maura, Cecilia, I don't know. For example, the women in my family have the kinds of names you should have. Alba is perfectly Latin, and so is Fermina."

"What about Cordelia?"

"That's good. Your cousin Cordelia has a real national name. Which makes yours all the more shocking. And besides, your whole family is Catholic. So why Gladys? Is there a Saint Gladys somewhere?"

"I don't know, dearest. In our family we only celebrate birthdays, not name days."

Gladys wasn't sure where to look. Who could she ask? How did you tell a Latin word? Suddenly she thought of the photo romances. There were hundreds of characters in those stories, all kinds of girls, and they had romantic names. She asked Alvaro if he liked those names.

"Who cares about romantic? As long as it's national."

Gladys envies her friend. The name Alba is so pure, so clear, so light. She envies her in the same way that Alba envies Gladys for her slim waist, her weight, her svelte figure. They envy each other as they sigh and go through all the issues of *You and Me* of the last few years. They look at the pictures—nothing but handsome men—and read what's in the bubbles. Gladys gets a clean sheet of paper and the two girls make a list of the names they like that seem most Latin: Cleo, Chloe, Emma, Messaline, Isadora, Leila, Farailda, Gemma, Solange, Mimosa, Hebbe, Marly, Esther-Lola-Lola-Esther, Caprice, Coccinella, Balduina, and Fabiola.

Alvaro, who had come back to the city secretly for two days, didn't like any of these names. He found them either dubious or pretentious. The wife of a man of the people, he said, had to have a name of the people.

———

A L V A R O, a man of the people. Of course, his fiancée said to herself, but when he's a businessman in León or, better still, in the capital . . . Sometimes she found him confusing, particularly since he had got involved in politics. For her, politics was like walking through a forest with no path, walking in darkness. Men got involved in politics the way certain ladies got involved in fortunetelling, and these men looked at the world the same way the ladies looked into their crystal balls. So you could be involved in politics just because you called yourself Marilyn (another cousin) or Juana. Because of the way you ate, too, Alvaro added (there was one kind of politics for the person who nibbled popcorn and another for the nationalist who stuffed himself with bananas). Because you prayed or didn't pray. And maybe there was a politics of cockfighting, too. In that case, she realized suddenly, her fiancé had gone north to do politics. And Gladys, the temporarily named Gladys, had no choice but to wait for him. For better or worse. She consoled Alba, she embroidered, she read photo romances while her beloved and his comrades, the survivors of the group, stopped marching, at last, and set up their camp. And once they were set up—and had launched their first attack—they were sure they would see new recruits arrive, would develop their logistics, would enlarge their base.

The first attack took place on a rough, partly wooded hillside. In effect it was only a counterattack, but what a counterattack: one dead in their column and four in the ranks of the enemy.

The guerrillas were going down a slope overgrown with shrubs. A peasant who had been paid ten cordobas to walk ahead of them opening a path with his machete was guiding them toward a damp, grassy basin the men thought would be more hospitable. But it had rained, and the vegetation was growing in a layer of mud. The grass was high. It was evening by the time they were ready to cross the basin. Alvaro was following on the heels of the guide, then came Paco, and after him came two survivors from the earlier team. For some time now, having been warned by the peasant, no one had breathed a word, but pieces of dead wood cracked under the men's feet, and though the wind in the trees was loud it didn't muffle the sound; they had to be careful where they stepped—they had to avoid tripping, sliding, falling. Most important, they had to keep their flashlights turned off, except for the comrade following the guide. This was a strict order, for, as everyone knew, batteries were hard to come by in these remote spots, and the peasants were very sparing of them. Whole groups of mountain people would go around at night sharing a single light. Many lights together indicated the presence of soldiers, poachers (even clever ones), and guerrillas. And someone would always tell the woodcutters, the head of the village, or the police about the strange sight. Unfortunately, in every column of future heroes there were scatterbrains, cowards, undisciplined elements. Sooner or later a flashlight would get knocked to the ground accidentally and roll on by itself, revealing the whereabouts of the column by glimmers of light like flashes of lightning.

Though neither he nor his comrades knew it, Alvaro's light had been spotted by the Guard. They had entered an area of high grass, a pool, a sea of plants. The men maneuvered their way across it, stirring up eddies of hard, sharp water. They swam as best they could, holding rifles in their hands. And it wasn't easy, for these were real popguns, antique blunderbusses without slings or safety catches. Some of the men were rowing with their rifles. With only their heads above the grass, they hardly made any progress at all. They dragged at their anchors, let go of their weapons and flashlights, fell flat in the mud. Guns went off, lights went on. Men swore, complained, cursed the ground, the plants, and their friends. They fell and got up again, covered with muck. They trailed across a slimy surface, dark, narrow, bare as a beach, before they finally reached the hillside where they intended to set up camp. Halfway up the slope they could make out a brighter, cleared area where a little hacienda squatted between clumps of trees. The estate, now abandoned, had belonged to an uncle of the dead "doctor," who had offered it to his friends back in León.

Alvaro instructed the guide, still armed with his machete, to go on. He seemed very much at home in the area, and in a hurry. The column had trouble following him.

All of a sudden he plunged off in another direction, bounded away, and disappeared from sight in the dark underbrush. At this point, a series of gunshots echoed in the air. Shouts rang out, and the column panicked: the shots were coming from the hacienda, which was occupied; they had been led into a trap. They pulled themselves together and divided into two groups. Someone shouted, "It's the Guard. Sons of bitches—we'll corner them, we'll get them from two sides!" And the two groups took off. They climbed, they aimed their rifles at the building in the woods, and, drawing closer, they counterattacked. Now the soldiers seemed to panic: some came outside, probably trying to run away, surprised by the strength of the counterattack. The guerrillas let them have it. Some of the enemy fell; then Paco was cut down. The two branches of the column withdrew, one man carrying Paco's body. They retreated to the basin and went around to another hillside. By morning everything was under control. Some men were panting, some groaning; some were washing minor wounds with spit; some were burying Paco.

"That son of a bitch of a peasant," raged a man who had a nosebleed. "That traitor, that son of a fucking whore, if I ever catch him I'll rip his guts out."

Had he really been a traitor, or had he simply been surprised by the soldiers like everybody else and tried to save his own skin? Was it treachery to save oneself for other battles? The men disagreed about it, they argued, they were ready to fight. But someone threw in another question: how was it that the Guard knew where they were going and got there ahead of them?

"That's simple!" exclaimed a close friend of Paco's. "Our footsteps, the noise we made falling down, our lights, our clumsiness, our stupidity, our idiocy, our blockheadedness."

"Hey, take it easy! Anything else?"

"Our cowardice."

"What cowardice, you idiot? What did you want us to do? Get ourselves shot?"

They got mad, started shouting, then abruptly everything quieted down. They were extremely tired, their nerves were frayed, they mourned for Paco. But they also felt a sense of victory. They had won, they told one another; they had dislodged the enemy from the camp, and the first battle was theirs—their retreat had only been a tactical one.

The news of the victory spread. In León, students organized impromptu meetings, stirred up trouble, printed leaflets. Vocations were born and volunteers turned up. Among the recruits there were two women, a journalist and a nurse.

The nurse's name was Claudia, Abel says. She was twenty-three, and immensely courageous; she had worked for the Front in the city for two years. One day she had gone up into the mountains with her fiancé, a man named Omar who was a militant in the city's working-class neighborhoods. Omar was apparently a complicated guy. He loved Claudia—and other women—plus alcohol and politics. The party wasn't sure they wanted to keep him. The threat of expulsion drove Omar to join the guerrillas. Confined in the forest, the man stopped drinking and hardly ever touched Claudia. He died in a suicide operation, strapping grenades all over himself and throwing himself at one of the Guard's patrols. The group his fiancée belonged to adopted his name. Three weeks later, the Omar T. column attacked the first of the Madriz garrisons. Claudia died in the attack. The survivors, eight men out of twenty, tried to form a new column. They would have named it after the two lovers, but since they had not attracted any recruits, they had to give up the idea and join another group, the one Alvaro and the journalist belonged to.

Abel knew the journalist by her pen name, Leonor. Denounced to the police, who were looking for her, Leonor had broken off all connections with her newspaper. She had rented a room from a widow in Managua, in a neighborhood called Villa Fontana. To the widow, she passed as a welfare worker, and she looked the part: she was about thirty, of average height, slender, and hair cut short, and she wore no makeup. She sometimes appeared in modest dresses, more often in dark pants. Her bearing, which was so sober, almost poor, would have looked sad on anyone else, but it made Leonor seem even more distinguished, especially whenever she opened her mouth. Then the former journalist showed some spirit: her voice was warm, her eyes intelligent, almost mischievous. She might not be pretty, Abel thought, but she had a lot of style.

His leader, Itamar, had given Abel a message to take to her. At that point he had been in the capital for only a few days, and he was lonely and obsessed by the memory of Toca. He was looking for a new friend, but he hadn't found one. Although he suffered, he didn't talk to anyone about it. Leonor was the first militant from the Front that he opened himself up to. She reassured him and told him about her own life—"single," she said, "against my will. The only guys I meet wear their balls on their sleeves. . . ." She told him how lucky he was to have Itamar as a leader.

"Why?"

"Do you know of anyone else in the party who isn't completely macho? Your brother, maybe . . ."

"Awful! His balls show like a pair of headlights!"

He gave a quick description of his family. An odd bunch— different from the families of his comrades. He was sure no other militant came from such a mixture of bigotry and brutality, narrow-mindedness, childish emotion, and especially political disagreement. "Are your parents still alive?" Abel went on to ask.

"Yes," Leonor said. "But they're separated. My father lives with his mistress, who also works with him at the bank. My mother still lives in the house, with my two sisters. My mother's great.

She's a teacher, she's political. She and her neighbors started the first Committee of Housewives of Matagalpa against the rise in the cost of living. And now the city has a dozen. It's a whole movement, those committees, they're not just protesting."

"Does your father know about it?"

"Of course, and he makes fun of it. He says his ex-wife is an agitator. He couldn't care less about poverty or politics. He's a sensualist, my father. He's only interested in "women-women," as he calls them. He likes tarts. He thinks any female who can think, who can discuss things, smells of the male, and he can't stand that."

"What about Itamar's parents?"

Until then Abel hadn't known much about his leader's past, his background. And now he found out that Leonor and Itamar came from the same city, an isolated town lost in the mountains, where everyone knew everyone else.

His old man was different, Leonor said. He was a widower. Itamar hadn't lived with his mother very long: she had died when he was only three. Nor had his father remarried. A pious man, he had entrusted his son to a Catholic colleague. He himself had become a sacristan—he had never liked secular life. And as for politics, what a shock it had been to find out that Itamar, then a student, had been arrested. The Front had been infiltrating the university for a long time, and cells had formed. One day the police rounded everybody up. The newspapers published the names of the "propagators of communist ideas," and Itamar's was among them.

His father's reaction was to do penance. He made a pilgrimage of atonement on foot to Suyapa, the Virgin's shrine—more than 125 miles through the middle of Honduras. What the pilgrim brought back from this pilgrimage were books on God, morality, and the social doctrine of the church, and he begged Clara, his son's fiancée, to take them to him. But Clara was a timid young lady who didn't know anyone in the capital, so in the end Leonor, a relative of hers, had been the one to make the trip. As soon as Itamar was released, Leonor had taken him the books.

"And Clara, was she pious?" asked Abel.

"She was pious, too. She believed that if people practiced charity all problems would be solved. So she prayed that the rich would give away their possessions."

"What an idiot! How did Itamar get involved with her? Was she very pretty?"

"She was sweet, she was motherly. And for Itamar, because he didn't have a mother, that was important."

There was Itamar the leader, the patriot, the "prof," the militant—a strong guy with a will of his own. But there was another Itamar, and it was this one, Abel realized, who made the leader human. When Itamar was firm, sure of himself, Abel was upset and antagonized. When Itamar seemed fragile, Abel warmed to him. Thus Abel was alternately mortified by Itamar and touched by his gentleness. This simple story of his private life made Abel thoughtful, as did all family stories, with their dramas, their deaths, their vices, their consolations. And Leonor talked about these things in a slightly ironic, detached, compassionate tone, a tone he had never heard before from any woman's mouth. He liked this tone and he was attracted to Leonor; the bogus welfare worker and he were clearly destined to get along. Secretly Abel cursed the fact that this new friend had to go off and join the guerrillas.

9

What was it like? Months later, Leonor was still living in the midst of a nightmare. Up there in the mountains there were no holidays, no Sundays, no Tuesdays, Wednesdays, or Thursdays. There were only days, nights, and infinite quantities of the color green. The months, weeks, and days were green; the ground was green, the stones were green—because of the moss—the tree trunks were green and even the air was green; they were swimming in green like fish in an ocean. Because everything they saw was green, they forgot that there were any other colors. And in these wells of green, these green rises and green descents, onto level places greener than grass after rain, these clearings, woods, labyrinths, and recesses, these holes and gorges like those in an aquarium—nothing but greenery and water—at the bottom of these damp, green thickets, with their feet in the omnipresent mud, what were the guerrillas—male and female—doing?

They were scrambling around, complaining, looking for a cache: Oh, shit, Christ's blood! Where are the weapons buried? They were searching through the slime, tearing up plants, digging under trees, baring roots. According to the password—"Six feet to the west of the oak, Augustus Caesar"—the first column had buried a whole case of ammunition here.

What else were they doing? Hunting monkeys. They would shoot, the animal would fall in the slime, they would skin it; now it would be all pink, like a baby. They would cook the baby without salt—they didn't have any—or spices. Every day—every day invented by God who was not God and by the guerrillas—they ate monkey; they chewed, ruminated, belched, and smelled of monkey. They did have recipes: Stuff yourself Congo-style, and since you don't have coffee, drink water from the river—watch out for dysentery—mixed with coarse roasted ground corn.

What else were you doing, brave Leonor? And where did you sleep? And whom did you sleep with? Did you make love? Did other people get jealous? Only, sometimes, a leader, an old lover. There were privileges, then? It was a matter of discipline. Anyway, the guerrillas were learning to touch themselves again. They were returning to adolescence. At first it was politically correct to masturbate. Then they began to enjoy it (the men, who made more noise, stifled their groans by covering their mouths with whichever hand they weren't using). These private sessions at night were just as valuable as the group sessions of political commentary: they calmed people down. Afterward, after some good, prolonged, vigorous masturbation, they were ready to submit to all sorts of training when they got up in the morning.

Naturally, they aimed at the monkeys the way they would aim at soldiers. A few imbeciles also practiced on cows, which made the peasants turn against them. That was why some peasants would lead the guerrillas into ambushes, or inform on them, or lose them. At best, the guerrillas trained in "camps," but these camps were just more greenery, probably not so thick, but still provided with the same eternal carpet of rank weeds, walls of shrubbery, and roof of leaves. Armed with AR-15s, old Mausers, rare Galils —taken off the enemy—they would select as a target a bird, the tip of a branch, yet another monkey (bad luck, you're going to have to eat it—you'd be happy to miss it), or a twig or a piece of fruit. That's what you do, if your heart dictates, sighed Leonor when she got back. And the best shots, the boldest, strongest fighters, are sent in to the attack by the leaders. The others stay on the mountain as though they were still in school. School makes them stronger. They come down more hardened, firmer, more stubborn. The mountain sends back to the towns cadres who are ready for anything, who are pure and purified militants.

A F T E R Leonor left, some propagandists, an organizer, and two other young women took off, followed by some students and a few unemployed men recruited in the outlying districts—those "colonies" that had gradually been won over to the cause. Finally Ignacio and his protégée also went up into the hills of the north, the mud, the rain, and the hopelessly tangled chaos of trees, bushes, and lianas.

She was little and brown. An Indian, a real Indian, joked Alvaro, who saw her coming by the side of her white man. She was a peasant, that girl. Here in the mountains she must feel she was in her element. Ignacio, he thought, was a more complicated case. Did a vicar live like other people once he was out of his robes, once he was a heretic clinging to a woman? Alvaro also figured that the guy was a foreigner and his country had to be just as different from this world of muck, these thickets, as a tilled field is different from a virgin forest. He didn't know that Rosario— this was the name under which the prostitute had carried on her profession—had been born in the city, where she had grown up and been sweet-talked, deflowered, and rejected by some individual. That her lovers of one night, her liars, thieves, and pimps, were guys from the city. In short, that she had never known anything but the dirty, dusty air and the din of the city. And, of course, the sidewalks, the asphalt or concrete sidewalks, twelve years of sidewalks, first in her own suburb—at the age of fourteen, comrade—then near the railroad station, then among the heaps of rubble—there were still some pieces of sidewalk left after the earthquake—and finally on the gravel in the area around the stadium. So the underbrush, the shrubs, the snakes, the dense woods . . .

"But am I the only woman?" she asked.

"No, though physically some are in better shape. They run through this godforsaken place all night long, they carry their own weapons, their grub, their reserves, their bundles of clothes."

"And we love each other," Ignacio insisted. "Love is good for us, keeps us fit; love is strength."

The words of a priest, Alvaro thought. Only a priest would equate love with walking twenty miles at a stretch through the ferns, the sludge, the couch grass. "We love each other"! And only a priest would fall in love with a tart. On the other hand, if the tart can clean our guns, wash our rags and cook monkey, if she can talk to the peasants, reassure them, get them to help—seasoned whore or virgin, it doesn't make much difference once she becomes a partisan, as long as she fights and does what she's told.

And Rosario did what she was told. She walked when they were told to walk, stopped when everybody else stopped, and built fires. She would set to work cutting up pieces of monkey, run a stick through them, bury the bones, and start walking again. But she didn't know what to say to the women on the mountain, and she would forget the phrases that had been spoken during the instruction sessions—she couldn't grasp politics any more than she could technical instruction or the alphabet. She had never been to school: she held the leaflets and the tracts upside down.

And the words the instructor used—"productivity," "alternative," "primary contradiction"—were so strange. No one had ever used these words in her mother's house or around the stadium. And so Rosario began to worry. It wasn't so serious, her priest assured her, she would learn; for a new woman or man, a new language.

And while they were waiting for this new woman to be born, there was always love. Only in the mind, of course, for among the guerrillas, it was each to his own hammock. But her past life had created certain needs in Rosario, and so she hung back, arranged things so that she would be at the end of the column, and tried to hold her man back. He didn't dare slow down: he was afraid of losing his group. So they had to take advantage of the stopovers, a few siestas, some brief excursions into the brush on which they pretended to be hunting macaque. There were also the cleaning sessions—when they disinfected sores and scrapes, took private baths, deloused themselves—and the hours of the watch. But all this was uncomfortable. Someone or other—envious of them? a voyeur?—was always hanging around. And they needed their hands to swat the mosquitoes. They also had to be careful not to sit on ants, and to look out for snakes. During the watch, together or alone, they had to be on the alert. Soldiers could appear at any moment, and you never knew if woodcutters, peasants, or hunters were friends or enemies.

Ignacio wasn't at all used to doing things on the sly or in dangerous situations. Besides, where love was concerned, with complete humility and some embarrassment, he considered himself a beginner. Rosario, with her years of frolicking about in all sorts of places, with or without an audience, in all kinds of weather, at all different tempos, was naturally less wary. She was hungry, and when she was hungry she had to eat: quickly or at her leisure, resting or in the midst of the march, lying down or standing up. This simple and worthy comrade didn't care about relishing her man in total security, in a state of meditation, as a communicant would his host. She was quite the opposite of the still-clumsy Ignacio, who made a great fuss over what she called "hitting below the belt."

In some sense, he wanted to consummate the union the way a priest would—slowly, ceremoniously, with refinements. Not the way a crude man, a proletarian, a warrior would. Ignacio had too much respect, he said, for the pleasures of the flesh. After the revolution, they would have the leisure to copulate in peace, to make children, and then they would have sons, handsome little boys, copper-skinned like their mother. Rather than give himself in haste, Ignacio refused altogether. Rosario returned to the charge. He refused again. This man would never satisfy her. Yet could she switch to another in this godforsaken spot, in the midst of this gang? She was a guerrilla's woman, and the guerrillas respected one another's rights. To cuckold a comrade was to sow discord, hatred, turn a brother into an enemy. Revolution had its own morality, comrade. The only way Rosario could become someone else's woman was if she became a widow first. And for her to become a widow, there would have to be a fight, and Ignacio would have to die in the fight.

T H E priest was a good shot, he hit the bull's-eye almost every time. Even he was astonished. No one in his family had ever handled a gun—not his father, a peaceful grammar teacher; not his brothers, one of whom was a law student and the other an architecture student. At the modest hacienda his family owned somewhere in the region of Antigua, people didn't hunt; they didn't even practice archery, but were content with snaring an occasional hare. The priest had a good eye, even if he hadn't known it before. When he lifted his rifle he just naturally stopped it at the right height. An excellent student, in the instructor's opinion. Ignacio was sure of his aim, his arms didn't move, he didn't hesitate, and he scored. This priest-guerrilla was full of promise, and if the enemy came up against him they would regret it.

They did regret it. As the marchers advanced, following the Yali River above San Sebastián, they stumbled on one of the Guard's patrols. The ground was marshy, and the guerrillas were getting bogged down. Rosario had lost a shoe in the muck. Barefoot or with shoes on, it didn't make any difference. These marches over mountains and valleys, these endless marches through interminable greenery—the woman had had enough of it, she couldn't take any more, and she was beginning to miss the city, her neighborhood, even the ruins. Besides, what did the mountain have to offer her? Making the revolution meant walking and more walking, nothing but walking. When she asked Ignacio where they were going, Ignacio didn't have time to answer, because a company of soldiers had appeared on the other side of the river.

The guerrillas weren't expecting this. The enemy was also surprised and stopped short, dived into the grass, and started firing. Alvaro and his comrades in turn put their guns to their shoulders and fired back at them. Both sides yelled, swore, loosed volleys of insults. The firing paused for a moment, started up again, and went on and on. No one was winning or losing, but there were more and more casualties on both sides. Since they were equal in strength, and doing equal damage, why go on? Did they want to massacre one another down to the last man, commit suicide?

Partisans and soldiers both withdrew. The fire died down. Each side collected its dead and wounded. Ignacio was lying on the ground, a hole in his head, one eye socket empty and red. Before they buried him, they took off his bag, his cartridges, and his boots, and stripped him of his full black canvas parka with its front pocket, which he never took off except to wash. In the pocket, Rosario found some letters, a pencil, and his *Guerrilla Manual*. Slipped in between the pages of the little book, like bookmarks, were sheets of paper covered with handwriting. Were these messages, she asked, more letters? And who were they addressed to? She gave them to a comrade who knew how to read. On one was copied out the fragment of text that spoke of men who took on "the color of stones, of the earth." On other sheets—had these also been sent to Ignacio by the seminarian infatuated with the ancient culture?—the following text was reproduced:

Then the warriors went to the designated places. This will be as our wall, as our clan, as our palisades, as our fortresses. That such may be our valor, our gallantry, said all the leaders in the afore-mentioned places, each for his clan, with the aim of fighting the enemy. When this was ordered, they left for the designated places to occupy the land of the tribes; it was for this that they went to those regions. Do not be afraid if there are warriors who march toward you to kill you; come quickly and tell me; I will go and I will kill them, said Quicab to them when he gave his orders to everyone and to the Eminent, the Speaker of the Men.

This text, perhaps even older, was also found copied out:

In his time is the wild turkey, in his time is Sulim Chan, the man of Chakanputun. They will seek their food in the forests, they will seek their food among the stones, those who have lost their harvests, when the destiny of Katun 11 Ahau comes.

The 11 Ahau begins the count, for it was the Katun who resigned when they arrived, the foreigners who came from the East, those who brought Christianity. In the East his word is done, the Katun is established at Ichcanziho. Then the sky will weep and the bread of the Katun will be full of bitterness.

The comrade who knew how to read—and who tried to comfort the widow, saying "Gibberish, my girl!"—also deciphered, at the bottom of the second tale: "Pp.-Vh., 44." And at the bottom of the third, these words: "Chilam Balam Xupan Nauat." And then—were they gaga, these people?—"Katun 11 Ahau."

1 0

Abel had disappeared in the middle of the week, in the small hours of the morning.

In Corinto, his parents were asleep and Alba was, as usual, having a dream in which she had lost weight, men were flocking around her, and a troop of admirers was fighting over her. Alvaro wasn't persecuting Abel—he was off with the guerrillas—and the rejected man was spending his last night in his own city by himself. He hung around the quays, sad and uncertain what to do. Should he try to see Toca again? Good-byes made people feel sorry for you: the most hardhearted would soften, and ex-lovers would give in and agree to one last favor. Yet Abel was afraid of being hurt again. He prowled around the soccer player's house, hesitated, refrained from knocking. Finally he tore himself away from the neighborhood—the house was all dark, Toca was asleep.

The boy headed back toward the lights of the port, toward the station. The first train of the day left at about four o'clock, going from Corinto to León to Managua. At León a crowd of passengers always got on—students, salesmen, middle- and lower-echelon civil servants, young men infected with wanderlust.

Abel had the car to himself until he got to Chichigalpa, a filthy town where a filthy, puffy-faced soldier got on, along with three noisy adult males wearing filthy, worn baseball caps. Fortunately, these individuals chose a seat together far away from his.

The train started up again. Abel went on looking out the window at the cordillera and the plantations of corn, cotton, sugar cane. The fields were turning green. The blue-green plain, spotted with black and planted here and there with groves of trees, extended to the base of the volcanoes, and the volcanoes lay there like a gigantic sculpture. Curtains of fog hung in shreds around the mountains and some of the peaks poked up through the clouds—it had rained so much the last few days. Chonco, its summit broken off, stood up against a more powerful, more precipitous mountain called by the Christian name of San Cristóbal. Then came Casita, longer, squatter, with gentle, wooded slopes, a curve like a hip.

My country is beautiful, Abel said to himself. My land . . . And he was filled with emotion, a vague sadness. As the train rolled along, the land on either side flattened out again. This spectacle of nature, this unfurling, this uprising of primordial forces, became fixed in him, turned into an inner landscape: Abel became his land. He became a plain, a volcano. Was this what it meant, then, to be a man, to be a man from this land—that one became living matter, peaceful waters, fire? And this fire was smoldering, smoldering everywhere: in the mountains' cores, in people's lives, in history, under the lagoons, under the green-and-brown crust of the fields, under the long twisted neck of the isthmus, under the ocean, the vast ocean with its stirring depths, its sudden bursts of heat. The smoldering fire broke out in eruptions and in revolutions. Central America, and this country, were uneasy places. You came from Nicaragua just as the devil came from hell: it was the same kind of thing. The very substance of Central America was rage, liquid torment, frozen torment, and Abel's uneasiness was the uneasiness of his world. Yet all this remained confused in him, unformulated; he felt things, but he couldn't articulate them, because he didn't have the words or the understanding. Only one notion—the notion of fatality, fatality as the key to everything—occurred to him, in a crude form. Most likely this fatality was the same as the fatality of earthquakes, tidal waves, stone. The train went on. Now the ground was dotted with slabs of concrete, walls, whole houses, iron structures; wires appeared, and pylons. Here and there stood isolated fences, then more walls, then larger buildings crowded together: the train was arriving in León.

W H E N Itamar got on, he spotted a seat to his left where only one other person was sitting. He introduced himself. And you? López Pastora? Not the brother of that daredevil back there in the Sierra de Estelí? The atmosphere relaxed and Abel joked: his brother was a López, all right, a wanderer, a stubborn go-getter— he had inherited that from his grandfather. As for himself, the younger brother, he belonged to the other, more discreet side of the family, his mother's side. The Pastoras led quieter lives, some would say slower and more surreptitious lives.

"I see. Alvaro . . . I had already left León when he came through. What a pity. I would have liked to ask him some questions."

"Theoretical questions? I hope you don't expect—"

"No, questions about terrain, climate, hygiene, diseases."

"Are you a doctor?"

The train shook back and forth while the two talked on and on, keeping their voices low since you never knew who might be sitting nearby, pretending to sleep—bogus students, "ears." Abel

1 1 7

laughed. Then he yawned. Itamar asked him if he had been traveling for a long time.

"Yes," he said evasively. "But I intend to move on, start all over again, from square one!"

They went on talking, confiding scraps of information to each other—numbers, dates, ages. By the time they arrived at their destination, the fugitive and the professor were calling each other *tú*. The professor promised to help Abel; he would give him names and addresses. Itamar described the pension where he lived—not bad, a bit of greenery, only six guests, not too inquisitive, an interesting neighborhood. And that, said Abel, was how he came to know the Estadio quarter, the little hotels and cheap restaurants, the ruins, La Perla. He went exploring. Naturally, as though in spite of himself, the boy had crossed the vacant lots, the area of the epicenter with its rubble, its shacks, its pellets of scrap iron. Quite naturally, he had walked around a warehouse, a square with broken benches, a little auto graveyard, and headed for the lake.

"Yes, in Managua, when you're bored you head for the lake."

You, too, the frustrated volcanologist—you are more and more frustrated, aren't you?—and discoverer of new, secret worlds, hidden fires . . . you, too, head for the lake. Militants, lovers, men out of work all go down there, as well as prowlers, homeless people, a few stray tourists—stranded geographers?—and a handful of melancholics. Water attracts some people, and the Xolotlan is more than just a lake. It's a sea; you can't make out either its periphery or the hills beyond. Its horizon is an interminable thread of liquid silver. They say there are sharks in it—the only freshwater sharks in the world.

Other people are attracted by stones, and high banks of cinder and scoria, by rocks and hardened earth, by fire under the stones. But for weeks now, even months, the volcanoes have seemed inaccessible to you, standing there so far from the city, so far from the worries of the people of the city, from your new friends, from the uprising, from these violent feelings. The volcanoes have become mere objects of nostalgia for you: there was once a love, and now this love seems to have been put in parentheses. Is it going to be there long? How can you know? And now other forces have aroused your curiosity, and they're pulling you in different directions. You are drawn by Abel, by Abel's life, by the rebellion these men are waging. You watch and listen. Your fellow boarder at La Perla, Abel's leader, already considers you one of them, and yet you're not committing yourself to anything, you're not carrying leaflets or messages to anyone, you're not agitating or demonstrating, and you're not writing on the walls such slogans as "Down with tyranny," "The mob is God," "Guerrilla, guerrilla, guerrilla" (which appears even in La Perla's toilets), and "Long live the Front!" Yet Abel is pressuring you.

You look at him. Are you from here? Are you going to stay here? Are you going to find yourself a new woman? And are you going to die here? The truth is, you disembark from a planet, you wander around, do some climbing, zigzag over another planet. Can you zigzag back and forth for long on land that is so convulsed, so burning hot, always standing its men on their ears? The answer will come, some day. From whom? How? For now, you give in again. Abel says he has nothing to do this afternoon, and the weather is too fine for you to molder between the walls of the pension, so you go off with him to wander around the edge of the lake.

T H E wind is blowing, churning up the water. Waves collapse on the rubble. A block of concrete sticks out of the grass and the two of you sit down on it, facing the rounded peninsula of Chiltepe with its row of gray-and-green hills containing old, flooded craters. A superb setting, you point out. Such a splendid place . . .

". . . is made for happiness, I know. All foreigners say that.

But happiness . . . I've tried, see? As soon as I came to Managua I started hunting."

Abel had had his share of adventures and misadventures here as elsewhere, nice surprises and disappointments. The first one was right here, on the banks of this bogus sea. To the right, behind them, stood a higher piece of ground covered with grass. Often, at about five o'clock, when the sun was beginning to set, a guy would come along, climb up, and sit on the hillock. Abel thought he had to be a poet; he looked serious, and he must be coming here to get away from the crowds and seek inspiration. But when Abel went up to him, the poet turned out to be stupid. Stupid but handsome, unfortunately. His name, he said, was Demóstenes, and he added that his father was a police commissioner. It was an interesting profession, he went on, and he was going to be a policeman, too, just like his papa—he was impressed by the uniform. It was the classiest thing you could be, he declared. Besides, didn't he have the right physique for it?

"Sure, you have a nice build."

"And when you have the physique, you have everything."

This braggart was sure that once he was in uniform he could have any woman he wanted. And when Demóstenes talked about women, he was talking about sex. At his age, eighteen, he already had a nice list. Better still—he'd already had the clap twice. Twice, my friend! You have to realize that when you've had fifty girls . . . Suspicious, that number; the kid was lying, thought Abel, hiding something.

All of a sudden he wanted to test him. The skeptic asked if he wanted to go swimming over there in the part of the lake off to the left, beyond the "beach" of rubble and debris. Demóstenes said he would, and climbed down from his embankment. The two of them went to a spot that was filled with little dunelike mounds. The shore was deserted. It was midsummer; the sun was still strong, though its rays fell obliquely on the water, dust, and grass; the heat was oppressive. The boys stripped and dived in, swam, came back to shore; dived in again, swam out vigorously, drew away from the bank, crossed paths, swam back in parallel lines, and touched ground again.

"I think I'll sunbathe," Abel said.

"It'll be a blood-red sunbath." Demóstenes thought the sun was too low: at that hour it was a waste of time—you couldn't get tan. "And anyway, to get tan you have to be so patient! It gets on my nerves. I'm going to put my clothes back on."

"Oh, come on, not right away."

"Why?"

"Because . . . because, see, Demó, you're a real pal, I can say it to you: I like looking at you this way. You're right, Demó, you're a real looker, you're handsome."

"I know."

"So when someone's good-looking . . ."

"Shit, you're getting hard!"

"Demó . . ."

"You're nuts!"

And now Demóstenes, too. But he was embarrassed, and to hide his embarrassment he started joking around. To get like this, all stiff, and in front of a guy . . . really . . . to think you're tempted by that, how stupid! And he grabbed his clothes, slammed them down on his belly.

"With a friend, a pal," Abel went on.

"But I want to be a commissioner!"

"So? You don't think that policemen . . . ?"

"Maybe, but not my father. He's a man who gets promoted. And he's handsome, my father is. He's like me. He's the most handsome policeman in his department and even in the whole district."

The boy started boasting about the uniform again, about what a good physique you needed, how you had to stand, what an effect it had. And he enumerated the advantages: the way you looked, the prestige, the respect of other men, the women who gave themselves to you. Abel grew tired of all this and his sex drooped. He finally understood that he would get nothing from this Demóstenes, not even a little companionship, a little fooling around. And what did he expect from an aspiring cop, anyway? He got up and said it was the sun; he was sorry, but even when the sun was red, even when it wasn't strong, it still heated the blood. It was like alcohol: it put strange ideas into your head. Demóstenes listened, puzzled.

"Really?" he said, apparently not understanding at all.

The two of them, not friends, not enemies, got dressed, walked away from the lake, and headed back toward the city at a steady pace, talking once again about women and the clap.

A B E L happened to run into Demóstenes again, on another day when he was wandering aimlessly around, coming from the endless field of ruins between the stadium and the González movie theater, which had survived intact and was repainted a very pale green, almost a pistachio color. Evening was falling, and a lot of men, plus a handful of women, were waiting to go into the movie theater. Demóstenes was in line with a friend, a policeman of about thirty. The two of them were approaching the ticket window when Abel appeared, slapped the boy's shoulder, and said: "Hey, handsome, still in civvies?"

The boy seemed embarrassed. His friend the policeman looked annoyed. Abel glanced at the posters that were plastered all around. They showed a Chinese—or maybe Japanese or Korean—adventure movie inspired by the martial arts, called *The Triumph of Kung Fu.*

"Enjoy the fight," said Abel, slapping Demóstenes's shoulder again. Then he said good-bye, ignoring the friend, and took off.

"That idiot," he said to himself. "I'll come across him again, but he'll be wearing khaki and I'll be on the other side of the bars."

For the final phase of the revolt would be coming soon. The whole city would rise up. The Guard and the police would become ruthless and start killing, and everything would be over. The guerrillas would enter the capital and the dictatorship would yield. The bigwigs would hightail it, while the little ones, people like Demóstenes, the foppish suburban police and the neighborhood police—they would be the ones to pay. But the time for open war, for a general, urban war, hadn't come yet. Is it going to come? you asked, skeptical, and more curious than upset. At the pension people talked about it every day, and yet it was still distant, abstract. Itamar was the only one who could really imagine it, with its different stages, its logistics, its powerful rhythm. For Abel, war hovered like a rumor: depending on his mood, sometimes the rumor seemed right to him, and at other times he rejected it. The boy believed in it when things were going badly for him, and doubted it when things were going well. And his doubts encouraged him to go hunting.

I F he had time, he hunted in the afternoons, between propaganda actions—scrawling graffiti on walls, attending *ad hoc* meetings, distributing leaflets—because at night he had to go to work. As soon as he had arrived, Abel had looked for a job—in a brickyard, in an air-conditioning repair shop, in restaurants, in garages. He had also investigated civilian construction, the Transportation and Water Departments. Eventually he was offered a job as night watchman at an open construction site in the northern part of the city. In this dusty, rocky area they were building houses for government employees, and there were an increasing number of thefts of boards, bricks, sand, and cement from the worksite. The watchman they had hired complained that he couldn't oversee the whole sector all by himself. To help him, the boss hired this ex-docker, who was given a kepi, a belt, a holster, and a revolver. Thus equipped, he was transformed into a cop.

"Can't be helped! I have no choice," he said to his new fellow worker, a good-natured man of about thirty who had fixed up a sort of room for himself in the basement of a detached house under construction.

"Well, I like this better than being a mason. It's easier, believe me. I know, because I was a mason for fourteen years. They used to oversee me; now I'm the overseer. And now that there are two of us, we'll be able to bring women here to my digs."

These digs really looked more like a storeroom than a bedroom. Part of the floor was covered by a straw mattress. Crates were piled up, their bottoms to the wall, to form a sort of cupboard, and in them were stacks of old newspapers, metal scraps—broken tools, fragments of car engines, shattered locks, other debris from various sources—and pieces of rubber cut from worn tires. On the ground was a hodgepodge of jam jars that had been emptied of their original contents and filled with water spotted with rust and oil, sometimes bluish and greasy, sometimes red. In among the jars stood a camping stove with a little kettle, and between the mattress and the crates a line of beer bottles, also empty, and some four or five glasses, one chipped.

"Well, this is my kingdom," declared the night watchman. "In this room you can screw in peace. No more forking out your dough in whorehouses."

"But you still have to find someone willing to walk all the way here."

"That's not so hard. Waspán City isn't far and there are heaps of women there without husbands—widows, old ladies . . ."

Why confess that his tastes were different? The thing to do was to be friendly, joke around, win your fellow worker over. And Abel joked, laughed, spun his revolver in front of the other guy.

During his first night on the construction site he wandered around among the buildings, dozed an hour or two on the mattress in the basement, went back up above ground, listened to the story of Farabundo's life.

Farabundo had been born in the flat country of the far south. His village was poor, and everyone worked in the fields—an endlessly green, vast space crossed by the Pan-American Highway. His father, who was of mixed Spanish, black, and Indian blood, died young, and his mother and he left the village. They went to live in a small hut at the edge of the city of Rivas, where the widow found work as a servant in the home of a reserve corporal who made everyone call him "lieutenant." This man spent his time buying and reselling old motorcycles. Farabundo grew up with his children. When he was ten, the corporal took him out of school and made him work in his shop, sweeping, cleaning engine parts, and running errands, though the boss didn't pay him anything—he said the boy's work just barely covered the cost of his food and bed. Farabundo's mother didn't protest—in fact, she was madly in love with the corporal. She thought she was his only woman, except for the wife.

Then one day she learned that he had two other mistresses. She cried and thought of leaving, but where do you go when you don't own anything, don't know anyone, don't have a job? So she stayed where she was, in his house. At the time Farabundo was fourteen. To get back at the corporal, she sent her son away and told the boss that the boy was tired of working for nothing and had run off. Furious, the corporal drove her out of his house.

Farabundo didn't find out about this until a few years later, when he happened to meet one of his old boss's kids in the market place. At that point, he set out to find his mother. He knocked on all sorts of doors, trying to get information from priests and sacristans, from brothels, farms, and the police stations. The only information he got was vague, because in this country it was all too common to run into women who were out looking for a brother, a husband, a child, and many people had encountered them, women of all ages, all colors, usually very poor, old, or crazy. Unfortunately, none of them seemed to answer to the name of Farabunda—which was actually the name Farabundo's mother went by. He never saw her again.

In the meantime he had become a mason, and now he roamed from one construction site to another. While he was building a store for a contractor from Belén he got to know a girl named Rina. She had nothing to do, and spent her days avoiding the shouting, crying, and quarreling of her twelve brothers and sisters. She complained that she hated knocking around and wanted to settle down. Farabundo took her in to stay with him in his shack, and for a year they lived there like man and wife. Then Rina, who was light-skinned, presented him with a daughter who was almost black. He became suspicious and wouldn't go near her. Finally he went off to work in another town, where he had another child, this time with a single mother who did the laundry for the men and was a great barfly. In all, Farabundo had had five women, not counting the one-night stands—"hundreds and hundreds of girls," he claimed—the excursions into brothels in different towns and villages. In other words, he had been around.

"Are you thinking of settling down now?" Abel asked.

"To settle down I would need a house. I don't have one. I've always lived in temporary places—huts, cellars, workers' quarters. I even lived in a tent while we were enlarging the main barracks of the department."

"And all these changes don't exhaust you?"

"I'm free! Free as a bird! And I intend to stay that way a few more years," he announced.

After this conversation, Abel made his rounds while Farabundo went down to the cellar to rest. The construction site was dead quiet, as quiet as the edge of the lake at nightfall. Between the half-constructed walls, around the cement mixers, among the little mounds of sand and piles of brick, nothing moved, not a shadow. The air was still. All that could be heard were the crickets— there were always crickets, wherever a little grass grew. As he walked, Abel thought about what Farabundo had said, about his conquests, how men were racked by this never-ending desire. Suddenly Toca's face swam back into his mind. Abel had had some of the best times of his life with Toca. Now he was tormented by the memory of those encounters, those intense, risky, and ultimately dangerous encounters—and the torment was as physical as a headache or the need for a drink. In the night, on the construction site, the boy was overcome by a growing desire to be touched. What tough luck that there was no one with him. He stopped walking and did it by himself, his belt unbuckled, his revolver beating against his thigh, alone behind one of the cement mixers.

T H E night watchman would head back to the pension at eight o'clock, when the masons arrived. There were about twenty of them, and they came in on a truck. Usually masons sleep on the sites where they work, but too many bricks, blocks of fiberboard, and sacks of cement had been stolen from this site. The contractor began to suspect that the workers were taking this stuff at night and selling it cheap to the people from the "colonies" and the working-class neighborhoods. So he had workers' quarters built on the far side of the city, and it was there that the masons camped now, crowded in between cardboard, sheet-metal, and wooden walls. Thefts from the site hadn't stopped since the second night watchman was added, but they had been reduced. If they were reduced still further, the boss had promised to give the night watchmen bonuses. With that money, Abel daydreamed, he would be able to travel.

When he wasn't discussing politics, Abel listened to songs in his room at La Perla. With his first paycheck he had bought himself a little transistor radio; and he specially loved the variety shows. In the morning, when Abel returned, the pension was emptying out. Itamar was going off to teach his classes, as was the mechanics instructor with his untidy hair and his rumpled clothes. The bank clerk, who had gone on a spree the night before, was dragging himself to his office, and the high-school students were on their way to school. As for the geometrician, he was leaving to go survey his plots of ground. The night watchman could sleep undisturbed.

The owner of the pension would wake him up at about three o'clock, at which point the place was deserted. Abel showered, ate something, and, back in his room, beguiled his loneliness by listening to popular singers. This was the period when, after a long absence—he had followed some woman all the way down to Argentina—Ramón de Dios, creator of the poignant song "Our Happiness Has the Flu," was back in the limelight, as sentimental as ever. It was the period when one could hear, twenty times a day, the great successes of José-José, Adalberto Lesbia, and the light and inspired tenor Celestino Celeste. It was also the period when the charming singer Rony Castro and the duo Los Dos were making names for themselves, and all the airwaves were full of the "hot rhythms" of the orchestra of the so-called brothers Eddy and Teddy Sánchez.

And, lastly, it was the period of the unforgettable Afrodita Cruz, nicknamed "the Heartbreaker" because her voice—deep, almost masculine, full of pathos—deeply touched anyone who heard it, brought back his most agonizing memories, plunged him into a blue mood. Afrodita Cruz was more than a singer: she was a priestess of the heart, an oracle, a reader of entrails and memory. Anyone who heard her sing the romantic song "My Love, We Will Go to Tegucigalpa" would feel something knot up and then loosen inside him; he would be overcome by a powerful desire, a tidal wave. Whenever Abel heard it, he dreamed of going away, of going to Tegucigalpa. Just think! To go to Tegucigalpa! Traveling through the countryside, through different departments, different towns, crossing rivers, bridges, the border, and rushing down the Pan-American, hour after hour, a whole day, a whole night! My love, we will go. . . .

"You know Tegucigalpa?" he asks you.

"I've been through it."

"It's pretty, isn't it?"

According to Afrodita Cruz, it is a refuge for runaway, outcast, and illicit lovers, very special lovers. Tegucigalpa must be a glamorous city, exquisite, like the places in fairy tales, different from anywhere else. . . .

"It's the middle of nowhere, a big nothing town, but the hills around it are beautiful."

And you describe the hills. You describe the roads with their hairpin turns that go up to the groves of pines, the haciendas, the country houses. You talk about the high brownish scree slopes and the little pale-blue or cream-colored houses that lean up against them, and about the precipices that line the tortuous road on the other side, the road with its few horses and cars climbing up. And finally you tell about the immensity of the panorama that meets your eye at the top of that road, an immensity of ocher, cleared of trees, on which stand the powerful, gray basilica of Suyapa and some squat buildings, beige cubes set on a surface of beige dust—an immensity covered by the endless urban zone of Comayagua.

"Well, I was right—the city is beautiful."

"When you see it from high up and far away."

But Abel never saw Tegucigalpa, not from inside the nothing town, not from the edge of town, not from the hills. He didn't have the money—or the time, since the vacations promised him were always postponed. The roads weren't safe, either: new guerrilla centers had sprung up, there was fighting in the north, the insurgents were setting up ambushes. The roads in the cordillera had been blocked, traffic interrupted, the border closed off. Abel was reduced to making excursions in the city on Sundays, to the neighborhood of the lagoons or around the lake. A new friend took him to other towns, fields, and *his* volcano, as he said proudly, a mountain he had climbed a hundred times—the imposing, the unique, the sublime Momotombo.

11

Abel's new friend lived in Managua, in Xolotlan City, a mile
or so from the construction site. An apprentice in a garage,
some sort of mechanic—he patched blowouts, tightened brakes,
replaced light bulbs, tubes, cables, mufflers—the boy was a year
older than Abel. He lived with his mother, who was a cleaning
woman. Because he had slanted eyes, eyes like a Miskito Indian
(or a Sumo, a Rama or a mixture of all three), he had been afflicted with the nickname Chino.

Chino was often bored. His employer didn't pay him very well,
and he was laid off half the time. Tired of the boss, of the filthy
garage, which was built of planks and cardboard, had holes in
the roof, and was organized in a completely haphazard way, the
apprentice had decided to seek a more brilliant career for himself. In a fit of mingled rage and hope—or hopelessness—Chino
had applied for a position in one of the corps of the Guard. While
he waited for an answer, the mechanic went on with his appren-

ticeship as best he could. He kept his application a secret from everyone—the head mechanic, his co-workers, his mother, his friend. He could always tell them about this promotion later if it happened. If he was turned down, no one would blame him for it or be sarcastic, because no one would know a thing about it. So Chino was like all young men, rich in dreams and desires, as comfortably settled in civilian life as any soul of the party is in his own life.

When he was little, only one job had impressed him—driving a tractor-trailer. And tractor-trailers did go by on the main road to La Paz Centro, the town where he was born, not far from Momotombo. Despite its ruts and potholes, he thought that road was the famous Pan-American. When he was an adolescent, the boy dreamed of becoming a guide, because he loved climbing the mountain. With friends from school he had often played at being a real mountain climber, an explorer, and he had discovered ways to get through the scrub brush and chunks of lava. He knew how to plunge through the ash and the scoria, which stones to grab on to, when to take a breather. He knew where the niches were, the faults where you could take shelter from avalanches. When he was big, he would lead scholars, poets, geographers, and other curious travelers to the top.

The young man tried it, but found out that in this country people who climbed mountains weren't willing to pay anything. They thought anyone who worked as a guide did it because he had no real job, because he was bored, because he had nothing better to do. Disgusted, Chino quit. His mother, who thought he was at last going to start helping her out, called him a "shitty son of a shitty Indian," as she always grumbled when she was at the end of her tether. Then she would pull herself together, and after that she would start crying. Her husband had deserted her long ago, and this son of hers was the only man in the world who could protect her.

Together they fled their neighborhood, "the asshole of the world," as she called it, a jumble of straw huts and shanties, a kind of rural appendix attached to the town. They went off to seek their fortune in the capital.

"But now and then," Chino said emphatically, "I go back to Momotombo. It's crazy the way you feel. You climb, your mouth is full of dust, your feet are worn out. When you get up there you're all black, you look like a chimney sweep, you have a little cough, you're spitting mud, your eyes sting from the gases, the stinking vapors, but you're the king, man!"

"The king of what?"

"The king of the countryside, the rocks."

"And hot air."

"Well, shit—you don't become king of America!"

And yet what a feeling of power it gave you to sit at the top! You were high above the towns, the down-and-outs, the dirty bosses, the factories, the whole rest of the world. In one glance you could take in the lake and the ocean, the two Leóns—the old one, which a history teacher would describe as the local Pompeii, with its low, reddish walls, and the new one—as well as Managua, the "colonies" around Managua, and the eight volcanoes of the cordillera of the Marabios. Then, true, his eye would fall back on his garage, the pit of his lousy garage, dug out of the beaten earth, where he was mired in mud and grease.

"So you can understand why I want to go back up there. As high up as possible."

You like the idea. Momotombo is an excellent volcano, an incomparable peak, a masterpiece created when the planet was forming, a legend. And you haven't explored it. The idea of getting to know this place rekindles a flame in you. To scale this colossus would restore a little of the original meaning of your coming to this country. It discourages Abel to think of climbing such a long, rough, high slope, but what can he do? He would go anywhere with Chino.

All three of you set off over a terrain choked with clusters of wine-colored stones, between which grow stunted shrubs with dark leaves. There is something unreal about this sparse grove sprouting from the ore. Thin treetops poke up near the mountain. A possible path appears among the shrubs. It leads to a drier, even more rocky, brown-spotted area where the vegetation is thinner. You take this oblique path, which hardly slopes up at all. The bushes become smaller; the plants shrink, redden, are coated with dust. Suddenly the slope is steeper, and you go on, trampling the half-dead grass, a long bed of slag, lichen. Now the sides of the volcano are carpeted only with ash and bits of straw. The tawny colors, the last tongues of green, give way to gray and straw-yellow. Then the patches of yellow disappear, and Momotombo is a formidable cone of cinder. The summit, which is emitting smoke, seems inaccessible. You're out of breath, you can't go on, and you want to go back down. Fortunately, Chino decides it's time to rest, and stops on a narrow promontory overhanging an abyss, with several other platforms down below and, at the bottom, the three lagoons carved out of the thick scrub.

Then you go on climbing. This time you have to follow the stream of solidified lava, an enormous round black vein that runs down from the summit to the base. As you climb higher, the stream of rock narrows. Where there is only ash underfoot, it disappears into the warm, powdery substance, in which you all sink up to your ankles, sometimes up to your calves.

The final stage turns out to be the most difficult. You're panting, sweating, the soles of your feet are burning, the small of your back hurts. It takes a full two hours to cover the last two hundred yards, which is an area of pure carbonaceous powder, gravel, and scoria. Sulphur vapors rise from a hundred fissures. Your mouth is full of dust and smoke, you're spitting out as much as you can, swallowing the rest, while your eyes sting, redden, keep filling with tears so you can't see.

"Well, here we are, we're the kings!" exclaims your guide, who is the first to pull himself up on the crest.

"You've already said that, fellow. The kings of what—death?"

"Shut up. You could have stayed down there on the grass."

Feeling like kings—even Abel—the three of you contemplate the world below you. It is dark green, brown, and gray, with a delicate film of silver above. You study:

> the plain
> the three lagoons (puddles)
> the lake and
> in the middle of the lake, the younger volcano: Momotom-
>   bito.

You study:

> an immense grassland
> rivers
> mouths of rivers
> the foreground of the countryside
> the background and
> in the farthest distance, the mountain chain of Dario.

"God, what emptiness," Abel insists.

"What fullness."

The one who doesn't like emptiness is the first to start back down. Sliding seems to be the best method—crouching if you can manage it, but more often sitting on your rear end. The thing to do would be to ski, without poles or skis, on the layer of ash and slag. But this black snow crumbles. Banks of powder and gravel collapse, carve out pits, produce sudden unexpected dropoffs. You fall head over heels, you try to get your balance, you grab at the dust, at the wind. You travel the whole stretch of pure mineral on your backside. You land on a semblance of a narrow, concave *piste* overgrown with the stubby high-altitude plants. Skier without skis, painfully you get back on your feet, totter, move with measured steps toward some feeble shrubs. You tear off one branch, then another, break them, fashion some ski poles for yourself, and go on. Abel plunges in the direction of the strips of grass

and pebbles, toward the belt of little trees, the long green decliv-
ity. He leaps—he would love to slalom down—but falls backward
and lands at the bottom of the volcano, his shoulderblades and
ass burning. His two friends join him, as dirty as he is, coated
with soot, the seats of their pants threadbare and torn to pieces.

"Long live the three kings of rags!" says Abel ironically.

"Sure, I can see your ass. . . ."

As for you, you're daydreaming, reliving your first few climbs
again, comparing. Yesterday you scaled the desolate, rough heights
of Masaya. The altitude, the nakedness of the rocks touched your
soul and you were uplifted, intoxicated. You wandered around by
yourself, and this frozen heap of stones, this world, existed only
for you. No one could see you. You took your clothes off—now
your nakedness matched the nakedness of your surroundings; there
was no separation between you and the elements, no barrier; your
flesh was the flesh of the earth; you were an extension of all things
mineral, vegetable, animal. Your rapture was boundless. Your
solitude freed you—nothing prevented you from wandering aimlessly, baring your body to the wind, the dust, the rain—and the
volcano's everlastingness made you ecstatic, gave you an ecstatic
love for matter and a feeling of power over matter. In stone, in
fire, omnipotence lay buried. Alone up there, you were walking
right on top of God.

This time there hadn't been any ecstasy. Colossal as it was,
Momotombo, too, gave an impression of great strength, and it was
everlasting in the same way, but for you to tremble, to yield yourself, you had to climb alone, attack the giant without anyone else
present. With no witnesses, you could let it intoxicate you. The
presence of Abel and Chino had stopped you from plucking the
secret of those deserted brown heights. There had been no exaltation, no explosion.

You're sorry you conquered the mistress mountain with other
men. "I'll come back," you promise yourself. It's possible. Is it
certain? Yesterday you were enjoying not only the solitude but

also the freshness of it. Now the freshness has been killed. Your love of volcanoes, your curiosity about the fiery heights could wear out. It's the same with places as with people. But what would you substitute for climbing? Hunting? For what? Watching fights? Men fighting, cocks fighting? Would you get involved in guerrilla activity? Revolutionary activity? When you started out for Momotombo, you were excited. You come back full of doubts.

In Managua, they leave you in front of the pension and go on, even though night is falling. It's true that Abel has to go off to the construction site.

Two weeks earlier the apprentice had been coming back from his garage to Xolotlan City at the same time as the night watchman was leaving for work. They got on the same bus, which was always packed and wobbling on its wheels. There, in the aisle between the seats, they started to play. Everyone knows the scenario in this city: it's a game for shy or reserved people, for novices, for hicks, for anyone who finds it hard to talk. And there were certain words Chino couldn't say. Abel wasn't sure what the looks they were giving each other meant, but there were also games you could play with your body. They went at it: one returned the stare of the other, one slipped between the other passengers to bump against the other, as though accidentally, one rubbed up against the other whenever the bus jolted, looking at the ceiling, the other people, the flies, the ghosts of the flies; then, since his rubbing was answered with an answering rub, he did it again, rubbed again, and look! He got off at the same stop, and now they know: everything's clear, the business is settled.

Ever since, the young man from the garage has gone to find Abel at the worksite after supper. The night watchman waits in front of the entrance to the site, leads Chino to a spot far away from Farabundo's cellar, then comes back, alone, to Farabundo and suggests he go sack out on his mattress if he feels like it, or trail around after some lady walking in the Waspán neighborhood. Rid of his co-worker, Abel rejoins his friend.

1 3 6

T H I S friend has some strange notions. For him life is only a succession of damned nuisances. If it weren't for sex, he thinks . . .

"Sex and the great outdoors, right?"

"Volcanoes."

"Sex and volcanoes," Abel sums up.

". . . it would be better to be done with it."

"And what about love?"

"It's the same thing," says Chino. "It's sex with the same person every time. Only that's full of bloody nuisances, too. You have to hide, hide, hide."

"Don't you think you'll get married some day?"

"Why?"

"So you don't have to hide any more!"

"There would be other nuisances, even more, probably—women cause plenty of trouble. You should hear my brothers. They're all older than me, all married. If they had it to do over again, all four of them say they'd stay bachelors."

In the shadow cast by the moon, the night watchman and the visitor are lying on the grass near a roofless house at the edge of the worksite.

"Take out your revolver," says Chino. "You're hurting me."

Abel removes his weapon and his belt.

"What would we do if thieves suddenly appeared?"

"I would shoot," says the night watchman.

"At them?"

"First I would fire in the air."

A breeze stirs between the sections of wall. The air is soft. Abel takes off his shirt. His friend unbuttons his own.

"If an animal came by, would you let me shoot at it?"

"What kind of animal?"

"A dog, a rat . . ."

"Why not?" answers Abel, intrigued by the question.

"What kind of revolver is it?"

"A Smith and Wesson, I think."

"Does it really kill?"

"You want to try?" the night watchman says, joking and challenging at the same time.

Chino looks at him, a little embarrassed, hesitating. All of a sudden he stands up, grabs the gun, points it at his temple, and says softly: "One shot for me, one shot for you, and all the shit, the games of hide-and-seek—finished! No more, no more, no more!"

On his knees, without moving the barrel of the revolver, the boy starts laughing, softly at first, then without restraint. Abel, uneasy, tries to take the gun away from him. Then he gets angry.

"Shit. Come on, don't behave like an idiot, Chino. Give me that!"

Chino goes on laughing, saying over and over again, as though he can't hear Abel, "One shot for me, one shot for you . . . one shot for me, one shot for you . . ." At that point Abel, trembling with rage and fear, and forcing himself to be very gentle, moves close to him, strokes his chest, embraces him. Chino throws the revolver away as quickly as he had seized it and clings to his friend's body. This amorous wrestling match may go on all night.

C H I N O has two brothers in the Guard. Before joining, one had been unemployed, and the other had been a seasonal worker, harvesting cotton three months a year, from January to March. Sometimes he worked for a fourth month, if there was some coffee left somewhere that had ripened late. The two other, younger boys in the family were also unemployed. All four had left home long ago. The seasonal worker had drifted from plantation to plantation between León and Chinandega. He would take lodgings here and there, knocking up girls along the way. Then, almost simultaneously, the two oldest were conscripted into the Guard. One of the two younger brothers followed in the steps of his brother the harvester. The other, who is still out of work, is probably being supported by someone, in the capital or elsewhere. Their mother has lost all trace of this son, and Chino can't find him, though he searches.

His military brothers, he goes on to say, wanted to be policemen.

"Is that what they're doing?"

"Hard to say, at least in the case of the one who was sent somewhere near the frontier. But the other is guarding public buildings in León. As for me, if I'm accepted . . ."

"What? You want to go into the Guard?" stammers Abel.

"Yeah."

Abel is not only surprised but also disappointed, thinking Chino has hoodwinked him out of spite. Chilly, distrustful, he moves away. His friend tries to reassure him:

"In the administration."

"Administration, hell! They'll make you part of the bureaucracy with a machine gun in your hand, up in the mountains, face to face with a bunch of guerrillas!"

"You think so?"

"Instead of scratching paper you'll be scratching bullets!"

"I'll quit."

"They'll make you do it!"

The argument may go on for a while. The two will never agree. It's pointless for the apprentice to remind Abel what a life he has in the pit—a filthy, oily, pit of black liquid manure—useless for him to talk about his mother's lamentations, his future. Abel can think of only one thing: one more soldier and then, soon—who knows?—a torturer, an enemy. It's really too much, especially after Demóstenes!

"Bitch! What's the matter with all of you?"

"Abel, calm down."

Abel won't let himself be calmed down. He's getting excited, he's pale. Tears are coming to his eyes, tears of rage. He asks: "When are you leaving?"

"How do I know? First they have to take me."

There is still hope. Chino is too unstable, too unrealistic, Abel tells himself: they won't want him. Soothed by that idea, he goes into the construction site with his friend. A shadow appears in front of them, projected against the façade of a house that has only two walls. The night watchman Farabundo has come up out of his cellar. The boys make a detour and go to the far side of the enclosure.

T H E game of hide-and-seek and the tricks are repeated almost every night. Eventually Farabundo discovers what is going on.

"Why do you like to make the rounds alone so often?" he asks when Abel has once again urged him to go down to the cellar and take it easy.

"Well, I sleep all day in my pension, and you don't sleep much. It just feels natural to me to stay outside at night."

"That isn't the real reason. You're hiding something from me. Someone's coming to see you."

"Well, you have visitors, too," Abel points out.

"But I don't mind sharing my women."

"I don't have any women coming to see me at night," Abel assures him.

"Liar! Listen: last night I came up from the cellar a few minutes after I went down, and I watched you. I saw you waiting at the entrance. Then someone came. You hugged this person, and I saw your two shadows disappear between the houses."

"All right, yes, I wasn't alone, I . . ."

"Are you jealous? In love? I'm not handsome enough for her? I'm too old? You have to pay? What?"

"Nothing like that, Fara."

"Are you fucking around with me?"

Farabundo is getting impatient: he's angry. Abel is afraid of an outburst, a quarrel, a fight, and he's afraid of losing his job. But he's worried that he'll also get fired if he deceives Farabundo. What should he do? He plucks up his courage, stakes all he has, and says, "It . . . it's not a woman."

"Fuck all! What is it? An angel? A ghost?" He laughs strangely. "Is it a werewolf, maybe?"

Trying to speak in a very steady voice, Abel looks at the ground and says, "His name is Chino." And he explains who Chino is, how he met him, why he likes him. Anyway, he adds as an excuse, as though relieved, the boy is going to get himself conscripted into the Guard. He's going off to join the army. The relationship can't last. . . .

"There," he concludes. "Now you can despise me if you like."

"Despise you? I don't care, you sleep with whoever you like. Besides, you're not the first guy like that I've met. I even think one of my brothers—one of the ones my father had with some other woman—well, I think he was also . . . I didn't know him that well."

"What did he . . . what would your brother do?"

"Whenever we played war, when we were kids, that brother always wanted to be the nurse. He took care of the fighters who pretended to be wounded—he liked to. He would make bandages out of paper."

"That shocked you?"

"Why should it? You have to have nurses in a war. But one day the leader of our gang said that kids who played nurse were homos."

"He said it in front of your brother?"

"I don't know. I don't remember any more. But that phrase stuck in my mind."

"How old is he now?"

"Twenty-seven, twenty-eight. I don't know where he lives or

what's become of him. When I left my family he was about twelve. I never understood why there are homos."

"Me neither. I know what I like. That's the way it is. But I don't know why it's that way."

"It's really like life," Farabundo says, suddenly philosophical. "Why is life the way it is? And why is it full of misery and then one day suddenly it's over?"

This thought plunges him into meditation, and as he meditates he nods his head gravely, lost in a sea of abstractions. Finally he heaves a sigh of defeat; it is all too much for him.

"What's the use of thinking about it?" he says. "Let's just live, since we're here. I have some beer in my digs. Come have a drink."

When they are sitting on the mattress with bottles in front of them, Farabundo goes on: "Maybe there are homos and straights in the world just like there are blacks and whites."

"And all kinds of colors in between," Abel adds.

"You're right. Just like there are very white people and very black people there are hundred-percent males and hundred-percent homos. And between them there are all the people who are more or less one or the other. In your case, Abel, you don't seem to be a hundred-percent homo. You wouldn't have told me you were, and I would never have thought you were. I would have thought you were zero percent."

"The hundred-percenters are crazy," Abel says, enjoying his friend's analogy.

"So what percent are you?"

"Fifty, fifty-five, something like that."

"That's already a lot. Fuck it, you hide it pretty well."

"And you, what percent male are you?"

"A hundred percent, shit!"

"You hide it pretty well, too, don't you?"

"Go on, bastard!"

"Really, no one is ever a hundred-percent white or black, especially in this country. There's always a drop or two of different blood in our veins, no matter what color we are. You even have quite a lot of mixed blood."

"Hold on!" Farabundo protests. "Are you trying to say I'm really half a male, like you?"

"More than half—three-quarters, even more if you like. Let's say . . . nine-tenths male."

"And what about the other tenth, huh, pal? What do you want me to do with that? Isn't your Chino enough for you?"

"Yes. I like Chino."

"If necessary, if it's dark enough, I can always hump a crazy woman. But you, a fifty-percenter and a guy in the same job on the top of that . . . no. Impossible!"

"But I wouldn't do it," Abel says.

"That's better. I was afraid I'd have to change the way I acted with you."

The two night watchmen empty their bottles. They've already talked more than enough, the older one thinks. And he says that by now Chino must be hanging around in front of the entrance. As for that, he adds, Abel can bring his pal back to the cellar if he likes; they would be better off here than lying on the ground.

"It's nice under the stars."

"But the ground is pretty hard," Farabundo objects.

"That's kind of nice, too."

"Well, everyone to his own tastes, that's for sure. Do what you like. I'm going to go make my rounds. We've got to keep an eye on this fucking construction site some of the time at least."

They go back up. No one is waiting in front of the gate. Chino doesn't come every night, but when he's not coming he lets Abel know the night before. Hoping Chino didn't have to take off suddenly for some barracks, Abel strolls around alone among the piles of materials, the bare foundations, and the half-built walls.

12

Itamar arrives unexpectedly, creating a sudden confusion. He says the heat is on everywhere and they'll have to meet in some safe place. They try to think of one. Abel suggests the ruins, Leonor a parking lot, and Comrade Superior, Ignacio's colleague, the sacristy of an oratory or a chapel. They opt for the most protected spot and hurry off to the church.

Leonor, who is now a liaison agent, knows a lot about what's going on. News is pouring in: the guerrilla war is expanding; there is fighting in the north, the Front occupying a border town, the Guard fleeing. People are taking over haciendas and giving the land to the peasants, while the owners are running away. Things are also stirring in the middle of the country: new guerrilla centers have been reported, and roads have been blocked. They say Matagalpa is in a state of wild excitement and people in Estelí have shut themselves up in their houses and are disobeying the law, even committing murder, while in the countryside peasants are mobilizing and awaiting orders and ammunition. In León, students are arming themselves, strikes are proliferating, and buses and trucks are being set on fire. They say the city is on the point of an insurrection. The fun is beginning on the southern border, too, with public unrest in the area of Rivas and San Carlos, where a column of fighters has already formed and equipped itself and is ready to march on the capital. They say the dictatorship is panicking and, comrades, it shows.

The Guard is increasing its numbers; policemen are everywhere—in front of ministries, headquarters of corporations, administration buildings; in police stations and barracks the squads are being reinforced. In the meantime, officials are flocking here from far away; they are supposedly advisers, experts—but experts in what? No one knows exactly. One minister, and only one, has stated that they come from the great sister nation, the United States. And some of these North Americans—what are they dreaming of?—have brought along their wives, their children, and their bedside rugs. For example, Leonor says, a house near her has been rented by a family of four (with four bedside rugs), all charming to look at (rugs and people). They're from Texas, she goes on to say. They smile all the time, and all of them, father, mother, and children—a boy of seven and a girl slightly younger—have blond hair. So much blondness surprises the people in the neighborhood and fills them with admiration.

From time to time in this country a child is born with a lighter mop of hair than usual, chestnut or red instead of black like everyone else; he or she will be the family favorite, success in love will come easy, potential girlfriends or boyfriends will abound, the privileged individual can pick and choose. And to find four people with golden hair under the same roof is a miracle. From the moment they arrived, the Texans have been surrounded by a glow of friendly feelings.

Though their house stands back to back with a "colony" that

keeps growing, sprouting new huts in the adjacent bit of country-side, they are protected by a wall surrounding their large, flower-filled garden with its swimming pool. The beautiful Texans own a long car painted a metallic sky-blue, also from the United States. They are always well dressed and spanking clean, the very pic-ture of well-being, good health, and success. The whole neigh-borhood thinks they are nice, aristocratic, superior. No one worries about what they're doing here in this half-destroyed city—so aus-tere, so tiresome—in this country consumed by violence and pov-erty. They are looked upon as good people.

The very day they arrived, the people in the neighborhood had seen something that caused a lot of talk and enhanced their pop-ularity right away. The family had driven up behind an enormous moving van, and as the vehicles came to a stop, homeowners in the prosperous part of the neighborhood rushed outside, along with their gardeners and maids; they were joined by urchins and itinerant saleswomen from the colony. Everyone who witnessed the spectacle, whether from the curb or a doorstep or from an open window, seemed enchanted. They all watched as ultra-modern furniture was carried inside, plus an assortment of other objects. They counted two tall refrigerators, a freezer, a large washing machine, a machine that could slice up whole kilos of bananas at one time, another machine to fry the slices, and ap-pliances to suck up dust, water potted plants, perfume the rooms, beat the bedside rugs, and wash the dishes. But the high point of the show was a grand piano. It caused some trouble to the mov-ers—it was too big to be taken in through the double doors—and it was pink, to boot. The gawkers were fascinated: few of them had ever seen a grand piano, and no one had ever imagined that anyone, even a rich person, might own a pink piano. If the neigh-borhood had been intrigued by the color of the newcomers' hair, it was positively fascinated by the color of the piano, and every-one agreed that this family was very distinguished. Straining their ingenuity, the movers at last took the piano in through a ground-floor window.

Eventually the neighborhood found out that the instrument belonged to the mother—therefore she must be a musician—and later that she taught music to her two children. Soon, they would her her playing the piano and singing scales almost every day, while her husband was away teaching classes in certain public offices in the city.

The plaque fixed to the garden gate reads "SAM LICHTENFELS, Specialist in Social Education." To most people this specialty seems rather vague. But the word "education" is a fine one, and that's what they remember: it makes the expert an honorable man. What's more, this Sam Lichtenfels is a practicing Catholic. They say he inherited his faith from his paternal ancestors, who were Bavarians from around Munich. It was his grandfather, Ludwig Lichtenfels, who emigrated to North America at the beginning of the century. The educator's wife has an Irish background. But Sam and June apparently don't like to talk about their family backgrounds: they live in the present, are interested only in the future, and consider themselves pure natives of the United States.

"Which means pure Yankees," Itamar observes, "pure imperialists."

T H E professor has just come from another meeting with his own boss. The night before, his boss met with the right arm of the leader of the Directorate. And the Directorate has been investigating: its informants made inquiries about the so-called experts even before they arrived. Ten of these men from Miami, Houston, and Washington have already settled in the country and others are following. They are in every city where agitation is rife. The precise role of these experts isn't clear: some call themselves educators, like Lichtenfels, or social advisers or instructors of administrative staff; others, more mysteriously, say they are trainers, managers, or sociologists. In short, there is a whole network of Yankees. And it's very important to understand the missions they're carrying out. These radiant men, with their strangely tall wives and little milk-fed children, obviously have the confidence of the regime.

"They're creeping in everywhere. They're sprouting up all over the country!" exclaims the professor.

"They're infiltrating us," says the Superior.

"They're watching us."

"They think we're Negroes; it's disgusting," says Abel.

"Well, we really are a little."

"Not me—in my family . . ."

"Quiet! We're here to make decisions, not to argue."

"All the same, passing for a Negro . . ."

"I say there's a whole network," the professor persists. "What are we going to do about it?"

"Dismantle it," suggests Comrade Superior.

"Not before we know what its role is, the role of each of these guys," Leonor stresses. "This is a crucial task; it fills in the gaps in the Directorate's investigations."

"Then we'll force these fine fellows to leave."

"Do we have the means?"

"Shall we kill them, then?"

"Whoa! Not so fast! Let's investigate first."

They argue and debate, between damp walls that were once white and are now covered with long patches of mildew. The two seats in the sacristy have been taken by the Superior and Itamar; the other members of the group are sitting on the ground, and they have sore bottoms. They stand up and lean against the tall black wooden cupboard in which vases, vestments—not used any more—and packages of hosts are stored.

"Since this guy Lichtenfels is a Catholic, you could be the one to deal with him," the professor suggests to the priest.

"A traditional Catholic . . . What do you expect me to say to him?"

"Maybe his religion is only a cover."

"All the more reason to unmask him," Abel put in.

"He'll be suspicious."

"And suppose he's a real believer, sincere and all that?"

"Belonging to the old school, speaking the language of the old school," the Superior remarks. "You mean spirituality floats above history, Jesus, and me, in a bottle. Impossible! Those people get on my nerves. They seem foreign to me now, terribly foreign. Comrades, I have nothing in common with them any more; there is no basis for even a semblance of a dialogue. I have nothing to say to them. Nothing."

The theologian is categorical. Outside of *materiology*—if only the revolution would come and make this new truth official!— outside of this conviction, there can be no exchange. It would be better to look for some other common ground, but what? What can serve as the basis for an understanding with this man Lichtenfels? How can he be outwitted, how can he be approached?

"I've got it!" cries Leonor. "I'll ask for piano lessons."

"Terrific," Abel says. "You approach the wife . . ."

". . . and you take care of the husband. There's one thing: the guy is trying to make himself popular, pal around with people; apparently he goes to the cockfights."

It's all working out nicely. A few more details are settled—the security rules, the assumed names: the former journalist will introduce herself as Anita; Abel will use his father's name.

The next day Anita rings the doorbell at the Yankees' house. The wife herself comes to the door. Unfortunately, June Lichtenfels speaks only English, and the visitor doesn't know a word of it. To make herself understood, she moves her fingers, imitating the motions of a pianist. The foreign woman thinks that Anita, like another native the day before, wants to admire the instrument, and she takes her into the living room, where the large pink piano occupies a place of honor. June smiles, and the militant smiles, too, feeling as if she were in a museum. Embarrassed by the silence, she says, "How pink it is!"

"Excuse me," says June Lichtenfels, "I don't understand."

"It's pink," the visitor repeats in Spanish. "P-i-i-n-k! Piano big baby. You understand? Big pink baby?"

Anita feels stupid. She'll never get any information out of this woman; the visit is a waste of time, her mission a failure even before it starts. To cut the visit short, she goes up to the piano as if it were a fat, gentle cow with three legs, strokes it, and leaves.

A B E L is luckier. He has talked to the gardener, who has confirmed that Lichtenfels is interested in cockfighting. The gardener himself told Lichtenfels about the most famous fights in the region and gave him the days, the times, the places.

"The ring at Nindirí?"

"There's one that's even closer. Things get really hot there. People bet like crazy. It's at the edge of the city, in the hills, on the Santo Domingo Heights."

He has heard about this ring. The birds don't have their crests removed, and metal spurs aren't allowed. The spectacle is bloodier, because the crests get torn, but it is less dramatic, because a bird's natural spur may wound but almost never kills, unlike a steel spur, which is longer and sharper. Abel prefers fights to the death. The spectators get more fired up and the atmosphere is more charged, more animal, more exciting. But since the enemy is going up to the Heights, who knows?

Abel spots him right away. He's all pink and blond and impeccably dressed in sporty light-beige pants and a white shirt, in the midst of the herd of dark, hairy men. The militant, who came early, pushes his way through, trying to get near him. The fights have begun, and two cocks, wing quills and lancets bristling, hurl themselves at each other, peck at each other furiously, tear each other's feathers out, stab each other's necks and sides. Releasing sharp, syncopated cries, they sweep the dusty ground with their sickle feathers. The two of them seem to be equal in strength, and driven by the same rage. The fight goes on, and now it threatens to become monotonous. It isn't clear how either one of them can win.

"This is a fake," says Abel, who has elbowed his way through to the Yankee.

"You think so?"

"All these beating wings! It's never going to end. This is no way for males to behave. What's going on here? Are these hens, or what?"

"Well, I don't know. . . ."

"Neither one is getting the better of the other!"

The birds go on fighting, but gently now, as though tired; the pauses get longer and longer. And the spectators protest, threaten to take back their bets, insult the cocks. The discontent becomes so great that the owners intervene. They pick up their birds, praise them, then set them down inside a white chalk circle drawn on the ground. With a clap of the hands, they goad them into a new confrontation, and the cocks respond. The first to step outside the circle is the loser, and this is the feeble outcome of the fight. The audience, after booing the cocks and their owners, leaves the arena.

Abel has not budged from the Yankee's side. He tries to keep him from leaving, proposing that they go for a drink at the small roadside bar across from the arena.

"I should get back. My wife doesn't like to wait up for me," Lichtenfels answers, in his Texan drawl.

"Just one glass. Come on!"

The man gives in. Abel explains to him that among the Latins, women always wait; they complain, too, but they love it.

"You sure they do?"

"Absolutely. Here, if a man is obedient, docile, he's taken for a weakling. The women say they want husbands who are attentive and gentle, but if they are, the women get tired of them. A guy who doesn't make his wife suffer lets her think she doesn't have a real man. Here in our country, a man who listens to his wife isn't a man."

"I'm not from here, and my wife isn't, either."

"Sure, but this is where you live, and you'll probably be living here for a long time."

"What makes you say that?" The foreigner is surprised and suddenly cautious.

"Christ! The whole neighborhood was there when you moved in. So much furniture! So many machines! Enough to set yourself up for life . . ."

The Texan smiles. He orders another glass and remarks, "So we're neighbors?

"No, but I know someone who lives there. Do you play the piano, too?"

"That piano! Everywhere we go people talk about it."

"Not surprising, given the color."

"I know. In Latin countries pianos are black and they always have to be black, as though people only played funeral music on them."

"How many Latin countries do you know?"

"Yours is the third."

"Does your wife know three countries, too?"

"No. This is the first time she's left the States. That's why she thought she had to bring so many things."

"How was it in other places? Did you do the same work as here?"

"Yes and no," says the foreigner, mistrustful again; he calls the waiter over, pays, and stands up.

"Now I have to go," he says. "I've got my car here, if you need a lift."

Abel declines. It isn't worth the trouble, he says. He lives near the arena, down the hill from the bar. The boy won't reveal the fact that he lives in a rooming house, works on a construction site, sleeps in a basement—he would be ashamed. Besides, as a militant, he would be committing an error. Abel, like his comrades, is duty-bound never to reveal the places where he lives and works, where he could be found and arrested. He tells the Yankee he'll be back the following Sunday to watch the fights again. The Yankee remains evasive.

I N the countryside, the guerrilla fighters are suffering various fates. One column, to the south, is advancing; others are marking time or confronting strong counteroffensives. Groups of fighters are withdrawing into the sierras, into the cordillera. Certain commando units are reorganizing, bringing in new, fresh militants and sending anyone who is exhausted, too hesitant, or a bad shot back to the city. The columns, re-formed, strengthened, move toward an enemy position. They choose as a target a garrison or an entrenchment that's off by itself, isolated. The guerrilla fighters spring up, rush in, surround the position, and seize it. They reject shock strategies, pure confrontations, in favor of these surrounding maneuvers, which pay off because of the nature of the terrain, especially to the west and even to the south. The large open spaces and the underbrush are conducive to making wide encirclements. The dips and hollows in the land allow the guerrillas to go to ground during counterattacks. Harassment tactics prove equally profitable. Little by little, Alvaro's group becomes expert in these actions, which require mobility, flexibility, bold strokes, and quick withdrawals.

They also require young fighters, and Abel's brother doesn't feel young any more. His stay in the mountains, the hardships, the forced marches, the fevers, the fatigue, have aged him. In six months, he says, he has aged six years. He can't run as fast as he used to, or for as long. He has lost his capacity for endurance. What is still vigorous is his hatred of the enemy and his desire for war, and his state of mind is colored by these feelings when, having been wounded, he is ordered back to the city by his leaders.

During a raid on a cantonment, Alvaro took a bullet in the middle of his thigh. He had just fired, and an enemy soldier returned the fire. Because the soldier was younger and more agile than he, Alvaro was hit before another guerrilla fighter could kill the enemy. He was evacuated at night, secretly, to Corinto. From there, he would go hide in the capital.

I N Alvaro's town the atmosphere is oppressive, the port paralyzed, and people are tense. A new strike has been called. The cranes aren't working; the tugboats remain at their berths; the warehouses are closed; the trams and railroad cars are blocked on their tracks; the dockers appear on the quays only to argue endlessly with one another. The reason for the work stoppage is the transfer of Chepe the Shirtless.

Suspected of belonging to the Front, the leader was questioned and at first kept in the local penitentiary. Then, without warning, he was sent to a prison in Managua. The presence of the agitator, even though he was locked up, had been inciting the other trade-unionists to demonstrate. The police removed him in the belief that this would bring the demonstrations to an end, but it only gave them a new impetus. Another worker, Pedro Gama, took over the leadership of the movement, and the Guard tried to arrest him. But this man, mistrustful, had changed his address and plunged underground. A third docker had succeeded him, one whom everyone calls Bolívar. And Bolívar is careful to stay behind the scenes: he runs the union through intermediaries and transmits the orders of Pedro Gama, who has become a relay of the Front at Corinto.

Gama, of course, has left the port neighborhood. The docker—who is really a schoolteacher playing proletarian and assigned to infiltrate the trade-union organization—has changed his occupation to carpenter. Under a false name, he is working in a shop that stands at the edge of a slum on the outskirts of the built-up area. This old, modest establishment belongs to his brother-in-law, a rustic fellow who admires the former teacher and shares his ideas. Walls of bare muddy brick topped with a roof of sheet metal form an extension of the workshop, and this is where the carpenter lives with his wife and children. This is also where the agitator holes up, and where Alvaro appears one evening.

An advanced post of the Front has directed him to Bolívar, who has served as his guide. The wounded man intends to get himself treated before worrying about his family. Afterward, when he has healed, he will arrange to see his fiancée, and maybe Maritza or some other woman, and even his parents. For the time being, he has to recover his strength and attend meetings and discussions with his secret comrades. These meetings are disguised as special work sessions to fill large, unexpected orders that require extra manpower. The increased activity of the workshop doesn't surprise any of the neighbors. In this noisy, populous part of town, it passes more or less unnoticed. Also, no one finds it either strange or excessive that an annex should be built behind the shop. The new room, made of boards, will provide a refuge for outlaws.

Pedro Gama is the first to use it; then Alvaro takes his place when the ex-teacher leaves for the capital. The wounded guerrilla is treated by a retired doctor, a simple soul who describes himself as a "positivist and therefore an enemy of the dictatorship." The wound closes, the sore heals. The young man comes out of it with a limp that the doctor hopes is temporary. But if he walks too much, if he leans on the bruised leg, the pain will revive and stiffen the limb. Before long, he won't be able to run or jump any more.

"I won't even be able to jump women?" he asks, half joking and half grumbling.

"Not even women—standing up, anyway," the doctor specifies, sighing.

Four months in the depths of nature with no one to fool around with, not even an old hag . . . ! Four months of marinating in the same old stale smells of men, without being able to savor any real perfume—the women guerrillas either smell like men or have their own men. Four months of making believe he's a pimply boy of fifteen and screwing his fist. Alvaro is hungry. His body is hungry—his hands, his lips, his sex. When night falls, he slips out of the workshop, limping. The streets are deserted outside the area of the port. He hesitates to go to Maritza's: guards patrol the dock area, and the house where she presides stands at the edge of it. Besides, is it prudent for an outlaw to show himself to the woman?

He would blame this absence—"this long absence, my hot little one"—on his fighting cocks. He would say that Jesús and Macho won every fight, or almost every one. Invitations poured in; he was running all over the country. Match followed match in the north, the west, and on the Atlantic coast. But Maritza might be suspicious; she might ask questions. Worse still: the prostitute, affected by the social climate, must have seen her business fall off somewhat, and certain houses that catered to the longshoremen have had to close down; all this will cause her to make a connection between her client's disappearance and the strikes, and ever-growing troubles, the guerrilla movement. Alvaro, who is mulling this over, suddenly turns off in a different direction.

He leaves the street known as "the Boulevard," which leads to the port, and takes instead a dirt road that winds away toward an endless stretch of uncultivated land. On the way out of town, at the edge of a banana plantation, buried in the vegetation, stands a brothel well known to traveling salesmen, students, and truck drivers who make regular trips to León. The outlaw introduces himself as a taxi driver who has recently been in an accident and has come back to his mother's house to recuperate. He receives a warm welcome: they feel sorry for him, make a fuss over him.

Soon Alvaro is a regular visitor to this brothel, and the frequent partner of one of the women there, who is as redheaded as an Englishwoman but endowed with swarthy skin and the exotic name of Claudine. This woman, born of a half-Indian mother and a mulatto father, dreams of her next life, when she will have hair that is naturally tawny, milk-white skin, pale-green eyes, and French nationality. This is why she has adopted the sparkling name of Claudine for the exercise of her professional talents. Such renunciation irritates Alvaro.

"Why in hell do you all want to have foreign hair and a foreign skin color, and why do you adopt foreign names?" he asks one night.

"It's prettier to be called Claudine than María. And also men would rather sleep with someone called Marilyn or Magali or Brigitte than someone called Josefa or Teresa, which are names that remind them of their wives. Just think: would you like it if I had the same name as your wife?"

"I don't have a wife. I'm not married."

"Your fiancée, then. You do have one of those, don't you?"

"Yes."

"And what's her name?"

"It's . . . it's Fermina," the boy lied.

"And it wouldn't bother you to sleep with me if my name was Fermina?"

"Not at all," Alvaro lies again.

"Well, you're different, that's all."

"I see," says the outlaw, worried. "How can you tell?"

"I don't know. Sometimes you seem to be somewhere else. To be running away from something."

"My future wife?"

"You can run away from her, but then you always go back to

her—all men do. I have a feeling you're running away from something that isn't a woman."

"I'm trying to get out of a rut, like everybody else."

"There's more to it than that."

"When you find out what it is, let me know," jokes the visitor. "I couldn't forgive myself if I missed a chance to find out who I am."

T H I S conversation has bothered him. The days pass and Alvaro hesitates to return to Claudine; he also refuses to resort to Maritza. There's too much malice in these women, he thinks. In their eyes you can read either distrust or a tacit, insistent interrogation. At least this is his impression, as strange as it is new, and it ought to be enough to make him conceive a dislike for all whores. Except that he's a man—and does a man give up a man's occupations? Maybe he's ripe for married life now. Under different circumstances, in peaceful times, Alvaro would have been married by now. He's twenty-two—after eight years of going to professionals, hasn't the time come for him to start his own family? But how can he live underground with a delicate, innocent wife? What right has he to drag her—who is so dutiful, so anxious to please her family—into the turbulence of a persecuted existence? Alvaro will wait, against his will, against the demands of his instinct. With these thoughts running through his head, he goes to Gladys's home. There he finds the girl agitated, consumed by anxiety.

"My love, what torture! Where have you been all this time?"

"I . . . my tour is finished. The cocks . . . none of that interests me any more. One of them died; I'm through with lugging the rest of them around the country! I'm going to do something different now."

"Did you make some money from the fights?"

"Quite a bit."

"So we'll be able to get married, dear?" Gladys concludes, suddenly brightening.

"Not right away. Let's wait until the troubles are over, until the work at the port starts up again, the soldiers of the Guard go away. They say it brings bad luck to get married in a troubled city."

"That surprises me. Ever since the patrols have been out on the streets I've felt protected."

"Against whom?"

"Well . . . the subversives, as they call them, the communists, the terrorists."

"There aren't any terrorists, in Corinto or anywhere else. Have there been any explosions?"

"No, that's true. But you know how I am about politics."

"I understand. Forget it. Just think about keeping yourself beautiful, and don't worry about anything but your pots and pans."

"And your love, right, my love?"

"Yeah."

It is dusk. Gladys and Alvaro are talking on the veranda. The girl's parents have retired to their bedroom, where a light has just appeared in the window. The boy hasn't been near the brothel for a week now, and his abstinence is weighing on him. The darkness that envelops the two of them incites him to change the way he is caressing Gladys. From squeezing Gladys's virtuous and tender hand in his own, he abruptly lifts it and puts it on his fly. The young lady, shocked, wants to pull it away, but Alvaro keeps it there.

"Darling, you're frightening me," she pleads.

"What are you afraid of? That thing you feel under your hand isn't thin and it isn't short, true, but it belongs to you, you can take it."

"Not now! How shocking!"

"We're alone, it's dark, your parents are in bed. What's the danger?"

"My love, don't you want me to be a virgin when you marry me? Don't you want to wait until we're married? You want me to faint here, on the veranda, almost in the street?"

"You won't faint, I promise. I know how to do it gently. Come on, I know you want to—your hand is all hot."

"Darling, I want to wear white when I get married!"

"You'll get married in white, with a veil and a crown of orange blossoms."

And he continues to press the girl's hand against the zipper of his pants, while she tries to pull away, moans, breathes heavily, and seems to be panicking.

"Alvaro, it's hard!" she exclaims.

"That's normal, sweetheart."

The boy wants to satisfy himself, but he also wants to spare Gladys's maidenhead. He therefore has to make sure of the artifices—sweet talk, skillful caresses, gentle and imperious force—employed by all fiancés who want to possess their future wives and at the same time preserve the conventions. In the shadows of the veranda, after a long and uncertain resistance, after certain contortions, extreme and passionate language, and a few tears, the fiancée turns over and yields to her beloved the only side he feels he can visit honorably for now. Afterward, looking at once frightened and delighted, her flesh sore, her heart pounding, Gladys experiences that curious sensation of having become Alvaro's wife without being truly married to him, and this sensation bewilders her. She cries a little more, and Alvaro, calm now, kisses her chastely on the neck, calling her "my little virgin." These words, along with one last intimate touch, reassure her.

T H E guerrilla is still limping, and stabs of pain sometimes pierce his thigh, but there is no more risk of infection. The doctor delivers his diagnosis to Bolívar, to Gama the carpenter, and to the patient. The advance guard of the Front is summoned to discuss the situation. No one can remain underground for long in a town where he has once lived openly. Too many people know him and would recognize him, even if he changed his hair and his skin color and hid behind glasses, carpenter's dungarees, and a mustache. For the outlaw to prolong his stay would be to forbid himself all action, to become a dead weight, to languish. The moment has come, they decide, to dispatch him to the capital. The organization gives him three days to say his good-byes. That is more than enough, thinks Alvaro, who will see Gladys but who doubts that Jeremías, his father, will receive him.

To tell the truth, he hasn't missed the old man, or his sister, Alba. He used to think of his mother, though, when he was lying in his hammock in the middle of the mountains after a day's march. It would be raining, and he would be hungry. His stomach rejected the monkey meat that had been cooked once, cooked again, and served up every evening. And the famished boy, swaying in his net above the mud, would curl up under his overcoat, close his eyes, and in his mind's eye see the housewife in her kitchen. And he would be overcome by a strong desire to eat fried bananas with cinnamon, rice pudding, all sorts of cakes. The boy would also dream of his fighting cocks.

It would be hard for him to leave without finding out how they were. When night comes, therefore, Alvaro takes the risk of going to the dimly lit yellow house where his parents live. He leaves an associate outside to keep watch. Fermina opens the door, lifts her arms, can hardly speak:

"My . . . mmm . . ."

"Is he here?"

"Who? Abel?" asks his mother, trembling and recovering some speech, and staring at him with amazement. "Christ, no! He's as good as dead for us!"

"My son," she manages to say next, "my son . . . Your father is sick."

"Is it serious?"

"His heart. All worn out. The poor man, he has worked so hard!"

"With his tongue, too."

"Shut your mouth!"

Jeremías is resting in his room, says Fermina. Before going in to see him, Alvaro goes out to the courtyard. A large cage stands in the back of it; only two birds are hopping about in it, Alvaro II and Macho.

"Where's Jesús?" Alvaro asks.

"He was stolen."

"What? My best bird stolen? My favorite? You're lying: no one stole him. Someone made him fight. Someone took advantage of my not being here. He was put into a fight with tricksters."

"Ask your father," Fermina says, defending herself.

"You wanted to collect big stakes," he accuses her desperately, "and you overdid it. You made him do too much, and you got him killed."

His mother holds her own against him, sticking to her first explanation. She sits down and waits for his anger to flag, begging him to spare the sick man the spectacle of his fury.

"Steal! Steal Jesús!" he repeats like a man obsessed, "That's crazy! At best, he was brought back to you completely drained of his blood and you ate him."

The father hears the shouts and gets up, emerges from his bedroom.

"Did you come back here to give us some of your mouth?" he hurls at his son.

"I just came to say hello, that's all."

"You're not staying?"

"I have to go away again. My leaders . . ."

"They're up to some pretty tricks, your leaders!" Jeremías interrupts. "They're the ones organizing all these strikes, aren't they?"

"They propose, the proletariat disposes."

162

"Nonsense! One good agitator can lead your proletarians by their noses."

"You talk like a boss," Alvaro retorts, "and you aren't even a boss. What a pity!"

"I forbid you . . ."

"You're talking like an imperialist."

"The big word! That's the magic formula, isn't it? You shout 'imperialist' the way the priests shout 'Satanás!' You point to the evil, and you think you're explaining everything; once you've played the exorcist, your conscience rests easy. Imperialist! If only I had the means! Unfortunately, I have to settle for being a modest nationalist."

"Then you should support the demands of the dockers."

"Never!" the old man shouts. "Strikes and disorder won't help the country move forward."

"Striking serves the revolution."

"And revolution serves progress—article one or two of your catechism."

"Madman!"

"Enough, you little idiot, enough!" orders the sick man.

And suddenly his hands begin to tremble, then his arms and his head, and he wavers, gasps, looks for somewhere to sit down.

Fermina rushes to him, pleads with him: "Jeremías, don't get excited." Turning to her son, she adds, "Shame on you! You're upsetting his nerves."

"And he's upsetting my reputation," Alvaro retorts. "To have a scab in the family, to be the son of a scab! What will my comrades think? A scab! It's not enough to have a fairy in the family?"

"I'm not a scab," Jeremías protests, more and more excited. "I . . . I'm a worker . . . an honest . . ."

"A scab and a fairy! Nice family!"

The father, livid, feverish, straightens up again. He raises his hand, choking with rage, tries to hit Alvaro, and faints. Hysterical, crying, the mother makes a terrible racket, and at this point Alba appears, having just come back from Gladys's house. Now she sees the old man on the ground, her brother back against the wall, his eyes hard, an expression of disgust on his face. Overcome with horror, she throws herself into Fermina's arms, and the two women clutch each other. Alvaro moves imperceptibly toward the door, then vanishes.

The night covers everything: the houses, the street, the entire city have slipped into a thick, inky blackness. The only light shines far away, a short necklace of lamps, and a band of mauve and gray chafes the sky above the port. The rebel has stolen away without banging the door. He hurries toward his friend, the man keeping watch, who is concealed in a recess in the wall between two houses. Without a word, with a simple tap on the arm, the boy leads him toward the neighborhood where Gladys lives. They reach that tranquil, semiresidential area where no patrol ever turns up, an area where placid middle-class people like Gladys's parents live cloistered with their families. The security of the place makes an escort unnecessary, and Alvaro sends his guard away. He walks alone for a few minutes, his nerves raw, his mind tense, then presents himself before Gladys. She is worried to see him in such a state. Thinking of what has been happening over the last few days, she imagines vague dangers and wants to know what is going on.

"Don't ask any questions, please," he counters.

"But I love you, Alvaro, and I'm afraid."

"No reason to be," he interrupts her, almost roughly.

The dryness of his words and his tone frightens her, but she forces herself to be gentle and says, "Do you want some milk, some coffee?"

"Milk."

"With honey, my love?"

"Not too much."

She heats up a half-filled saucepan of the white liquid—not very thick, because it come from the store diluted with water—then adds a good portion of honey to it and pours the whole thing into a bowl, which she sets in front of him on the table. Alvaro glances at the pendulum clock hanging on the wall between the image of the Sacred Heart and a chromo depicting the volcano Chonco. Gladys looks at her fiancé; she is upset, and can't help trying to make sure he loves her. . . .

"That's obvious, isn't it?"

"A lot?"

"Gladys, I want to go to sleep."

"Where?"

"Anywhere except in my house. I had a fight with my father this evening."

"Really! You two! You see where politics gets you?"

"Don't worry about that. That isn't your role; you don't know anything about it! What matters now is that I want to go to sleep."

"Not here—my parents would never allow it. Right now they're in their room. I don't think they saw you come in. Just think of the scandal if they found you in this house tomorrow morning, even if you were sleeping all alone on the living-room sofa! And the neighbors, if they saw you leaving!"

"What shit!"

"Darling, do you want people to say I don't know how make you respect me?"

"No, of course not."

"You don't have any friends?"

"They're married."

"Go to a hotel. If you don't have any money on you, I'll lend you some."

"Hotels depress me. They're anonymous; you feel lonely."

"If you could, you'd marry me this minute, wouldn't you?"

1 6 5

Alvaro, distracted, shrugs his shoulders. He is haunted by the scene with his father. And he has been ordered to leave—soon and for a long time, maybe indefinitely.

"You'd do it, wouldn't you?" Gladys repeats.

Alvaro sighs. "Come on, give me the money," he says, "I'm going to the hotel."

The girl, afraid of making noise, slowly closes the door behind him and blows him kisses. After a few dozen steps he looks back and then stops. The street is deserted. All he can hear is the rustling of the leaves in the few thin trees along the sidewalk, and, at the end of the street, the growling hum of a car. Alvaro watches the lights go out inside the house, first in the living room and then in the bedroom. Plunged into darkness, the house seems as inaccessible to him as a palace to a beggar. Yet Gladys's parents' house is nothing like a palace. It's a narrow detached house like millions of others, with two stories, rough-coated in beige and embellished with a plastic porch roof above the veranda that happens to be green and is meant to imitate rippled sheet metal. The porch roof is actually the only thing that differentiates this house from his own family's house. And, like his own father, Gladys's father is a civil servant: he handles the Water Department accounts. His salary is scarcely larger than Jeremías's. Alvaro has no reason to envy these people.

Even so, he feels a distance, a gap between him and the house, where the sheltered girl is getting ready for bed. This sensation, perhaps caused by the darkness, bothers him: the distance feels like a provocation. And the idea of shutting himself up all alone in a hotel room only increases his feeling of rejection. Without admitting it to himself, Alvaro had hoped to spend this, his last night in Corinto, with Gladys. After the intimacy of the other evening on the veranda, he had dreamed of sleeping in her house— who knows, maybe in her bed? Her refusal arouses his scorn. Alvaro is annoyed with himself. In spite of the girl's explanations, her refusal feels like a slap in the face; it upsets him to be beaten;

the thought is, in fact, intolerable. But this warrior, this ladies' man, has other resources: now certain memories come back to him, certain images, and he relaxes. He has Gladys's money in his pocket, and he squeezes it in his hand, against his thigh. He'll go sleep with Claudine at the brothel.

13

Recruit, recruit, recruit: the order is quite explicit. The revolution needs men—in the guerrilla forces, in the parishes, the towns, the "colonies," the plantations, and the factories. More combatants are needed in the mountains, more militants in the cities. The spirit of rebellion is spreading. Young people and adolescents form groups spontaneously, without leadership, without officers, and they agitate, demonstrate, hoot at the soldiers of the Guard, the police, even the cops directing traffic. The unrest is growing: Estelí, León, and Managua are seething. The working-class neighborhoods seem to be on the point of revolting. Leaders appear, factionists without strategies or tactics. The duties of the Front multiply, expand, diversify.

Should they attack right away, ransack the garrisons (and maybe the supermarkets, too), steal arms, ammunition, provisions, cars? Should they restrain the guerrillas, let them mingle with the crowds, release them in the city like mad thiefs? Should they prevent fires from breaking out, or encourage them? Should they organize housewives, train them to be canteen managers, nurses, and messengers?

And there are some guys who can't keep their mouths shut— the rioters, the adventurers who blend in with the demonstrators and deflect the protest. There are the muddleheaded, undisciplined characters who seem better behaved in the guerrilla forces than in the suburbs, where they go wild. There are the crazies, the potential suicides, and the delinquents. There are the dregs who drift up and mix in, poisoning the movement and playing into the enemy's hands.

The truth is, any sort of excess, any form of disorder is a threat. The country is falling apart, the state is disintegrating, the dictatorship seems to have its back against the wall. Now that it has become urgent to fight anarchy and the regime at the same time, the organization gives priority to morale, discipline, and the enrollment and training of cadres. The Front asks each militant to recruit at least three people and instruct them.

Abel hopes to bring in his friend before Chino goes over to the other side. He also tries to sign up his colleague at the construction site.

"Overthrow the government?" says Farabundo, astonished. "And what about the new one? What is it going to give me? Money? Women? A roof over my head? No big shot is going to give anything to a little guy!"

"But afterward there won't be any big shots."

"After what?"

"After we've taken power from the big shots."

"There'll be new big shots," the night watchman assures him.

"But we'll have a revolution!"

"Then we'll have the big shots of the revolution."

Farabundo's theory is simple: little guys remain little guys, the poor stay poor. And a poor man doesn't attack a rich man head-on; a weak man doesn't attack a strong man—it wouldn't be a fair fight. The little guy doesn't resist the big one—instead, he cheats him, for unscrupulous trickery is his only weapon. He, Farabundo, doesn't know any other; the only way he has survived so far is by swindling the big shots.

Abel has never actually thought of this "strategy of the little man," as the night watchman calls it, nor has his leader, or Leonor, or Comrade Superior. Guile as a tactical method or line of defense doesn't appear in the Front's manuals. But that's not surprising, says Farabundo. Who writes the manuals? Doctors, professors, guys from the city. And the notions that have the most validity for them are called "opposition," "grouping," "rallying," "striking," "boycott," and "rebellion." Deceit is for peasants, not students; it is the continuing, silent, invisible war fought by the peasants century after century in the depths of the countryside. And Farabundo is a peasant. Neither Abel nor any other city dweller, however friendly he may be, will make Farabundo join. It's useless to go on trying, he says. Look somewhere else.

S H O R T L Y afterward, Chino appears, dragging his feet. He can barely say hello and seems not just tired, but sad. The older of the two night watchmen disappears into the cellar. Chino and Abel walk a bit and then sit down on a stack of fiberboard. The worksite, with its sections of wall, its roofless houses, and its scattered bricks, looks like an extension of the ruined city center. Chino is silent. Abel tells him about the threats that are looming, the "prospects" (as Leonor and Itamar call them), and the needs of the Front. Then he broaches the subject of signing Chino on.

"Organize me?" says Chino. "Unfortunately, I'm leaving in a few days: I was called up."

"You can't!"

"We knew this was going to happen."

"But you're joining at the worst time—your leaders will throw you into the thick of it; they'll make you do some really dirty work!"

"What choice do I have? Can I desert?"

"Why not?"

"They'll shoot me. Anyway, who can say where all this confusion is going to lead?"

Abel feels defeated, discouraged, helpless. Fate. Oh, to hell with fate! Why couldn't his fate have taken a different turn!

"If you hadn't had to join the Guard now," Abel asks, "would you have joined us? Would you have supported the Front?"

"No. I would have stayed out of it. Out of everything—you know that. I don't like getting into a bloody mess any more than I like being poor. Anyway, what's the point of being organized?"

"It's essential!"

"You're obviously involved in politics. All politicians need followers, troops—without them they're nothing. But I don't give a damn about politics. I'll never be involved in politics—not in my neighborhood or anywhere else."

"That's easy to say," Abel answers. "What do you have to defend? Not a scrap of land, no convictions, no family."

"And I'll never have a family. You don't like that idea, do you?"

What can he say to that? Abel has several contradictory feelings at once. His friend's indifference to social struggles—even though he is a proletarian—makes Abel angry, and the news that they won't be seeing each other any more disheartens him. But the fact that Chino wants to reject any idea of marrying, which means he wants to save himself for Abel, delights him. Abel suddenly feels the desire to forget everything, cut his moral and political ties, turn his back on his obligations. Go away! Go far away, leave the country, take Chino with him. It's a crazy dream. To do that would be to betray his friends, ruin himself. After all, Itamar is an intelligent and a good man. His obsession with being a militant probably makes it impossible for him to feel any joy in life, but that must suit him. As for Abel himself, does he really have to give all his time, the best part of himself, to politics?

"Chino," he pleads, "I want us to spend every night together until you leave."

Chino doesn't answer, doesn't promise anything. Sadly, and with a look of determination, he manages a feeble smile.

T H E last few nights together. Abel is afraid Chino won't come back, and he goes out looking for him—it takes him hours to find his hut.

In a conversation one day, Chino had mentioned the place where he lived. His neighborhood, he said, was full of peasant families, people who had fled the troubles, the extreme poverty of the back country. Only one specific part of Xolotlan City fits this description. Abel goes there. Remembering his friend's favorite recreation, he tries to find the soccer field. He asks around and is shown a refuse dump near which, in an oddly shaped vacant lot, some kids are running after a ball.

"Do you know a guy called Chino?" he asks.

"Chino what? There are loads of Chinos here. All the guys who have eyes like buttonholes are called Chino," he is told by an adolescent, a beanpole who seems to be the captain of the team.

"I have no idea," Abel confesses, suddenly surprised that he doesn't know his friend's real name. "Well, the guy I know is eighteen; he works in a garage, and he's about to go into the army."

"Is he queer?" asks a slender, dark-skinned boy, no taller than a table top, and he wiggles his ass, while the other kids laugh. "If he is, your guy is Pretty Boy Chino," the team captain says with only a trace of contempt. "And he lives near the reservoir, in a little place with flowers in front."

"The guy I'm looking for isn't a queer," Abel retorts in a dry, superior tone. "He'll be in the army in a few days, and he's certainly too old for your babyish games. So long—go play with your toys."

These words embarrass the group. Abel, still disdainful, spits on the ground and turns on his heel. As he walks away, he hears yet another brat say to his skinny pal, "You think he's one, too?"

A FEW yards from the reservoir, he finds the right Chino, his own Chino, sitting in the doorway of a tumbledown cottage made of unpainted boards topped with pieces of rusty sheet metal. Chino jumps to his feet, amazed.

"Well, son of a bitch! How did you find me?"

"Sense of smell, my friend. I'm a dog, I have a dog's nose, and since you have a unique smell, all I had to do was sniff the air."

"Shit! And what do I smell like?"

"Someone I've been missing."

At this, Chino smiles and confesses in a subdued voice, "I've missed you, too, Abel."

"Go on!"

"I swear."

"Then why didn't you come see me?"

"My mother doesn't sleep when I stay out all night, because she's frightened. Anyway, I'll be locked up in a barracks soon, so what's the point? It's bad to get so used to each other, to get so attached—we'll miss each other, and that won't be much fun."

"So it's better to live alone?"

"Or make love with people you only see once, people who go away, so you never see them again."

"Like dogs."

"Didn't you say you were a dog?" retorts Chino. "With your famous sense of smell."

"Skip it. There'll always be time to lift my leg in every corner when you're gone."

"That way you'll forget me."

"I certainly hope so," Abel interrupts.

"Shut up, prick! Go on home. My mother's going to ask what I'm doing out here. Wait for me in front of the gate tonight."

"Your mother's really sick?" Abel asks, unwilling to believe this promise that they'll see each other again.

"She's an insomniac—even when I crash at home. But if I'm not here it's worse: she lies awake and hears thieves prowling around and wings beating, some kind of vultures, and she thinks souls from purgatory will come whimper in her room. In the morning, when I show up she makes a hell of a scene."

"When you're in the Guard she'll have to get used to living alone."

"My mother doesn't know I'm joining. I haven't said anything yet, but she'll get used to it. She thinks the souls don't come when I'm away for a good reason."

"Your reasons for staying out are perfectly good: making love."

"Souls from purgatory don't like love," Chino interrupts. "When people here on earth are happy, it means the souls have to cook longer in the fire."

"Do you believe all that nonsense?"

"No, but my mother does. She thinks that if the souls come it's because I'm spending the night in sin."

"And what if you sin all alone in your bed? Does jerking off make the souls cry, too?"

"Doesn't look like it, because I've been jerking off the last few nights, thinking about you, and, well, my mother hasn't said anything."

"But some priests say jerking off is more serious than fucking. If you masturbate, God will make you deaf, they say, but never if you fuck, not even up the ass. As long as you stay near her, your old lady doesn't care if you sin, and the souls don't, either. It's all blackmail. If we made love here, in your bed, the souls wouldn't visit us any more than Chinamen from China or the King of Spain."

These words drive away Chino's last scruples—if he has any, that is, Abel says to himself on the way home. And as he walks, he wonders why the kids in the neighborhood call his friend Pretty Boy. Chino isn't any better looking than a lot of other guys. He's of average height, average build for a boy his age; his skin is coppery, which isn't unusual in this country; his carelessly combed hair is black—not very exciting—and cut in an ordinary style. Even the shape of his eyes, which some people—in the magazine *You and I*, for instance—might describe as "bewitching," isn't rare enough for Chino to be able to pride himself on it. The smoothness of his hair, and his straight, delicate nose, are less common features, perhaps, but they're not exceptional. In other words, Chino's physical charms are shared by a lot of other people. Which makes his nickname seem all the more arbitrary.

"They call me that because of my mother," Chino eventually explains. "When I was a kid, she would talk about me, and she would say to the whole neighborhood, 'That one's my handsomest, he's my pretty boy,' and the name stuck."

"It's flattering."

"It makes me puke. Fuck, I'm not a doll! You're not bad looking, either, but does anyone call you Pretty Boy or Pretty Face or Handsome?"

As always, Abel and his friend make the rounds of the construction site first, talking as they walk along the fence, which is full of gaps, stakes pulled out here and there, though it is supposed to enclose the worksite completely. Once Farabundo has come up from the cellar, the other two go down and collapse on the straw mattress. That night, one of the last nights—what a terrible, sweet thought—Chino has brought along some beer.

"You'll see, it's neat," he says to his friend. "We'll have a contest."

"What? With six bottles it won't last very long."

"The point isn't how much you can drink—that's a game for boozers. What I like is a good contest of skill."

To engage in this contest, first they each have to empty a bottle, which doesn't take long, since the bottles hold less than half a liter. Then they have to put the bottle down on the ground in front of them at a distance of about three feet and try to get as much urine into it as possible.

"You stand up, you spread your legs, you aim, and you piss," Chino says. "The one who gets the most in wins a bottle of beer."

"Fine, OK," Abel says unenthusiastically. "But if you don't aim very well you get the place all wet. We should play this game aboveground."

"It's dark," says Chino.

"There's a moon."

"And we'd have to get dressed again."

"Not necessarily," says Abel, who, at the thought of cavorting around the construction site naked with his friend, finally begins to get excited about the idea.

As soon as they were alone together on the mattress, the two boys had stripped, as they always did. Now they go outdoors, bottles in hand, and stand naked in the night, in the moonlight, like living statues. They urinate into their bottles, and Chino, being the experienced player, wins and goes down to the cellar for his reward. He comes back up and offers to share his bottle with his pal. Then, still naked, like soccer players in a locker room, like beggars surprised among the rubbish by the lake, they drink the other three bottles. Between swallows they wrestle with each other, pour beer on each other's chins and chests. Finally, like drunken colts, they collapse and roll on the sandy, cement-covered ground.

Every night! Sure! Abel rages. Every last night! If you had only known—complications and more idiotic complications. You say to yourself: This time I'm staying here, I'm going to sack out with my pal, peacefully, far away from everything. And then all hell breaks loose: your comrades, his mother, fights. Because Chino's mother, when she learns that her son is going away, first collapses in tearful resignation, then goes from resignation to stupefaction and from stupefaction to agony. Suddenly the woman won't let him stay away all night. She makes scenes, crying and refusing to be separated from him. The future soldier is forced to make Abel come to him for an hour or two late in the afternoon, before he goes to the worksite. She cries and grumbles at this, too. While her back is turned, while she's cooking, the boys give each other intense looks, full of heartache, wanting to squeeze each other's hands hard, until they hurt, wanting to try to . . . Until the very end, they will have to make do with cruelly brief caresses, ambiguous punches, hasty, rough gestures that only make their desire more painfully acute.

And finally the last night comes. The night watchman has sworn he'll drag his friend out of the house, sworn they'll be alone together, for God's sake! They'll go out at night, behind the house, behind other huts, behind the reservoir, to a vacant lot or even, taking a big risk, to the patch of ground the neighborhood kids use as a playing field. They'll be alone, tell each other things, do things to each other.

But none of this happens. Just as Abel is leaving the pension, Itamar comes back. The professor's face is tense, his eyes uneasy; he's nervous.

"It's serious," he says, "very serious. We must have a meeting right away." And he asks his comrade to go tell Leonor and Comrade Superior. Abel can't leave, because a man has been killed—worse, a prisoner has been killed. Chepe the Shirtless, who was being held in Managua's central prison, has apparently committed suicide.

"Impossible. A proletarian doesn't commit suicide."

"Especially not a revolutionary proletarian."

"And a leader, to boot."

"A handsome man."

They talk about it, mulling over what the next step should be, trying to think how to respond. This death, when all is said and done, is hardly surprising. The docker's imprisonment caused public unrest, the affair grew in importance, and there was clearly trouble ahead.

A few days before, Itamar reports, a hundred or so people were gathered in front of the prison to demand that the union leader be released then and there. They shouted out slogans and marched on the guards' post. But the sentinels had brought in a group of soldiers to back them up, and the soldiers, standing guard along the walls, threatened to use their weapons. The troop of civilians stood their ground and shouted Chepe's name all the louder, this time demanding that all political prisoners be freed. At that point, a spokesman for the prison director, a stiff young NCO, came out and read a prepared statement.

"There are no political prisoners here," he said. "No more here than in the rest of the country," he added, which set off a new wave of protests.

"Where are they, then?" someone shouted.

"The docker and his accomplices have committed common-law crimes; they are no different from the other prisoners."

"That's ridiculous!"

"The judges have made their decision, and the guilty men have recognized their wrongdoing. Furthermore, one of them has already punished himself."

"Which one?"

"The leader," says the spokesman. "He slashed his wrists—he killed himself."

The news shocked and disconcerted the protesters. Everyone rejected the idea that Chepe the Shirtless, that solid worker, could have killed himself.

"You killed him," shouted a young man to the officer, but the officer was already re-entering the building, and the sentinels, their bayonet-tipped rifles at point, drove the demonstrators back. The next day a messenger from the prison made the rounds of all the newspapers, delivering photocopies of a medical certificate which testified that "the citizen José Monimbó, alias Chepe Monimbó, alias Chepe the Shirtless, has succumbed to an arterial hemorrhage due to a deliberate severing of his wrists."

"The statement was just issued," Itamar says, "even though Chepe was buried three days ago."

The burial took place, he explains, in the eastern cemetery, the largest in the city, in the part reserved for the poorest of the poor and people without families. No one was told about it, especially not the sympathizers.

But many of them would have stayed home anyway. The announcement of the suicide, whether true or not, had made people uneasy. A certain discredit had fallen on the group: these prisoners didn't deserve to have people fight for them, the protesters decided. No—all the more reason to go on, the professor insists. "Nothing about this rings true: there never was any suicide. We have to investigate."

"Who do we talk to?" asks the night watchman.

"The other prisoners."

"You're dreaming. We'll never be able to get near them."

"Not us. But in Managua there must be one honest lawyer, even if there aren't any honest judges."

The meeting goes on and on, while Abel fidgets, thinking about Chino. He wants to leave: it's already past the hour when he was supposed to be at the construction site. He'll be late, and Farabundo will be getting impatient—he'll chew him out. And Chino is also waiting for him, in front of his house, and getting worried. Abel doesn't usually miss appointments. Besides, it's their last evening. He'll wonder what's going on. The night watchman, sitting in front of his cellar, will also wonder, and he'll be irritated that Abel hasn't shown up, because he has a date with a woman this evening in the Waspán district, and here he is stuck. Farabundo hates waiting.

As for Chino, he goes back inside the little house, tired of waiting and defeated by the complaints he imagines will come from his mother. He doesn't want to listen to his mother talk and groan and snivel—that kills him. All he wants is to fall into a deep sleep right away, not think of anything until the time he leaves. But when he goes to bed, he can't sleep. Even though Chino tells himself not to do it, he is straining to hear the sound of footsteps, a whisper.

Day breaks, and light filters in between the boards. Chino hasn't closed his eyes all night. He gets up, dresses, and drinks a cup of coffee—he's not hungry, he says. Then he picks up his bag, a sort of haversack containing some underclothes, his toothbrush, and a rosary his mother has slipped in without telling him, even though neither of them ever prays with a rosary. Equipped with this faded, patched piece of luggage, Chino goes out, his mind strangely empty. Almost running, he leaves his house and his neighborhood.

Meanwhile, Abel is trying to placate Farabundo, who was beside himself with anger when Abel arrived, because he had missed his date and therefore lost the woman, lost all trace of her—and she was a good one, idiot, a hot one, that was obvious, and he doesn't have her address. It's out of the question for Abel to leave him and go to Chino now. He paces around the construction site, dead tired, his heart full of rage, cursing everything at once— Farabundo, Farabundo's women, the army, and politics. And suddenly a novel, unexpected idea invades him: by spending all that time with the people from the Front, he betrayed his friend. He opted against Chino, he thinks; he was unfaithful. And this was their last night. How can he face what he's thinking now?

T H E Y have dug up an honest lawyer, maybe the only one. Comrade Superior knows another theologian who is married and belongs to a certain Church of the Parousia. This Parousian has a certain interest in the juridical sciences and is studying law with the help of a professional, apparently a Freemason—and perhaps a man with some principles, the Superior observes.

Itamar goes to see him where he lives in a little detached red-brick-and-fiberboard house behind a tangle of banana trees and bamboo in the chaotic, summarily urbanized district called Garden City. The lawyer has added the semblance of a tie to dress up his short-sleeved, white nylon shirt. He takes the visitor into his office, a room that looks out on a kitchen garden where nothing is growing but rank weeds. Portraits of Voltaire and Benjamin Franklin hang on the walls.

"Yes, I know, they aren't from here," the lawyer says. "But I've looked for people from here, and I can't find any, except maybe Morazán—only one in all of Central America. And even so, you'd have to study his case. . . ."

"And what about Sandino?" Itamar protests.

"Yes, Sandino was a patriot and a brave man. But if he had lived, what would he have turned into? A great republican president? He would have turned into what everyone turns into in our country: a *caudillo*. You know very well that free minds, democratic leaders, don't come running to our volcanoes!"

The lawyer clearly honors the thinkers, the great men who illuminated his life as a student at a time long past, a time when people didn't talk about Marx or Martí. For he is over seventy, this defender of freedom of thought who has fought for thankless causes and people without money, generally in opposition to the dictators. He listens while the professor tells him Chepe's story.

"That's a lot to take on, and I'm tired," the old jurist grumbles.

He urges Itamar to ask the help of one of his colleagues, a young one, an ardent one. But Itamar proves stubborn, and the lawyer gives in.

"I'm weak," he sighs, "I'm weak." And he sets to work.

He immediately begins by harassing the director of the penitentiary, pestering reporters, and besieging the newspaper owners. He also ferrets around in various offices and sifts through files. In a casual way, he questions soldiers ordered to watch the prisoners. Then he tries to chat with the prisoners, but the head of the prison won't allow it—orders from higher up, very high up, he apologizes, official orders. The lawyer is fully aware of what this intransigence is hiding: that some of the men are being kept in solitary confinement—always used to cover up shameful practices, the old man explains. Every dictatorship does it.

"Young man," he adds, "the prisoners are being tortured."

"So Chepe didn't kill himself—I was sure of it!" cries Itamar, almost happy.

"My dear fellow, restrain yourself. Citizen Monimbó still may have ended his life himself. And it would be understandable: either he found the idea of torture intolerable, or he didn't want to be put back on the rack, or maybe he was afraid of breaking down and talking. All three hypotheses are plausible."

"There's one more," the professor says.

"What's that?"

"His executioners tortured him until he lost consciousness. Then they took him back to his cell, and before he came to, they cut the man's wrists."

"That has been known to happen."

"It's the only possible version," Itamar decides. "The sympathizers have to be told."

Several evenings in a row, the professor visits the lawyer to hear news and to seek comfort. This time, he seizes the old man's small, spotted hands and, despite what he has said about Sandino, in his heart blesses the Freemasons, the freethinkers, the Voltaireans, the Franklinians, and everyone who resembles them.

"*Maître*," he concludes, "since people are being tortured, we have to unmask the torturers. Let me report all this to my organization."

"You mean the union?"

"The Front."

"Not very Voltairean, your Front—I don't like it." And at that, the lawyer dismisses the "young man."

T H E demonstrations in support of the prisoners start up again. The revelation about the death of the dockers' leader has shocked people, and those who had recently quit change their minds now, and are angry at themselves for believing in Chepe's suicide. They regroup and return to the charge, flanked by new members. Another rally is in preparation. The sympathizers intend to make the authorities wary of committing other such murders. But the authorities accuse the protesters of "destroying society's peace" and they ban demonstrations. At the same time, they order the newspapers not to print another line about the deceased trade-unionist or his friends. Also for the sake of "society's peace," the incident must be forgotten, recriminations must cease, and nothing must be said about prisoners' being kept in solitary confinement.

In spite of this, their friends decide to demonstrate. A hundred or so men and women, mostly young, form an escort and head for the prison. Soon they run up against a shock troop. The soldiers make a tactical retreat of a few yards, then throw tear-gas grenades. The demonstrators don't budge. An officer with a megaphone warns them that more dangerous projectiles will be used, then immediately orders the soldiers to fire a round of rubber bullets. A friend of Itamar's who teaches in the same school is hit under the eye. His cheek starts bleeding, his eyeball fills with red liquid, and he can't see. Other protesters are bruised in various parts of their bodies; Abel, struck in the top of the thigh, thinks a bullet has torn off his genitals. He howls, then faints. Two men pick him up and the group beats a retreat.

When Abel regains consciousness, he is lying on a sofa in the house of a comrade named Leticia. Itamar and the woman are watching him. They have undressed and washed him; the woman has surrounded his penis and testicles with compresses soaked in warm water.

"Oh, God, my balls," Abel groans, "they've destroyed my balls!"

"Calm down," his leader says. "You haven't lost them. You have some hematomas; they've only turned blue."

"Blue balls? Shit! Who's going to like me with blue balls!"

The crippled man thinks of the face Chino would make if he could see him. The picture makes him laugh dryly for a moment; then he's seized with fury again.

"What luck! How would you like having indigo nuts?"

"Could've been worse," Itamar says, trying to soothe him. "The bum might have aimed an inch higher."

"Thanks!"

"Don't worry, they'll turn white again," Leticia says gently.

"How soon?"

"I'm not a doctor. I don't know—maybe a few months."

"In the meantime what am I going to do?"

"You'll do it . . . in the dark," the professor answers.

"I'll do nothing at all. Shit! Do you hear me? Nothing!"

Abel continues to rage. His friends decide to say no more; Leticia changes the compresses and the two of them go away. Alone now, Abel bursts into sobs. It makes him feel better to cry, and he lets his tears wash his cheeks, run along his mouth, slip down his neck. It isn't his habit to feel sorry for himself when he gets hurt. He has suffered all sorts of blows in his life and has been badly hurt twice: once falling on the shards of a smashed bottle in Corinto, when he bled copiously, and then during a brawl between two groups of fans during a cockfight, when he hurt his jaw. In neither case did he shed a tear—he simply cursed the pieces of glass and the fans. But this time he feels his spirit has been broken, his morale damaged. The bruises on his genitals have only revealed another, deeper, more private wound that isn't healing despite the days, the weeks that have passed: Abel is crying because Chino is gone.

14

Should he run away from the city, his comrades, his memories? Should he turn his back on the revolution, on the struggle, and leave behind the pension, the construction site, the lakeshore, the ruins, and the adventures he might have in the vacant lots (since he no longer has Chino)? Should he desert and go back to his family in Corinto, ask their forgiveness, change his life?

Abel isn't sure any more. Too many telescoped pictures pass through his mind, confusing him. Certain faces upset him, sear him. Others make him sad or thoughtful. His overburdened memory is pushing him in too many directions. Suddenly Alvaro's face appears to him, with its hard eyes: his brother insults him, and Abel immediately appeals to his sister's timid smile, his mother's tired smile, Chino's ever surprised smile. Then the image of his father drives all the others out, fills his soul with a smell of death; the boy swears that he will never again lay eyes on that tyrant, that failure—as he convinces himself his father is—even if he goes back to Corinto.

Abel often remembers scenes from his childhood, a time that has ceased to seem real to him. His brother goes out with his father or hangs around, playing in the street, fighting with the kids. The younger brother gets along well with his sister. The two of them prefer the company of their mother and, following her example, are pious. They say their prayers together; they go to catechism class; and in processions Alba plays the part of Saint Rose of Lima, the virgin who rubbed hot peppers over her body, while Abel is Saint Anthony of Lisbon.

One Christmas they played the roles of Mary and Joseph in the nativity scene. It was hot that December—summer was at its height—and the church was stifling. Abel was sweating under his brown robe and his pepper-and-salt wig; his beard, which was made from the down of young hens, tickled him. He tried to scratch his cheeks, keeping his hands joined, while his sister sighed—worshipping her celluloid baby Jesus for three hours was too much for her. Too much for her . . .

How long ago that was! Today the poor thing doesn't play Mary any more—in fact, she doesn't play either of the two Marys, the saint or the sinner. She hardly ever prays and she doesn't sin: she doesn't do anything but help her mother a little, daydream about having a man, and get bored. Though she likes Abel a lot, she doesn't dare speak his name: if she talked about her brother, her mother would cry and her father would blow up. Abel and Alba used to see each other secretly sometimes, after Jeremías drove him out of the house and before he left the city. And Abel would make her laugh, reminding her of the time when he played the part of the chaste Joseph. Then, abruptly, Abel would take off—night was falling, and in the dark, he said, he would change into a very strange Jesus indeed.

———

F E R M I N A can hardly bear her son's absence. In the depths of her town, of her house, of her kitchen, she moans to herself and weeps as she waits for news. At church she lights candles in front of Saint Anthony and Our Lady of Sorrows—Saint Rita is turning a deaf ear. She pleads with the Virgin and with the blessed patron of lost people and things to bring Abel back to her. When her other son is away and her husband out of the house, Fermina talks to Alba all day long about her affliction.

"Where do you think he's gone?" she asks. "North to Chinandega? To the big cities?"

"Maybe he's gone to sea—who knows? Abel could have signed onto a ship the way Rony Palma did last year, when his father kicked him out of the house. Don't you remember, Mother?"

"Yes, my daughter. Oh dear! And he hasn't written once. No one knows where the ship took him. Maybe Rony lives with the gringos now, or in Europe—in France or in the Guineas."

"Maybe they were shipwrecked and he drowned and now Rony Palma is walking on the bottom of the ocean with the sirens."

"Be quiet, Alba. Rony was a Catholic. If he died he's in heaven with the Blessed Virgin."

The girl doesn't say any more. The father comes home from the office and Alvaro from a cockfight. The mother sets the table and Alba serves the food. The women don't dare mention what's bothering them. Once, just once, Fermina sighed: "Oh, if only he would write to us!"

"What 'he' are you talking about?" asked her husband, irritated. "Write . . . write . . . What are you dreaming about, woman—dead people don't write!"

"He isn't dead," Alba protested.

"Are you trying to contradict me, you idiot? Get out of here—go to your room. Instead of worrying about dead people—yes, dead people, I'll say it again, once and for all—you'd do better to dig up a husband for yourself."

"And a real one," her brother hastened to add as Alba fled, "a husband who likes to take you to bed."

"Alvaro! For shame, to speak that way before your mother," Fermina broke in.

And she, too, having lost her appetite, left the table. The two men went on eating in silence, united by their common instincts, their reciprocal suspicion, the bitter attraction of male for male.

A T last a note comes from Abel. Fortunately, the postman brings it after father and son have gone out. Alba is the one who reads it, because she has good eyes and, unlike Fermina, who was pushed through school too quickly, she's used to reading. In his letter, Abel writes:

Dear Mama,
Dear Little Sister,
    I'm writing to let you know that I'm in excellent health. I arrived safely in the capital, I'm eating salad, tomatoes, corn pancakes, chicken. I'm working, I'm earning my living. I sprained my foot by slipping on some rotten coconut shells but now it's better, I'm beginning to walk again. I live with educated people—here everyone knows more things than back home. I've even got to know a teacher who has good ideas about politics and our country. This teacher is young, twenty-four or twenty-five, but he reads lots of books and likes to talk—he doesn't have time to wander around and run after girls. He's a serious man and I'm learning lots of things from him. There, dear Mama, dear Little Sister, that's what I've been wanting to say to you for weeks, but I was always afraid my letter would fall into the hands of my brother or the old man. And I hope it won't. Anyway, I'm not giving you my address—I don't want them to come and make trou-

ble for me here. Write me care of General Delivery, Main Post Office, Post Office Square, Managua. With embraces from your homesick son and brother,

                                                    Abel

"He writes so well, doesn't he?" the mother observes. "Eating chicken—how lucky he is! We'll have to answer him. Tell him he should watch out for that teacher—let's hope he's a law-abiding fellow!"

"Maybe he's against the government . . ."

"My God! You think so?"

". . . and he would agree with Alvaro."

"About politics, maybe. The rest . . . well, nobody can change his ways completely!" sighs the mother.

And she takes the letter, folds it, and stuffs it down under her handkerchief and keys in the bottom of the pocket of her dress, a sleeveless, beltless garment that she uses both as a housedress and apron.

A B E L has gone to the General Delivery office a few times. The pigeonholes always contain dozens of letters, but none of them ever has his name on it. They've forgotten him, he decides, and he won't write any more. He'll keep his homesickness, his doubts, his sorrows to himself. With Chino gone, he won't unburden himself to anyone—not to Farabundo, not even to Itamar. Anyway, Itamar seems too busy to listen to him.

Now that his courses are over, the professor leaves school as promptly as a student eager to go play. He stops by the pension briefly, then goes out again at triple speed to organize meetings, talk to people here, argue with people there, instruct cadres or set up a Secondary School Student Movement with the help of a high-school boy whose efforts have already done a great deal for it. The boy, beardless, skinny, a big reader—but only in the old days, he says apologetically, when he had time to read, and then his favorites were Lenin, Malraux (whose name he pronounces Malrawks), some Yankee poets (yes, Walt Whitman), and some Jamaican poets (who?)—the boy already has a reputation as an extremist. But he considers himself only an "important militant," and one who intends to remain anonymous from now on, which is why he has adopted the most anonymous sort of pseudonym. The driving force behind the student movement calls himself Seventeen. Why that number? Well, he explains with a smile, he's seventeen years old.

Like the professor, he devotes himself entirely to politics. And, like him, he doesn't seem to have a girlfriend or fiancée or any pals—all Itamar and Seventeen have in their lives are the comrades. Abel and the professor talk to each other now only as comrades. In their conversations at La Perla, Abel's leader warns him about some of the other guests, especially the geometrician and the landowner's two sons: these people are increasingly hostile to the trade unions, the students, to all the protesters. The geometrician invokes religion and "the dignity of the family" and approves of repressive measures. The boys echo this approbation: all they really want is to safeguard their patrimony, the land. This makes them dangerous, the professor says. If they suspect that he and Abel are militants, they'll denounce them. Itamar and Abel will have to act like imbeciles, pretend to be indignant, be even more vociferous in their ranting and raving than the others. But Abel does none of this. He seems distracted, evasive, sullen. His mind is elsewhere; he's having trouble getting used to the fact that Chino is gone. He keeps wondering what Chino is doing, what barracks they've quartered him in, if he's thinking of Abel, what sort of mission they're preparing him for, what kind of training they're putting him through. Little by little he's slipping into a state of utter dejection.

O N the construction site, Farabundo is worried: for two nights now, Abel hasn't shown up. That restless soul has surely gone to León or even farther. Two more nights go by. Still no sign of the boy. This time he's in trouble, Farabundo decides—something bad has happened, and he won't be coming back. But after a week, Abel appears. He's walking slowly, his legs apart.

"Christ! What's the matter with you?"

Abel is recuperating little by little, though it's taking a long time. He has also been instructed not to tell anyone the real cause of his injury.

"I . . . I fucked too much," he answers. "I hurt my balls."

"I'll be damned! Who with?"

"Uh . . . a girl who was passing through, traveling . . ."

"Hey, have you switched?"

"Yes and no . . . Well, I mean, an asshole is an asshole."

Farabundo hasn't been idle himself—he never is. In the past week alone, he says, he has slept with seven women—a new one every night. He gets infected by this kind of madness from time to time. It depends on the season: at certain times of the year, as soon as he goes out hunting he captures someone. The same was true of his uncle Ezequiel, and Ezequiel attributed *his* sudden appetites to the phases of the moon.

"They must have the same effect on you," the night watchman continues. "I bet you ran into your traveler just when the moon was entering its last quarter."

"Its last quarter . . . Yeah, maybe. I wasn't walking around with my nose in the air, so I didn't notice."

Astronomy leaves him cold; he doesn't give a damn about the phases of the moon. As far as that goes, he might add—grimacing sarcastically because he hurts—as far as the moon is concerned, Farabundo can go off and point his telescope at it if he wants to. Abel will be happy to watch the site alone; after all those nights of overdoing it, you see . . . (he thinks unhappily of Leticia's useless compresses). The senior night watchman doesn't wait to be asked a second time.

A B E L strolls gingerly between the buildings, the little heaps of sand, and the piles of bricks, advancing cautiously and stopping when the stabs of pain shoot through his testicles. He sits down on a patch of grass by the edge of a foundation hole. Then he lies down and looks up at the sky. For the first time he really studies the moon, observes its contours, its shadows, its nimbus. Strangely, this contemplation awakens memories. Certain specific parts of Chino's body come back to him: he sees his hands again, his back. This upsets him and makes him nervous, and he moves suddenly and carelessly, causing fresh stabs of pain. It hurts to get an erection, like getting a cramp, like spraining something. Abel grumbles, stands up, moves off again. Oh, if only he could think about other things, erase these pictures from his mind, drop out of everything for a while. Once again he thinks of leaving his friends, his work. Managua is oppressive, and the construction site gets him down: it's hard for him to wait like this, the way other people sink into poverty—and what's he waiting for, anyway? He ought to be able to stave off his loneliness; he has to distract himself from his unhappiness, steady himself, enjoy . . . what, anonymous bodies? Abel is wandering among the unfinished walls, the scaffolding, when suddenly he stumbles over a bottle. He sees the glass shining in a ray of moonlight, spots other bottles, and recognizes the labels: littering the ground are the beer bottles he and Chino tried to fill with their water. The memory hurts him, and what hurts even more is the memory of making love (what pain, pain and the blues, pain without the blues) after their game was over.

J E R E M Í A S died one night in his sleep. During the evening, as usual, he had spat on his life—what an idiotic thing it was!—on his family—what a disgrace!—on his sons, those perverts who should have been expelled stillborn from their mother's womb. And his wife, as usual, had crossed herself and moaned, begging her man to calm down. Alba came back from her friend Gladys's house just in time to ask for his blessing, and though Jeremías made fun of religion, he clung to this ritual: he had so few ways left of showing his authority. His daughter said her prayers as mechanically, as absent-mindedly, as she would say good night.

"Bless you, you sausage," answered the old man.

Despite the insult, the mother congratulated herself for keeping up the pious custom, which she saw as a last vestige of belief on the part of her husband. Afterward, she took Alba to her room and comforted her.

"Your padding is starting to melt away," she told her. "You're losing weight." And she helped the girl get undressed, wondering out loud about where Abel might be and what would become of Alvaro.

"Has Gladys seen him?" she asked.

"Mother, I don't know!"

"Ask her next time, featherbrain!"

Fermina tucked her daughter in, turned out the light, and left the room. She tidied up a little in the kitchen, went to the bedroom, and then, wearing her eternal tan rayon nightgown, lay down next to Jeremías, who grumbled at her heavy sighs, the weight of her body sinking down on the bed, and the squeaking of the springs. He shifted, groaned, and automatically turned his back on her.

Usually he was the one to wake up first in the morning: he would reach out to Fermina and shake her until she got up and went to make the coffee. But this morning Fermina was the first to open her eyes. According to the alarm clock on the night table, it was seven o'clock. Her husband seemed still to be asleep. She turned to him, disheveled, stiff all over. His face was serene. She patted his cheeks; she hadn't done that for years, and it made her feel tender. But her Jeremías remained impassive. Fermina leaned over him and rubbed her foot against his bare calf—all he wore to bed were his old cotton underpants, worn and covered with biscuit-colored spots. Finding his leg abnormally cold, she began to tremble. Fearfully she put her hand on the sleeper's mouth, and no breath came out: her husband wasn't breathing any more. She gave a long, dramatic cry, the cry of a bereaved woman, jumped from her bed, and rushed in to her daughter.

"Alba, darling, this is terrible," she cried. "This is terrible— I have been sleeping next to a dead man."

Torn from sleep so abruptly, the girl had no idea what was going on. She yawned. Her mother, becoming impatient, shook her and pulled her off the bed.

"My little girl, my poor little girl," she moaned, "your papa is no longer with us."

The girl threw herself into her mother's arms and the two of them cried. Neither dared go back into the room where the dead man was lying, ice-cold and stiff. They washed their faces hastily, put on their dresses, and ran to tell the neighbors. Women from the neighborhood washed the dead man, dressed him in his only suit, an old pale-gray flannel, and in the evening helped the coffin maker lay him in the coffin. The same neighbors, a few old men, and some children escorted the remains to the cemetery. Without the support of the other men of the house, Fermina and Alba felt too weak to accompany the hearse, and so the old man was borne to his grave by strangers.

A S the worries of the living supplanted the memory of the dead man, mother and daughter soon stopped talking about him. What they talked about now was Abel's return.

"Write him that we're waiting for him," ordered Fermina. "Explain that we're alone, that we can't live like this, that we need a man to protect us."

"And what if he doesn't get the letter? What if he's not in Managua any more, what if he's gone off somewhere else?"

"In that case we'll have to make do with Alvaro, but that certainly won't last long. As soon as he gets married, he'll be off again. Besides, even if he wanted to go on living in our house with his wife, I wouldn't let him."

"Why? Gladys is nice."

"She's a proud woman, and I won't have her giving the orders around here. Two mistresses can't rule one house. With Abel, at least, we wouldn't have to worry about that."

"Even if he brought back a . . . what's it called? A soccer player like Toca?"

"Shut your mouth, you foolish girl. I want to see him come back alone. Whatever company he keeps, let him keep it somewhere else. For a family, that kind of thing doesn't exist; it isn't part of your life, you ignore it, you shut up about it."

"What if Abel tries anyway?"

"You're the one who has to bring us a man, not him!"

A L B A doesn't write to her brother immediately. The bureau drawer is empty, she says: there isn't a piece of paper or an envelope in it. But she'll buy some, and her mother will dictate the letter to her later. Right now, the girl must see Gladys. She leaves.

A few soldiers of the Guard are strolling in the street. Ever since Chepe's death, the dockers have seemed discouraged, and they're not agitating any more, so the port area is peaceful, but the troops remain in the city. As the days go by without any great upheavals, the patrols don't do much patrolling, the sentries relax their vigilance, and the orderlies perform their duties indolently. People are getting used to the presence of men dressed in khaki—men who have nothing to do. Some of the soldiers prowl around, and when evening falls they lie in wait for a young woman to go by and try to draw her into a corner.

As Alba prepares to cross the square named after the priest-poet Azarias Pallais, the daylight is fading and the shadows of the houses are lengthening, doubling in size, darkening the streets and courtyards. Soldiers loiter around the statue of the poet who wrote about roads after rain, burials of the poor, the hands of humble people. The girl hesitates, her heart thumping. She is afraid of the mobs of bantering males, who may be violent.

Seeking protection, she lifts her eyes to the priest's white stone face with its delicate, peaceful features, feels comforted, and walks on. The men in khaki call out to her and whistle, but the way she looks at the statue of that sacred figure discourages them from making indecent propositions or lewd gestures. Alba passes them quickly and, still trembling, enters the deserted tree-lined avenue that leads to Gladys's neighborhood. A few empty cars are parked at long intervals by the edge of the gutters. The girl hurries along under the trees, keeping close to the buildings. Suddenly in front of her looms a thick tree trunk. She stops. A lone soldier is leaning against the tree, smiling at her. He motions to her to come closer. Alarmed, out of breath, Alba doesn't dare go forward or back. In her heart she cries out to Pallais the priest. But the statue of the poet is far away, its back turned. Alba stands frozen stupidly, a few yards from the young man in the green uniform. Now he detaches himself from the tree trunk and whispers:

"Hey, come on, come see. Don't be afraid."

At first the girl doesn't react; her speech dies in her throat, and she breaks into a sweat. Then she manages to move: she takes a few steps toward the soldier—not to get a closer look at him, but to leave this dark spot and find a brighter place and then run, run as fast as she can, with all her strength, to her friend's house. The soldier, however, interprets her movement toward him as a sign of consent. He walks up to her, still smiling—and what does Alba see suddenly rising in front of her, horribly swollen, massive, threatening? She sees—as she will later tell Gladys—she sees the . . . the . . . It was enormous, she blurts out, sobbing, deeply impressed by this vision, so unexpected, so unprecedented. That man—it was impossible! Her friend tries to calm her down, telling her that it's quite normal, that this is the way things are.

"Luckily he didn't touch me," Alba goes on. "The guy would have killed me."

How did she get away? Faced with that dagger of brown flesh, the girl let out a strident, doleful cry, the cry of a cornered animal. The soldier, furious, put his hands down over his weapon, and Alba took to her heels. She ran without turning around, splattering herself with mud and tripping twice, until she collapsed in her friend's arms.

Gladys soothes her; Gladys is so calm—in fact, she is surprisingly calm. The truth is that for several weeks now Gladys has considered herself a woman. Yet she doesn't dare confess that Alvaro also knows how to expose himself. And that as far as candles go—poor Alba had used that word; she had called it a dirty, dark candle, a short, awful, thick, black candle—he had frightened her, too, but then . . . ! Gladys doesn't want to say anything; she pretends she's imagining what it must be like, and she says, "I think . . . I think you get used to it."

"But it's like a huge club—it's so long!"

"We're deep enough, sweetie."

"It's so fat!"

"We're wide enough; we're built to be mothers, Alba!"

"Gladys, doesn't it scare you to think of a man going inside you?"

"Why? I know your brother will help me."

"Well, I think it's frightful. I think I'll never . . ."

It's getting late. Alba refuses to go back home alone. Anyway, deep down, she isn't sorry about what happened, and she takes her time getting over it: it gives her an excuse to sleep at Gladys's house, which she loves to do.

A T last Fermina has dictated her letter and sent it. Abel, who is keeping his distance from the post office now, hasn't received it. The letter has turned yellow in its pigeonhole behind the counter, along with other letters addressed to people who aren't expecting them any more, who have gone away, disappeared. After a month, the post office returns it to the sender.

"Maybe Abel is dead," Alba ventures.

"Impossible!" her mother answers. "If my son had passed away, I would know it."

"Well, then, he's moved; maybe he's gone to La Calamidad, or Wiwili, or Costa Rica."

"Or they're holding him somewhere, in some barracks, in the country, in prison—you never know with all this mess, all this political business."

"Do you think he's forgotten us?"

"You, maybe. Not me. Whether he loves her or hates her, a son doesn't forget his mother; it's impossible—it would be like forgetting himself, forgetting his own life."

The truth is that Abel is changing. A day comes when he swears he's finished with it all, finished with feeling abandoned, missing his papa, his mama, the roosters, his little boyfriend—and how he used to cry over them at night, all alone, and how he used to daydream and give up and think of going back. He's finished with thinking about Papa, Mama, Chino, and his wound. Enough sop, enough soup, enough shit! He's perfectly happy to be empty, alone. Good-bye, home—and it was pretty, that home! See you tomorrow or later, my friend, my lover! Or maybe never. And with all his strength—is it an energy born of despair?—he plunges back into agitating.

He attends meetings again, he commits himself again; almost

frenetically, he accepts every mission, every service, every task. And one of these tasks in particular means a lot to him: Itamar has asked him to tackle Lichtenfels, that evasive and probably dangerous character, one more time.

Abel finds the foreigner outside the Santo Domingo ring, surrounded by cocks and fans. They watch the fights together, betting, pressing up against the low boards of the ring wall, jostled by drunkards. The rum drinkers—still loyal to the Caneflower brand—spoil the fight and invalidate the betting; the bettors get mad and the spectators protest. At last the fight is over. Abel follows the Yankee and tries yet again to pump him for information.

"Where do you work?"

"It's always different; I move around to different agencies."

"You don't specialize in anything?"

"Not really."

"That's strange. On the plaque attached to your gate it says 'Specialist.' "

"You have to put down something!"

"It also says 'Social Education'—that's pretty specific."

"Let's just say I oversee the last stage in the training of certain civil servants. But let's not talk about that any more; I can't stand talking about work in my free time."

Lichtenfels has eluded him once more, and Abel can only repeat his suspicions: the gringo, he thinks, plays an important role, maybe—who knows?—a crucial one. But what role, under whose authority, in which administration? Too hasty, too quickly exhausted, he doubts that he'll ever find out. Others are hunting the man down, the professor says. Leonor is continuing to make investigations, along with Seventeen, the high-school student who has recently joined their little group.

The former journalist found it hard to accept her failure with the wife—the one with the piano the same color as her ass, Leonor said ironically, because she believes all blond women have pink asses spotted with acne from eating too much rich food and not getting out in the sun. She found it hard to take, and now, like Seventeen, she is twice as assiduous at tailing and making inquiries. She trades impressions, pieces of information, or questions with other informants of the Front. In this way, the network of agents gradually draws up a list of the Yankees who have arrived recently, along with their titles—their "covers"—and their true missions. And now, Itamar announces, the organization knows which of these men is a propaganda expert, which an ideologist, which ones specialize in repression, which in intelligence, and which are instructors in the art of torture.

"What . . . ?"

"Torture. It's a technique, they say, almost a science, with its own laws, its own development. It's a more discreet and, if possible, a more secret method of governing. A torturer is the same as a revenue agent, an inspector of weights and measures—just another civil servant—and he does his job like any other civil servant. . . ."

"I . . . Christ Almighty! I was trying not to let myself think that," Abel confesses.

"Of course. The blond children, maybe the cockfights, the piano—Lichtenfels 'educates' in the central penitentiary."

Abel isn't listening any more. His imagination is heating up. In his mind, he sees the tortures inflicted on Chepe the Shirtless.

"The Front has already condemned him," Itamar adds. "We have to find the executioners. We need two people. I'm a candidate."

The night watchman hesitates. To kill a man, such a well-groomed, sporty guy—it bothers him, the idea of taking justice into his own hands; it paralyzes him, sends a shiver through him. But if it has to be done . . . The high-school boy volunteers immediately, before Abel has a chance. Now the group has only to decide when, where, and how the execution will be carried out.

15

You wake up very early that morning, before anyone else in the pension. You get up at dawn, the hour when Bayardo the porter is returning from his errands in the neighborhood. The man is agitated, running to the maid and the cook, and bumping into the owner. As he hurries across the hallway, you meet up with him and he shouts to you, too, "Oh, those poor kids, they'll pay dearly for this! Very dearly! My God, they'll pay for it."

"Pay for what?"

"The dogs."

"What dogs?"

"Go to the square and see. They'll pay for it, it's going to be awful."

And you hurry down the steps and head for the square. Road-workers and other working people are rushing in the same direction, curious. You overhear snatches of talk:

"They're all over the place."

"How did they ever do it?"

"Hanged? With ropes?"

Knots of people have formed on either side of the tall, circular ruins. And the curious, usually so talkative, eye one another silently, suspiciously; they also gaze with bewilderment at the bizarre, unprecedented, and horribly eloquent spectacle before them, this immense *tableau vivant* of death.

On the stage, as large as the square itself, dozens of dogs are hanging from the ends of wires, cords, and ropes of all thicknesses. Basset hounds, pugs, black dogs, white dogs, mongrels are suspended from trees; mastiffs and puppies dangle from the arms of the streetlights. The air is already warm, and the sky is whitening. Rays of sunlight pierce the foliage and paint yellowish spots on the pavement. Nothing moves around the trees except the birds. Some species of long-tailed blackbirds hop and flutter between the tree trunks and the lampposts. Above the tableau, vultures are gliding. Like garish votive offerings, large animals decorate the branches near the statue in the middle of the square. One of the dogs, swollen, has a head so small that you would expect the neck to snap and the body to separate and crash to the stone, like a bag stuffed with slaughterhouse offal. During the earthquake, the statue, a monumental, powerful work, had remained intact; the ground had shaken but the pedestal had stood fast, so that the father of the present dictator, also a general, continued to survey his city and the rubble of his city from high up on the back of his bronze horse. The founder of the dynasty (as implacable and sweet-tongued as his son, they say) is holding the reins of his charger in one hand. His other arm, the left arm of the "benefactor," is raised horizontally, and from the wrist of the august arm hangs a fat, pot-bellied, dark-colored animal—a bulldog. On the bas-relief of the pedestal someone has carved these words with a drill: TO THE SUPREME DOG, TO THE SON OF THE DOG, TO THE DOG OF DOGS, CANISSIME, the whole punctuated with a death's-head. Very Latin, that *canissime*, you observe. Is it a return to the original identity, is it poetry? Maybe only an accident of language . . . Hold on there, you won't voice any doubts, friend; you won't wax ironical. You will have faith: the revolution must be your inspiration. You think about the spectacle, the people who arranged it, the executioners.

"Where did they get them?" someone asks, worried.

"From the bourgeoisie, probably."

"From the vacant lots," ventures another spectator. "It's a good thing. There are so many of these mangy mutts."

"Why didn't they hang them all?"

Maybe they didn't have time, someone says, or they panicked. Maybe there was a false alarm. A few dogs are lying on the pavement around the stone pedestal. One large animal with rust-colored fur, soaked in blood, occupies a bench—the same bench where Ignacio used to sit with the whore. Other animals, most of them small, too small to be hanged, are strewn over other benches.

"It's a healthy kind of slaughter," continues the man who approves of the whole business. "Too many dogs in this city, and no one feeds them; they steal food from the beggars. All in all, an excellent hygienic measure!"

"So we should congratulate the people responsible?"

"In the name of public health, yes."

"Was that the point of it?" you ask, playing the naïf.

"That, my good man, you will have to find out from the kids."

The kids—those "poor kids," as Bayardo calls them—are the kids from the opposition—the only true, dangerous opposition—the Front. They will pay dearly for it, the porter says again, they will pay dearly.

You don't move. In the square the spectacle continues, a great still life: everything frozen, the statue holding its arm up, the dogs hanging. The onlookers linger, fascinated by what they see, by the imagination of the head artisan (the Front is an artist), by his audacity. All of a sudden you hear the noise of an engine.

The crowd stirs. Is it a police car, a truck from the barracks of the commandos, spearhead of the fight against the street protests? The rumbling draws closer and people shrink back, but it's only a bus, the first of the day, coming from the south, passing in front of the little restaurants and modest hotels, disappearing between the sections of standing wall, the little heaps of earth, and the high grass of the no-man's-land to the left of the gigantic stage set of collapsed tiers of seats.

The circle of spectators closes in again, then is almost immediately broken once more, this time by the eruption of a dozen jeeps. The vehicles pour in from both sides of the square, loaded with braying infantrymen weighed down by grenades and cartridge belts and holding submachine guns in their fists. The columns converge, catching the onlookers in a pincer movement. The latter, panic-stricken—and you, too, you overly curious foreigner—try to run away. The soldiers fire in the air, jostle people, kick them, hit them with the butts of their guns. An officer shouts orders; one group of soldiers seizes a few young men at random to serve as examples, and the rest of the elite commandos run over to the statue, the trees, and the lampposts, and set about removing the dogs. You and the man who was in favor of this slaughter head for the ruins, reaching what was once the main entrance to the stadium. You run into an arcade, under a long slab of concrete, then wander around, looking for an opening, a hole, until you spot a gap in the wall opposite the entrance, between some mounds of rubbish. Some shrubs growing outside mask the straight, low passageway where you have to crawl on your hands and knees, followed by the man who doesn't like dogs. Without being seen, apparently—at this hour the street is hardly crowded—you escape from the circus of the dead.

T H E half-dozen or so young men—schoolboys, clerks—who were arrested at random are taken away by the Guard to the usual field, which lies below street level, behind the old cathedral. Even six years after the tremor, people still empty rubble into this wasteland, still leave abandoned cars here, along with all sorts of other debris and refuse. And the area—attractive seen from far away, with its bright green grass during the rainy season—reaches all the way down to the lake.

Wielding their weapons, belaboring the kidneys of the unlucky men, the soldiers of the Guard force them in the direction of the shore. There, of course, they shoot them.

From now on, reprisals will be swift. In the capital, vagabonds, militants—when they can be caught—and indifferent or distracted citizens are indiscriminately imprisoned, tortured, and killed. But no type of repression can restrain the Front. No campaign of terror, Itamar stresses, should stop them from performing the tasks they are assigned. And the most urgent of these is still the execution of the Yankee. The only thing they're not sure of now is the place. Would it be suitable to kill Lichtenfels in front of his house, in his garden, on his front doorstep? It would be convenient—there aren't any police or army sentries guarding the house. But the trouble is, the place isn't political enough. The reasons for the assassination wouldn't be obvious, and the population would be scandalized to see the father of a family murdered right in front of his wife and children. Even more shocking would be to shoot the man when he was coming out of Mass. To kill him in front of the church or his own house would be to deprive the justice seekers of the social benefit of their gesture. In the end, for the sake of morale and propaganda, it is decided that the torturer should be put to death where he does his evil work—in front of the prison. The five members of the cell agree about this. Leonor rents a car using false identification papers. Comrade Superior and Abel will keep watch not far from the prison. Itamar, who is a bad shot, will drive. Armed with a sawed-off shotgun, the schoolboy Seventeen will sit in the back of the vehicle.

At about five o'clock, toward the end of the afternoon, the ed-

ucator Lichtenfels leaves the institution where he gives his lessons. He avoids, however, leaving by the main door or even by
the smaller door in the side of the building, choosing instead an
inconspicuous door discreetly set in the wall of an annex behind
the prison. Two steps away stands his metallic sky-blue limou-
sine, parked with other civilian cars in the little square nearby.
Itamar will park his car at the corner of one of the three streets
leading into the square, and he and Seventeen will wait there for
the executioner to appear. The moment the man crosses the
threshold, they'll roar out and the schoolboy will take aim and
fire. Then they'll make their getaway, taking a right turn at the
spot where Abel and the priest, as though they had nothing to do
with it, will be pretending to be outraged, cursing and getting in
the way of any help that may come. The car will drive around the
block and enter the district of shops and street stalls, where traffic
is heavy, and here Seventeen and Itamar will abandon the car,
separate, and lose themselves in the crowd. The group will not
meet until the following night, when, for the first time, they will
meet at the home of one of the military leaders of the Front.

A T the appointed hour, the teacher left the prison and Itamar
drove the car out. Seventeen fired, and Lichtenfels collapsed on
the sidewalk. A burst of machine-gun fire sounded from a turret
that overlooked the prison annex and was barely visible from the
street. Itamar accelerated abruptly. Seventeen crouched down on
the floor in front of his seat. The vehicle charged ahead while
gunfire echoed all around it; just as it was about to leave the
square, a van appeared, going slowly, its roof loaded down with
cages full of chickens. Itamar, unable to slow down, tried to ma-
neuver the car around the van, but he couldn't avoid hitting it.
The collision produced a brief, dull crash and a sort of explosion,
but the two men were able to get out safely. Suddenly an army
van appeared. Seventeen turned around and faced the van, firing

at it, and crumpled, his belly covered with blood, riddled with bullets. His comrade, also wounded, fell down onto the asphalt but managed to drag himself behind the chicken van. But the poultryman, who had only been slightly bruised, threw himself on Itamar, subdued him, and handed him over to the soldiers, who kicked him and tossed him into the army van along with the dead man. Stunned, as though they, too, had been riddled with bullets, Abel and the Superior did not try to act offended or vengeful— they took to their heels.

Y O U didn't know about any of this: you come back to La Perla and find everyone in a panic. Soldiers are standing guard in front of the house. Suitcases, bags, and cartons overflowing with books and notebooks are being taken out of the pension. Everyone is being arrested: they're taking away the pension guests, the staff, and the owner. A few people are grumbling; the cook is crying; the bank clerk, a little the worse for drink, is declaring loud and clear his sympathy for "our most illustrious general, His Excellency, who . . ." The mechanics teacher is away (oh, blessings on supplementary courses and mental exertion!), and so avoids being arrested. The porter, his jaws clamped together, his eyes bright, remains calm, while the geometrician, bewildered, protests his innocence, mentions his religion, and crosses himself, to the jeers of the soldiers.

You want to get your things out of there. You walk up, thinking that since you are a foreigner . . . But they don't care about that. A Frenchman! What the hell could a Frenchman be doing in this shitty country! exclaims the leader of the commandos—is your occupation really volcanologarbage? Or is it agitation?

"It's sex, Commander," says another idiot. "The French are all pigs."

The so-called commander pushes you into the police van, and it moves off. The jokes continue:

"Is it true that the French do it everywhere?"

"Is it true that the French don't wash, even before they do it?"

"Is it true that when Frenchmen fuck, they make their women stick their fingers in them?"

These questions, and the way they're asked, and the gestures that accompany them, make the Christian geometrician turn successively red, white, and green. A whole new world of different customs and unsuspected acrobatics is revealed to him suddenly and plunges him into a silent, uncomfortable turmoil. Taken away despite their important family name, the two schoolboys listen to the commandos' questions and, rather cheered up by them, begin to relax.

At the barracks, you are all locked up in the same overheated room; it has a window in the shape of a long, narrow opening up near the ceiling. An NCO comes in and reads off the names: the landowners' two offspring are released—*Cómo no, jefe?* What could be more natural?—as well as the bank clerk, the cook, and the one who expected it least—the porter Bayardo. The owner stays, as does, strangely, scandalously—as he dares to grumble—the land surveyor, the zealous fanatic of cadastral surveys, the law-and-order man.

As for you, they lead you into another, brighter, furnished room and the interrogation starts up again, in a tone intended to be detached, slightly disdainful:

"What about this Itamar Lobo—do you know him well? A teacher—a real one? Anything to confess? And what about the other prof, the technician? And what's-his-name?" The man goes through the registration forms taken from the pension. "This López, first name Abel, no profession . . . Hold on there, no profession—a professional? A professional militant, I mean, sir. La Perla! You live in a jewel box. How many red pearls there? Who came to visit? It seems there was quite a bit of coming and going. Meetings? Secret sessions?"

The questions rain down. How should you answer them? You

ape astonishment. Then you bristle. The torrent is unending: question follows question. You try to keep on your feet.

"As a volcanologist, Inspector . . ." As a man of the solitary, unpeopled heights . . .

"But, for God's sake, you've been living in the capital for five months now," says the inspector, becoming impatient.

"It's . . . I'm waiting for the end of the rainy season."

You try to convince him: rain on miles and miles of black dust; the thick layer turns to slime, and you sink down in it; you can't get anywhere, and you vanish along with your equipment, your borers, your thermometers, your pyrometers, your seismometers or graphs, and eventually your transcribers, your planimeters, and your goniometers. When it rains the mountain liquefies, you drift, you drown in brown mud with your planimeters, your tachometers or your theodolites, orogenetically speaking, sir, with your top——

"That's enough!"

"Men pass on, volcanoes remain."

"Go back to your volcanoes, but not here—go back to the ones in your own country!"

"They're . . . they're extinct, sir," you confess, shamefaced. What yearning you feel suddenly—what a strange fit of sadness!

"What? Not even a little one?"

"The Old World, sir."

"And it certainly deserves its name, by God! If everything is going extinct there, too bad for you—it's not our fault."

They release you and advise you to leave—"Its your skin, Mr. Volcano-Ass"—and the sooner the better. Your mind is in a whirl—filled with a dizzying confusion of ideas and plans. Can you clear out, tear yourself away after all these months of discoveries, of metamorphoses, of fears and passions? Can you turn your back on these friends, these life stories, leave the stage in the very middle of the play? It's hard to make up your mind. You waver, you think about it, you try to find out a few things.

You would at least like to talk—for one last time?—to Itamar, and to Abel. But where are they? News of the professor comes quickly, by way of the press. One newspaper, in fact, publishes an official statement from the Minister of Justice in which he announces: "Following a murder committed on the person of a guest of the government, an adviser on social questions and a native of a friendly country, the accused, a certain José Itamar, aged twenty-six, wounded superficially and treated at the military hospital, was tried in a closed proceeding. Found guilty, the accused received a life sentence."

You close the newspaper, wondering what to do. Do you have a choice? You know the name of the parish where Comrade Superior lives, and you go to see him.

The man's home is a shack built of planks and fiberboard at the back of a fenced, overgrown garden behind the neighborhood church. Barely visible, situated as it is at the edge of the property, it looks like a gardener's shed or some other kind of outbuilding. What impresses you much more when your arrive is the parish house, all of concrete, plastered in white, a true villa. There seems to be no relation at all between this house and the other.

"The people who live in the parish house close their eyes. Either they don't know or they don't want to know," is all the explanation the militant theologian gives.

The two of you are alone, sitting in the larger of the shack's two rooms, which has to serve as living room, dining room, and meeting room, on rocking chairs made of ordinary, unpainted wood, the kind of chairs found in all the houses in this country, even the poorest. You're alone, and the street noises—dogs barking, children shouting, the rumbling of engines, the cries of itinerant tradespeople—are muffled. This seclusion, the austerity of the place—the cement floor, the bare walls—as well as a certain mystery, a certain silence surrounding it, make you uncomfortable, make you want to be noisy. You'd like to talk, make him talk, fill the house with explosions of voices, ask a thousand questions. All of a sudden, the door to the bedroom opens and Leonor appears. Was she expecting to see you? Apparently not. Her short jet-black hair is tousled, her features are swollen, and she's wearing a bathrobe—she has just got up. She looks at you, mildly surprised. Forestalling any embarrassment, the priest tries to make light of it:

"The theology of the Incarnation, taken to its extreme . . ."

". . . makes you like everyone else," Leonor concludes in a matter-of-fact way, no doubt quite content to interrupt the extemporaneous moralizing.

You smile, thoughtful. Do priests throw themselves into the revolution because they have first thrown themselves on a woman? Or do they throw themselves on women because they have thrown themselves into the revolution? When they were young, these priests renounced the world and worldly things and took a vow of chastity. But now worldly things have gradually attracted them, and two of those things are power and the pleasures of the flesh. Which of the two forces came first? Some priests must have first succumbed to sex and others to politics. All the rest—philosophy and cosmology, the Ministry of the People, Divine Matter (divine rocks, divine buttocks), the Blessed Sacrifice of Violence, the Sacrament of the Class Struggle—is no more than a kind of poetry justifying the transgression, tranfiguring (or intended to transfigure), making the break easier.

There are plenty of things to talk about, plenty of questions to ask. You find this "Superior" intriguing. You would like to be able to contradict him, but aren't you already submitting to questions about your intentions? There is also the presence of the woman, who knows you by name, she says, because Abel has

2 1 2

often talked to her about you. She adds that if you want to see him again, you're going to have to be patient.

"Oh—is he hiding?"

"No. He's exhausted, but that'll pass. The comrade has taken it into his head that going back to Corinto for a while may do him some good."

16

Leonor doesn't live with Comrade Superior: they see each other and spend the night together now and then. Convenience, the body's needs, and a certain mutual affection are a sufficient explanation for this casual relationship. The word "lovers" would be too strong for what they are to each other—the passion that consumes them doesn't come from love. The theologian, and Leonor even more, live for an idea, a struggle. It is simply that their political comradeship is paralleled by sexual comradeship. The woman pays her partner a visit from time to time; she is likely to go home with him after evening cell meetings. Otherwise she goes home to one of the houses that the Front's treasurer has rented as lodgings for the permanent members, the fanatical militants, the guerrillas transferred from the country to the city.

When she lived with the widow at Villa Fontana, Leonor would not have men friends visit or stay with her. But her leaders assigned her tasks involving many moves, meetings, encounters with other people. They asked her to live in one of the hiding places designated by numbers and known as "bases." This was how the former journalist happened to move into Base 14. Two restless, ill-shaven young men, proud of their long months of wandering and fighting in the mountains of the north, were already living there.

The younger one limped, and for that very reason, out of defiance, the militant, who was supposed to be on leave to rest up, could not keep still. He talked in a loud voice, drew up plans for raids, envisaged surprise attacks. The situation was ripe and the masses were ready, said the impatient man, who felt it was urgent to carry out guerrilla operations in the middle of the capital, since this was the way—the only way, he stressed—to spark off the armed insurrection of the population at last, to strike the decisive blow to the dictatorship.

A political tendency, a military tendency—it's a typical situation, rife with commonplaces, litanies, and various kinds of posturing. The revolutionary party is up to its ears in it. Our line, says one militant, my "masses' line," the Front's line . . . To hell with your line, another, underground militant counters. Your line is too soft. The enterprise of war requires that . . . Priority to arms, comrades! The level of the struggle . . . Enough agitating and debating! Hell, the Front isn't empty-handed now. So let's move on! Hurray for this line! But the "politicals" resist. Their current . . . Our current is vast, we're in the majority. Right, the "military" say in counterattack: greater numbers are soft, that's fatal, and—a major tenet of the Sacred Gospel—what are the masses? The masses are stupid, the masses are dear little ignorant souls, they're not the avant-garde. Stupidity of stupidities! What's the avant-garde without the masses? A gang! A band of looters! Adventurers! With "the advance of the struggles" (are you stumbling through it?) the debate grows more intense. At the top they are working out the Synthesis as best they can. Long live our (sacred) Political and Military Directorate! Clichés continue to be voiced by the flock. The students, the fighters who are on leave in order to get some rest—the kind of rest cuckolds get, they fume!—fidget with impatience, try to force things. At Base 14, the former mountain fighters defend the military line.

Better: they put into effect an operation that is supposed to strike a significant blow and whose object is to kidnap a prominent member of the regime. It will be carried out with very few men, very scanty resources. Its professed goal: to exchange the hostage for political prisoners. Its covert goal: to prove that their line is correct. There will be five people involved—a shock commando unit, including the two guerrillas from the north, Anthony—What's with the Yankee name? It's an assumed name, friend, to make it easier for him to infiltrate—and Alvaro, for he is indeed the limping man from Base 14. They will be joined by Ramón and Oscar, two students from León hidden away in another base. A woman, Comrade Ofelia (a Trotskyite infiltrator, someone said), will be the fifth. The prominent member of the regime they will abduct is Minister Alonso. The operation will be carried out on a Saturday evening, at the entrance to the residence of his colleague, Minister Schnick.

Every weekend, Adolfo Schnick and his wife hold a dance for their friends and acquaintances. Alonso is a most faithful attender of these parties, as is his wife, the beautiful Eugenia, formerly Miss Country Club and the daughter of an important family, the Chamorro de Cortéses. The guests always show up about nine o'clock, arriving gaily in front of the house at the foot of the pretty flight of granite steps with its white landing.

At eight-twenty the commando starts off. Three of the members, Ofelia and the students, take their places in the car. Alvaro and Anthony follow them on a motorcycle. The job of the first three is to seize the minister, overcome him, force him into the car, and take him away, while the others, armed with revolvers, cover them.

The evening is mild, monotonously mild, and fortunately, in spite of the season, there is no sign of a storm. On Saturdays surveillance around the residence is relaxed. When the soldiers on guard relieve one another, they often bring along, hidden in their pockets, little square bottles of rum; slinging their weapons across their backs, they booze and take it easy. This evening, as always, the guests are a select group—senators, more ministers, a general, some colonels, and a few ambassadors, all accompanied by their lawful wives and older sons and daughters, except the man who always brings along his Philippine "secretary," formerly a masseuse, according to malicious gossip. They all go into the marble foyer—Schnick is crazy about marble—and then into the reception rooms, decorated Austrian-style—Schnick's father was born in Vienna—with candelabras, gilded wood credenzas, and velvet hangings. The most elegant of the ladies is still the haughty Eugenia, though the Philippine rivals her. Still young and slender, Alonso's wife can wear any sort of dress, and she goes in for décolletage especially, since her skin is faultlessly tanned and she likes to reveal her shoulders, throat, and back. She and her husband are always punctual at these parties, invariably arriving on the stroke of nine. The minister parks his car in the private parking area to the right of the residence. He and Eugenia walk to the semicircular steps that lead up to the granite stoop. Before passing through the door, the wife lingers a moment on the steps, just long enough to straighten her necklace, smooth her dress, and tidy a few locks of hair. This is the moment the commando unit chooses to take action.

The car stops at the foot of the steps, with Ofelia at the wheel. The other two, leaving their doors open, have jumped out even before she stops. They leap up the steps and throw themselves on the minister, who panics and clings to his wife, while the wife starts screaming, suddenly hysterical, and struggles, glued to her husband like a bird with its feet caught in lime. The woman's bawling and her disordered, wild motions interfere with the kidnappers and allow the minister to fling himself around and resist them; it looks as though he may even be able to get away.

The other members of the commando, sitting on their motorcycle, are following the action from a distance. The operation threatens to be a failure—this is obvious, and it's unacceptable, Alvaro says. Something has to be done. He and his partner expect the guards, the soldiers, and the other guests to come out of the villa at any moment. The idea that the minister is getting away from them is intolerable. And the kidnappers are still there, trying to separate the couple. It's risky, it's dangerous, it's crazy. A few more seconds of this stupid scuffling at the top of the stairs and their comrades will be captured, lynched, killed. Alvaro raises his weapon, aims for Alonso, and fires. The confusion is such that he hits the wife. Taken by surprise, the kidnappers retreat. Eugenia stumbles down the steps and falls. Her husband rushes into the foyer of the house. The members of the commando unit manage to slip away before the soldiers appear.

"Eugenia didn't get up again?" Leonor asks, when they tell her about the incident the next day.

"The radio said she died on the spot. She lost a lot of blood."

As one reporter wrote, the victim's dress, a long white silk sheath, had turned red. The crime allowed the minister and his friends to make a heroine, a martyr, of the dead woman. The former Miss Country Club immediately became a saint, a Joan of Arc. Her husband, more respected than ever, was apparently going to be given a second portfolio.

Leonor makes her point of view clear. She argues, retorts, counterattacks. Despite the failures, some of the comrades continue to support the military line. She and her friend the Superior defend the political line. And the bogus social worker runs around, stopping in at all the bases, convincing others that her position is the correct one, winning followers, unsettling the opinions of a number of leaders. The operation against Alonso was too careless, they decide. It was unpopular, suicidal. Something would have to be done, because this was adventurism. If they let it go, they run the risk of having a catastrophe on their hands. Finally they talk about what should be done to the men from Base 14.

A leader summons the undisciplined men. They can't be sent back to the country, unfortunately—too risky—nor can they be moved to a different city or sent home. In the end, the leader suspends them from the organization for three weeks. He then gives Leonor the job of writing and circulating the document that gives notice of the punishment. She is delighted to do this, and gives a copy to the two men in her cell. Comrade Superior thinks it is good: it shows the supremacy of reason, of time, of endurance. The Directorate is clearsighted. No salvation apart from the Directorate. As for Abel, "pre-eminence," as the text calls it, is not what really interests him. What he would like to know is the names of the suspended militants.

"One is called Anthony," Leonor tells him; "then there's Ofelia, admitted a short time ago, a suspect woman, I'm sure of it, maybe a spy. There's this other guy from the north— all these people from the north—what a nuisance! His name is Alvaro."

"What? My brother! He's a hothead, a real dangerous guy, I swear."

Abel isn't at all surprised. In fact, he has expected it, sooner or later, because Alvaro was made for terrorism—it suits him perfectly. During that operation Alvaro must have felt overjoyed, drunk with pleasure. Abel has expected this, but not here in the capital, and now, discovering that his brother has been right here in the same city, he becomes uneasy. He's afraid of more craziness.

"Did he accept the punishment?" he asks.

"Not really. He and Anthony are sticking together."

Leonor explains that this man Anthony called the political line "a cowardly line." Alvaro contrasted it to the "men's line," balked, advertised his disgust with submitting to the "female line."

"So he's going to reject the punishment?"

"I've warned him—he runs the risk of being barred."

A B E L didn't go back to Corinto, or at least not right away.
He kept changing his mind. Over the last few days he had changed
his mind fifty times. Too many things were preoccupying him,
upsetting him: how long was Itamar going to be locked up? Five
years? Ten years? Forever? Or would they learn that he, too, had
"committed suicide"? Chino in the Guard—another parting and,
given the situation, probably another death. Then, too, he had
had to leave La Perla, which was in some sense his home, the
only place he could live in some peace. He thought of running
away, but where to, and for how long? He thought of going back
to a bitter father, a martyred mother, and the vague, very vague
hope of meeting up with Toca on the soccer field after a game, of
following him into the locker room the way he used to, speaking
to him, making him relent, beginning all that again. . . . No!
Just as he was about to get on the bus, Abel changed his mind
again. From now on, his home, his lair, would be the construction
site. He would turn into a mole and live there full-time, like
Farabundo. The fence, the buildings, the cellars would be his
territory, his permanent address. The night watchman moved in
and endured a week of dejection, hesitation, and confusion before
deciding to leave again.

A F T E R talking to the Superior and his friend in the little
house at the back of the garden, after being exposed to these new
considerations—the manly line, the reasonable line, the bold line,
the protracted line, the flexible or hard line or "the idiotic line"—
after the instructions and the resolutions and the new tasks, Abel
gives himself up to the only thing that soothes him: strolling around
in the open spaces with the wind in his face, enjoying the sweet-

ness of wasting time. Anyway, what else is there to do? Somewhere, Chino is being trained in the art of killing—slogging away between four walls in some barracks, or on some drilling ground. He's languishing or fidgeting in some garrison, but Abel doesn't know where. He doesn't even know if Chino is still in the capital. Abel drifts toward the area of the ruins with its fringe of whores in the evening, the area of rank weeds, of wandering dogs—the ones who weren't hanged—and on toward the lake.

I was wrong, he thinks, not to go to Corinto. For only two days, one day, a day trip. Just staying long enough to see the house again, walk in front of it, walk around it. The house with its yellow walls (dirty, too, probably, and gray seen from a distance), its concrete doorsill, the window—the only window in which a light shines late into the night, whether because of his father's insomnia, or arguments, or his bad health, or his bad moods, or when nature calls him (Where is the toilet paper? he shouts, trotting from one room to another, and he gropes for the light switch in the kitchen, where the rolls of paper are kept), or because of the mania he has for rereading the newspaper in the middle of the night.

That's where Abel was born, after all. . . . Eighteen years in the (once) yellow house. He grew up there, he raised his first cock there; as a child, he delighted in possessing a mother, toys, a courtyard of trampled earth and a few plants, a world all his own, his world, and, until he was fourteen, a family, too. But the old man is lurking within those walls. And he would take the return of his son as a provocation, an insult. Jeremías would cause a scandal—a dead man doesn't come home again, he would scream, and would threaten to hit him; and Alba would run away crying, maybe calling on the neighbors, and the police would come.

I was wrong, I wasn't wrong. . . . A few days later, for no real reason, idly, Abel turns down a different street and goes into the post office. A letter is waiting for him. How many days has it been there? He can't see anything but the circle of the postmark.

In the letter, Alba tells him his father has died. Then she describes Alvaro's prolonged, incomprehensible absence—incomprehensible to Gladys, at least. She goes on to talk about the decimation of the poultry yard, her mother's fears—mainly at night, when her hands start to tremble—and promises to God, to Saint Rita; about her mother's heart wearing out, more about the nights, which are so long, longer than they used to be—how strange, the planet is changing. She talks about *loneliness*, about how the bathroom faucet doesn't work too well. Fermina has her daughter underline the word "loneliness." "We are alone, Abel," Alba repeats. The lonely women beg him to come back.

He answers their pleading. Is it pity? For himself? Or weakness? A mistake. The bus is slow, the road endless, and it's hot, very hot, because there's a storm coming. The dust rises from the ground, as thick and abundant as a crop of grass. The fields are beautiful, a long layer of green, and because the sun is beating down on this layer of green, because the heat is so intense and the sky so silver, the green looks almost white. Then the first huts appear, standing crookedly on the sandy clay. Abel catches a glimpse of the ocean, then loses it, then sees it again between the shacks. Without waiting to reach the terminus, he jumps off and makes his way through the streets. Suddenly he finds himself face to face with Alba, who is coming out of the house.

"God have mercy! My br——" She turns around and calls to her mother.

"Saint Rita!" cries the mother. "Your poor old . . . the poor old man, you know, we loved each other so much. . . ."

"I know."

The son lets himself be pulled inside. Fermina and Alba never stop talking, and they both talk at the same time. They get excited, weep, dry their eyes. And what about Alvaro, who doesn't send any news of himself? Where is he? Has he bought a business? If this goes on, Gladys—she's growing thin; it's not fair; she doesn't need this. If it goes on . . . Times are difficult, we're

2 2 2

mending thread and bobbins, even medium bobbins cost a lot now—not to mention meat and flour. And it rains so much. Storms break, always in the middle of the night, and you tremble so hard the bed shakes, too, you think the earth is moving, you wait for the shock, for the walls to collapse. But now that Abel is back . . .

"But I'm leaving again."

"What! Why? Are you mixed up in politics?"

"My own life."

"Your life? You don't live alone? Are you planning to get married?"

"Why do you always want me to get married? Is Alvaro married? What about Alba? Is she about to get married?"

"Well, so it's politics."

"What's the difference?"

"All that will come to a bad end, my son. If you're alone . . ."

"That's enough! I'm not alone," he interrupts, exasperated by the interrogation.

Politics or no politics, making the revolution or having nothing to do with it, being committed or staying on the sidelines—what difference does any of that make, if you live alone? Yesterday there was Toca, Chino. Will there be someone else tomorrow? A soccer player, a soldier? If he had to choose, which . . .? One thing is sure, obvious, as clear as though his father were still here: I'm leaving again, Abel repeats. His life, his mother, Alba . . . They put their hands together and beg, they grovel, they crawl on the ground. Fermina announces that she's going to bake a cake. The boy tears himself away from their yellow arms—so fat, so soft—from Fermina's heavy, trembling flesh. Alba . . . His mother . . . He promises to come see her "as often as I can."

17

It's always like this, it seems. You wait months—it never comes. You watch the clouds, you lose hope, the ground wrinkles, splits open, the countryside turns gray, dust gathers on roads, plants, and fences. Everything is blanketed—windowsills, benches, roofs—with a layer of dry dirt. The city turns to dirt, the asphalt turns to dirt, the dogs turn yellow, and the people grow tired. And then, suddenly, within a few hours, everything becomes even grayer, the sky especially, exaggeratedly, and that enormous black belly hanging up there over the city swells up, cracks, and breaks open. Water drops from it and rushes down the sheet-metal roofs, the tiles, the tree trunks, the roads, everything. Ten torrents, fifty torrents flow together. Gutters turn into rivers, vacant lots into swamps. The rubble-chocked plain by the edge of the lake becomes another lake. People can't walk in Managua any more: they paddle with their feet, they slide, they let themselves be carried off. Good-bye to taking walks until next season!

Street singers and lovers go to ground and take shelter as the rain continues to pour down. Itinerant vendors flounder about, their carts sinking into the ruts as they push, pull, swear, curse the sky and its rains, and finally give up. Skirt chasers and drunks hang about under lean-tos. Prostitutes hug the walls of the stadium. Men plunge across the square, driven by their increasing need, the excitement of the storm, their soaked clothes like a second skin. They disappear into the ruins with the women. Though the downpours make it impossible for people to flirt on the street corners and under the trees, stroll about and serenade each other, exchange civilities on lawns and benches, joke around and simper, no rain is heavy enough to stop sex; no storm is powerful enough to keep people from making love. Love or war. They would even do it under water—make love, kill one another; getting soaked doesn't bother lovers or gunmen.

There's a lot of shooting in the eastern parts of the city, in San Judas, where street fights take place every day now. The avalanches of water don't do much to contain the action of the insurgents. The fire from the weapons isn't extinguished. The cataracts don't make either the guerrillas or their supporters retreat. The occupation of the periphery continues, courtyard by courtyard, sidewalk by sidewalk, block by block. Victories make the timid brave. Power wavers; in certain parts of the city and country the Guard quakes with fear. There is talk of desertion—of arms and ammunition diverted, and of growing numbers of soldiers in retreat. The end-of-the-reign atmosphere gives another dose of courage to the pure "politicals." The "military line" crops up again, and this time the others leave them alone. The most circumspect of the militants become daring. Leonor does more and more things that she would have condemned only the day before. Her friend Comrade Superior abandons his lair and makes the rounds of the fermenting neighborhoods, visiting parishes and trying to bring the priests over to the side of the Front.

The theologian knows a Spanish priest who has taken in another Spaniard, a defrocked priest who had once been involved in a peasant movement in the department of Boaco. Each of the two men has his own philosophy, his own private life, his own ways. But they come from the same region, almost from the same canton—they are Asturians. So, for the sake of their native land, Reverend José Luis provides a room for the other priest, who arrived in America under the name of Father Francisco Xavier and who has been transformed after six years—and some internal upheavals, crises of conscience, hard struggles—into Comrade Francisco.

In his rural parishes—the priest was in charge of eight villages—Francisco, moved by pity and certain things he had read, had helped to create the beginnings of a union. The leader was a knock-kneed, merry little man, a peasant named Epaminondas who lived on a piece of property belonging to Don Lázaro, the biggest landowner in the area. From the father, who also endeavored to educate his flock, Epaminondas had learned to read and had discovered new words and phrases—"God's people" and "God's class," "contraceptive" (what a word!—he often said "contrastive"), "socialism," "self-defense," "condom," "trench"; he also learned that "the rural areas are the garden of the revolution." All these teachings, so new in the country, spread and reached the ears of Don Lázaro. And when the union was set up, the landowner intervened. First he tried to thwart the priest, then he tried to buy him, then he started threatening him. Finally, because the priest "persisted in agitating," as the judge later explained, the hereditary and legitimate owner of the soil unleashed his guard, his private police, which the villagers called "the black dogs."

These animals first burned the place where the union held its meetings, a cottage made of lime-covered earth. Then they set fire to Epaminondas's hut and those of his companions. The dogs beat the "agitators" black and blue, roughed up their wives, and casually, openly, raped a few of their daughters. One of the dogs carried off Teresa, Epaminondas's timid concubine, a girl of sixteen who had been handed over by her father in exchange for twenty pounds of beans at the market in the town of Camoapa. Finally the private police attacked the priest. They demolished his van, an old Chevrolet, and undressed the driver, beat him, and left him naked in a field. The Spaniard and his lieutenant, convinced that the dogs would go as far as murder, had to leave.

From then on the peasant followed his leader everywhere. He found a new woman in the parish of the other Asturian, a woman just as young and timorous as Teresa—Epaminondas didn't like his women to be brash or mature—and, still with Francisco, he is militating for the Front in his neighborhood. For weeks now the two of them have been trying to persuade Reverend José Luis to join the revolutionary forces, but he is resisting. Only the moral and intellectual weight, the prestige, of Comrade Superior—his theology, revised as necessary, may not be entirely convincing, but it is disturbing—makes him close his eyes to the activities of his compatriot. With the help of Epaminondas, the former priest now arranges meetings of young people in a little outbuilding next to the church that serves as a storage room for the dais, the banners, the movable altars, and the lanterns used in processions. Amid these church trappings, Francisco and his congregation discuss the documents of the Front, describe the strategy to be followed, and assign tasks. They also learn how to construct little incendiary bombs like Molotov cocktails.

In this way, Comrade Superior has managed to neutralize a number of priests, vicars, and even monks. Where the people had already come around, the theologian had only to enlist the pastors. Two months short of the final uprising—and a few days before Epaminondas, his concubine, and a resistance fighter who wasn't fighting just then were killed in an ambush—Leonor's friend could count on the support of almost half the parishes in the capital. He had a brilliant future; the Front's Directorate congratulated him. The leader of the "political line" made promises to him.

W H A T is there for an out-of-work combatant to do? How can a suspended militant, a strong young man, fill his time? He wanders around, he gets into discussions, and, in a roundabout way, secretly, he schemes and plots. In order to kill his boredom (cover up his failures), he looks for women.

At Base 14, Alvaro had done his best to seduce Leonor. Tired to death of fighting—fighting rain, hunger, disease, and the forest; fighting mosquitoes and the enemy—the warrior had rediscovered what it was like to have a real bed, a real kitchen, a real shower: here in the city, his feelings came alive again. Suddenly he wanted badly to make love. He paced around the house, sighing, his nerves knotted up, and then he made his advances. This was in the midst of the confrontation between the "military line" and the "political line," and Leonor refused him point-blank.

Now the young man's mind is all on fire, filled with the memory of the humps and hollows, curves and slits of certain bodies; of Maritza's mouth and Claudine's breasts; of the soft bellies, the hot recesses of the girls of Corinto. . . . These images torture him in the very depth of his being, and he is subject to violent, imperious attacks of homesickness; his continence racks him like a fever. He leaves the base and goes down to what they call the shady parts of town. The penis has its own sense of smell, and Alvaro follows where it points the way. Very quickly, driven by its intense needs, it picks up the trail, and the wanderer wanders only a short while, ending up, the first evening, at the square near the stadium.

Is it too late, or too early? Ever since the dogs were hanged here, the superstitious whores have been afraid of the place. Are the voyeurs and clients afraid too? Beyond the square, near the cheap restaurants, there is a lighted window. The rectangle of light stands out from the wall of a two-story house—a family house, says the wanderer, a sheltered, peaceful house like the one where the impressionable Gladys is pining away, her body still full of secrets. Impressionable and far away, and yet . . . she is his fiancée, after all. Another era? Probably, but soon it will be possible to return to that era. Things look hopeful—at the rate the Front is advancing.

But for the fiancée, nothing looks very hopeful. Deep in her part of town, in her little bedroom—so clearly a girl's bedroom—what does Gladys know about the failures, or about the final, glorious victories that the leaders, in confidence, swear are imminent? What does she know about offensives, a new deal, priority restored to arms over discussions? She doesn't know anything any more—she weeps, her head in Alba's lap, consumed by one fear:

"I will never call you 'sister-in-law,' " she laments, her head against her friend's shoulder. "I'll never marry him; I'll end up an old maid."

"Some other man will turn up."

"I won't have anything to do with him; I'll send him to you."

"That's sweet of you, Gladys, but if he likes you he won't like me. You're thin. Or I'll just have to lose weight somehow."

"Eat slices of pineapple, without sugar, and nothing else."

"Not even shortbread?"

"Especially not shortbread. It's very crisp, I know; you feel as if you're eating air. But it's deceptive—it's loaded with calories."

"And fritters? They're empty inside; there's nothing in them."

"Forbidden! Fritters are rich."

Again and again, Gladys and Alba spend all evening talking, about everything: marriages that have taken place in the city, the troubles that are starting up again, the rounds of the Guard; about dresses, about losing weight, about different stitches in knitting, about their families. And Alba regularly harks back to the incident in which that brazen soldier tried to seduce her, exhibiting his thing. The size of that thing still inspires her with the same thought:

"It grows so fast! How do they do it?"

"It happens all by itself," her friend assures her with a delicate, falsely modest air, a touch of melancholy in her eyes.

"And does it fold up again? After all, they have to be able to put it back where it belongs."

"It deflates—it's automatic."

Alba is quite aware that a woman's body, with its strange discharges and its ability to bear children, has its own mysteries. But a man's body is also full of mysteries, and everyone pretends to know nothing about it. The girl could muse endlessly about the reasons for this silence, but she prefers to go on to something else, the most important event of the last few days and the big news: Abel's visit.

"And what does he say? Has he set up house with someone? Does he have a lover?"

"Oh no! My brother would rather live alone. I think he likes that."

"Alvaro claims he's a failure."

"According to *him*, the whole family is a failure."

Gladys, distracted, her mind on something else, is barely listening. She is suddenly afraid: is her fiancé going to come back? Will her whole youth pass by this way? And will she be able to preserve her eggshell complexion, her slender figure? Alba sympathizes. She, too, has so many reasons for grieving; she, too, is filled with misgivings, uneasiness! There's nothing the girls can do but sit and cry together. Outside on the veranda, they hold hands, letting go only to wipe their eyes; in the distance the night is torn apart by flashes of heat lightning.

W H E N evening comes, Alvaro leaves the base. He will pay no attention to warnings to be cautious, or to any talk about the threat of a storm. The danger of a sudden shower or a stray bullet is nothing compared with being forced to stay inside doing nothing. That's a kind of death, an unending private agony. Pulling himself together, he goes out and finds his way back to the ruins, paces around the square, and slips in between the collapsed tiers of seats and grandstands.

One day he crosses a tilled plot of land—there's still some wire left here, and the remains of a border, but was this place really a vegetable garden once, before the quake?—and as he crosses it he sees a man emerge from between two stands of bamboo.

"Hey, you know the way, too?" this man asks him, surprised.

"The way to what?"

"Come on, don't pretend."

"To what, for Christ's sake?"

"To the whorehouse," the other finally confesses, unnerved by Alvaro's sudden ill humor and his rough appearance.

Among the bamboo trees a narrow, barely visible path choked with bricks leads to a cement house, the only construction that has been restored or has survived in this corner of the city, where wooden inns, windowless private houses, and huts made of boards, rags, pieces of sheet metal, and bits of tar-lined cardboard are scattered in the greenery. The cement house itself is painted green, as though someone were determined to conceal it from the eyes of envious intruders, or the poor, or maybe the police. And someone who didn't know better might take it to be an army shelter, an outpost on the frontier of the shady zone, of the no-man's-land, a little, camouflaged fort with a special purpose. Alvaro likes its military appearance. The fighter who isn't fighting any more has the feeling he is laying siege to a sort of garrison, only one where the soldiers are women.

There are six of them, and not one of them looks like a canteen manager. They're all civilian women dressed in civilian split skirts with bold floral patterns, and they even seem rather refined.

"Yes, we're indoor girls," one of them says. "We have nothing to do with the hookers on the square."

An indoor girl. Like Gladys. With her own room, her own clean sheets, her little knickknacks, and her slippers carefully placed next to her bedside rug. A lady, a home, a nest. Alvaro wouldn't want to be taken for some vulgar client—fucking, paying, then leaving. But the lady is in a hurry.

"OK, come on," she says.

"Let's chat a little first."

"That'll be more money."

The price—it's all a matter of price. This outpost is only a more fashionable, more expensive brothel, after all. The nest has some nice birds in it—vultures. The visitor doesn't have enough money on him, but he tries anyway. He meets with resistance; the woman won't budge. Alvaro pushes past her roughly, knocks over the low table with its flowers—which don't snap, for their supple stems are made of some pale-blue, solid, flexible substance—and leaves, braying rustic (militant?) obscenities.

A S for you, homesick for the mountains but forced to be sedentary, to witness the unrest, to stay when you didn't mean to, blown about by contrary winds, you often walk near the green house. You go around in circles, wandering about inside the perimeter of the same chaotic area. And although you feel more left out of things than ever, you cling to this, you stubbornly remain here. It's as though some strange mechanism were keeping you here, as though you had become addicted to this drama. A suspect, dangerous curiosity rivets you to this city, makes you wander this field, soon to be a battlefield, and you can only be driven out of it by a real disaster.

After nightfall, you pass near the "little fort" but don't notice it. You stay outside the formless area, walking through places thickly covered with underbrush. The screen of shrubbery, the high, unscythed grass with its suspicious rustlings, and the rotting garbage, the holes, the sharp pieces of wood, the debris of rusty iron, the poisonous plants—all this forms a barrier. You won't let yourself make a breach in that barrier, out of laziness, timidity, superstition, and also fear of the unknown, of its perils and attractions, and of yourself. A cautious explorer, you walk around these haunted thickets, then return to your new pension.

This establishment, which has the pretentious name of Central Hotel, is smaller and squatter, and has less vegetation around it, than La Perla. In front of it, on a strip of sodden, black earth, stand several posts of different heights, without wire or rope between them, a pointless decoration. Above the front door is a translucent, lemon-yellow, Plexiglas porch roof. An electric bell, the hotel's one great luxury, embellishes the doorframe. This is where you have holed up—between these walls of boards (beautiful, unbroken boards, not painted but carefully laid)—since your trip to the police station, with its summonses and the prospect of another interrogation, and after long hours of walking, a night of doubt and hesitation. There aren't many guests at the pension; you feel alone there. Your friends have vanished completely. No more volcanology—it's been months! No more discoveries, no more discussions, no more friendships. What else is there for you to do in this country? Vegetate another few weeks, wait for calamities, wait for the war with all its intensity, wait to die? It's clear; your mind is made up. What's left of your savings is gone now—because you've bought your ticket. The destinations are written on it. You will change planes once, in Mexico, and you'll be in Paris in eight days.

You're soothed by the purchase of this little package with its delicate slips of paper, these names of cities, these dates, these hours. Your fate, this new stage in your fate, is recorded here. You won't get moldy staying in one place, you won't die in this land where everything is changing so fast, coming apart, melting into the insidious chaos of lives, landscapes, and things. You will leave again, traveler, you will start off again. This should make you feel cheerful, but vestiges of perplexity continue to cling to you. You stroll around, thinking of what is going on right now, in a present that is at once empty and full, and also of your future, which is so uncertain (or perhaps it is already filed away in one of the pigeonholes of an obedient, fixed, orderly world). You think as you walk. You think some more lying on your bed in your room in the Central Hotel, and you smoke—you smoke a lot these days. Then, one evening, strangely, the hotel servant comes and knocks at your door. A visitor is looking for you, he announces. He's outside, waiting for you. A visitor? This is the big event of the week, of the month. Who in the world . . . ? You go out. Abel rushes up and throws his arms around you.

"Finally! Hey, it's been a while. . . ."

He seems happy, but tired. He was afraid you had left the country, after Itamar was thrown in the clinker, after all those misfortunes, the repression. But a vague hope, an intuition, something like the voice of friendship had caused him to persevere. He had gone around to all the little hotels, inns, pensions. What made him even more determined, he confesses, is that he has "fabulous news" to tell you: Do you remember Chino? Well, he has found the bum!

"I've found Chino! It's crazy! If you only knew . . ."

You have rarely seen him so radiant—Abel, who is as indecisive as you are, your companion on outings. Is it really true that you went to Nindirí, and does the place still exist, with its sticky smells, its blood, its shouting, its fondling? This guy you chatted with and strolled around with and climbed mountains with, though all too rarely, drags you off to commemorate the rediscovery of all this—he can hardly bear it.

Here's how it all happened, he explains: Three days ago, Abel was wandering by the edge of the immense wasteland of the Santo Domingo neighborhood in the late afternoon, when he noticed a knot of soldiers at the far end of the field, on the level strip of ground in front of the church. He went up to them. The men were laughing, enjoying themselves. Little kids were fluttering around them, women were running up to them. For the moment, they weren't repressing anyone, they weren't arresting anyone—they were having fun. Abel joined the soldiers and the gawkers. People were clapping and shouting. A few idiots were betting. The kids slipped in among them, jostling everyone to get a better look, though some of the passers-by, mothers loaded down with babies, took off in disgust.

The circle was tight, but Abel elbowed his way in. In the midst of the spectators, on the ground—in shadow, since the sun was low—two drunks were flailing at each other.

One was young, with a bit of a mustache. In his torn shirt, missing one shoe, he flopped around like a puppy and kept pulling up his pants, which made everyone laugh. The other one, older and stronger and maybe less drunk, was fighting bare-chested; on his feet, half laced up, were the stout black boots they wear in the army. The fighters rolled around in the dust, filth, and motley garbage, coating themselves with earth, their faces gray and sweaty. They grabbed each other, let go, then pounced on each other again, whimpering and cursing. It was like a cockfight. The spectators were excited, keeping track of how many blows had been struck.

Though Abel watched the scene, he couldn't get very enthusiastic about it. But as he was turning away, what did he see? Two guys dressed in the uniforms of the Guard talking, joking—two younger-than-average soldiers, their backs to the light. And one of them looked like Chino. The soldier had the same slightly stiff way of standing, and his motions were abrupt. Unfortunately, it was hard to make out his features. The two guys still had their backs to the light, but when they laughed, Abel heard Chino's laugh. And his hair was like Chino's hair, smooth and falling untidily over his forehead. Abel waited for the boy to pivot around, for the sunlight to fall on him; when at last he moved, Abel really did see before him Chino's eyes, his cheeks and cheekbones, his skin, his nose, his mouth, and his profile. It was Chino.

"Chino!" Abel called out, unable to stand it any more. The soldier looked up at Abel and his face froze. Then, all of a sudden, he backed off, separating himself from his colleague. Chino—it really was him—moved away from the group and Abel walked after him, calling out again. Chino hurried on, left the road, and took a path through the grass. His pursuer rushed on. The soldier turned around. His friend came up to him, caught him by the arm.

"Let go of me," ordered the soldier.

"Chino, don't you recognize me? I'm . . ."

"You have a beard! I don't like beards!"

"I'll shave it off, Chino."

"I hope so."

"It's crazy—I never would have thought . . ."

"Oh, shit!" the other interrupted. "Let's go over there—people are looking at us."

Do you change the way you look in order to change your life? Or do you let your hair grow out of apathy, carelessness, on a whim? With a different head, who knows? Wearing a mask makes it easier to infiltrate, Abel explained. But the young man in uniform wasn't listening; he was more concerned about avoiding the people who were loitering around. Chino begged his friend to calm down, to walk with him as if they didn't know each other. Fortunately, the sun was setting behind the hills. The soldier turned off onto a path that led to the vast field beside the lake, without buildings or even shacks. The field was all in shadow, bathed in the darkness that had just begun to descend, a dirty, inky night speckled with gray. The air stirred a little, and a light breeze shook the stems of the wild plants. The ground was riddled with pockets of slime because of the morning rains. In spite of that, on this inhospitable, perhaps dangerous soil, Abel and Chino fell on each other like drunks suddenly losing their balance. They clutched each other and thrashed about, but even in his passion Chino kept his face away from his friend's. And he told him again how he had a horror of feeling the hairs of a beard on his cheeks and lips.

"What an idea!" he said. "You look lousy that way. I'm not sure I would have recognized you."

"You've changed, too. You've got fatter, haven't you?" Abel observed.

"Yeah, we eat pretty well at the barracks."

"I've missed you, Chino."

"And I've missed you, you bastard! I was down in the dumps for weeks, especially at night: I thought of you, you and your construction site. I was petrified they would send me into the middle of nowhere, and then I found out I would be staying here, and that gave me hope again. I thought we'd run into each other sooner or later."

"What's your job?"

"Patrols, rounds."

"In dangerous sections?"

"Not even."

"But it's becoming dangerous everywhere, Chino. You ought to think about . . ."

"About what? Deserting? You'd like that, wouldn't you? But who would help my mother? I've had water installed in the house, and I have to pay for that, and she's eating meat for a change, and what the hell did I used to eat, anyway, except for grease and oil?"

"That didn't kill you. Now, meat . . . water . . . they may be costing you your life, my friend. The Front is preparing an offensive, and not just outside the city."

"They've been saying that for weeks."

"The vise is tightening, Chino. It's even dangerous for me; I have to stay on my guard."

"You're still messing with politics? Jesus, how can anyone go asking for trouble like that?"

"It's a good question. How can I answer it? All I can say is, I have certain obligations."

Then Abel told him about the bad things that had happened to his friends. He described the crimes of the American expert, his punishment, the bad luck of the justice seekers, and Itamar's sentence. After that, he said, he couldn't stand back. He felt obliged to continue the struggle.

"In that case," Chino concluded, "we won't be able to see each other again."

"Not in public, no. If we meet in the street it would be better to ignore each other. But now I live on the worksite; I've fixed up a cellar for myself. At night you can come to where I live."

"Dressed like this? It's risky. The whole neighborhood would find me out in no time."

"Come in civvies," Abel suggested.

"There's no way I can change my clothes. Those idiot sergeants say it's not allowed when we're on a campaign, and since it seems we're on a campaign . . . Besides, I don't have any civilian clothes at the barracks, or at my mother's; she passed all my rags on to one of my cousins."

"I'll lend you some. We'll meet after dark in a deserted spot, a vacant lot or the ruins, and you'll change. I know some hiding places. You'll leave your uniform and then we'll go to the worksite."

"You're really determined to do this?"

"Come on, Chino, here we can't even wash."

They've seen each other many times since then, Abel tells you. Night would fall, the soldier would leave his barracks, a vast place near the old airfield, and come to the spot they had agreed on. His friend would be waiting for him there with a bundle of clothes. As a precaution, each would take a different route to reach the edge of the Xolotlan. As soon as they arrived, Chino would strip off his uniform, dance around with his buttocks bared to the breezes, laugh, leap about, and then pull on a pair of pants too big for him and one of his friend's shirts. He would hide his uniform in a hollow between two slabs of reinforced concrete. Then he would go to the worksite with Abel.

"What nights we've had, man!" Abel resumes. You're sitting together on the terrace of a little bar.

These nights would actually last until dawn. To talk about them is to reduce them to something smaller than they are, Abel feels: you can only recite banal phrases that have been used a thousand times, scraps of song, the words "happiness" and "pleasure," but when it's real, when it happens to you, there's nothing ordinary about it. It becomes unique; these times are very rare experiences. You feel a complete joy, and your body is a precious object, a musical instrument, in perfect tune; it gives everything that it usually hides or holds back, and it overwhelms you and overwhelms the other body, which also overwhelms you, in its turn, at the same time, with the same intensity, and these bodies play with such harmony, your mind or soul or consciousness experiences a state of profound, total, unimaginable tranquillity. And once you've felt this tranquillity, this peace, once you've stolen this fragment of eternity, you want only one thing—to find it again. And they will find it again, Abel swears to himself, they will find it again, because Chino and he want it with all their heart and soul.

"So you're still seeing each other?" you ask then.

"Well, actually, he didn't come yesterday. But that can't be his fault. Something must have happened that kept him from coming; something must have prevented him. I'll have to find out."

Abel did find out. You couldn't see him again, because you were leaving in just a few days. Not for several years would you find out what happened, find out about the catastrophes, the pieces of good luck, the hours of exaltation, the hours of tragedy that were experienced by Abel and his little world, a world you would never rediscover anywhere else. You wouldn't find out about all this for several years, and then it would be in circumstances you couldn't possibly have foreseen, at a radically different time in your life from this period right now, when you are being forced to leave the country.

18

The militants resume their armed combat. There are repercussions: arrests by the police, searches, reprisals. The followers of the "military line" find this reassuring—it tells them their blows are striking home. Triumph will be their reward for enduring the worst suffering! But for the militants of both lines, the struggle is becoming complicated, as is their existence and their very survival. Soldiers and ordinary civilians look suspiciously at one another. Sentries have been added around the barracks. Sympathizers of the Front systematically avoid encounters with members of the Guard, whether they're on their way to work, to the movies, or to the market. Even those who haven't taken sides keep their distance. People are intrigued when they see the occasional civilian walking with a soldier—this sort of association seems abnormal, questionable.

Chino and Abel feel the oppressive weight of this climate of distrust and unspoken hatred. The soldier still dares to slip away from his fellows, but it makes him uneasy to walk through the abandoned part of the city by himself at the end of the day. What he dreads even more is the patrols: it would embarrass him to be found walking with a civilian, and he would be finished if they caught him in his civvies. That's why it would be better, he explains, if he didn't take off his uniform; that's the only way he and Abel can go on seeing each other. Agreed—the militant acquiesces. They have to invent a new trick: from now on Abel will change his clothes.

"Bring me a uniform," Abel says. And he specifies—the whole outfit, with boots, undershirt, and underpants.

"I don't have a spare one," says Chino. "I would have to steal one."

"Well, then, steal one!" the militant retorts.

Chino hesitates, perplexed.

"Steal the rags," Abel repeats. "It's easy, for God's sake. You're right there!"

Chino gives in. All that remains is to decide how the bundle of clothes will be delivered. That's easy, too, according to his friend: he should wrap them up in newspaper as if they were dirty laundry. And instead of walking around for a long time with his little bundle—and maybe meeting up with a patrol—he should go directly to the Santo Domingo church, which is close to his barracks. There, behind the choir, standing on the ground by the wall, half buried in the grass, are two large urns. All Chino has to do is deposit his package in one of the urns.

T H E parish priest had ordered the two receptacles from a local manufacturer. They were meant to decorate the short gravel walk leading to the church. Crudely fashioned, striped with uneven lines, the urns had been a disappointment, and the priest had relegated them to a corner near the sacristy door. Since then, no one had put any fresh flowers in them, and all they contained were a few black stalks of wilted, rotting gladiolas.

One evening, Chino comes and wedges his package down among the flower stalks. Abel retrieves it and takes it back to his cellar. When he opens it, he sees that Chino has forgotten to put a beret in with the uniform. Damn! It would have been better if the scatterbrain had forgotten the underpants, but the underpants are there, rolled up with the socks and the undershirt—a pair of faded khaki underpants with a spot on the front, and too big for him, of course. Never mind! Abel tosses them aside and pulls on the pants, which fortunately fit. Dressed as a soldier, he goes out again.

At this hour, Chino should already be waiting for him at the usual place, where apparently the only other creatures wandering about are the dogs.

Abel hadn't been sure his friend would carry out their plan. He was delighted that it had worked. Now he is thinking about other kinds of theft. Maybe Chino would be willing to repeat the crime.

"You behaved like a good militant," he jokes, once they're back in the vicinity of Xolotlan. "That made me happy, you know. I even think you should collaborate with us."

"Oh no! I don't want to get shot!"

"I'm only asking you to do little things for us."

"And then you'll want me to do big things. You bug me sometimes! Is that why you're so anxious to see me?"

"Chino, you can't think . . . You have no right . . . Our friendship . . ."

"Then why do you want me to take risks?"

"If you come over to my side, I'll love you even more."

"Blackmail!"

"No. You'll see: we'll win in the end, and you'll be glad you worked for the Front."

"And what will the Front give me? What would your leaders say if they learned why we see each other?"

"My leaders? Except for Leonor and Itamar, I hardly know them. And I'm sure Itamar would treat us like brothers."

"If he lives long enough! And what about Leonor?"

"I have confidence in her."

"And the others?"

"I don't know, Chino. Anyway, it isn't any of their business. What matters is to carry out certain actions, to have an effect."

"And what do you have in mind?"

"For you to do the same thing you did with the clothes I'm wearing."

"What? You want me to filch some more clothes?"

"I want you to steal arms."

Abel and his friend are sitting on a large rock. The moon shines dimly on the countryside and is reflected in the tin-colored lake. Chino turns toward his corruptor and gives him a hard, heavily charged, almost evil look out of the corner of his eye. Then he sighs, stands up abruptly, and begins walking. Abel follows him.

"Wait, Chino, let me explain."

"Keep your explanations to yourself. Go away! Go change your clothes!"

Grumbling, the soldier moves off, plunges into the grass, trips over bits of rubble, heads toward the black mass of the ruined cathedral. His friend hurries after him. Chino starts running, and Abel runs, too, over the abandoned field that served them as a bed the first night they found each other again. Abel charges ahead, catches up with Chino, and throws himself at him. Without saying a word, the fake soldier and the real soldier, giving way to a desire that has an element of brutality in it, tumble to the ground.

I N the end, for two successive days, Chino does steal arms. Abel is proud: his friend has come over to his side, he thinks, and the thefts will continue. Dressed in khaki, the militant goes to the church. He walks in, anxious to create an excuse for his nosing about the building. He lingers a few moments at the back, in the last pew. A handful of worshippers come and go, pleased to see that there are still some Christian soldiers left in the country. Even the priest, who has come in to hear someone's confession, smiles at him. And Abel goes out again, reassured.

He walks around the building, stops by the urns, and then, inspecting his surroundings to make sure no one is coming, thrusts his hand in among the black stalks. The first package contains two revolvers and some bullets—and the militant would have given way to his feeling of triumph if the hour, the place, and the nature of his booty hadn't required great discretion. The second package contains another revolver and more bullets. The third time he comes, the cement crater is empty. The fake soldier is surprised, but he goes down to the lake all the same, the way he did the day before and the day before that. And, just as he did before, he waits for his thief until very late—but in vain. Despite this, he comes back to visit the urns the next day. Again there is nothing in them but the thin, withered flowers. This time Abel is alarmed. The fact that his accomplice hasn't shown up is inexplicable, especially since Chino did stop by the church twice. What does it mean—that the thefts have stopped? Does the soldier have nothing more to steal? Has he given it up? And what about his failure, twice, to keep his word? What does that mean? Abel puts the stolen weapons into a cardboard box. This is his trophy, a kind of security that he will hand over to Leonor. He is seeing her that same day, at the Superior's house. Before leaving, he puts his civilian clothes back on.

T H E residents of the Front's bases have fake identity cards, fake work cards, and, some of them, falsified birth certificates. Now the most wanted cadres move to rooms rented in private houses, either in neighborhoods that have been won over to the revolution or, better still, in those that are apparently loyal to the regime. Apparently . . . for certain bourgeois families have recently been feeling the wind shift. The caches of arms in the bases have been cleared out. At Base 14, the housecleaning is nearly finished—except for a suitcase full of leaflets that has to be removed.

"A job for you," Leonor says to Abel. "There couldn't be a better hiding place than your cellar at the construction site."

And she asks him to stop by and pick up the suitcase the next day around noon.

"It's the base in the Larreynaga district," she says. "If I'm not there, wait for me."

Abel knows Alvaro is hiding out in the capital, because Leonor told him. And they must have been in the same places without knowing it, crossed the same no-man's-lands, wandered around the ruins near the cheap restaurants, each driven by his own needs, his own worries, his own boredom. More than once, probably, they just missed running into each other. Yet Abel has no idea, as he sets off for the base, which is a good half-hour's walk from the construction site, that his brother lives in the same house as Leonor—she did not think to warn him.

Abel walks through the narrow, zigzagging streets of the "colonies," picking his way past the eternal shacks, the eternal lines of yellow-gray, piss-colored cardboard hovels, and the eternal clouds of dust floating around the shanties. He heads for the center of town, with its jumbled blocks of little houses, its grassless yards, its patches of caved-in asphalt, its roadsides that vanish into open sewers. He walks through a labyrinth of blind alleys, crossroads, dead ends, and at last reaches the house. An unshaven man with thick hair answers his knock at the door: it's Alvaro.

"You . . . you . . . here!" the younger brother barely manages to stammer.

"Come on in. I was expecting you. Leonor told me everything."

The guerrilla closes the door. Abel, still dumbfounded, keeps standing stupidly in front of him like a schoolboy before the teacher.

He's expecting his brother to question him, but Alvaro only accuses Abel of being late and then tears into him:

"You haven't changed, have you? I know it, they've told me."

"I have changed. Now I've turned political."

"Which side?"

"Yours."

"Oh, sure—playing the sissy with soldiers!"

"I only see one. I've won him over—"

"Into your bed!" Alvaro breaks in.

"And into our camp," Abel adds, lifting his head and raising his voice; suddenly he is prepared to stand up to his brother.

"It's one or the other."

"You can do both. What you did with the guerrillas—did that stop you from going to a brothel?"

"That's not the same thing. Whores aren't enemies, they aren't army spies."

"Chino isn't a spy; he's one of us."

"If he were, he would desert."

"Maybe he will."

"To do that you have to have balls, friend."

"He has balls!" Abel retorts.

"Shit! So you're still the one who gets fucked up the ass? I was right: you haven't changed."

"None of that means anything."

"That soldier is using you. He has you where he wants you. Because he shows you a good time, you think he's working for us."

Alvaro stubbornly sticks to his accusations. He mixes everything up and makes it impossible for Abel to explain anything. Leonor has to come back, Abel says to himself. Without her, it's useless to go on. They're bickering for nothing. How much longer is she going to be?

"Doesn't matter. She has nothing to do with this," says the guerrilla.

"Why? It's a political problem."

"Shut up! We'll settle this business of your ass between us; it's a family matter."

"Leonor is the only person I answer to for my political behavior."

"You'll answer to me for your behavior pure and simple."

"No. I will only talk about my life in front of her."

"I order you . . ."

"Nothing!" says Abel. "You won't order me to do anything!"

"I order you not to see that dirty soldier any more."

"And what if the Front asks me to do the opposite?"

"I'll take care of that. My God, I would be ashamed to tell my comrades what you are, but I'll stop you from seeing him anyway," the older brother warns.

"You don't have the right. You can't go against the decisions of the leaders."

"Those decisions would be different if they knew you."

"Maybe they know me better than you think."

"A queer! They would kick you out of the Front, you imbecile!"

Abel can't take any more. His brother is locked inside his hatred. And he, Abel, only wants to leave. There is no one else in the house. The younger brother moves toward the door. Alvaro rushes at him, grabs his shirt under the chin, shakes him, and, his fist trembling with rage, says again: "I'll stop you from seeing that soldier of yours. You hear me? I'll stop you, faggot!" And he throws his brother out.

I S hatred infectious? Abel is filled with nausea, disgust, regret, spite. He's mad at himself for urging his friend to steal arms. Those thefts of revolvers and ammunition have created a kind of net that is binding him even more closely to political action, even though he hasn't seen Chino again. But once again Abel is beginning to detest politics. It was politics that led him to his brother, that drove Chino to the front line, that put both of them in grave danger. Without politics, he says to himself, his friend and he would be living together peacefully, far away from the brutes and the crazies, in a little house in a lonely spot somewhere in the country where nothing ever happens. Because they would leave. They would go off beyond the hills of Chiltepe, beyond the peninsulas, beyond the lake. They would settle in a hut, their own hut, which they themselves would build at the foot of Momotombo. Their only nation, their only family, would be each other; their only reason for living, friendship; their daily occupations, tilling the land, fishing, climbing the mountain, having adventures. And they would never come back here, where they have suffered so, where people have insulted them, tried to separate them, destroy them. They would run away without turning back; they would desert all of it, shaking the dust from their shoes, shaking off the omnipresent filth of this bewitched city.

I T is noontime, and the fiery sun shines down from its zenith at full strength. In this stormy season its fire is golden and weak; the light has lost some of its whiteness, its steely glint. Yet Alvaro's brother flees from it. He has gone below and thrown himself on the pallet in his dark cellar. And on the ground, lined up against the wall, are the carton of revolvers, the box containing the stolen uniform, another box filled with leaflets, and a pile of newspapers.

Abel wants to sleep. He tries, but he's too uneasy, too fearful; he needs to know where Chino is, what he's up to. There's only one thing he can do now: wait until night, surface again, and go off looking yet one more time. How often he has done this in his miserable life, and in what places, what tangled fields of rubble and underbrush? He'll go looking yet again, in those lost parts of the city peopled by beggars, hooligans, crazies. He'll walk, ferret about, climb, go back down, turn in circles, start off again to find the soldier. . . . At last he gets up, after hours of struggling against the unpleasant ideas that fill his mind, against his fear and the gloomy pictures that arise from it. He rolls up his pallet, hesitates between his two sets of clothing, civilian and military, puts on the civilian, and goes out.

Abel crosses his worksite, with its long shadows, calls out to Farabundo, and walks away. Where should he go first? What spot should he investigate first? You never know. Abel heads for Santo Domingo. He'll go to the church, he says to himself, walk around it, inspect the urns. Maybe there will be a little scrap of paper slipped in between the stalks of flowers, an envelope, some message from Chino. His friend may have encountered unexpected difficulties, and the best way of warning Abel is still to use one of the urns as a mailbox. So he hurries toward the church, steering clear of the barracks on his way.

At that hour of the afternoon, not many people go into the church. The evening Masses are held later, after working hours. Abel reaches the field in front of the building, crosses the flat piece of ground, walks around to the side. The place is bare; there is nothing left but two large spots, two circles of black earth in the grass where the urns had stood—nothing left but the imprint of their massive, circular bases, scattered with the brown stalks of the dried flowers and the mixture of dust and pebbles that had accumulated in them. The urns themselves are gone. They were apparently difficult to wrest from the ground: among the stalks are shards of hardened cement and even a large piece of an urn with its awkwardly drawn lines.

Abel tries to figure out why they're gone. Were they transferred somewhere else? Did the priest give the order to his sacristan to remove them? Or were they stolen, and in that case, what could thieves want with those crude objects? Or was it the police? Or a bad joke? Or was it the Guard's intelligence service? One thing is sure: the secret mailbox no longer exists. And Abel doesn't know where Chino might have left a letter—in what niche, what other jar, what flowerpot. There are hiding places all over, in what used to be the gardens of Managua—abandoned, often broken vases, cracked pots, pits, hollow or split stones. It would take months to comb those expanses. It would be agonizing work for an impatient man, enough to drive him mad.

Abel goes away. He is beside himself, almost wild. Even though night is falling, he plunges into the wasteland, with its holes and thorny underbrush. Now the sun is red, shadows cover the whole of the north, the sky is darkening above the "colonies," above the lake, above the endless, temporary—they say—district of tumbledown shacks. And the dying of the day adds a special kind of anguish to what he is already feeling, an anguish that always threatens Abel when nightfall takes him by surprise.

It's an old story. Every time it happens, it kills his ability to think, to reason, driving him on so that he doesn't care where he runs. This is why he usually tries to spend the twilight hour in a place where other people are moving about noisily, talking, playing, or working. Even as a child, Abel dreaded the disappearance of the light. It worried him to see the street, the little garden, the courtyard of the house be swallowed up by the darkness; he would run to his father and mother. The boy hated to see the sky's beautiful color vanish as the world inexplicably toppled over into the nothingness called night. Later, when he was an adolescent, he learned that some people went into ecstasies over the dying of the light. He could never understand why certain poets liked to stand in a lonely field or meadow and contemplate the setting of the great star that dispensed heat and light, why they were so moved and, even worse, would celebrate its disappearance with tears of joy.

In the old days, in Corinto, Abel would make sure to be home before it happened; he would play with his sister, argue or chat with his brother or his parents. Then, later, he would hang around after work with the dockers in the port district, talking, joking, distracting himself so that night would come without his realizing it. At the pension where he lived next he did the same, knocking on Itamar's door or going down to chat with the guests in the dining room. Sometimes he would get on a bus just when the sky was turning red, and there, squeezed up against the passengers, feeling sheltered, he would watch the sun slip down behind the houses. Witnessing this spectacle surrounded by other people, safe behind windows and moving along, gave him the sense that he was triumphing over something inevitable. At those times he could contemplate the dying of the day with a sort of irony and scorn.

When he arrived at his destination—the end of the line, not far from the construction site—the battle between the light and the shadows would be over. After that nothing could bother him. The shadows no longer hesitated: night had taken possession. He could settle into the darkness as though it were a room or a bed or a mother's lap or the arms of a loved one. Alone on the construction site at that hour, Abel wasn't afraid of anything; the darkness, so full, so manifest, had become familiar. And Chino would be coming soon.

But this time Abel has let himself be taken by surprise: the battle between day and night has broken out too suddenly, and the sunset has come down like a sudden rain or a storm. Preoccupied with his thoughts, his search, Abel didn't notice the time passing. And now here he is plunging through the grass, stumbling over the rocks. He leaves the wasteland for another area, which is just as desolate and rough—a dangerous area, he says to himself, because the loss of his friend now seems threatening to him. The color of the sky, which is changing so fast, the vacillations of the daylight, the uncertainty of the world, the twilight's blood—all this fills him with panic. Panic makes him walk straight ahead, not knowing where he is going, not even thinking that he might run across his friend.

He does find Chino, eventually, though it is a different evening, and not in the jumbled meadow by the side of the lake. He sees his silhouette, realizes who it is, and rushes toward the soldier. Chino can't avoid him.

"What in hell happened?" Abel asks him.

"Where do you mean?"

"Behind the church. Someone's got rid of the urns."

"Good!"

"What are we going to do now?"

"Nothing," the soldier breaks in, authoritative, irritated. "If we'd gone on like that we would have got ourselves into real trouble. And you know what I think of trouble."

"But, Chino . . ."

"You want to lose me?"

The soldier seems angry. He threatens to leave Abel standing there and go on to his barracks. He forces Abel to keep silent, and this silence is oppressive, upsetting, only lightening little by little as they walk along. And so, without saying a word, they push their way into the wild crop of grass and into the night, which is now total. The two part the tufts with their feet and kick their way into the underbrush. There, still in silence, they stop and sit down on top of a slight undulation in the ground. Once again, unable to help themselves, the soldier and his friend touch each other, cling to each other, swear to each other that . . .

The next day they swear again, and the day after. They go into another field, closer to the streets, the field on whose edge stands the green house with its curtain of bamboos, near the square, the monstrous stage set of the crumbled stadium. It is here, in this field they hardly know, that Abel's brother finds them.

Alvaro is furious at having been snubbed by the girls in the green house. He's mad at them and at himself, and he keeps coming back and loitering nearby. He prowls around the fortress-like house and then paces the field, where a shabby underbrush grows. As he moves away from the house, he sees two shadows. A couple making love: people who are doing it secretly, in the middle of nature, he thinks, the way they always do when one of them is married. And the idea of spying on them excites him. Without making a sound, he moves closer, gliding between the few shrubs. The couple stops. It seems there is some sort of disagreement—an argument has apparently broken out. Unfortunately, he's too far away to hear what they're saying. Yet he can hear very clearly that the voices rising through the darkness and the warm air are men's voices.

He is intrigued. He goes closer, hoping to make out some of what they're saying. Then Alvaro notices that one of them is wearing a beret. Shit, a soldier, he says to himself. Luckily, his revolver is in its holster, strapped to his leg above the calf. It's a habit, an elementary precaution: a guerrilla never goes out unarmed, even when he's on leave. And he doesn't take off his weapon except when he washes or makes love—and not even then if he's copulating standing up, or doesn't trust the place, or is in a hurry.

Alvaro stops, listens hard. The soldier is talking more loudly than the other man, whose only answer is to slip his arm around his companion's neck. And now the soldier seems to be calming down. Maybe these guys are going to the whorehouse. And one of them, probably the private, doesn't have enough money and is trying to extract some from the other. But the guy in civvies starts talking again. He withdraws his arms, turns, and stands in front of the soldier. Facing him, he waves his hands and raises his voice. Alvaro recognizes that voice: it's his brother's. In a moment he has raised his pantleg, torn the pistol from its holster, and leaped out of his hiding place. The guerrilla points his weapon at the soldier.

Abel, dumbfounded, cries out, "Don't shoot! Listen! Let me say something!"

"Shut up, pervert!"

"Please! I beg you."

"You, too, soldier—you're a traitor, too."

"He's a comrade!" Abel protests.

"Fairy comrades! Nobody wants to have anything to do with you!"

While the brothers are quarreling, Chino is backing away. He says nothing, just watches. In a flash, he has caught sight of a dip in the ground, a hollow where he can hide. Alvaro lifts his pistol as the soldier moves toward the hollow, Abel at his heels. The guerrilla fires and Abel falls on the dusty grass at the edge of the slope.

19

In the whorehouse beyond the field and behind the bamboos, the girls and the madam are sitting and drinking their after-dinner coffee in the room they use as a bar and parlor, when the gunshots echo through the room. Everyone jumps. A few of the women are curious enough to go outside. Now the firing stops, and they go back into the common room and start talking again. Each of them has her own explanation:

"It's a crazy person, some guy trying to scare people."

"Something is going on between the Guard and the rebels."

"Of course! The Front! Didn't I tell you they were coming?"

"Really? The rebels are alone?"

"They have leaders."

"Students, teachers, from what they say," one of the women adds, thrilled.

"Yes, but changed into warriors. Hard men, believe me—hard and pure."

"My God, what are they going to do to us?"

"Girls, my dears, now calm down," the madam intervenes. "It's normal to hear gunfire in this area. I've always heard gunfire. It's only hooligans, thieves, people settling accounts. As for the Guard and the pimps, no danger from them. Those dogs all come from the same kennel."

The girls aren't comforted by their madam's words. The discussion starts up again. Strong words are tossed around: there is talk of a "war of nerves," "males avenging themselves" (and—Lord save us!—for what?), "lost militants," "gangsterism," and—this is the limit! thinks the madam, getting angry—one girl uses the word "capitulation."

"Capitulation to what, if you please?"

"And why?"

"Idiot, you think you're a fighter?"

Fortunately, a visitor rings the bell at this point, the first of the evening. The man is a frequent customer, and they trust him.

"Ah, Mr. Mario! What luck! You're a good, brave man—now we'll feel safe," the madam jokes.

"Sure, I'm brave," laughs Mr. Mario, "but not brave enough to walk straight toward a man with a gun! I just saw a soldier running and he was shouting, 'Watch out—there's a crazy man back there, a crazy man!' I almost turned right around and went away. Then the soldier disappeared very fast," the visitor continues. "Everything is quiet, nothing was moving. Maybe the soldier himself was shooting; then he stopped." As for the customer, he is "ever faithful, isn't he, my dears?" and he knows how to live up to his motto. . . .

C H I N O did run like a crazy man. He plunged into the underbrush, crossed the field and more abandoned, debris-choked fields with their vestiges of roads. He was losing his head as he ran. His heart was beating so hard he felt he would suffocate. He bounded straight ahead despite the roughness of the terrain. And then suddenly he stopped short. He had lost the killer. There wasn't a sound—no footsteps, not even distant ones, no crackling of underbrush disturbed the silence of the night. Exhausted, the soldier collapsed on the grass.

A hundred different ideas crowded into his head. Should he go on as far as the built-up area, run farther, pass his barracks, keep running until his heart exploded? Should he desert? Should he betray Abel's friends, should he reveal what his brother had done? Maybe the moment had come to turn his back on everyone, on everything, go to ground like a sick man, a man whose powers are failing him, in a shanty somewhere, in his mother's hut. He was dizzy, and he hurt all over—in his feet, his stomach, his soul. He wanted to faint. Or sleep for two nights, ten nights, forever. He was paralyzed by lassitude, bewilderment. How could he decide anything, and what should he decide? He stood up anyway, walked a few steps, and stopped again. He lay back down in the middle of the field. The sky was dark—why look at it? It was like the bottom of a hole. Within a few seconds, sleep descended on him and he lay utterly still.

A L V A R O telephones the police station from a bar or a post office. Disguising his voice and withholding his name, he says there's a dead body lying in an old, grassy park between the ruins and the stadium square. After making the call, even though it isn't very late, he goes back to his base.

Leonor is holding a meeting, and at the moment she's arguing with Anthony, the guerrilla. A student named Flora and Comrade Superior are also joining in the debate, along with a certain Modesto, a man worn out by his years of experience in social struggles and still active in the masons' brotherhood. Leonor is recommending that they form units of at least five people, believing, she says, that they should concentrate their efforts, merge different groups and tendencies, and consolidate the organization. Once her cell is formed, they go on to the order of the day, which has already been drawn up. It concerns security questions. Here Leonor is insistent—why didn't Abel pick up the leaflets?

"Even though he promised me he would come by," she stresses.

And, turning to Abel's brother, who has taken his seat, she asks: "Didn't you see him?"

"No, but I'm not surprised. That guy can't be counted on; he's unreliable, and he always has been. I know him—I've known him for an eternity! No one's more of an authority on that man than I am, unfortunately! He plays close to his chest."

"Sure, sometimes he gets confused; he worries about things," Leonor concedes. "But apart from that, what could he be hiding?"

"Is he in trouble?" the Superior asks. "Does he have health problems?"

"Money problems?" Leonor asks.

"Maybe some woman is after him," Flora suggests.

"None of those things!" retorts Alvaro.

"Tell us, then!"

"What an affliction! What a dishonor! It demoralizes me to talk about that guy. Think of all the times he's been evasive, all the times he's forgotten to do this or that—don't you think it smells just a little of treason? There's something even worse," Alvaro goes on, almost snarling. "Don't you think there's something else concealed behind this theft of arms, which he carried out with the collaboration of the enemy?"

"What?" Leonor asks indignantly.

"It's a cover. All informers need a cover."

"You mean Abel . . . ?"

"He's a spy," the brother announces in an exalted tone. "And the spy deserves to be shot. In fact . . ."

"In fact what?" the woman says impatiently.

"I've executed him. It's done."

The confession drops like the blade of a guillotine. The group is speechless. The former journalist and her comrades look at each other open-mouthed, stupefied. Alvaro straightens, clenches his teeth, and tries to compose himself.

"This is horrible!" Leonor says at last.

"It was necessary."

"You can't expel a member of the Front without a trial," the Superior intervenes at this point. "*A fortiori*, you can't kill him, either."

"But his case was already tried—a long time ago!" Alvaro defends himself. "Shit! The guy was my brother, my younger brother. I have information about him you don't know of."

"You should have given it to the leadership."

"There are things you don't talk about."

"Secrets?" asks the leader of the cell, who keeps returning to the charge. "If they have political implications, you are obliged to transmit them." And the woman concludes, "Comrade, you'll have to explain yourself."

Alvaro, still confident, says he's ready to appear before the authorities of the Front any time. Leonor answers that she will arrange it. But right now, she continues, the leaflets have to be moved. Flora offers her services: she'll make the transfer by car, and she can keep the suitcase at her house. One more question is worrying Leonor: what has happened to the victim's identification papers? The police have no doubt discovered the body and found certain documents on it bearing his name and address.

"They haven't found anything," the brother interrupts. "I took his papers: here they are."

He removes them from his pocket and tosses them on the low table in front of the woman. She picks them up and examines them. There are three cards: the green one, issued by the Corinto prefecture, shows his civil status; the second, a larger one folded in half, dates from the time when Abel worked as a docker; and the third is his old red Cristal soccer-club membership card.

———

T H E Front has chosen seven people to pass judgment on Alvaro's action, and sent Leonor and her cell two comrades from another group: an agriculture student and a woman named Glenda, a teacher and mother very active in the working-class neighborhood of San Judas. The jurors are charged with deciding the fate of the militant, who is unafraid, unreflecting. They gather and prepare. Should they absolve him, keep him in the movement, expel him? And if they expel him, will that be enough of a punishment?

The former journalist goes over the facts, giving a general description of the actions of the two brothers and pointing out the contribution that each in his own way made to the struggle against imperialism and the dictatorship. The woman rejects out of hand the idea that an older brother has life-and-death power over a younger one, an idea that offends the principle of equality between men and the morality of socialism. She also feels that the murder goes beyond the bounds of a simple family matter.

"The person you have eliminated from our ranks is first and foremost a militant," she concludes, addressing Alvaro.

"A suspect militant."

"Why suspect?" the teacher asks.

"He was in collusion with a member of the Guard."

"An officer?"

"A common soldier," Leonor specifies. "A young, low-paid worker."

"Did this soldier know that the army was exploiting him?" Flora asks.

"Probably. He was working for us," the former journalist answers again.

"He was working for himself," the murderer contradicts her, "and indirectly for the government, for the Guard. If he stole ammunition, it was so that he could win Abel over more effectively, so that he could corrupt him and corrupt us along with him."

"What kind of corruption are you talking about? Was he using these arms to buy information from your brother? Was he trying to infiltrate one of our cells?"

"I don't know anything about that. But what I'm sure of is this: neither of them deserved to be called 'comrade.' "

"What did they actually do?" the woman interrupts, becoming impatient.

"It was a farce. If you want to know everything, this shit of a brother of mine just played at being a good militant. And you, all of you," he adds, looking around the room, "you all fell into the trap; you reacted like idiots!"

"My dear friend, now you are making accusations without cause," the theologian intervenes, anxious to restore a little peace to the discussion.

"I repeat the facts: Abel and his soldier didn't deserve either to be called comrades . . . or to be called men!" The murderer seems to be ridding himself of an old anguish, a sense of oppression, a disease, the kind you don't dare name but that belabors your heart and mind, tortures you.

"Those so-called comrades slept together! Yes! Those brave militants were . . ."

"Horrible!" exclaims Anthony.

"Nauseating," adds the agriculture student. "If anyone had told me that when I first joined the Front, I would have left."

"I can understand that," the murderer says with approval. "I find it disgusting, too, to fight side by side with perverts."

"Well, it doesn't disgust me," Leonor says firmly. "I knew how Abel lived."

"He told you about it?"

"My predecessor talked to me about it. Maybe you know him—Itamar, the cell leader who got a life sentence? Itamar never wanted Abel to leave our organization."

"That's ridiculous!" Anthony protests.

"If the people knew . . . ! And these individuals claim to

represent them? I mean, these guys claim to fight for the people?"

The future agronomist is getting impatient; the faces he's making show his feelings clearly. But that isn't enough—he's determined to "make a statement."

"And it's important," he says, "for the course of the trial."

"Go ahead; we're listening."

"The victim, or I should say the so-called victim," the young man says, "identified himself with indications of bourgeois decadence."

"Well, well," Leonor says, feigning astonishment.

"Abel was not bourgeois," Flora corrects him. "He did not live as a bourgeois. But his family belonged to the middle class. Isn't that right, Alvaro?"

"Yes, our father wasn't really from the working class," he confirms with a look of regret.

"Your brother's friend, this soldier, was the child of a worker. . . ."

"In my opinion he was only a marginal person, one of those guys—I don't know what you call them in your texts; it's a strange name, a German or Russian word. I don't remember."

"A lumpen?"

"That's it. That bugger of a soldier is a lumpen."

"And not a proletarian," the agronomist insists. "Besides," he adds, very sure of his theory, "that would be impossible."

Each of them gives his opinion, protests, argues. Some are accused, warned; some defend themselves. Only the oldest person in the group, the old truck driver Modesto, hasn't spoken. Is he too tired to talk? Too indignant? Does he have trouble understanding what the youngest woman on the jury has been referring to as "modern life"? But Leonor wants him to tell them what he thinks.

"What I think is quite simple," the old man declares, "and maybe it will disappoint you. You know that I never had an education, but, well, I know what life is. At my age, you've seen a lot of things. I've learned that you don't have control over your body—or over your heart, for that matter, and everyone admits that. So if a man goes after another man, well, goodness, I think . . ."

"It's scandalous!" Anthony cries out.

"To you, yes, because you're young. But I think that as long as no one's forcing anyone else . . . Anyway, are you sure that people who are attracted to other people of their own sex find it pleasant? Maybe some fight against it, torment themselves, and then one day nature is too powerful for them. In the end, it's the same with desire as it is with growing old: our minds can't do anything about it. Our minds would love it if the bodies they inhabit stayed young; but our bodies decide to grow old. It's the same with alcohol, or tobacco. There are some people who would so much like not to drink or smoke. Their wills know what they want, but their bodies refuse to go along. Their bodies want the opposite, and sooner or later they get what they want. Comrade, I tell you again: when you get older you'll understand that we don't have any control over our bodies."

"So you excuse that bugger Abel?"

"Yes. And I disapprove of what his brother did," says the old militant in a level, slightly weary, completely unemotional voice.

These words give new impetus to the indignation of some, delight others. The debate threatens to start up again, even more hotly, which is dangerous for the political unity of the group. However, Leonor intervenes at this point: she's the one who has met with the spokesman of the leaders of the Front, and so she is presiding over the meeting. In this capacity, the woman opposes the resumption of the discussion. She decides to have a vote on the proposed punishment—to expel the guerrilla, a proposal that also comes from the Front, as formulated by the spokesman. That man didn't reproach Alvaro for his ideas about love and manliness. What he could not countenance was lack of discipline. Alvaro had concealed his brother's associations from the leaders, and that was unfortunate. He had killed him, and that was intolerable! The killer had not been given either a mission or any kind of permission to do this. No militant could arrogate this right to himself, whether the intended victim was a libertine or a traitor. Having transmitted this, Leonor waits for each person to speak. The other two women and the old fighter choose, as she does, to expel Alvaro. Comrade Superior prefers to abstain. Annoyed, Anthony and the student laugh derisively, making fun of the "sentimental vote" of the fair sex. Alvaro joins in, glad that only one man out of four condemns him.

"I'll fight without you," he proclaims to his critics. "It's people like me who make the revolution—not old men, not females!"

So saying, Alvaro stands up, furious. He bumps into Leonor on his way out and slams the door behind him.

F E R M I N A doesn't take it very well. She won't be able to look at the dead boy's face or make the sign of the cross over him; she won't be able to touch her son's forehead or lips, or kiss him. By the time the police came to tell her the news, the body was already beginning to decompose. It had taken the authorities four days to identify the dead man—and how zealous they were! They transported the body to the morgue, took his fingerprints, compared them with the ones they had on file, leafed through all the papers in the registry. In short, the mother should be pleased. The research was successful: now she would be able to bury her son. What's the good of complaining, protesting, crying like this? It's true that the investigators haven't found the murderer—they can't pick up his trail. But if they caught the killer, would that bring her son back to life? Fermina must be reasonable. After all, she has another son, and some day that son will come back. When boys grow up a little, the policeman assures her, they stop running around: the mother won't grow old without seeing him again.

Grow old? Jeremías's widow is only forty-six, but all of a sudden she looks sixty. The woman doesn't eat any more, and she hardly sleeps. She goes around clutching a piece of Abel's clothing in her hand: she wipes her eyes with one of his old shirts, or an undershirt, or a patched pair of pants. She spends hours taking his clothes out of his closet, unfolding them, looking at them, rubbing her face with them, folding them up again.

Little by little she slips into a peaceful, silent delirium. She grows thin, and her skin acquires a yellowish hue. She consumes nothing but a little coffee. This long fast and this sorrow weaken her so much that she dies only a few weeks after Abel's death.

The only one left is Alba. The house seems too big now, and she feels as alone as a prisoner in a cell. Everything torments her. She hides in her room, sitting on her bed, and listens to the sounds that come in from the street and the rest of the house—a dog barking, a bird chirping, a piece of furniture creaking, the neighbors' footsteps. Every splash of water, every ringing of a bell, every backfire makes her jump. She sees shadows moving above her bed, in the kitchen, in the hallway.

Because the girl finds it very hard to stay at home, she goes out often. She goes from shop to shop, walks down the street to the church, attending every service. At the slightest excuse, the lonely girl runs to Gladys's house. There she lingers, then begs her friend to walk her home, invites her to dinner, contrives to keep her there, and asks her to stay the night. Eventually the friend gives in; Gladys and Alba become inseparable.

But this shared life, this wonderful understanding, is doomed. After a few days, Alvaro causes another explosion and everyone everywhere is talking about him. The young man does something that upsets people, makes the press indignant, and covers his fiancée and her parents with shame. After this new crime, this unpardonable act, Gladys and her family refuse to receive Alba, because to continue associating with someone close to Alvaro, even if the girl is an orphan, would be to bring dishonor on themselves.

O U S T E D from the Front, the murderer is prey to all sorts of obsessions. He is filled with disgust and hopelessness, and he dreams of taking revenge while at the same time proving how courageous he is. The idea plagues him, agitates him. Abel's brother has been wounded and his pride hurt, and he feels like a hounded animal. His private demons tear into him—and how can he free himself of them except by doing something that will at once restore his honor, remove him from this lousy life, and give his detractors a slap in the face? He turns over in his mind various plans, all of them spectacular, as they must be. He imagines ambushes, murders of politicians or army officers. . . .

He also thinks of suicide. To kill himself would be to turn his back disdainfully on his former comrades. It would affront them, force them to regret expelling him, make the injustice of it seem blatant. Unfortunately, a combatant who kills himself presents the adversary with an easy victory—the rejected guerrilla has to think of a way to crush both is enemies and his ex-friends. And this is how he comes to conceive of a twofold plan: to destroy not only himself but also a henchman of the dictatorship, a notorious leader of the regime. Alvaro opts for a useful, political suicide, sure that one day this kind of death will be called glorious, and for his target he chooses the commander of a crack regiment, a prominent colonel known as "Starch."

The condemned militant no longer has access to the house or the hiding place of any of his former companions. He can't sleep where they live, can't eat or take a shower there. He spurns the temptation to return to his native city, for by killing Abel the combatant has burned his bridges and cut himself off from those slimy, paralyzing associations—his fiancée, his family. For a few days Alvaro wanders around the city, sometimes going into cheap restaurants, swallowing some soup, nibbling at a sandwich. And he spends the night in one of the many cut-rate brothels—vast ramshackle houses—in the eastern part of the city. Here the guerrilla sleeps with a woman—it doesn't matter which one, whoever comes up to him—and he drinks.

Then, very early one morning, he goes out to get the projectiles he will need to carry out his plan. They consist of two fragmentation grenades he was given not long before; they were meant to be used to execute Minister Alonso. What a loss it would have been if the guerrilla had thrown them just to kill the beautiful Eugenia! Fortunately, he had managed to get away with these fruits made of powder and iron. He had hidden them in the bottom of a hole covered with dead branches in a vacant field. He finds them again, well preserved in their plastic bag, like new. They are also small enough to fit in his pants pockets. Thus armed, Abel's brother goes to the barracks where the crack regiment has its quarters.

To the right of the entrance is a recruitment office taking on volunteers. A line has formed, consisting of the idle, the unemployed, and the usual collection of peasants driven from their backwaters by poverty and hunger, most of them very young and bewildered. It is nine o'clock. Alvaro is standing at the head of the line. In a few moments, as is his habit, the colonel will appear. He arrives in a jeep; vigorous despite his age, he jumps out before it comes to a stop. Starch speaks peremptorily to the guards accompanying him, greets the volunteers, congratulates them, shakes some hands. Still irrepressible, always in a hurry, the colonel smiles at everyone and no one, grooming his image. The guerrilla pulls the first grenade out of his pocket. The colonel approaches him. The infiltrator takes the pin out, leaps from the line, and forcefully pitches the grenade a few feet away from himself between the commander's legs. Starch is killed outright by the explosion, and some of the men standing there are wounded. The condemned militant will die on the way to the army hospital.

EPILOGUE

You come back. Four years have gone by, four Tun years (as the sacrificed priest from Guatemala would have calculated), seventy-two uinal—lunar—months, and hundreds of Kin days. . . . You come back—in which Ahau since the dizzying beginning of the enumeration? The sons of the earth (the sons of the stones) have taken power, they have won. You are extremely curious: these men are fascinating. It is impossible *not* to come back.

You, the traveler, took off a few weeks before what they call the Victory, four days before Abel's death, eight days before his brother's. Your feet left that land, but your mind—disturbed, undermined, bewitched—took away with it words, a city (unreal), whole lives, and the land itself. You lived back there in France with all of this. In the evenings you would daydream about it. Your insomniac nights were peopled by crowds of all kinds, by militants, by young people exposed, burned, burning, by fighting cocks. You had to find the time and the means, you had to change your vocation, make your destiny swerve out of its path. For four years you ruminated about the time you had spent living among guerrillas and volcanoes. In the course of these four years, in Europe, a man of forty

settles his affairs (dangerously)
treats his arthritis
gets a divorce (it's a very slow process!)
elucidates his ideas, puts them in order, discards twenty-
    five of them
keeps two of them.

And he says good-bye, attends one last meeting, hands in his final report to his colleagues, the World Explorers. He takes leave of people close to him and people who used to be close.

Yes, good night forever, since all that is dead, my dear, quite dead. Of course we wanted to, but we couldn't. And underneath (in spite of terrific beginnings, good advice, different methods) it was all false. And so good night, my ex-wife, since you "are starting your life all over again." (With a sedentary man this time— and good for you! The two of you will flourish in your little garden.) Good night and good-bye. I'm leaving again. I will be leaving often. Mooring lines break if one wants them to.

And so, in the nth Katun—that's their calendar, my dear—you turn your back, you fly off, you fly over oceans, islands—the Caribbean Islands and the islands of the Sargasso Sea—banks, gray and mauve sheets of water under the clear water, archipelagos, coral reefs. You are still flying; the plane enters and is lost in a cloud of vapor. You seem to hover in this opacity for a long time, and then, suddenly, the cloud tears apart and you see it— you see it ONCE AGAIN: that little silver inland ocean. And on the edge of the ocean, in front of you, the color of tin, the unique and formidable god of ash and rock, Momotombo. The giant is a reference point, a limit, a guide. The plane seems to fly straight toward it. But what are you going back to, who are you going back to, really? Men, elements? Oh, the power of fiery mountains!

Once you touch ground, the volcano disappears behind a hangar, a banana tree, streamers declaring IMPERIALISM IS STILL ALIVE AND SO ARE WE (so that hasn't been wiped out yet), and THE FRONT IS IMMORTAL, and GREETINGS TO OUR SISTER REPUBLICS, as well as red-and-black flags, other inscriptions, and the verb that everyone is conjugating: WE ARE SANDINING, YOU WILL SANDIN (in a chorus), THEY WILL SANDIN (forever). Of course some people say WE ARE SANDINIZING, YOU WILL SANDINIZE, THEY WILL SANDINIZE. . . . But the volcano reappears around the side of another hangar that has collapsed and is surrounded by shanties. Momotombo reappears—or at least its peak does—above a line of huts. You see the summit of the cone beyond some ruins. And the massive size of it is impressive, triumphant, as you cross the first wastelands.

The volcano disappears again when you get swallowed up by the "colonies." No more contemplation for you; you swim in dust, stir up miasmas, crawl along. No more smoking colossus, divine, tutelary mountain. And then you are struck by another kind of scenery, new things, new place names. You read signs saying Dimitrov Quarter, Cuba Quarter, Libya Quarter (a former wasteland); farther along you see a section where, in the old days, nothing grew but some couch grass: "Unión Soviética," they call it, with its rubbish, its slogans, its "Carlos Marx Avenue," its dogs, its cocks, its pregnant women (two citizens out of three), and its attempts at streets. A taxi takes you off, arbitrarily making the trip longer than necessary, as it seems to you, and you protest, "But I'm going to the center of town!"

"Which one?"

"Are there new ones?"

"Anything they've given a new name to is a center now."

Then you describe the stadium, the square, the little hotels. . . .

"Oh, right, well, you should have told me!"

And the vehicle turns off between two fields, crosses a shantytown (still a novelty), avoids a large hole, takes a street paved with square stones, and comes out on a main road—Bolívar Boulevard.

"Oh, really!" you observe.

"Long live Bolívar!" says the driver. And he leans toward you and whispers in your ear, almost fearfully, "I'm a nationalist, yes, yes. . . . Well, you see what I mean."

"I see," you whisper, too.

You don't see anything except what looms up at the end of the road, a crowd carrying flags, machetes, rifles, notebooks.

"Another demonstration," the driver sighs.

"Against whom?"

"Against the war. Certain people herald it every day but, like the end of time, it never comes."

In France, too, you explain, the newspapers talk about it a lot. Reports, articles, files used to accumulate on your wife's pillow, on your rug, on your bedspread. And these clippings described the birth of counterrevolutionary underground forces and used words like "hardening," "confiscation," "Cubanization." One press correspondent would write, "They are encircled, the last hand is being played, the last card, there will be a headlong flight. . . ." Another guaranteed that "it's irreversible, the rebels will stand their ground," while a third, a news analyst and correspondent, announced that "Lenin has eaten Sandino." This was mere publicity, propaganda, a communications strategy, you thought—nothing but speeches, a paper war.

But the driver goes further.

"They're Sandinizing everyone; it's escalation, see."

Men, women, and even children are Sandinizing with all their might, the driver continues, pointing to the demonstrators. All different ages of people are Sandinizing, in families, gangs, corporations, schools, government departments, entire neighborhoods. Fathers are Sandinizing with daughters, sons with mothers. People Sandinize by twos, by threes, in groups, sitting down, standing up. People Sandinize in rows, in circles, stark naked, wearing pajamas, wearing blue work clothes, or wearing dresses (military-style dresses) with or without berets. They Sandinize on foot and on horseback; more than fifty at once Sandinize, jumping about, jostling one another, grabbing and lifting one another up in the full sunlight, streaming with sweat, onto those moving shields—the scoops of dump trucks. Little girls Sandinize with little boys, and little boys with their lady teachers. Soldiers Sandinize among themselves, and sometimes with volunteers, civilians. Even the invalids Sandinize; and old women, too, all the better because they started so late in life. Masons Sandinize with poets, gardeners with psychologists, street sweepers with bank tellers. People of all classes Sandinize in the daytime, in the evening, and sometimes at night. Some get up at dawn to Sandinize in peace, in the coolness of the wastelands and dumps. And the working people Sandinize just as much as the unemployed, even though they have less time. The Christian schoolgirls also Sandinize, and the maids at their schools, the teachers, and the nuns—who Sandinize in concert with the oldest pupils. . . .

"In short, sir, entire classes in every part of the city, people who had never done anything before, are going at it now."

"That's democratic," you observe.

"But the leaders aren't Sandinizing!"

"What are they doing?"

"They're Leninizing or Lenining, whichever you like. All the leaders are Lenining now. And the crowds go on thinking that the leaders are doing what they're doing and that they're following the leaders."

Yet there doesn't seem to be any portrait of the Russian in the procession, or any scarlet or blood-red standard, or any flag with hammer and sickle on it. Were these purely verbal maneuvers, semantic tactics and ruses? You're right: it is a war of words. All kinds of confusions descend on the country, accumulate within the country. There is disorder in speech and disorder in the streets, social disturbances and disturbances in ideas, in people's minds. Here it's definitely true that words spring from geography.

The taxi brushes past the tail of the procession—with its placards reading: WE ARE THE REVOLUTION . . . THE FRONT STANDS FAST . . . LONG LIVE THE PROCESS . . . !—makes a left turn, and goes toward the South Road. Ah—now you're seeing the old parks again, the lake in the distance, the dumps! Heaps of rubble appear. On a section of beige wall someone has written in black tar: "The bourgeoisie will die of nostalgia." Farther along, again in black, on a housefront: "I, Nono, am fucked." On another wall, this time in white: "Only the peasants will go the whole way" . . . In this part of town words sprout everywhere, the war of sentences flourishes—on a workshop in ruins, on a fence, on the asphalt—history is literature. The taxi is getting close now; you recognize the trees (a chilamate, some palms), the little mounds of garbage (what staying power they have!), the little auto graveyard, the tall clumps of bamboo, the square, and lastly, already half restored, monumental, familiar, the stadium—what a surprise! Long live the revolution!

But what's the use of dreaming, feeling regretful? What will you embark on tomorrow, you volcanologist—extinct, though your cinders are still hot? The car moves on. A tricolored flag flaps on its pole before an austere, massive, oblong, whitewashed building.

"This is where they Sandinize most thoroughly," the driver tells you.

"How do you know?"

"The neighbors. They see everything, and they talk, especially the ones who live in the back."

You'll see if he's right. This embassy gets talked about a lot in

France. They say it's full of shrill, politicized diplomats, people with an investment in the Left in power. One of them is the essayist and storyteller Arnaud Strée, appointed to be information attaché. In Paris, two of his readers, one lady (a great traveler, mature, a Third World expert) and a civil servant in a moderately good position, have recommended you to him.

But Arnaud Strée will have to wait. First you have to find out about the fates of certain local people, people with roots and heavy burdens here. What has become of Leonor, Itamar, and Comrade Superior? What metamorphoses has the country gone through, how are people living, who is still alive? Did Chino stick it out, or did he allow himself to be crushed? These questions haunt you, determine what you do. Where are the former victims of persecution, the rebels, holing up? You don't know, but you tell the cab driver, "Take me to the La Perla pension."

The car turns around, passes houses, workshops, shacks. A fence appears, made of stalks of bamboo, stakes, mismatched boards torn from other fences, huts, dismantled shacks. Thick, abundant banana trees lean against this fence, choked with gray leaves, never pruned. Behind the rampart of greenery and filth, the building is still there, the same as it was before, with its outside staircase. Its function, however, has changed. Attached to the wall is a sign saying HOUSE OF THE NEW MAN. Farewell La Perla; the name was useless, smelling of old men, the old regime, sin. Whitewashed now. Is the building still being used as an inn? At the entrance—what luck!—you come upon the porter Bayardo.

"Professor!" he cries out. "After all this time! So you didn't leave after all."

You explain. Bayardo always called you "professor." To come from so far away, to cross seas, to run from one crater to another, examining humps and hollows, comparing boulders and blocks of scoria—that's certainly a professor's passion. Anyway, wasn't it because you were teachers that you and Comrade Itamar . . . ?

"As a matter of fact, I'm looking for him. Is he still alive?"

"He's still alive. Prison aged him a good deal. He's working at the Bureau of Political Orientation."

"And you, Bayardo?"

"I fought; I'm still fighting."

He's the only one who stayed till the final stage of the insurrection. The owner, who had fled to the country, came back, thinking he could start up his business again just the way it was before. After a few months he realized that there was a revolution going on. From now on there were unions, laws, sacrifices to be made. The man tried to deflect the process, ignore it, but the process is like a dog, Bayardo says, and when a dog takes a dislike to the seat of your pants . . . Well, the process caught up with the owner. Then he resisted, stiffened, and, after a year, cracked. He went to Miami, an exile, to join other hotel owners. At that point the government, at the request of the employees, confiscated the pension. Today it's a shelter for people from the Front.

A T the moment, he's drinking—he's drinking a great deal. You have to understand, Leonor will say: he has suffered so much. Rum came into his life like a woman; it moved in with him, and they won't ever leave each other. The first approaches did not take place until a few months after the Victory. They became more and more numerous, just as the arrests and decrees became more and more numerous. He gave way to alcohol more and more rapidly, just as history gives way to revolution. Rum conquered the lover as the ideology conquered the minds of others. Each consolidation of doctrine, each prescription, each new ordinance increased his need for the bottle. Each "deepening," "clarification," "rectification" measure drove him to seek consolation in the bottle.

An old militant who drinks—what does that mean? Is the revolution moving too fast, is it deviating, is it destroying itself, is it going to end in nothing? Is it necessarily treacherous, does it become denatured when it triumphs? If that's the case, it's a cruel discovery—one has been cuckolded. The old combatant, the fighter who has created it, sees in it his own offspring—and once this offspring is set in motion, it flies away from him. A revolutionary in love with revolution either plays false with her or divorces. And the one who breaks with her doesn't make up his mind to leave the roof they share. He remains, witnesses the licentiousness, and drinks. Itamar arrives with his bottle (wrapped in a newspaper and enclosed in a satchel) at the Bureau of Political Orientation. The man is still just as thin, and he looks old now. His hair is beginning to turn gray. At the age of thirty, he looks forty-five. His cheeks are furrowed by wrinkles; his neck is sunken between his shoulders and he stoops; his gaze seems to reach beyond the person he's talking to, beyond the walls, beyond any horizon. The former professor can't admit that he was expecting you, obviously. But he's not astonished that you're back.

"You saw some fine things here, a short time ago," he says.

"Some terrible things, too."

"It was a time of love. . . ."

"And of hate, it seems to me," you risk adding.

Itamar doesn't hear that word; suddenly he seems deaf. Something far away but strong is drawing his mind elsewhere, cutting him off from you, from his office, from the present. His gaze hovers, loses itself in a vague infinity. You're not there any more: he has forgotten you. He is speaking to himself now, only to himself. He says, "Abel is happy."

There is a long silence. A broad ray of sunshine enters and brightens the room. A fly is struggling against a windowpane. Its buzzing makes the silence oppressive. An empty space opens up, a sort of gulf. Then Abel's former leader bends over one of his desk drawers, takes out a bottle, opens it, and holds it out to you.

"Golden rum, see, a good brand."

One swallow, only one swallow, you say, that's enough. The militant takes two or three mouthfuls very fast and puts the flask down on his work table behind a stack of files. Silence again, and his eyes go back to staring at the invisible point.

You think of what Leonor has said: he was kept in solitary confinement for two years, without anything to read, without being allowed to receive a single letter; his torturers would appear unexpectedly in the middle of the night; the hardest thing, she thinks, was not the bad treatment or the isolation, because it was only his body that they put to the test and wounded. Other, more pernicious blows, with more consequence, undermined his morale. Itamar really cracked at the end of the third year, when he was visited by his father.

The old man came from his native town in the north—seventy-five miles away—on foot, in order to expiate his son's abjuration. The penitent begged the prisoner to return to God, to prayer, to the devotions of his childhood. Itamar was expecting this; he had prepared himself. He wanted to please his father, see him go home happy, and for this he was ready to lie. Unfortunately, the old man kept on talking, insisting. His extreme submissiveness, his mental slavishness, upset the militant, and Itamar's compassion deserted him: he gave way to indignation. Rejection took the place of pity. The old man gently answered that the only kind of son he could have was a Christian one, and therefore he no longer had a son. He stated it as a simple fact. Itamar had lost him; he felt immensely sad. His father left, a broken man, plunged in mourning. For a long time, Itamar was mad at himself, reproaching himself for being so frank. He still regrets it, Leonor assures you: he will always regret not having deceived the old man. But the evil was done, the truth spoken. The pious father did not leave his town again, or his house, according to certain people. He just allowed himself to die.

The ray of sunlight has widened. A long pencil of light brightens the wall opposite you. Itamar looks at the pattern—a bright corner, volumes of shadow with perfect edges. And then there's the fly, still stubbornly trying to get through the windowpane.

"Will you have some more?" asks Itamar, moving his fingers to the neck of the bottle.

You decline—you have a right to, don't you?

"You're wrong, my friend," Itamar jokes feebly. "You may even be committing an error."

You smile. The drinker goes on: "It's true: Abel is happy."

Then he asks you if you've seen his friend yet. That Chino— what a problem! It took a year to get him out of the clinker, poor man. A year of vegetating with the convicts of Palo Alto! For that was where the Front had locked up the soldiers of the Guard, the ones who hadn't fled to a foreign country, the ones they had caught still in uniform, the ones the people had captured and handed over. And Abel's friend had been picked up with the other soldiers, a group of terrorized boys who had been shoved into huts and were begging for mercy. Only one of them had unearthed a civilian shirt, navy-blue with little pale-blue sailboats on it, but he was still wearing army pants. Chino had turned up—no one knew why—without a gun, without shoes, and bare-chested. He had been sent off with the other soldiers, and like them he had been judged and sentenced. These "enemies of the people" had been sentenced to three years. There was no choice: to excuse them, to take into consideration certain exonerating circumstances, such as hunger, would not have been appreciated by the citizens, the militants, especially the other poor people. And Chino, the idiot, had never mentioned his collaboration with the Front. He had kept his friendship and his thefts a secret. Obviously it was embarrassing to him to talk about Abel, to explain the whys and wherefores. They would have laughed, accused him of being a comedian, a liar, and once he was back in his cell the other prisoners would have insulted him. So Chino said nothing and simply put up with his situation. And then one day Leonor located him.

Like everyone else, like me, Itamar confesses, she had at first thought the boy had escaped to the country, into the forest, that he had gone to ground somewhere in one of the villages beyond the swamps and the mountains, some remote spot behind the lakes, near the Atlantic or Honduras—that he had escaped or that someone had killed him. Then, by chance, she became acquainted with a young woman who happened to say that every time she visited her husband in Palo Alto, he would talk about a dead man named Abel. She was a distant cousin of Chino's named Domitila, barely out of her teens, and she was living with his mother, who had arranged the marriage.

A rumor had been going around that ordinary prisoners would be released more quickly if they had children. Chino's mother therefore dug up this cousin and told her how wonderful Chino was. She took the cousin to the prison one Sunday, on a visiting day, when the guards would leave the prisoners alone with their wives or fiancées for a few minutes. For the revolution understands—yes, it really does! Itamar adds—that this is the best way to hold down the number of fights, rapes, and sudden fits of madness, and also to reduce the risks of murder. The mother still thought of Chino as a kid. "Tomorrow," she announced, "I'm going to visit my Pretty Boy." And Domitila saw that he deserved the nickname. Chino himself figured: I've lost everything, so what does it matter?

After a few weeks, the cousin was pregnant. She declared that she was married, and proudly showed her belly. Domitila explained to her friends, her brothers, everyone, that her husband was the victim of a mistake. He had worked for the Front, and he had even militated with a martyr, the one he talked about, Abel, who—blessed Virgin!—if he could talk would explain to you all, Miss Leonor . . . And with "Comrade Miss," as she called her, the future mother went to get Chino out the next day. The child was born, and all three of them left the city and went back to the boy's native town, off the road to León, not far from

Momotombo, a road that was always congested with buses and heavy trucks.

"Abel is happy," the professor repeats. "Chino, too, in a way."

"And you, Itamar, if I may be permitted . . ."

"I?" he breaks in, bursting into laughter, rather the worse for drink. "What do I do? I orient! I orient, my dear. We're needed, we orienters, orientators—what a word! It's new, isn't it? The word, I mean. In the old days, elsewhere, what did we say? Guides? Mentors?"

Are they spying on him? Are they watching him? Are the walls stuffed with hidden microphones? Maybe his comrades, his leaders, don't trust him any more. Does an orienter who doubts still orient? And if he does, toward what and whom? And, then, everyone knows Itamar has gone downhill; he is exposed.

Or Itamar is delirious. The man grabs the bottle, drinks one last mouthful from it. He would like to continue the conversation elsewhere, he says, outside the office, outside the building, in a little bar he knows well, without walls or fences, open to the breezes, lost in the vegetation in Tiscapa, above the lagoon. You leave the building. Itamar calls his driver, a shy fellow, a recruit from the Liberation Army. The car turns down a two-lane avenue like all the others, running as straight as a railroad track across the same wastelands, the same formless neighborhoods with their scraps of shantytowns, their patches of abandoned earth, the beginnings of dumps. And then, all of a sudden, the car comes out on the Bolívar Boulevard. The lagoon lies very low in the crater that opens up at the far end of the road. The little bar by the side of the water, at the bottom of the hole, feels like a hiding place. The only way down to it is a steep path. Its thatched roof is supported by wooden pillars connected by a balustrade, also of wood but painted. A few tables are arranged on the terrace, a short rectangular landing made of boards that hangs a few feet above the species of pond. Without consulting you, Itamar orders a half-bottle of rum. Golden rum, of course.

"Comrade, there isn't any more, we've served—"

"Silver rum, then—can't be helped! Rum and revolution: nice program, isn't it? Imagine this symbol: you see a bottle in the shape of a woman, and the woman is waving the Front's flag. Like Marianne, the symbol of the French Republic, a Marianne of the *sans-culottes* of Central America. At the bottom of the picture you would write: "Rum Transfiguring the Revolution." But maybe that isn't even a new idea. In your country, in 1789 and the years after, wine flowed like rivers, according to what people say."

"I don't know anything about that. There are so many legends."

"That's normal, that's healthy. You have to encourage legends. They count for a lot in orientation work. You have to imagine, you have to charm."

"Propagandize . . ."

"Obviously you don't like it—it reminds you of things. I know what they think of our revolution in Europe. Our press service receives stacks of newspapers; they're cut up, translated, put into files. What a hodgepodge of accusations, such adjectives! All those big and little reporters, those 'special correspondents'—really! Special correspondents! I ask you: why is every one of them 'special'? Those faraway pen-pushers know us better than our closest friends, than we know ourselves! Partisans! Totalitarians! Traitors! That's what some of them fulminate. Others, not so many, say we're original, unlike anyone else. Still others say we're extremists, we're possessed. And the worst of all, though flattering for such an underdeveloped people as we are, are the ones who say, 'They're nomenklaturized!' Pretty, isn't it? Sophisticated in an anathematic sort of way."

"And what about the ones who think you're original?" you ask.

"They're naïve!" Itamar says. "Useful, of course, as Papa Lenin said before me."

"Useful for what?"

"That's a good question, my dear friend. And I've been asking myself that for months, ever since I learned, ever since I saw that everything is part of everything else. . . . So tell me what revolution is good for, where it's going, where it should be taken?"

"There are texts."

"The catechism, yes. But why not dare to dream of different things?"

"Is sinning against orthodoxy a serious thing here, among you?"

"I don't want to know!" Itamar says, suddenly angry. "And just between you and me, they can go to hell, those orthodox types."

Orthodox! Nomenklatura. It's all a matter of false sophistication, importation of ideas, imitation! These words stick in his throat; he fumes, screwing up his eyes, waxing ironical. Since they stick in his throat, he's got to try to wash them down. And in one gulp the grumbler empties his glass. Drunkenness. Imprudence. Talk, talk, talk, on and on, and no more control. Itamar becomes confused, mumbles phrases, bits of phrases, "philosoph-hic-al and pol-polit-hic-al" phrases—also enigmatical. He makes certain "connections" between the "cat-echism," the fools, the masses, "dialec-tical con-nections," of course, the "imb-eciles, the ortho . . . fools—that's it, the orthofools"—and tries to lift his glass again, brings it toward him, swallows—"revol' and rum"!—and collapses, his forehead resting on the table.

You and the driver take him back to Clara, his wife, who never stopped waiting for him and who is still waiting, who was born to wait, who doesn't understand, who accepts everything. Clara also forgives—that's her religion. Clara expects to understand some day, expects to see him change, forget, disappear. She helps you lift up the drunken man, calls him "my son," asks you to carry him to the bed. Then she falls silent, like the driver—probably a peasant, an Indian—who still seems shy and hasn't said a word, though whether out of scorn, indifference, or superiority, you don't know. And gently, obstinately, this silence drives you out of the house.

———

T H E way south: you take a long avenue with shoulders wider than the road itself, embellished with stones, trails of tan dust, and black spots, and planted with chilamates. There is a bend in the road; after you climb a little, you overlook a plain dotted with villages. A gulf appears, filled with water—the Asososca reservoir, immense and delightful to the eye. The lake, opaline in the light, darkens: a thick cloud has stopped directly above it. You continue to climb, drawing away. Now the sea drowns the horizon, the false sea of old Xolotlan. Traces of forests, sandbanks, slopes—and the yellow grass that grows everywhere, stuffing holes, crowning stones and pieces of wood—and various other plants, grayish and blond, form a wet, spongy shore.

The road to the south never goes down there. The ribbon of asphalt assails one last slope, rises, all at once divides the whole plateau. You go on peacefully, engine purring, pass through motionless towns, fields, meadows, and arrive at La Paz Centro.

"It's over there, sir, toward the volcano." A man selling dead iguanas points out the way to you. In your rented Land Rover you go down a straight, hump-backed dirt road full of potholes and as dusty as a baker's table. The land is scattered with leafless, scorched shrubs and different kinds of thornbushes grow between blocks of hardened lava in the hollows. Huts appear, standing on the rare level patches of land or leaning up against massive rocks like walls. The distance separating the highway from Momotombo seems greater than it used to be.

Today you're traveling alone, free to think your own thoughts, surrounded by silence. The world is mineral, empty. The only living things you see are birds, in the distance. Nothing makes a sound except the engine. There's a sudden fork: to the left you see a mauve road made of unevenly heaped slag, to the right another made of scoria. The slag leads more directly to the volcano, to its base, to the land around it, to the hamlet they say came into being when Chino arrived—a minuscule place, with its three huts and the little sheds next to them, minuscule and very exposed. Straw roofs, walls of branches and dried mud—the smallest landslide would flatten the whole thing like a cow patch. The huts are occupied by families: young fathers, young mothers, children. One man plants sesame, he says (but where, for God's sake?); another is out of work; and Chino climbs. "Now foreigners come," he says, also barely surprised to see you. "I guide them, I help them; they climb with cameras, boxes, rolls of paper."

"Empty boxes?"

"Some of them, yes."

"And what do they put in these boxes?"

"Whatever they pick up—pebbles, soot, bags of dust."

You chat about the crater, the debris, the heat—which is increasing only by a few degrees but continuously, one explorer has discovered—the mountain, smoke holes, eruptions.

"It was nice up there four years ago," you say after a moment's hesitation. "The landscape, the site."

"It hasn't changed," Chino interrupts.

And the young man looks away. He pivots, stares at the stones in front of him, stones thrown to the ground farther away, the base and the cone of the mountain, everything stony, the plain itself stony as far as the eye can see.

"Stone doesn't change," he goes on. "Stone is like bone. Too bad we're not made entirely of bone."

"Yes, that's a thought."

"We would last a long time, such a long time! We wouldn't wear out so fast; we would die slowly and easily, without noticing. Every year we would produce our little thimbleful of dust. And an adult has enough for a thousand," he laughs, "so we would live a thousand years! We wouldn't worry about bullets, about getting shot. Just a little hole, that's all it would make, an opening."

Still joking, the boy has glanced back at you. He has moved closer and, looking for a shady spot, has sat down on a sort of quarrystone near the car. You have settled down on the running board. Out of the blue, without thinking, you ask him if wants to come with you.

"Where?"

"To Corinto."

"I dream about it. *He* is dust now, isn't he?"

"And bone. Or stone, if you like."

Is this thought, this image of endurance a kind of consolation? The young man seems detached. True, you're still far away from the dead friend's city.

N O T many people have ever seen Leonor hesitate. She has a healthy outlook on things, they say, and her nerves are steady. They may bend, they may twist, they get pulled this way and that, but they never snap. Flexibility in her relations with people and firmness in her commitments: this is how she honors her contract as militant and leader. The former journalist has become the editor-in-chief of a large daily paper. Her mission is to explain the new measures, support the government, and defend the gains of the revolution. The class struggle is at its height. The petite bourgeoisie, the middle classes, are disappointed. There are fewer Front sympathizers, especially in the cities. Some militants are withdrawing. Some are joining the underground forces opposed to the regime. The confusion in some people is increased by threats from others. A certain famous leader, who only recently was Sandinizing alongside his comrades, is henceforth Sandinizing against them: the latter aren't Sandinizing any more, he declares. And the man has collected old and young combatants around him. A guerrilla camp has been formed in a damp, inhospitable area that the official propaganda situates beyond the border, in the marshes of Costa Rica. A broadcasting station has been set up in this same region, which the dissidents call the "first liberated territory." Every evening, over the radio, their commander denounces the treason of his former companions. He, the "authentic Sandinist"—the "nonaligned," the "*latino*," the "nationalist"—glues on them the label of "Sandino-communists"— "aligned," "Russianized," "satellite." The Authentic Sandinist chooses to address the soldiers of the Front and appeals to them to desert.

"His revolution is impossible," Leonor says. "His plan is chimerical. This 'Authentic Sandinist' is another Don Quixote; he's half crazy. There's only one revolution: the one that *is* possible. You're either for it or against it."

"It's as simple as that?"

"It's not simple, it's clear."

"It's reasonable," Comrade Superior says approvingly. Leonor has made a point of telling you that her visits to him are purely political now. "And reason is clear. You know that, because you're French. Otherwise reason isn't reason any more."

"So it's clear, but it's complicated," you persist. "I saw Itamar, and for him the reasons of the heart . . ."

"The revolution is no longer a matter of the heart," Leonor interrupts. "The heart mattered before we took power."

"Today the heart is the enemy," says Comrade Superior, once again going even further.

The theologian speaks distinctly. His new functions have made him self-assured and intransigent. The man is now a minister in the government. Since his appointment, the militants have been calling him "Comrade Father," because there is no longer any such thing as superior or inferior—everyone is equal. The presence of a priest in the government seems infamous to the opposition, who believes it's purely tactical: the government is trying to divide the faithful, lure them in, use them. They're mixing politics with religion and saying, "You see, we aren't atheists." Of course, they're forgetting the theses of "materiology."

In private, what is more, the priest confesses that his "ideas are evolving." They're coming into line, Leonor thinks: to be a materiologue is to be materialistic. The opposition—and the Authentic Sandinist and his partisans—still say the government is trying to make the good people think the priest-minister has remained a Christian. The trick has worked: they are pluralists.

"The heart again," says the theologian. "It can possess five truths . . ."

"That's its luxury."

". . . while reason has only one—that's clear, too."

A luxury revolution—Itamar's dream. Luxury and feelings. Poetry . . . But revolution is a science, the priest-minister warns. Enough. He no longer has the time—or the inclination, probably—to argue about these things. The revolution demands that one accomplish it, and by doing so, one becomes enlightened. Practice is the science of revolution. The revolutionary is a technician.

All Chino retains from this conversation is that one word. You have brought him back to the capital, still in the Land Rover. It was agreed that Leonor would go with the two of you to Corinto, so you had to come get her. At the moment you were leaving again, the telephone rang. It was Comrade Father calling. He was waiting for the editor-in-chief at his ministry. He had to discuss an article that had appeared that same morning and which he found disturbing. In this article—"The Sacred Nature of the Proletariat"—he was quoted and described as the "subtle ex-theologian." This . . . inadvertence . . . could be harmful. The word was not part of the select vocabulary of the Bureau of Political Orientation. Either Itamar had become careless or he was playing a trick on the priest-minister. Whatever the case, Comrade Father wanted an explanation. Would he get one? Leonor first talked alone with the minister. Then both of them came and joined Chino and you in the antichamber of his office. This was where the "technician" sacrificed a few minutes of his precious time.

" 'Technician' is better than 'mechanic,' " the former apprentice says jokingly as they go out.

The Land Rover is parked under the lacquered emerald foliage of a gigantic chilamate. The sun is sitting up in the very middle of the sky. The air is warm, motionless, the light so heavy you wade through it as if through water in a swimming pool. The car moves forward, peacefully cleaving the layer of heat like the prow of a boat. Leonor is sitting in front, close to the driver. The Momotombo guide is dozing in the back seat.

"What about inviting Itamar?" you ask. "He would be touched to visit Abel's grave."

"He would be touched and we would all argue," Leonor retorts. "Itamar can't control himself any more. Every time we see each other we fight."

She goes on to say that the orienter is still one of them: as a former prisoner, as someone who was tortured, he deserves respect. But it is becoming painful to see him drunk and to listen to him. So critical, so insulting is he, occasionally, that it's impossible to feel he's a friend.

This time you don't make any stops or detours: the three of you go straight down the road to Corinto. The sun lights up plantations, trails—paths etched out of semblances of plowed fields—and volcanoes. Numerous khaki-colored trucks, sitting high up on their wheels, are in evidence, shuttling back and forth between the port and the capital. At the entrance to Corinto, a convoy has stopped and soldiers are scattering in all directions, some of them bounding off barefoot and bare-chested toward the ocean.

The cemetery you're looking for, the only one in the area, is on an island, and you have to take a boat to get there. Ferrymen are waiting around near the loading dock, which looks as though it had been taken by storm today. A crowd of men and women are jostling one another, several of them crying, and kids are running in all directions. A few men are bustling around dressed in ill-assorted uniforms; they look as if they were part firemen, part rescuers, part policemen. They are doing their best to get to the landing dock, pushing people aside and making a path through the crowd with their stretchers. The women, many of them young, none of them in mourning clothes, are protesting and shouting. Flushed, clamorous, the mob seems more interested in arguing than grieving. Chino observes that maybe the ferrymen are on strike, which would put the families of the dead in a real state. To prevent the living from burying their dead would be too much; people would rebel. Some strikes should be outlawed.

"You can't outlaw what doesn't exist any more," Leonor says flatly. "Today, in the middle of the revolution, strikes don't make sense any more. I think all this confusion, this crowd, is because there are too many people here and everyone wants to be the first to leave."

"Too many people and too many dead to bury," the boy deduces.

"Yes, it's too bad! But it takes longer than four years to cure a country that's been sick for four centuries."

You approach some ferrymen. Leonor questions them.

"Drownings, ma'am," answers a plump, middle-aged guy who seems quite calm. "Two boats capsized, which wasn't surprising, because there were too many passengers on board—twelve in an old tub! They're crazy! Twelve people in a boat with six places! Of course, it's more economical. But there were children—four children drowned, ma'am. That's a disgrace!"

"And what about the adults?"

"Two women, tarts from the port, but it wasn't their kids who died—they didn't have any. The drowned kids were the brats of other prostitutes."

"Who were probably on their way to bury one of their sisters?" asks Chino.

"That's exactly right, and the poor thing—her coffin went to the bottom, too. The rescuers tried to fish it up, but it's not easy: the box weighs a lot—the dead woman wasn't young and she was fat. She didn't sleep with her clients any more—she acted as madam."

"Madam!" the journalist says, astonished. "Comrade, you must be making a mistake. The brothels here, like the ones in the capital, have been shut down."

"She did it in her house with three, four girls who helped her cook meals for travelers."

The madam, the ferryman explains, had transformed her home into a canteen. And in the port area, with all the Czechs, Russians, Bulgarians arriving now, and arriving hungry, eager to taste some exotic cooking, dozens of canteens are sprouting up. And a lot of girls pursue their activities there, all the while passing themselves off as waitresses, dishwashers, chicken pluckers. . . . The revolution has simply imposed a double vocation on them.

"That's ridiculous! Love has nothing to do with money any more. . . ."

"For young people, sure," interrupts the ferryman, "and for guys who are good-looking. But there's nothing new about that— a good-looking man has never paid at a brothel if he didn't feel like it. The problem is the sick ones, the old ones, the twisted ones. What can the revolution do for them? Make women give themselves for nothing?"

"Impossible!"

"Create a body of professionals paid by the state?"

"Unthinkable!"

"Why? They would be militant professionals."

Leonor is growing impatient; she's sure the ferryman is trying to provoke her. He's a macho, the fat old guy, a misfit, a reactionary. . . . Have to shrug your shoulders, despise them, these males, even though they're proletarians. . . . Contradictions, critical passage, question of time. In two or three generations the New Man . . . And meanwhile we'll have to treat them severely. We'll have to . . . Enough talking to herself, enough interior monologue! It's pointless to try and manufacture new consciousness out of old penises!

"Let's get back to what we came for," she says dryly. "When can we go over to the island?"

"Soon, looks like. They've already fished out the dead people. As for the coffin, if they find it they only need one boat to take it back."

"Is your boat free?"

"We can try. If you can give me something extra . . . But we'll have to load over there, on the other side of the dune, where no one can see us."

The sum is handed over, and you all walk around behind a hump of black, micaceous sand. The ferryman, rowing by himself, brings his boat to where you are. Barely an hour across, he assures you, and you'll be on the island.

As the skiff makes its way forward, no one talks; you're all studying the silvery line in the distance, watching for the appearance of a mass of green, a shore, a cemetery. Chino walls himself up in his thoughts, cutting himself off from everything around him, already somewhere else, in front of or very much behind everyone. He's living through an hour that took place some other time, recently or long ago: he's lying next to Abel at the worksite, four years ago, next to the man who's going to be dead before long; he lies there, caresses him, then comes upon his grave. . . .

"Are you going to visit an old grave?" the rower asks. The long silence makes him uncomfortable.

"We're going to see the grave of a young man."

"A poor young man, then. No one is buried on the island any more except poor people and whores. The others are buried on the mainland. They have to transport the coffins quite far away, all the way to a cemetery in another city—in Chinandega—and it costs."

The expanse of land looks like an overgrown, neglected garden dotted with slabs of concrete that were once whitewashed, and with leaning, chipped steles on which names and dates are engraved. Lopsided wooden crosses rot between shrubs bound in tangled nets of creepers and ivy. Other crosses, also of wood or of stone, emerge from the grass; here and there, the trefoiled, rounded tips of plants are visible. All the brick ornaments—crosses, small columns, low walls—have crumbled. You're not so much walking on hallowed ground as stumbling across some sort of savannah. And in the midst of this savannah, small square or rectangular cleared patches open up suddenly in front of you. Certain poor people and certain prostitutes come here regularly to tidy the graves of their girlfriends, their families. One of these graves bears Abel's name, and below it, the dates 1959–1979. Chino says nothing. He feels as though the others are watching him, as though they had taken him by surprise during a moment of intimacy with his friend.

"It's dumb," he sighs. "What a stupid idea to bury people in the middle of all these dumb plants."

Having said this, Chino retreats into himself again—completely; he won't say another word. The wretched pearls have rolled out of his mouth and the shell closes up again. Leonor, though she is never at a loss for an opinion or a comment, remains silent, too. She only shakes her head no. No to what? You don't ask. You all leave the island and return to the mainland sad, embarrassed, like fishermen coming back empty-handed.

T H E little yellow house, the family home (caught up in politics, conflicting passions) of the late clerk Jeremías . . . Some of the locals know it, have heard tell of it, others look away. Some kids pretend to be astonished when questioned. A man laughs and says, "Oh, the family of crazies?" and walks away. A woman passes, makes a face. Another woman is willing to answer: the yellow house is on the second street to the left.

Evening is falling. Lights go on, but very few, for an austerity program is in effect and public lighting is being rationed. After five years (of economy measures, conscientiousness, development) light will stream forth everywhere, the Plan will be finished; people will be able to see as well at night as they do at noontime. But for now . . . Yes, the revolution is certainly a long march. And nothing but shadows so far, nothing but nasty aftereffects! However, they are going in the right direction: Leonor, the comrades—Chino, too? and Itamar?—are all going in the right direction.

As for Alba, she looks as though she's floating through the air. She doesn't hold on to anything, she doesn't lean on anything. A recluse in her house, puffy and turning gray, she seems to have detached herself from the world. The single young woman—when will she marry?—wanders from one room to another, waiting for it to get darker, as she says, because that's when her family comes back. They're not lost, explains the lonely, somnambulistic girl; they haven't abandoned her, they're just hiding from the light. Especially her mother: the good Fermina can only tolerate complete darkness. During the night, she stays and helps her daughter prepare her trousseau. As for Gladys—oh, that girl, she only likes the light, obviously; she does nothing but walk around alone in the sun, people say. Gladys is crazy, the crazy girl says.

"And what about Abel?" interrupts Chino, who is both drawn to and disturbed by the sight of the gentle madwoman.

"He doesn't come here much. He often goes away. He told me he was happy under his stone."

"His stone on the island?"

"His stone. I don't know which."

The young man has sat down. Alba stands up and walks across the room slowly, as though tired, wandering through the shadows with the ease of a person who is deeply familiar with her territory: the contours of nooks and corners, of doorways. As she goes by, she brushes against a chair, then a table. She stops and puts her hand on the journalist's shoulder—Leonor is still standing.

"Tomorrow is the day they're supposed to come," she announces, her eyes turned to the window. "We're waiting, we're waiting. . . . I've been waiting for this fiancé of mine for so long! But Gladys will never get married."

2 9 4

"You're lucky, Alba," Leonor answers, clearly uncomfortable playing this game. "You're . . . well, what really matters is that he will come in the end."

"But it'll be dark. Will I be able to see him?" asks Alba, suddenly worried.

"He . . . he'll touch you."

"My God, I'm so scared!"

Leonor can't go on with this. She tells the others, quietly, that she wants to leave. In all honesty, what can they do for the woman? Shake some sense into her? Take her out of the house and plunge her into this night of hers? Encourage her in her hallucinations? Strange role for a militant, or even for someone without commitments or credo.

"A role for a saint, maybe," says Abel's friend.

"For an artist."

"For a crazy person, yes," retorts the journalist.

And she takes her leave of the madwoman. You follow, and Chino trails behind, after pausing to ask one last question about the dead brother, or, rather, the brother who is gone but who lives under the stone. . . .

C H I N O will come back to Corinto by himself. Alone, he will visit the island again and return to the little yellow house. Alba and he will talk a good deal and even laugh together. And then, abruptly, he will stop coming. The young man will never again, or very seldom, leave his hamlet, his acres of slag and dry grass, his volcano. And it is there, in front of his hut, surrounded by stones, that you will see him for the last time. But before this last visit (when you are also visiting a life, a segment of your life and your obsessions, Momotombo), you see, also for the last time—and what a strange feeling of uneasiness comes over you—the newly named Comrade Father.

———

T H E former superior is doing very well. His ministry hums with activity: militants run from one room to another transmitting instructions and the slogans of the day, organizing demonstrations. Young people who used to be guerrillas appear suddenly between the houses, equipped with megaphones. They shout out the slogans—"The counterrevolution will not succeed!" "Put the traitors in jail," "Mobilization!"—and everyone leaves his office, drops his files, suspends his discussions and meetings. Minister, vice-minister, and Cabinet director, a variety of under-directors and first secretaries, second secretaries, subsecretaries, ushers, staid or trembling *pasionarias*, and natty and triumphant typists (who are also up to date with everything and know by heart the first page of the first volume of Lenin's works), typists in delicate khaki blouses striped with brown lines (like the outfits of the troops guarding the borders), typists who are merry but also uncompromising, severe typists (the wives of former priests), typists who have enlisted in the territorial brigades or militia (often on night duty, once a week), typists who are fervent worshippers of Mary, Mother of Proletarian Jesus, typists who are readers of the *Manifesto* and the Sermon on the Mount, the numerous delectable, demonstrative Marxist-Leninist-Christians, all these ladies, along with their leaders, their leaders' leaders, and officials even higher up than the leaders' leaders, the masters of the beehive, all go down to the central patio. They go down because:

—There has been an alert, comrades! (And they simulate a retreat to the trenches dug in the vacant lot behind the ministry.)

—An unidentified plane is flying over the country, comrades (unidentified even though it is flying low).

—A truck transporting nurses and soldiers has been blown up, comrades, by a mine thirteen kilometers from Honduras.

Because:

—They're distributing ration tickets, comrades (for soap, sugar, oil, rice, beans, corn, and toilet paper that tears apart when you unroll it).

2 9 6

Because:

—Comrades, we must prepare the people's revolutionary festival of the Immaculate Conception, called the Most Pure, consoler of the masses and the exploited.

Because:

—Comrade Father is going to speak (and raise our colors, darling).

Because (in chorus):

—We're going to do away with imperialism!

Because (still in chorus):

—Long live the Directorate!

And it's so mild, it's so nice on the patio, the sun is so golden, the sky so blue, all these heads filled with such red ideas, these hearts so warm. . . . And you're waiting (for a vocation?) for the ceremony to be over. Then, when the slogans have been shouted and the fists lowered, you buttonhole the minister.

"Just a courtesy visit," you explain. "I'm going back to France, and I came to say good-bye."

"My schedule is very full, dear friend. You've seen some of it already, and it's not over yet. My driver and Commandant Monica are getting impatient. We have to leave right away for the north."

"A visit to the front?"

"We're going to pay tribute—inaugurate a cooperative."

"Agricultural?"

"That's right. A wonderful thing!"

"But you're not the Minister of Agriculture."

"The cooperative will be named after Julio César Ramirez— you know, my young colleague from Guatemala. It's the second thing named after him. In the south they've already changed the name of a school that used to belong to the congregation of Marists. Now it's called the Martyr Ignacio Institute."

"That's . . . that's good, my father," you say approvingly (why not?). You even add, "Things are progressing."

"We're all making progress!"

And the theologian goes off to rejoin the elegant and coura-geous Commandant Monica—wounded twice during the Insurrec-tion, once in the hip and once in the thigh.

You won't be able to follow the career of the priest-minister except by reading the paper, Leonor's paper, and that for only a few more days. Leafing through it, you learn that:

—He has declared that atheists have a right to be atheists.

—He has laid flowers (narcissi and ferns) before the statue of Martí.

—He has said that he worships the people and the people's mother. . . .

And between one day's perusal of the paper and the next, you say good-bye to the orienter Itamar. Unfortunately, the day is nearing its end and the man is completely drunk. His orderly (who is scornful? indifferent? superior?) explains that Itamar has mixed brown and white rum. This makes him piss endlessly, and as he pisses the orienter declares that he is watering the revolu-tions that are being imported—along with their defrocked Spanish priests, their Bulgarian strawberry shampoo, their Polish wheel-barrows, and their Byelorussian forks. Itamar pisses while the Indian working for him (scornful? indifferent? superior?) helps his boss stay on his feet, says nothing, and watches the pisser piss-ing. You watch, too. What can you do? You glean your interpre-tations wherever you can. You remember the advice you were given in Paris. Good-bye, Itamar! Good-bye . . . You take the only road that's left to take, besides the road to the airport: the one that leads to the embassy.

T H E R E'S a beautiful red copper plaque on the cream-colored wall of the embassy building, and it bears one word (what exoti-cism!): FRANCIA.

You ring. Somebody inside parts the slats of a venetian blind rolled down behind a frosted-glass window. You ring again and another person's nose appears at a second window. Then you hear footsteps, doors slamming, the squeaking of hinges, and the murmur of voices. A third recluse shows his mustache in the half-moon judas, and then you hear various clinkings and hissings of electric springs, latches, bolts (and tongues and fingers?).

"What do you want?" murmurs the guy at the judas in a quasi-confidential, definitely diplomatic tone.

"I'm here to see Arnaud Strée."

Extremely proud and suddenly distant, the porter—or is he a sentry, or a spy, or a bodyguard?—announces, "This is the chancellery, sir. See the annex departments—they're in the annex."

"And where is this annex?"

"Beyond the garages."

The porter's mustache disappears at exactly the same moment as the eyes between the slats and the nose at the bottom of the window, as though they were three fragments of the same human body.

The annex containing the annex departments has some of the characteristics of a waiting room, a station concourse, a retreat for doubting militants, ladies alone, young men even more alone, uneasy or tired pen-pushers (French and native), nomads with problems. It is at once an inn, a brothel, a reading room, a church, a building filled with private spots suitable for true or false conspiracies, half-secret meetings, half-public debates, confessions, crying fits, and real or disguised, officially administrative psychodramas. The annex and its offices are the site of professions of faith—Oh, if only Jaurès would return!. . . Or Marx or Johnny Walker, my friend . . . The Son of the carpenter, right, Sister White, but even so, do you think Saint Joseph represents the modern proletariat?—and also a place for narrow ambitions and lofty dreams, for promises kept and broken, for the writings of born writers—"His Excellency would find it of great value if the Department would kindly send him its feelings about the properly reiterated and imputable order on the credits allocated in the prescribed manner—see our dispatch #534 S/C.I. in response to your TG #23456 DG/SM-B42, sect. 53—which order concerns firstly, given the difficulties the station is suffering, the generating set and the pencil sharpeners it urges that its services could benefit from. . . ."

It's the place where one presents things, presents oneself, represents things; in short, it's the front of the stage, if you like, Arnaud Strée says ironically. And this man—what a patter he has!—seems to be fooling. Yet he will confess that there is one function, the only interesting one, never mentioned except in textbooks and speeches, which represents the eternal function of embassies (and their mystery, the aspect of them that makes them like brothels or places of worship), the function no one talks about or wants to talk about, as appalling as the secret of the confessional: that of "backstage attaché."

"You know very well, sir, in history and especially in the history of revolutions, the high places, the holy of holies, are the backstage areas. The people who really count are the stage hands. Just think of the appearance and disappearance of sets, the lights that come on suddenly, the unexpected or expected (always tactical) darkness, the sound effects, the montages and special effects. The greatest diplomats are stage hands. The others—for, after all, the stage can't be empty—simply allow themselves to be placed in front of the sets. These are the halberd bearers, the Swiss Guard, if you like. There's the ambassador and there's the Swiss Guard of the chancellery like the guard of a church—familiar figures. They often have an air of great nobility; the ladies adore them. And the halberd bearers of the other embassies court them. Just think: France's Swiss Guard!"

The attaché "of information" as he is called (also backstage technician?) no doubt deserves some of the labels that have been applied to him recently by the Paris newspapers. One fashionable feature writer called him a speechifier. A certain gossip columnist called him a philosopher *manqué* but a clever man. A militant without faith but efficient, skeptical, loquacious, and pessimistic, a very active one (he does gymnastics), pronounced the critic of the only two works by Arnaud Strée: *The Passage* (which you haven't read), an "intellectual autobiographical essay" felt to be too modest to be truly honest, according to the same critic, and *The Truth*, a book praised for "the singularity of its writing." In *The Passage*, it seems, the attaché describes the stages that led him from a novitiate with the Franciscans (for four years he was a Minorite and devoted himself to the underprivileged who lived in the housing developments around Lyon) to leftism with Trotskyite coloration (a subfaction of a dissident group of the Fourth International), and from leftism to the reunified, rising, reassuring forces of the Socialist Party.

This essay was written by the author at the end of his journey, whereas we are told that he began the other work, *The Truth*, even before he left the Franciscans. It is a collection of four erotic novels all centering on the Mary Magdalens of the suburbs and a certain Saint Jean, who came from a poor family and who, since he had to earn a living after all, became an unenthusiastic actor in pornographic films.

After this the writer, still young—thirty-five years old—began traveling. While he reported on the (American) pillaging of the Third World, his party came to power in France, to Arnaud Strée's applause. He was offered this position between volcanoes and banana trees, a position as observer, they stressed, scrutinizer, analyst of a revolution that was upsetting the brains of half a dozen functionaries sitting over a map of the world in some palace by the Seine. And now the envoy has been analyzing for two years. Time helps, he admits. Eventually the outer layers get torn away.

"Between you and me, revolution really writes some fine chapters of literature. And what characters it creates! What great roles! It has everything: crime, gambling, sainthood. . . . Here, my dear man, we are at the theater. It is Year IV of the revolution,

Act IV. How many acts will there be? No one knows. Maybe five or even six, because of help from outside. But already one can glimpse the eventual fate of the protagonists. This is all quite traditional, you'll tell me—you've seen it before. But have you *seen* it or *read* it? As a matter of fact, I don't like to read Shakespeare—I like to see it. And here, finally, we can *see*.

The attaché settles back in his attaché's armchair (what a high back it has!). His talk is sometimes deliberate, sometimes passionate. In a word, he sums up, intelligence is *voyeuristic*. And the closer one gets to the actors, especially if one mingles with them, and most of all in the evening, after three glasses of rum or whisky, the better one sees. The attaché-cum-voyeur, attracted to the night the way others are attracted to policemen or alcohol, the attaché of Year IV (and Act IV), has seen plenty. According to him, there are five different sorts of destinies, roles that are as classical as you can get:

There are those who live for the revolution and may die of it. (You wonder if Leonor is one of them.)

There are those who live in the revolution but who don't die of it. (Comrade Superior?)

There are those who oppose the revolution to the point of dying of it. (Those barefoot people who joined the Authentic Sandinist?)

There are those who oppose the revolution but don't die of it. (The Authentic Sandinist?)

There are those who are at once in the revolution and outside it, surviving as best they can, and dying one day as a result of a car accident, a brawl, a quick or long-drawn-out suicide, a high fever. (Abel, if he were still here? The Arnaud Strées of the country? The "backstage attachés"? Itamar?)

But the play is more or less over. From this point on, in that famous backstage area, people will be yawning, stowing away the props, thinking of the next play.

"Thank you, Mr. Strée. I needed to talk to someone like you, who—"

"Quite all right, my good man! But you yourself must have made some friends here."

"Two or three. One is dead, one has had a breakdown . . ."

Maybe you were about to mention Chino when a woman's cry echoes through the annex. Arnaud Strée races out of his office. It's his secretary. The woman keeps saying "It's horrible! It's dreadful!" as she shakes her hair, suddenly fouled, of a rare or even an exceptional sort, visibly out of place. "Horrible! It's all over! Look at my typewriter carriage, the keys, the files, the chair. Oh, God, what a place this embassy is! Do something!"

The attaché calmly sets about doing something. With the help of an usher, he discovers that an iguana has gotten into the room's air conditioner. The animal has been electrocuted and has been putrefying for the last day or two. The carcass has become a swarm of maggots, and the machine, which the secretary has just turned on, has expelled a cloud of little worms along with the cold air.

"Oh, the tropics—I tell you, sir!" the woman complains, having taken refuge near you. "The tropics! Well, I hope to end my career in Bern."

The conversation with the analyst is not resumed. Arnaud Strée has his maggots to sweep up—and also reports to read, letters to write, telegrams to decipher, a vice-minister to visit, and especially, he stresses, a lecture to draft on the true nature of French socialism as opposed to its Russian variant. The conversation is not resumed, and you knew you won't be coming back. But you like people to like you, and you say, "I'll stop by again some time."

L A S T scene. The only really indispensable one. Last figures, last settings: Chino, a few kids, Domitila running after a dusty, skinny hen, trying to catch it, and all around, wherever you look, the chaotic reddish-brown earth, stones, more stones, the volcano. You're walking on a semblance of a path, a dark, uncertain line drawn on a gray and purplish-blue surface, and the path leads to a tangle of brambles. The brambles are reddish-brown, too, scorched by months of sun. And behind the brambles you can make out a field of rubble. Then, rising in a long, massive slope, you see the foothills, the formidable verdigris belt with its tawny pocks—Momotombo.

You could say "It's beautiful," but that's obvious. You could say "You're lucky," but that may not be true. You could say "Ah, yes, time moves on," travelers travel, one can't do anything about it, the sky is white, the sun beats down (and burns your skull where you're beginning to go bald, so that when you get back, like the last time, a new woman—or the old one, who loves reunions—will call you "the man with the red pate"). You could also say that volcanology is really a puzzle. And climb, climb once again. Survey, my friend, take measurements. And there are so many stones: the ones over there, from the lava lake, from the dome, from the cone, from the shield, from the plateau. The ones from the path, too, these bluish lumps, the broken stones all around you, under your feet. How restful it is? You could say . . . But Chino is the one who speaks:

"Are you going to stay in France?"

"No."

"Where will you go?"

"I don't know."

"To China?"

"Not to China. What would I do in China?"

"They have revolutions there, don't they?"

"They certainly do."

"What a pain. Are there cemeteries?"

"I would think there are."

"Oh, I thought they burned their dead."

"Maybe they burn some of them, the way they do in India and other countries."

"Well, if I had some ashes," he confesses, "I would scatter them under my bed."

"Why there?"

"How can I explain? I have a feeling I would sleep better."

What ashes was he thinking of? Why under the bed rather than on the threshold of the hut or under the table? It's good to spread a man's ashes under a table. Then you think about him three times a day, when you eat.

You're still walking, slowly, but you've turned around and are approaching the house. Domitila has caught the hen at last. She comes back hugging the squawking bird against her, triumphant, while the kids, several little boys of three or four, follow her into the hut, laughing. They get in Domitila's way and she drives them back outside, where they run around in the dust.

"Four years already!" sighs the young man, watching Abel, his son. And Abel, with his little friends, is playing his favorite game, the game all the kids like best—war.